STEEL
JUSTICE

Jenni Boyd

Jenni Boyd Books

Australia

Copyright © 2013 Jenni Boyd

The moral right of the author has been asserted.

All rights reserved. No part of this book may be reproduced or transmitted without written permission from the author.

First Edition

All characters in this book are fictitious and any resemblance to real persons living or dead is purely coincidental.

ISBN: 978-0-9872443-6-9

Publisher: Jenni Boyd Books.

Cover Image & Design ©: Jenni Boyd Books

www.jenniboydbooks.com

Queensland, Australia.

I would like to thank:

Adrian Bailey Photography
Cover Image

Michelle S.
Blake F.
Cover models

Sarah S.
Proofreading

STEEL
JUSTICE

Jenni Boyd

STEEL JUSTICE

PROLOGUE

It was a dark moonless night, making the yacht virtually invisible as she glided through the water, powered only by the wind in her sails and navigated by autopilot coupled to a G.P.S.

There were no lights to be seen; the only sound was of the yacht's hull slicing through the water, momentarily interrupted by a loud splash as she released her heavily weighted cargo.

Without pausing, the mission complete, they continued into the night, no one saw, no one heard... so they thought!

* * *

He wasn't a handsome man, but then he wasn't ugly either, he was what one would class as ordinary, but then that was how he liked it. Nothing about him would stand out in a crowd, it was only if one got close enough to see his eyes, so dark the irises blended with the pupils, like the black soulless eyes of a shark.

As he looked in the mirror, he lifted his hand to his cheek and a smile came to his face, even he could not recognise the stranger looking back.

Jenni Boyd

STEEL JUSTICE

CHAPTER ONE

With a drink in hand, Michelle walked out onto the deck of the beautiful white yacht. She took in the lavish surroundings; noting that no expense had been spared, from the highly polished stainless steel rails to the immaculately maintained timber deck. There were inviting sun lounges, with bold colourful cushions and music was being played through strategically placed speakers. *God this is only the front deck, I wonder what the rest looks like?*

As she stretched out on a sunlounge, she thought about the owner of the boat and a smile came to her face as she realised, her father would blow a fuse if he knew where she was, for the owner of this boat was her father's archenemy!

She quickly drained her glass of champagne as thoughts of her father came to mind which annoyed her, *when will he realise his past is his past and he is no longer involved in any covert ops even she is not allowed to know about!* She looked into the bottom of her glass and realised it was empty; *where the hell was Dan?* Suddenly angry with her father, Dan and most men in general, she stood as she realised there was only one person she could count on and that was herself. *If the drink doesn't come to the girl, then the girl shall go to the drink!*

Michelle combed her fingers through her long blonde hair and adjusted her blue bikini, making sure her assets were displayed to her best advantage, she was well aware of her looks and drew pleasure from the cold hard stares of the women, but more so, the admiration from the men, it gave her a sense of power!

Standing at five foot ten, her long slender legs and flawless skin the colour of warm honey caught many an eye, but her aqua blue eyes, fringed with thick black lashes were her most startling feature.

Upon entering the bar, she was hoping to have a chance to gain the attention of the skipper, his dark good looks and well-muscled, tattooed body, had not gone undetected by her discerning eye. Disappointed he was not there, she debated whether to get a drink or wander the decks in the hope she could entice him to get it for her when she suddenly noticed the stairs to the lower deck. Upon boarding, all guests were given strict instructions that the lower deck, apart from the bathroom, which was at the base of the stairs, was out of bounds; *but rules were meant to be broken!*

Quickly going down below, noting the door marked 'bathroom', she continued along the narrow passageway until she came upon a door that was slightly ajar. Suddenly she heard a deep sexy voice and instantly knew it was the skipper, a thrill of excitement coursed through her and she debated whether to walk right in or wait until he came out, when she realised his conversation was one sided. *He must be talking on the phone.* Deciding to wait outside until she could get his full attention, she leaned against the passageway listening to the sound of his voice, when something about his conversation penetrated her thoughts, causing her to listen more carefully.

"Boss you know Steel is suspicious, I've had reports he's been asking questions about the *Talisman.*"

There was a sudden pause in the conversation and Michelle realised the person on the other end was talking and that person could be no other than Malcolm Microbe.

"These daytrips with the tourists are not only very lucrative, but they should also keep Steel off our back."

Michelle's mind was racing, after realising they were talking about her father.

"Yes the door is locked and all passengers have been instructed not to venture past the bathrooms on the lower deck."

She realised he was ending the call and all previous thoughts of walking into the room were now dashed, turning quickly she bolted for the stairs, taking them two at a time and almost tripping on the top step, causing the barman to look at her strangely.

"My goodness, I just saw the biggest bug in the ladies room, I was so scared!"

The barman suddenly smiled at her, accepting her ridiculous lie, he grabbed a clean glass and a bottle of champagne from the fridge and poured her a drink.

"Maybe this will help you forget such a traumatic experience," he said with a charming smile.

As she reached for the glass, she was surprised to see a slight tremble in her hand and drank a good measure of the cool bubbly liquid. She was about to thank him, when the skipper suddenly appeared at the top of the stairs and she could physically feel her heart rate increase. He paused for a moment and looked at her as if he was going to speak, then thought better of it before proceeding outside. All sorts of thoughts were running through her head when Dan walked in wanting to know where she had been.

"Just had to go to the little-girls room."

"She was in need of something to calm her nerves, after encountering a crawly creature in the bathroom," commented the barman.

Michelle could see the confusion on Dan's face, then he started to laugh and she knew she had to act quickly before he gave the game away.

"You know Dan you can be so insensitive sometimes, you know very well how the sight of a crawly creature scares me and if it hadn't been for this nice barman, I would be one blubbering mess right now!"

Michelle turned her back to the barman and gave Dan a warning look, letting him know he had better play along with it, or else suffer the consequences. He stared at her for a moment and then a smile came to his face, before he enveloped her in his arms.

"I'm sorry baby; it was very mean of me to tease you. How about we go back out on the deck and forget the whole terrifying experience."

She nodded her head and walked quickly outside; making a

beeline for a sunlounge, trying to ignore Dan's questioning eyes.

"Michelle, what the hell was that about and don't give me that bull about being scared of a bug? I know very well nothing scares you!"

"Don't worry about it, it's nothing."

Dan kept trying to get an answer from her, but she wasn't listening, her mind was going over the snippet of conversation she'd heard between the skipper and his boss. *If the day cruises like the one today were purely for the purpose of fooling her father, then it could mean only one thing, Microbe was using the boat for something illegal, but what, what was the real purpose of this boat?*

She straightened in her chair and scanned the top deck and realised for the first time that all the passengers were being watched and her instincts told her it wasn't for their safety or comfort, but to ensure everyone was accounted for at all times. As the skipper's conversation came to mind regarding these day trips being very lucrative, she looked at each and every guest and it dawned on her; apart from Dan and herself, no one was under the age of fifty and by the amount of jewellery the women were wearing; they were filthy rich! *Was this part of the criteria to be given an invitation, if so why was Dan invited?*

"Dan, how did you get an invite on this boat?"

"Why?"

"I just thought it was strange that you are the only young person that got invited, but also have you seen the size of the rocks the women are wearing on their fingers?"

"Well to be honest the invite was actually for my dad and his girlfriend, but he couldn't make it."

"Is your dad by chance, rich?"

"Why?"

"Well the way I see things you have to be over the hill and have a lot of dough to get an invite on this boat."

Dan looked around at all the other guests then looked back

at Michelle.

"I suppose you are right."

"So I take it your dad has a lot of moolah, hence the invite, but I am surprised they let you take his place because of the age thing."

"Have you heard the term, money talks?"

"Yeah; but why would you want to go on a cruise with a bunch of oldies?"

"I figured it was the only way to get you to go out with me, if I waved an invite aboard the *Talisman* under your nose."

"Hmm, smart boy."

"Yeah, well."

I wonder how much a ticket aboard this vessel actually costs and whether the skipper is taking a sizeable cut. Then reflecting back on the conversation between the skipper and Microbe about a locked door, *what was in there?* The curiosity was killing her, she was to the point that she could think of nothing else, she had to find out, or else it would drive her crazy if she set foot off this boat without so much as a peak!

Finally, she saw her chance, Dan was busy at the buffet and the skipper was talking to a crewman at the front of the boat and for the first time no one was watching her. Grabbing her opportunity, she quickly ran below, going straight past the bathroom along the passageway towards the door where she'd heard the skipper talking on the phone. Gingerly pushing the door open, mentally crossing her fingers that no one was inside; to her relief the room was empty. As she looked around the room she realised there was another door with a sign fixed to it stating 'NO ADMITTANCE STAFF ONLY', *bingo*!

After trying the door handle and finding it locked, she quickly removed two hairpins from her hair and proceeded to pick the lock, something she had learnt from an old boyfriend who was now spending time behind bars.

In a matter of seconds, she heard the click of the lock and quickly opened the door, slipping inside and softly closing the door behind her. Her heart was racing and the adrenaline was coursing through her veins as she scanned the small room, which was virtually empty apart from a grey waterproof box about two metres in length and one metre high. As she walked over towards it she noticed it was fitted with remotely controlled inflatable devices to the sides and the box was padlocked. *This is definitely not a life raft!* The combination of the fact she could get caught at any moment and the thought of what was in the box caused her hands to shake as she inserted the hairpins in the lock. Moments later, she was rewarded with the sound of the lock clicking open and quickly lifted the lid. Mildly disappointed to see nothing but packing, she started to move it aside when she heard voices outside.

Holy Shit! She paused what she was doing, trying to decide whether to delve deeper or close the lid before being discovered. Suddenly she heard the skipper's voice, knew he was right outside the door, so she quickly re-adjusted the packing and relocked the lid before running over to the door. Her heart was pounding so hard she could barely hear what was going on in the other room. *Is he still there or has he left the room?* Trying to hold her breath and listen over the sound of the blood rushing in her ears, she could hear nothing and assumed he had left the room, so she very slowly opened the door a crack, when suddenly the skipper's broad back came into view, causing her to almost slam the door closed.

She stood there motionless still holding her breath, her heart was pounding so hard now it seemed as if it was resounding off the walls, her lungs were screaming out for air and she was starting to sweat. Realising she was losing control she slowly inhaled and closed her eyes, willing herself back into a state of control.

Once again, she slowly opened the door, relieved to see the skipper retreating through the other door. *It's now or never!* She quickly stepped into the outer room, making sure the door was securely locked behind her, then ran across the room and slowly opened the passageway door to see if the coast was clear, expelling a loud sigh of relief when she saw the passageway was empty.

She had barely closed the door when a voice boomed behind her demanding to know what she was doing, causing her to jump in fright and as she turned she looked directly into the angry face of the skipper.

"Holy crap you gave me a fright!"

"Well?"

"I was looking for the little-girls room."

"All passengers were clearly told before departure that the bathroom is located at the base of the stairs and no one was allowed to venture any further!"

"I'm sorry I mustn't have been listening."

Michelle tried her best dumb blonde act, something that had worked for her many times before. She noticed his eyes narrowed as he stared at her and realised he didn't believe her lie.

"Well I really must go."

Quickly ducking past him, she rushed off towards the bathroom, almost slamming the door behind her. Upon looking at her reflection in the mirror, she was surprised to see the frightened look on her face, something she was unaccustomed to. Splashing her face with cold water, she took a few deep breaths, then as an afterthought flushed the toilet. It was possible the skipper was still standing outside and the thought of him sent a thrill through her body, *perhaps now is the time to ask for that drink.* Taking a quick look in the mirror before adjusting her bikini top, she casually opened the door and walked out sensuously, but to her disappointment, the area was deserted.

No sooner had her feet touched the top deck than Dan demanded to know where she had been, instantly getting her back up; *no man ever demands anything of me!* Michelle realised she was already bored with him as his use had expired. Ignoring his voice, which suddenly reminded her of a yapping lap dog, she noticed the skipper watching her. Grabbing her towel and a bottle of sunscreen lotion, she sensuously walked towards him before laying out her towel on the deck and positioning herself ensuring he got the best possible view, before slowly applying the lotion to her long legs, sneaking looks underneath her dark lashes and delighted to see he was watching.

"Do you think you could put some on my back?"

Michelle held out the bottle of lotion to him, but before he could respond, Dan dashed forward and snatched the bottle from her outstretched hand.

"I'll do that! After all you are my girlfriend!"

Michelle saw a smile come to the skipper's face before he walked off, then, felt Dan's hand rubbing lotion on her back. Her hands instinctively clenched into fists and it took all her willpower not to hit him or throw him overboard!

All the passengers had left the boat and the crew were busy clearing away empty bottles and left over food, putting everything back in order for their next overnight trip. The skipper's mind wondered to one passenger, one very tall sexy blonde and then he thought about finding her in the bow section below decks. He didn't for a moment believe her story. *What was she doing there?* Suddenly he decided to check the locked room and was reassured to find the door was still locked and didn't show any sign of being tampered with but he felt the need to check inside. He unlocked the door, then walked over to the grey box and saw it was still locked. It didn't appear to have been disturbed; realising it was nothing but his paranoia.

He started to walk towards the door when a glint caught his eye, there was something shiny on the floor near the door. He walked over and picked it up staring at it for a moment, before realising it was a woman's hairpin. *How on earth did this get in here? No female has ever worked on the boat, nor has one been allowed in this room, even the boss's wife hadn't been here, in fact she had no idea what her husband was really using this boat for!*

Quickly unlocking the box, making sure nothing had been disturbed or removed, he re-locked it and then left the room ensuring the door was securely locked behind him. He walked around the room tapping the hairpin on his chin thinking, suddenly deciding to check the video surveillance; it was very cleverly hidden throughout the boat.

As he viewed the tape he realised his suspicions about Michelle were correct, there is no mistaking her in that blue bikini. He watched as she expertly picked the door lock and then the grey box and started moving the packing. He saw her suddenly pause and look behind her and then quickly replace the packing and close the lid. *She must have heard someone coming.* He zoomed in the vision as he watched her stand motionless against the wall and could see she was beginning to panic and then amazingly he watched as she managed to psych herself back in control, noting her deep breaths before she calmly exited the room.

I'll have to alert the boss, but first I'll have to find out who she is. How on earth did she get on the boat today, it was obvious she was no tourist, more like an undercover cop; but she looked far too young?

Damon Stokes was not only the skipper of the boat, but also Malcolm Microbe's right hand man and head of security, which required him to keep himself in good physical shape. Despite only being in his early thirties, he had seen and done many things and it was only because of Microbe that he wasn't currently cooling his heels in jail! Standing well over six foot with jet-black hair, his looks could only be described as handsome but dangerous, which tended to make people cautious about getting too close.

After making a few phone calls he discovered Michelle was not only a well-known local, but also well known to the local police, but what surprised him was despite the fact she gave the local police Sargent cause to drink more than he should, her private life was something of a mystery, causing him to delve even deeper. When he finally uncovered her secret, he knew his boss was going to blow a fuse!

"Boss, we have a problem!"

"I'll be there in five."

Malcolm was there in record time; he knew Damon would not call unless it was serious.

"We've had a security breach, one of the guests on our last trip managed to break into the room and open the box," he said before Malcolm could speak.

"How the hell did this happen, I specifically stated that all guests that step aboard the *Talisman* are to be watched at all times?"

"I know, but she managed to sneak down below undetected."

"She! It was a woman?"

"Yeah, look I'll run the tape and you can see for yourself."

Damon turned on the screen and played the video.

"My god she's only a girl, do you know who she is?"

"She goes by the name of Michelle Brown."

"Meaning?"

"Max Steel is her father!"

"Holy crap! How the hell did she get an invite?"

"I made sure there were no locals on the guest list and as usual we screened each person before an invite was sent out. We suspect one of the male guest's, who did have an invite, helped her sneak aboard."

"Didn't you do a head count?"

"Yes, but you see it turns out the guy who helped her aboard, his invite was originally for his father and companion, someone forgot to change the guest list."

"Find out who it is and fire him, I will not tolerate incompetence from any of my staff!"

"The matter has already been taken care of."

"Of all the people to have snooping on my boat, it had to be the daughter of Max Steel! Do you think she saw what was in the box?"

"I don't think so, she hadn't penetrated the second layer of packaging; what do you want me to do?"

"We can't risk her talking to anyone about what she saw;

especially her father; my god what if she has already told him!"

"I doubt it, firstly we would know by now and secondly from what I have learnt about her she would keep something like this to herself until she learns what the box contains."

"I suppose you are right on the first count and if you are on the second we have to make sure she never discovers the contents of that box!"

"So what do you propose?"

"Get rid of her, but make it look like an accident; I'm sure you can think of something."

"There are many options."

"The less I know the better! The first I want to know about it is when I read it in the paper!"

"Gotcha!"

Eden Cove was considered paradise to many, with its lush tropical surroundings that are skirted by a picturesque, azure sea on the doorstep of The Great Barrier Reef.

When Malcolm Microbe first came to Eden Cove, he too thought he had discovered paradise, but for another reason. It was a small isolated fishing village, there was no hospital only one overworked and under paid GP. The nearest city and hospital were many kilometres away. There was one small school, which could only cater for children up to the fourth grade. Many families had to spend time apart or move away altogether so their children could complete their schooling; but more importantly there was one police officer who was hungry for a better retirement incentive than his pension and at the time there was no watchful eye patrolling the ocean.

Microbe realised Eden Cove could be a potential money-spinner for him, so he gained the trust and respect of the locals by building a small community hospital and expanded the school. With the admiration of the town, but also with the surety of no interference from the local police, who now enjoyed a more comfortable lifestyle, he was virtually free to do whatever he pleased.

Malcolm Microbe is not a big man, if you hadn't heard the

rumours about him you would be hard pressed to believe he could be involved in anything illegal or sinister. In his mid-sixties, of average height and build with thin greying hair, he looks like a regular grandad. However nothing could be further from the truth, he is a man of no scruples, a man if ever challenged or crossed will make it his personal vendetta to destroy them or make them disappear altogether; a man Max Steel was determined to put behind bars!

STEEL JUSTICE

CHAPTER TWO

It was the 'Sunday Sesh' at the local pub at Eden Cove, a tradition with the locals every Sunday, a live band was playing and the place was filled to capacity. The music was loud over the din of voices, to the point you had to yell to be heard. Michelle was there with her best friend Jane; the two were so similar in looks they were often mistaken for sisters.

Suddenly Jane spotted two tall, dark haired good-looking guys and knew they weren't locals, as she hadn't seen them before. Nudging Michelle, she nodded her head in their direction.

"Check out the cute guys over by the bar."

"Oh yeah, definitely new arrivals!"

"Maybe they're here for the shooting of that new film they have chosen to make in our little slice of paradise?"

"Ah I think we just got sprung perving," laughed Michelle.

"Oh my god; they're coming our way!"

"Hi girls mind if we join you?"

"Sure, the more the merrier," said Michelle.

"We're new in town, I'm Josh and this is Tom."

"I'm Michelle and this is Jane."

"Are you here for the new movie their shooting in Eden Cove?" Asked Jane.

Tom shook his head as in no, but Josh nudged him.

"Looks like you've caught us out, but keep it to yourselves okay."

"Why what's the big secret?" Asked Michelle

"We've arrived a few days early so we can enjoy the sights of town before we start work, so we'd like to keep a low profile." Said Josh

"Don't worry your secret is safe with us. You know you couldn't have picked a better table to sit at, because Jane and I know this place like the back of our hand and if you're interested we could show you some places that even the locals don't know about!" Said Michelle

"Funny you mentioned that, because both Tom and I have our pilots licence and just happen to have a helicopter at our disposal."

"Wicked!" Exclaimed Michelle.

"So these places you mentioned are they only on the mainland or are you familiar with the islands as well?" Asked Josh.

"Both," said Michelle

"We want to hit some of the uninhabited islands, preferably ones that are not frequented by people; if you know what I mean," said Josh.

"I do, but you couldn't land there, you'd have to have floats on the helicopter." Replied Michelle.

"Our chopper is equipped with that, also we would like to camp there overnight, you girls interested in a sleep over?" Asked Josh.

"Michelle I hope you're not thinking of Lagoon Island, it's a definite no-no for camping?"

"Jane since when has the word no stopped me?"

"That's the spirit!" Said Josh.

"Look, what you guys don't realise, if we get caught camping there the fine alone is massive, but there is also a possible jail sentence!" Exclaimed Jane.

"Well I've always been one to live life on the edge, how about you Michelle?" Asked Josh.

"Definitely, you can count me in!"

"Well Jane it looks like it's three against one, the choice is yours."

"Come on Jane, it'll be fun!" Exclaimed Michelle.

"I don't know."

"Well put it this way, we're going with or without you," said Josh.

"Oh but…"

"Michelle, do you have another friend who might want to take Jane's place?"

"Ok I'll go, but promise you won't breathe a word of this to anyone else?"

"Our lips are sealed, in fact Tom and I wouldn't want it any other way. Do we have a deal?"

"Deal!"

All four shook on it and Josh bought them a round of drinks to seal the deal. Jane couldn't help worrying about the consequences if they got caught; she didn't seek danger the way Michelle did. It had been decided they would leave early the day after next, giving Michelle and Jane time to organise things their end, but also that's when their two-day break started.

While Michelle was planning her next risky adventure, her father Max was carrying out a very dangerous covert operation of his own.

Eden Cove was a town which thrived on its fishing and the reef, so the major business sector of the township was its boats. It was common knowledge the large sleek white yacht called the *Talisman*, which was moored at the forefront of the marina, was owned by Malcolm Microbe. What puzzled Max about this boat was why Microbe had never allowed a local to set foot on the *Talisman* and rumour had it that one had to be extremely rich, but also it was by invitation only.

Max had been keeping his eye on its comings and goings and often noticed it left the marina in the dead of night, when the marina was virtually asleep, sparking his suspicions. He wondered what the vessel's real purpose was and he knew there was only one way he could find out for sure, he had to attach a tracking device to the boat's hull, the only place he would be sure it would go undetected.

This in itself was extremely dangerous, because he could only do this at night as the boat and berthing area were well guarded during the day, but more so, the area the boat was moored was not only extremely murky, but frequented by crocodiles!

This didn't deter Max, he had carried out many dangerous

covert operations before and it was the sort of thing he thrived on, the thrill of the next operation, something his daughter inherited from him. Like his daughter he was tall, a good six foot two, with the same dark lashed blue eyes, but where her hair was blonde, his was as black as coal. He was in excellent physical condition for his thirty-nine years of age and had maintained his strict fitness regime even after retiring from the army's Special Forces division.

He launched his small runabout further up the inlet, trying to keep well clear of the public marina and Microbe's men. As he slowly motored down the river with his fishing rod and crab pots, looking like any other fisherman, he scanned the area for a good spot to anchor unnoticed but also in the vicinity of the *Talisman* and found the perfect spot amongst the mangroves.

Quickly getting into his diving gear, he clipped a small bag to his belt that held the tracking device he planned to attach to the underside of Microbe's boat and then armed himself with a torch, dive knife, spear gun and compass that he strapped to his wrist. After estimating the time it would take to swim the distance from his runabout to the *Talisman*, he set his watch timer, which flashes at the end of the set time. Suddenly he heard a loud noise, similar to that of a crocodile snapping its powerful jaws over its prey. Pushing this to the back of his mind he quietly entered the water, going down as deep as possible so his torch light would not be detected from above, but also knowing crocodiles are more likely to stay closer to the surface this time of year, as the water temperature is warmer and more to their liking.

After a while he realised his torch was virtually useless as the water was much murkier than first thought, so he had to rely solely on his compass and the timer on his watch. Suddenly he saw a bright green flash on his wrist, alerting him that he should be below his required target. Slowly rising to the surface, knowing this was the most dangerous stage of his mission. He had more chance of becoming a crocs dinner now, as it was common practice to throw any food scraps over the side of the boat, which was one of the things that attracted them to the inlet and the marina, if his calculations were incorrect, he could resurface and be totally exposed. As he looked up, he could see a distorted glow and knew it was coming from the lights of the marina as they shone down on the water. He slowly broke the surface not making a sound and was pleased to see the markings of the *Talisman*.

Having done this sort of thing many times back in his military training, he swiftly attached the device before making a careful descent below and headed back to the mangroves and his small runabout. As soon as he broke the surface, he swiftly pulled himself back into his boat, removing his dive gear and stowing it out of view. Before he started the motor, he threw his crab pots overboard, the mission was a success and maybe there would be a bonus of some crabs in his pots the following morning.

* * *

Max had an intense dislike for Malcolm Microbe; it all started years ago when he had come to a point in his life when he had seen too many battles and too many men killed. At that time, he was recovering from a bullet wound to his shoulder and had picked the sleepy little seaside town of Eden Cove to lay low. The relaxed lifestyle of the locals and the fact he was far from the noise of war, or the fast pace of the city had him hooked.

It was by mere chance he met Microbe, he had been browsing properties for sale in the window of a local Real Estate office, which happened to be owned by Malcolm Microbe. Buying a place of his own had never been a consideration before, but now he felt the need for somewhere to escape. Microbe had been watching him from inside, noting Max had his arm in a sling and a look of indecision on his face; he knew this person was ripe for the picking. After inviting Max inside, he began his spiel; about having inside information on an apartment that was about to go on the market. The owner was in financial difficulty and the place was going for a steal, the bargain of a lifetime. Max could sense he was being conned, but agreed to take a look at the property anyway.

His initial reaction to the place was one of surprise, sure, it needed a little work but the price the owner was asking was definitely a steal, *there had to be a catch*. As if reading his thoughts Microbe said he was welcome to have the place inspected by a reputable builder, an offer Max decided to take up.

Obtaining a builder for the inspection had been much harder than Max first thought. Of the few available builders in the area, they were all too busy or unable to carry out his request. Max realised he was fast running out of builders to call and was starting to wonder if there was another reason why they would not go near the place? He had come to the point of calling Microbe and telling him he wasn't interested when there was a knock at the door of his motel room.

His combat instincts immediately kicking in, as there was only one person who knew of his whereabouts and he knew that under no circumstances would he divulge that information. Grabbing his gun from under the pillow, he cautiously made his way to the window beside the door and moved the curtain a fraction to peek out.

Standing directly in front of his door was a young girl of fourteen or fifteen, with long dirty blonde hair and dressed totally in black, wearing long black boots and a ridiculously short mini skirt. He shoved his gun in the waistband at the back of his jeans before unlocking the door.

He noticed the unhealthy pallor of her skin and the over use of facial piercings and despite her young age he could see this girl had an attitude.

"Are you Max Steel?"

He was taken aback she knew his name, but also the fact she had a large bolt through her tongue.

"Who are you and what on earth possessed you to pierce

your face with all that metal?"

"I didn't come here for a lecture on my personal appearance, I just want to know if you are Max Steel; is that too hard a question to answer?"

He noticed the defiant look in her eyes as she folded her arms across her chest. There was something about her, something familiar, but he was sure he had never seen her before.

"First answer my question, who are you, what are you doing here and how the hell did you find me?"

"I'm not just a pretty face; you'd be amazed at what I am capable of!"

"You still haven't told me who you are and what you're doing here."

"My name is Michelle, Michelle Brown I am here to find my father Max Steel."

He raised his eyebrows at her, *were the hell did this girl get off?* Then as he stared at her, he remembered he knew a girl once and her name was Brown. *No couldn't be, that was years ago, we were only kids!*

"You're kidding me right?"

"Do I look like the sort of person who would kid around; OK don't answer that. Look I've got a letter here that will explain everything, do you want to read it out here in the open, or are you going to let me come inside?"

Max looked over the top of her head and quickly scanned the area before letting her come inside and then closed the door behind her. She quickly scanned the room before making a beeline for the small bar fridge.

"Have you got anything to eat, I'm starving?"

Without waiting for a response, she opened the fridge and found it devoid of food, but there was a six-pack of beer. She grabbed a stubby and expertly twisted off the lid before bringing it to her lips.

"What the hell do you think you are doing?" He asked as he took the stubby from her.

"What does it look like?

"You're far too young to be drinking; you couldn't be more than fifteen!"

"As a matter of fact I am almost sixteen and what do you care anyway, since when did you decide to play dad?"

"I had no idea I had a daughter and you haven't proven to me that I am your father, or produced this mysterious letter and by the way, how did you find me?"

Michelle looked at him defiantly, then rummaged in her handbag before pulling out a thick envelope and thrust it in his face. He quickly unfolded the letter:

Max,

I know this is not the way for you to discover you are a father, but the time had come for you both to know the truth. Firstly, the reason I never told you was we were both very young and you had just started your career in the army and by then we had gone our separate ways. I'm not sure if you remember John, but he was always keen on me, well he asked me to marry him, even though he knew I was carrying your child, it was only recently Michelle discovered John was not her father. She had always been a determined headstrong child and when she discovered the truth, she became even more difficult to control. Mainly due to this fact and her determination to meet her biological father, with John's help we were able to locate your whereabouts. I am hoping that with your guidance you might be able to steer her in the right direction, for I have exhausted all my possibilities. I have also enclosed her Birth Certificate, as I know you will want proof, but you only have to take a good look at her to know she is your daughter.

Sincerely,
Adele Brown.

He quickly scanned the Birth Certificate, and then looked at the girl standing before him and suddenly it dawned on him why she seemed familiar, it was her eyes, he saw those eyes every morning when he shaved. Her eyes were turquoise blue and fringed with coal black lashes, almost identical to his.

As he looked at her, he could see her appearance was all a facade, behind it all she was just a frightened little girl. The thought of Adele keeping such a thing from him, made him extremely angry and that moment had been the turning point in his life.

He realised it was time for him to face facts, he had seen enough war, it was time to retire from the army and face up to his responsibilities as a father and Eden Cove seemed to be the perfect place.

Once his mind was made up, things moved quickly, he finally located a builder who was willing to check over the property. The builder's report stated the building was structurally sound and was in actual fact valued much higher than the asking price.

It was not long after contracts were signed and Max and Michelle moved in, he realised he had been duped. The report was falsified; the apartment was overvalued, because it had numerous problems. It turned out the builder, who supplied the original report, was one of Microbe's shonky mates, whose license had been revoked, He was later to discover the other builders had been threatened by Microbe to stay clear, but by this time, it was too late, as Microbe had very cleverly imbedded a binding clause in the contract, one that Max had no hope of getting out of and it turned out to be a very costly exercise.

Never before had anyone so successfully pulled the wool over the eyes of Max Steel, so it became his personal quest to put Microbe behind bars and throw away the key!

CHAPTER THREE

It was early morning and Josh was driving, Michelle and Jane chatted in the back but for some reason the men remained silent in front. Michelle wondered where Josh was taking them as they were now on the outskirts of Eden Cove, which mainly consisted of bush and farmland, something Michelle thought strange as she assumed he'd take them to Eden Cove's small airport. She was starting to wonder where this supposed helicopter was or if in fact it existed, when an open paddock came into view and in the middle was a small blue and white helicopter

Without warning, Josh suddenly turned off the sealed road and onto a bumpy dirt track, causing the girls to be thrown about in the back. As they neared the helicopter Josh didn't make any attempt to slow down and Michelle was about to comment, when she noticed an old barn up ahead on the right *perhaps there is another chopper inside*. He was driving so fast the car bumped crazily over the road and it appeared he was going to drive right past the barn when once again he turned sharply and steered the vehicle inside the open barn door. The instant the car was past the barn doors he stamped on the brakes, bringing the car to a skidding halt, engulfing them in a large cloud of dust.

Apart from the ticking sound of the car cooling, there was total silence, as all passengers were still registering what just happened. As the dust slowly settled Michelle looked across at Jane, noting her face seemed to be frozen in fright and her hands still bracing the front seat. Suddenly the whole ridiculousness of the situation dawned on Michelle and she burst out laughing, causing Jane to snap out of her trance and looked at her as if she had gone completely mad!

"I feel like I'm in some B grade movie and I should drop and roll as soon as I get out of the car!" Exclaimed Michelle.

"It wouldn't be much of a secret if we landed the chopper

in town!" Exclaimed Josh.

Michelle thought about the many helicopters that came and went to the small airport, bringing the tourists from the city or taking them to see the sights of the Great Barrier Reef. *No, a helicopter would probably draw more attention out here in the middle of a paddock. As for driving the car into a barn, at a ridiculous speed, it was almost laughable, how many movies had this guy been in, because he definitely had one hell of an imagination?*

Trying to hide her smile, she thought it could only add to the excitement of the trip. It was a beautiful clear day and not a cloud in sight, perfect for flying, something she was well familiar with, as she had been flying many times with her father.

The girls were enjoying the flight and Michelle had to admit Tom was a good pilot; she never tired of the view of the reef from the air and was so enthralled it took her a moment to get her bearings to Lagoon Island.

"The best spot to land is just up ahead, so you better inflate the floats on the skids."

"If there is a patch of flat ground on that island, I can land this baby anywhere!" Stated Tom.

"I told you there is no possible place to land on the island; you have to land on the water!"

"I agree with Michelle, it too dangerous and I don't fancy a crash landing!" Exclaimed Jane.

"Relax girls if Tom says he can land here I trust his judgement; he's the best helicopter pilot there is."

"This is suicide!"

Michelle was angry, she knew Tom was trying to impress them, but needlessly risking other people's lives was a definite turn off! Josh took off his sunglasses before turning around and then with a smile, he stretched out his hand and put it on her leg.

"Just relax, trust me Tom has done this sort of landing many times before."

The look Josh gave Michelle and the suggestive way he was rubbing his hand on her leg, anything further she had planned to say, was effectively silenced.

As the helicopter made its descent, Michelle looked out the window and saw the small clearing below. Bracing herself, she could feel the machine shudder as the rotor blades were slicing through protruding branches and leaves, which were overhanging the small clearing. She looked across at Jane who had her eyes tightly shut and all the colour had drained from her face.

With the combination of the branches and the wind currents from below, the little helicopter appeared to be struggling to keep in its upright position and Michelle wondered if this was what it was like to be in a tornado. Finally she felt the skids touch the ground and expelled a lung full of air, not realising she had been holding her breath and Jane had been tightly gripping her hand.

Moments later Jane released her painful grip and Michelle quickly unbuckled her seat belt and ripped off her headset, throwing it to the floor and launched herself forward grabbing a handful of Tom's shirt and knocking off his headset as she pulled him towards her.

"You ever do anything like that again without my say so; I'll knock your bloody head off!"

"I got you down in one piece didn't I?"

"Lucky for you!"

"Okay enough, no one was hurt so let's set up camp and enjoy ourselves!" Said Josh.

They found a good protected area for their camp and then Michelle took them on a guided tour over a good portion of the island. It was a usual hot day for the tropics so Michelle suggested they go for a swim and a snorkel.

Later that night they all sat around a small campfire enjoying the food and drink Josh had brought, when he asked Michelle if she'd like to go for a walk. Needing no encouragement, Michelle quickly mouthing to Jane, '*don't wait up'*.

With Michelle and Josh gone it was obvious to Jane that Tom was jealous as he seemed distracted and had no interest in conversation with her, so she decided to go to bed.

* * *

Jane was suddenly jolted from her sleep as a hand clamped over her mouth; she tried to scream while desperately clawing at it trying to pull it away. She was so scared she could hear the blood pounding in her ears and started to feel faint.

"Jane it's me Michelle, don't make a sound, we have to get out of here!" She said as she slowly released her hand.

"What's going on, you almost gave me a heart attack?"

"I can't talk now, just follow me and keep quiet."

Michelle stealthily led Jane away from the camp, after about five minutes they stopped.

"What the hell is going on you scared me half to death, I thought someone was trying to kill me?

"I was trying to keep you quiet, I think Josh is dead, someone shot him and we could be next on the list!"

"Are you serious?"

"You really think I would joke about something like this?"

"Well you have been known to…"

"OK, OK, trust me this time it is no joke; obviously there is someone else on the island, someone who is not too happy about us being here!"

"What about Tom, where is he?"

"I don't know I wasn't bothering to find out; my only thought was waking you and getting away from the camp!"

"To where?"

"I don't know I just know we would have been sitting ducks if we stayed there!"

They sat in silence for a while, Michelle's brain was in overload *why would someone kill Josh and how did they know he was going to be here?*

"Do you think it's possible there's some weirdo living on the island that no one sees in the day?" Asked Jane.

"I don't know I certainly didn't see any signs of anyone else here; my instincts tell me it's got something to do with drugs."

"You mean their growing something here?"

"Hmm doubt it, possibly a drop off point."

"Michelle maybe this is why Josh wanted us to keep quiet about them being in Eden Cove?"

"Yeah come to think of it, remember when you asked them if they were with the movie crew and Tom was going to deny it?"

"Oh my god; how dumb are we; what have we got ourselves involved in?"

"I don't know."

"So what happened, did you see the guy?"

"One minute I was kissing Josh and then he said he heard a noise in the bush and ran off to check it out. I heard him argue with someone and then a gun went off. I wasn't about to wait and be next so I hid behind some bushes and waited to see if Josh came back out, but he didn't!"

"What are we going to do?"

"We have to go back to the camp."

"Are you insane?"

"We have to get our stuff; unfortunately we can't call for help, because we didn't think we would need our phones."

"Your idea, not mine!"

"Yeah well we don't have time to argue about it, this island is not big enough to hide for too long; our only chance is if we leave the island tonight."

"How do you propose we do that, we don't have a boat and you don't know how to fly a helicopter?"

"The only way we can, we swim."

"Are you insane, crocs cruise these waters at night and besides were the hell, are we going to swim to?"

"I know a place but I don't have time to explain now, first

we have to get our gear and get as far away from camp as possible. You can stay here if you want; you should be safe as long as you remain quiet."

"You're not leaving me here on my own, I'm coming with you!"

"Okay, but be quiet."

"Of course, but you might hear my knees knocking."

They slowly made their way back and as they approached the camp, they could hear someone talking and Michelle signalled Jane to hide behind a bush.

"I'm going to get closer and see if it's Tom." Michelle whispered

Jane nodded her head, but instead of staying put, she followed Michelle. The camp light was on and they could see a person lying motionless on the ground; Jane put her hand over her mouth and stifled a cry. Michelle once again signalled for them to crouch low, as she tried to listen to who was talking. Suddenly she realised the conversation was one sided as he was talking on the phone, but what sent chills down Michelle's spine; she realised it was Josh!

"I thought you said he was dead?" Jane whispered

Suddenly the talking stopped and Michelle scowled at Jane, dragging her finger across her throat giving her the hint to shut up! Not game to move a muscle both sat motionless, hoping he hadn't heard Jane; suddenly he started talking again.

"Don't worry both girls will be dead by morning, they haven't got any form of communication, we're just playing a little game of cat and mouse; this island isn't big enough to hide for long. Besides I've got the chopper and no one knows they're here!"

Both girls looked at each other, as it dawned on them the real reason they were brought here. Michelle saw tears well up in Jane's eyes and quickly grabbed her hand and gave it a squeeze; they couldn't afford to lose control now, not if they wanted a chance at getting off the island alive! Michelle signalled Jane she was going to try to sneak into their tent and get their gear. Jane nodded in acknowledgment and crossed her fingers before looking across at Josh, while Michelle crept silently towards their tent.

To Michelle's relief the tent was still unzipped, because of their earlier hasty exit. She quickly ducked into the tent, grabbed her watertight bag, and quickly threw in a pair of binoculars, a warm jacket for them both, bottled water and energy bars. She quickly strapped her dive knife to her hip and grabbed the other bag that held their flippers. She knew precious seconds were ticking by and could not waste any more time thinking about what they might need. As she quickly and silently made her way back to Jane, she signalled for her to remain quiet and follow.

After about twenty minutes, when Michelle was fairly certain they hadn't been followed, she found a safe spot amongst the bushes to rest and give her time to think.

"What the hell is going on, I thought you said you saw Josh get shot and who was that lying on the ground, he looked like he was dead?" Jane babbled in one breath.

Michelle could see she was starting to lose it.

"I think it was Tom."

"What, why would Josh kill Tom?"

"I'm thinking he knew what Josh was up to and tried to either warn me or stop Josh."

"Why does he want to kill us, what did we ever do to deserve this?"

"I wish I knew, all I know is we have to get off this island as soon as possible,"

"You still don't plan to swim out in the dark?"

"It's our only hope, if we wait till morning it could be too late. Remember he has the chopper and I know he won't fly at night; it has no lights. The darkness is our cover as there's barely even a moon tonight."

"What about the crocs and where are we supposed to swim to?"

"The crocs are a risk we have to take! About a year ago a

guy took me to Oyster Island and if my memory is correct, it's about two kilometres from here, it's perfect; no one in their right mind would want to go there!"

"Then why the hell are we?"

"Jeez Jane, its blondes like you that give us a bad name, THINK! It is called Oyster Island because very sharp and dangerous oyster-covered rocks surround it!"

"Well how do you propose we get on this Island, if it is surrounded by such dangerous rocks and what about the crocs?"

"There is a safe passage which we discovered and as for the crocs, we need to weigh up the odds. Do we stay here and definitely get shot and fed to the crocs, or do we risk swimming to the island and possibly get eaten by crocs along the way?"

"Isn't there a choice number three?"

"Afraid not. Look if we make the island there's a tree house there, it will provide us with some shelter until we are rescued."

"Big emphasis on if!"

There was the small issue of Michelle remembering where the safe passage was, let alone finding it in the dark, but she wasn't about to voice this to Jane, not yet anyway.

They kept walking till they came to a small beach on the other side of the island, one Josh didn't know about, she had been planning on showing them this spot in the morning; but obviously, that wouldn't be happening now!

"Michelle I've been thinking about what happens if we make it to the island; how are we supposed to get rescued when no one knows where we are?"

"Max is a smart man, he'll figure it out!"

"I don't know why you think Max would care if you were at the cottage or not."

"He has this thing about checking up on me."

"I know he always looked out for you and your mum because you lived in the cottage on his property, but you're a big girl now, why would he care whether you're there or not and besides, you left your car there?"

"Ah yeah, forgot about that, but trust me there's nothing to worry about, all we have to do is swim to the island and sit tight until the rescue party turns up."

"You make it sound so simple, but you're forgetting what we might encounter in the water!"

Michelle didn't bother to respond as she'd just noticed a small light on the water. She signalled Jane to remain quiet and got out the binoculars. *Dad's going to have a fit when he finds out I borrowed these babies with the night vision capability; who would have thought I'd really need them!*

Switching them to night vision, she could see a boat moving silently through the water. It was practically invisible on this dark moonless night and as she strained her ears she couldn't hear the hum of an engine, in fact she couldn't hear any noise at all. *They must be powered by the wind in the sails. Maybe help is already here, although they weren't displaying navigation lights, if anything they were trying not to be seen*!

"What do you see?"

"A boat."

"Oh thank god we don't have to swim with the crocs!"

Michelle assumed they were using GPS navigation, because it was insane to travel these waters at night and without lights to warn other boats of their presence to avoid a collision!

She changed the focus on the lens and zoomed in further, noticing two men carrying something out from the cabin of the boat. Assuming it to be heavy, as they appeared to be struggling with the weight as they walked over to the side and with one almighty heave, threw it overboard. As if in slow motion the box spun slowly in mid-air, before tilting end down and then entering the water like a diver, she could actually hear the gentle splash.

"Michelle what's wrong, why aren't you excited about the boat?"

Michelle suddenly remembered seeing such a box before and quickly scanned the side of the boat for the usual markings. It was like a form of registration, denoting the name and port of origin of a boat, but it appeared as though all such markings were covered up.

The hairs on the back of her neck suddenly prickled, as she was sure this was the very boat she had been on only day's prior. For the first time in Michelle's life, she felt real fear, as she noticed the men were all carrying semi-automatic assault rifles. *Was this the real reason Jane and herself were brought out here, because of what she had seen on the Talisman?*

"My god!" Gasped Michelle.

"What is it?"

"The guys on board are carrying assault rifles!"

"Are you sure, do you recognise the boat?"

Michelle brought the binoculars back up to her eyes, she was certain she knew the name of this boat, but couldn't bring herself to tell Jane. It suddenly dawned on her that her curiosity might very well get herself and her friend killed!

"All the markings on the boat have been covered up and being so dark, at this distance, it's hard to get a clear visual of the boat."

"Who would be out here at this hour and carrying guns?"

"Ah because they're obviously doing something illegal!"

"Do you think they're looking for us?"

"I don't think so, they dropped something overboard and I think it was weighted so it would sink to the bottom."

"Maybe a body."

Michelle felt certain it was the same box she had picked the lock on and one thing was for sure, if there had been a dead body in there, the smell would have given it away. Besides, if they had wanted to get rid of a body, all they needed to do was to throw it to the crocs; there were plenty of them around in these parts. *Dam, why did she have to remind herself of that!*

"Well?"

"Shush."

Michelle put her hand over Jane's mouth and they sat silently and waited for the boat to leave. When Michelle was sure there was no movement on the beach and confident Josh wasn't in the vicinity, she started slicing branches off the trees with her dive knife.

"What are you doing?"

"We are going to need all the protection we can get when we enter the water; I'm hoping these branches will do the trick until we get to the island."

"You're referring to the crocs?"

"Ah yeah, I hope it works, unless you have a better idea?"

"How about a gun and maybe some croc proofing armour."

"I'm afraid we are fresh out of those, these branches will have to do and I have my dive knife; just hope I don't have to use it, I don't really fancy doing the crocodile Dundee thing. Are you ready?"

"No!" Replied Jane nervously.

"It's now or never, just stay close to me; we'll have regular stops to check our bearings and keep a look out for crocs."

They slowly made their way towards the water and organised themselves between the branches. As they entered the water, both girls gasped not expecting it to be so cool and Michelle hoped they would not have to add hypothermia to their list of worries, but then the cooler temperature could be in their favour, as crocodiles where known to like the warmer water.

For the first time in her life, Michelle actually prayed. She had done some risky things in her life always looking for that big rush, but this was definitely not something she would have willingly chosen to do, as the odds stacked against them were far too high!

They had been moving slowly through the water for over an hour, constantly reassuring each other along the way, trying desperately not to think of what else might be in the water but trying to stay focussed on the island they were heading for.

It was a moonless night and Michelle was using the stars to

help navigate, another survival trick her father had taught her. Because it was such a dark night it seemed to make the swim for their lives even that much more frightening, but Michelle tried to look at it in a positive way and told Jane it would make it impossible for anyone on Lagoon Island to see them.

Despite Michelle having been a risk taker all her life, she struggled with a rising fear, as she had never attempted an open ocean swim before, let alone at night.

Suddenly Michelle felt the branches she had been clinging to start to move of their own accord and she struggled to keep a grip on them.

"Michelle, what's happening, it's like something is trying to pull the branches away from me?"

"I don't know, just don't let go!"

"I'm scared; I think there is something swimming underneath me!"

"Try to get as much of your body as possible out of the water onto the branches."

Michelle tried to do the same while angling closer to Jane who was panicking and thrashing about in the water.

"Jane, stop panicking your only drawing attention to yourself with all that noise!"

Michelle could hear Jane really crying as she struggled to swim over to her friend. *What the hell is going on, it's like I'm in a rip?* Michelle finally managed to get over to Jane and grab hold of her branches as Jane desperately struggled to get on top of them, when suddenly it dawned on Michelle what was happening.

"The shipping channel, we're in the shipping channel, quick get back in the water we have to swim hard!"

"Why?"

"I'm not trying to scare you, but we're caught in the strong currents, we have to swim hard to get out of them or get run down by a tanker!"

Both were fully aware of what would happen if they were still in the channel and a large tanker, many of which frequented these waters, came past. There was not only the risk of being run over, as despite their size they moved at amazing speeds, if the bow of the boat did not kill them, the powerful props churning the water would. They could be sucked under with no chance of resurfacing, or be cut to pieces by the massive churning blades!

"Jane do you remember when we used to have swimming races?"

"Yeah."

"Well I bet I can still beat you."

"What?"

"Bet I can still beat you!"

Jane realised what her friend was trying to do and instantly started kicking harder, trying to imagine she was back in the pool and not on a swim for her life! As soon as Michelle realised Jane had taken up the challenge she swum her hardest, all thoughts of tankers and crocs temporarily gone from her mind, her only focus was on their destination.

Michelle's legs were cramping from the exertion and she realised Jane was beginning to lag behind. She slowed up and moments later so did Jane, both relieved they could no longer feel the strong currents running underneath.

"Try swimming on your back for a while, give yourself a bit of a rest, I'll keep my eye on where we're going," said Michelle.

Jane thankfully turned on her back and Michelle kept a hold of her arm to ensure she went in the right direction.

"Michelle, do you think we are going to die?"

"The thought has crossed my mind, but I think it best if we try to remain positive."

"On the off chance we don't make it, can I ask you something?"

"Sure."

"You consider me your best friend don't you?"

"Of course!"

"You know real friends trust each other and tell them their

deepest, darkest secrets."

"Jane, what are you getting at?"

"You know when we first met and I used to come and have sleep overs at your place and Ann would bake cookies and make hot chocolate with marshmallows?"

"Yeah."

"She's not really your mother is she?"

"Where the hell did that come from?"

"Well for starters you always called her Ann, not mum."

"So?"

"Come on, it's the truth isn't it?"

Michelle's mind was racing a million miles an hour, it had been difficult keeping the secret of Max Steel being her father and the pretence he was just keeping his eye out for her and Ann, who was posing as her mother, *but Jane was right, they might not survive the night.*

"Yes."

"Why did you pretend she was?"

"It was supposed to be for my own safety."

"Oh my god, you're in the witness protection program, that's why Josh is trying to kill us!"

"Ahh, wrong. I really am Michelle Brown; it's because of my father."

"But he's dead."

"Wrong again, Max Steel is my father."

"I don't understand."

"Before I came to Eden Cove I thought my father was John Brown, but then I found my Birth Certificate. As you know Max Steel used to be in the army, apparently it was something very secret and he did a lot of real dangerous stuff, stuff that created enemies and he was afraid they would try to hurt me to get to him, hence the reason Ann lived with me in the cottage when I was younger."

"Is your real mother still alive?"

"Yes."

"How did she feel about Ann?"

"She was cool about it; she knew it was for my own safety."

"It explains a lot, but also why Josh is trying to kill us; it's because of your father."

"I don't think so."

"Why else would anyone want to kill us, there is no other explanation?"

Michelle couldn't bring herself to answer that, but she was almost certain this had nothing to do with her father. She noticed the blackness of the sky was slowly turning grey as morning was approaching and with the lightening of the sky the stars began to fade. Michelle paused, momentarily treading water trying to see if there were any landmarks ahead when she noticed something in the water ahead of them. Keeping her eyes focused on the shape ahead, her heart rate increased, desperately hoping it was not the one thing they had been afraid of encountering while in the water.

"How you doing Shell, want to have a rest while I keep look out?"

"Nah its ok."

Michelle tried desperately to keep the quake out of her voice and hoped Jane hadn't noticed. The shape was getting larger and there was no mistaking the lumpy ridges, of a crocs back, she instinctively put her hand to her dive knife, needing reassurance it was still there. Michelle swallowed the lump in her throat, as there was a strong possibly it was her doing that got her friend involved in a threat against their lives and now, apart from some branches, Jane had no form of protection.

She slowly pulled the knife from its sheath and firmly gripped it in her right hand before kicking her legs harder, trying to get in front of her friend. Michelle knew if she had any hope of winning a fight with a croc, she needed it to stay on the surface; she would have only one chance to sink the sharp blade of her knife so it penetrated the brain, but if the croc decided to go below the surface, then their odds of both surviving were definitely none.

Michelle was having trouble focusing with a combination of terror and tears that refused to stay in check. She noticed the shape was getting larger and almost screamed, as it seemed to loom above her. Suddenly her flipper made contact with something under the surface and Jane yelled out, causing Michelle to turn. *We're about to die and Jane is smiling!*

"We made it Shell, we made it!"

In confusion, Michelle turned expecting to be looking directly into the large jaws of a crocodile, but instead the lumpy shape that had been growing larger was in actual fact the rocky outcrop of Oyster Island, realising her flipper had come in contact with one of the oyster-covered rocks that surrounded the island.

Michelle turned back to her friend, no longer trying to hide her emotions, crying and laughing at the same time, quickly re-sheathing her knife before hugging her friend. She wanted nothing more than to swim her hardest and feel her feet on solid ground, but she knew she had to focus on remembering the safe passage to get onto the island.

"We can't go any closer till I get my bearings and remember where the safe entry is."

"Well don't take too long, I feel like I am being watched by something with more than two legs."

Think Michelle! Think! Marker, what was the marker? She closed her eyes and tried to remember back to the day she first came here. *A tree, palm trees close together, yes that's it!*

"Look for three palm trees that look like they're growing out of one base."

They both slowly paddled at a safe distance from the razor sharp rocks and as the light of the new day first began it provided a good silhouette of the island.

"Look over there, is that it?"

"Yes! Now the passage is very narrow, so I'll go in front and you follow close behind me."

They inched along slowly, as a cut from an oyster off these rocks would cause a serious infection if antibiotics weren't administered very soon thereafter, suddenly Michelle felt her flippers dig into sand.

"You can stand up now, but be careful it's still narrow, probably a good idea to take off our flippers so we don't trip." said Michelle.

Michelle never thought it could feel so good to remove her flippers and the feel of the sand as it moved between her toes; it was almost to the point of being delicious.

Finally they had made their way on to the small beach and found a safe spot to rest, Michelle unzipped her watertight bag and pulled out a bottle of water, an energy bar and two pairs of sandshoes.

"I'm sure you're as hungry and thirsty as me, but we have to stretch out our rations as much as possible."

"Well by the look of these rocks we won't go hungry, look at all the oysters?"

"Yeah, let's hope we can find some water and we'll be set!"

Both drank from the bottle and shared an energy bar, then put on their shoes and made their way through the bush to where Michelle thought the tree house was.

"Welcome to our new abode," said Michelle with a wave of her arm.

Jane stopped and tried to focus on what was in front of her, at first she thought it was just a tree with a lot of vines growing around it, but after she stared at it for a while she realised it was a well-camouflaged tree house.

"I'm so glad it is well off the ground at least it will keep out the nasty four-legged creatures, providing they also know the safe passage onto the island!" Commented Jane.

"Well thanks to Mother Nature and whoever built this, if Josh happens to fly over I don't think he will see it."

"I wonder who built it, what if they still live here."

"I wondered the same thing the first time I saw it, but after asking around, without letting on about this particular island, I found out that some Vietnam vets returning after years of living in the jungle, had trouble adjusting to suburban living. Legend has it; many could not cope with society and built shacks in remote areas to escape."

"Well whatever the reason I'm glad we have some shelter and hope it will offer enough protection till we're rescued!"

"So do I, now I'll go up first to check the safety of the ladder and make sure we are alone."

Michelle unsheathed her knife and slowly made her way up the ladder, then gingerly peeked inside hoping she wouldn't be looking directly into the barrel of a gun or a pair of some creature's eyes. Momentarily waiting for her eyes to adjust she looked into the darkened room. Confident it was uninhabited, she climbed inside and found that apart from dirt, moss and cobwebs the place was empty and would be a good place to hide, not only offering protection from the elements, but also making them virtually invisible to anyone flying over.

"It seems safe enough, although we might want to take some bushy branches up first and clear out the cobwebs."

When the tree house was reasonably cobweb free, they drank another ration of water before collapsing on the floor and within minutes, both girls fell into a deep exhausted sleep.

CHAPTER FOUR

"Hello."
"Boss its Damon, the package has been delivered."
"Good and the payment?"
"Everything went according to plan."
"Good, we might have to increase the shipment next time."
"No problems."

The line was disconnected and Microbe went and poured himself a drink, he had been tempted to ask Damon about the Steel girl, but then realised it was better he didn't know. He was sure her father would point the finger at him, so the less he knew about it the better.

His thoughts were now on Max Steel, god how he hated that name! He knew he had a vendetta against him for sucking him into that property scam; something he would regret for the rest of his days!

Charlene his wife walked into the room, causing him to pour himself another drink. God with all the money she had spent on a plastic surgeon he still couldn't look at her without needing a drink. He should have had the man killed for what he did to her face, it was pulled so tight her skin looked like plastic and one eye was higher than the other and to make things worse she continued over bleaching her hair so it looked like it was made of straw; no wonder he had a mistress!

"Darling, you haven't forgotten we're going out to dinner with my sister and her husband, have you?"

Malcolm poured himself yet another drink, *god what did I do to deserve this? I should have put a contract out on all three a long time ago and these dinners always managed to cost him.*

"Charlene just once it would be nice if that whining sister and her free-loading husband paid their way!"

"Don't be like that; it will get the evening off to a bad start."

Like it hasn't already! He poured himself another drink.

In the meantime, Damon was concerned, it was mid-afternoon and he hadn't heard anything further from Josh. Damon realised he'd have to go to Lagoon Island himself, he had to have this matter cleared up before he even thought about another shipment, he couldn't risk them crossing paths with any rescue efforts looking for two missing girls.

Damon had used Josh before and has never had any qualms about using him again, but this time Josh had insisted it wasn't a one-man job if they wanted to avoid any possible suspicion. Damon's first impression of Tom was that he wasn't cut out for this kind of work but Josh had convinced him otherwise.

The fact Josh had their only chopper meant he'd have to take the Van Witsen, but his real concern was if Josh had screwed up, the missing chopper was registered to Microbe, which would link him to the girls deaths.

* * *

Max decided to check the track log on his computer that was monitoring the tracking device he'd attached to the *Talisman*. It showed the boat had recently done a trip and when he checked these details on his maritime chart, he was surprised that not only did they not make any stops, but the area they had travelled in was far too dangerous at night, being frequented by large tankers, especially at that hour. *Why would they risk travelling these waters at night, only to do a loop back to port?*

* * *

Michelle rolled over and let out a soft groan, as there was not a single part of her body that didn't ache. Struggling to sit up she looked around her, taking in her surroundings, the dusty old shack, Jane still asleep on the floor next to her, realisation dawning on her of where she was and why her body ached. It came flooding back to her, their daring escape from Lagoon

Island, followed by a mammoth swim through dangerous croc infested waters.

She sat there motionless and listened to the noises coming from outside, straining her ears for anything that sounded remotely like an approaching helicopter. There was the noisy chatter of birds and the distant sound of the waves crashing over rocks and to her relief no sound of an approaching helicopter. Not sure if her legs were yet capable of holding her upright, she slowly and cautiously crawled her way over to the entrance, trying not to wake Jane but also not wanting to make a noise in case someone might be standing below. She gingerly poked her head outside looking in every possible direction, from her position she could see the small beach they had arrived on and wondered if their tree house was well camouflaged in full light.

As she hobbled down the ladder, the hot sun burned on her salt-caked body, making it itchy and sore. The thought of a cool soothing bath was almost too much to bear and as she tried to dust the worst of the salt from her body, it only inflamed the mosquito bites that covered her arms and legs. Standing back and taking a good look up at the tree house, she could see Mother Nature had definitely done her job in ensuring it was well hidden.

"What are you looking at?"

Michelle jumped at the sound of Jane's voice, as it seemed to echo across the island and was about to rebuke her for yelling, when she burst into fits of laughter at the sight of her salt-caked hair that was sticking out like a straw scarecrow.

"What's so funny?" Asked Jane as she descended the ladder

"You; if only we had a mirror."

"You're one to talk; if you could see yourself, you'd be hoping the rescue crew is all female!"

Michelle instantly stopped laughing and looked at Jane.
"That bad?"
"That bad!"

Both girls looked at each other, then they both burst out laughing, they were laughing so hard, they were crying and once the tears came, it was hard to stop, as reality dawned on them of what they had been through in the last twenty-four hours!

"How long do you think it will be before we are rescued?"

"Who knows? Hopefully my boss will be so pissed off tomorrow when I don't show up for work he'll call my dad, he won't waste any time and he will start a search straight away."

"What makes you think he will call Max?"

"When I first started working with Harry I had to list an emergency contact, which I stated was Ann Brown."

"But she doesn't live with you anymore."

"I know, but the call will go through to Max, he will put two and two together, trust me we will be fine."

"Don't you have to be classed as missing for twenty four hours, before the police will even consider a search party?"

"Come on, you yourself said Max is very protective of me, do you think he will let a little thing like that stop him?"

"I hope you are right. Why do you think Josh tried to kill us?"

"I have no idea, but one thing I am sure of, Josh is not his real name."

"Why don't we organise a signal, so when we hear them searching the island they can find us?"

"No can do. How will we know it's my father and not Josh? We just have to wait it out, now I don't know about you, but I'm thirsty and hungry, let's go back to the shack and sort out our rations."

As the girls placed out all their rations they both realised the greatest worry was running out of water, as the oysters provided them a good food source. Suddenly a noise penetrated Michelle's brain and as she sat there listening she noticed it was getting louder. At first it reminded her of the thumping vibration of a subwoofer, then her heart began to pound as it got louder she realised it was the thumping of a helicopter's rotor blades.

"Shit, it's a helicopter!" Exclaimed Michelle

"Thank God!"

Jane made a dash for the ladder of the tree house, but Michelle tackled her to the floor.

"What the hell are you doing? We need to let them know we are here!" Cried Jane.

"It's too soon, no one will know we're missing yet, it's obviously Josh!"

"Oh my God, what if he sees the shack, what if he lands on the island?"

"It is well hidden from the ground and hopefully from the air, I'm just hoping the foliage it too thick to land on the island."

"That didn't stop Tom!"

They both moved well away from the opening and huddled in the darkest corner as the noise became louder and louder as if it was heading straight for them. Suddenly dust started to stir in the tree house and leaves and debris started blowing everywhere. Michelle realised he was very close and as the tree house began to shake she knew he was virtually on top of them. Suddenly Jane reached out and clutched Michelle's hand, as the helicopter appeared to be hovering right above them.

Both girls huddled together, making themselves as small as possible and keeping their heads down and eyes closed from the ever-increasing swirl of dust and leaves. After what seemed like an age, the helicopter climbed to a higher altitude and appeared to be moving away as the sound grew fainter, until they could no longer hear it.

"Do you think he's gone?" Asked Jane in a hoarse whisper.

"I hope so, I think we should go outside and do our own search, just in case he saw the tree house and found somewhere to land."

Michelle walked over to her bag and grabbed the energy bars and bottles of water, throwing one to Jane, then strapped on her dive belt.

"We mightn't be able to come back here, so we need to take some supplies."

"Then shouldn't we take everything?"

"It will weigh us down too much; we're the ones being hunted, remember."

"I wish you hadn't said that!"

"Well get used to it, cause it's a fact. Now I'll go out first, then when I'm sure it is safe, I'll give you the all clear."

As Michelle made her way slowly down the ladder, she scanned the area and hoped she wasn't being observed. When she reached the bottom, she walked a small distance away from the shack, keeping her eyes peeled, before signalling Jane to come down.

"Now I've never really explored this island before, so we need to not only look for any signs of Josh, but fresh water and possibly another shelter."

"I hope we find enough to have a wash, my skin feels like it is on fire."

"I know how you feel! Now stay close and keep your eyes and ears peeled, I think it best if we don't speak, just grab my arm if you see or hear anything and I'll do likewise to you."

Jane nodded and followed closely behind Michelle who was using her dive knife to carefully mark a trail, but not so it would be visible to anyone else, the last thing they needed was to get lost. It was a clever trick her father had shown her on one of their many camping trips. She remembered back to the time when he had shown her, she had been bored and not really listening, she could still hear his voice.

"Michelle listen and take notice, it could be something which could very well save your life one day!"

She had rolled her eyes and thought her dad was so paranoid, as if she would need to do such a thing, but he made her take notice and tested her later on. She sent up a silent prayer of thanks to her dad and then wondered if she was feeling alright as that had been two prayers she had said in the space of twenty-four hours.

After walking for about an hour, Michelle suggested they stop for a break and a drink.

"Okay we'll just have a quarter of an energy bar each, we need to stretch out our rations as much as possible."

"Well if anything good does come out of this nightmare, it will be losing those extra kilos I didn't need!"

"That's the spirit Jane, stay positive!"

They both sat in silence while they ate, when Michelle suddenly jumped up and ran over to a clump of bushes.

"Look, do you recognise this plant?"

"No should I?"

"They need constant fresh water, there must be an underground stream, look how lush they are."

"Are you suggesting we dig to find it?"

"Not unless we really have to, but it does mean we are near a water source, come on let's get moving!"

Jane moaned as she got to her feet, she ached in places she didn't know she had, but Michelle seemed to have a new lease on life. After about fifteen minutes, they came upon another cluster of the same plants, bigger than the previous lot.

"You know what would be even better than finding water? A water hole or lagoon that we could swim in and wash off this salt!" Commented Jane.

"Now you're talking!"

As they moved forward, both had to stop themselves from running and making a noise as they moved through the bush, because they still didn't know if Josh had landed on the island. Michelle knew they were getting closer to fresh water, as the plants were becoming more abundant and the ones, which seemed to thrive closer to the ocean edge were almost non-existent. Suddenly Michelle heard a noise, grabbed Jane's arm and held a finger to her lips.

"Listen, can you hear that?" Whispered Michelle.

Jane listened for a minute and a smile came to her face as she realised it was the sound of running water. They moved slowly forward and suddenly came upon a clearing, causing

Michelle to grab Jane's arm and held a finger once again to her lips.

As the girls ventured cautiously out into the clearing, both gasped in amazement. Michelle wondered if she was hallucinating, as there was a small rock pool of beautiful clear water that was surrounded by lush green plants and flowers. It appeared as if there was an underground spring, as water was bubbling up through the rocks above and overflowing to the pool below.

"My god is this real or am I dreaming?" Asked Jane.

"I was thinking the same thing."

Both girls looked at one another then ran forward, but before Jane plonked herself in the water, Michelle stopped her.

"This could be our only water source and I don't want us to contaminate it, let's fill the water bottles and pour the water over us."

After ridding their hair and skin of salt and dirt, both girls rested for a while before refilling their bottles and continuing on their search of the island. After the girls had been walking for a time, Michelle was feeling pretty confident, realising the bush was so dense it would have been impossible for Josh to land.

"I think it is safe to say, there is no safe place for anyone to land on this island. It is almost impossible to walk through, let alone land a helicopter!"

"So you think it is safe enough to go back to the tree house?

"Yep, you know I've been thinking about how low he was flying over the tree house, Tom is dead so there is no way he could have maned the controls and get a good visual of what was below."

"So you don't think he saw our hideout?"

"No, I reckon he was just flying low trying to disturb the foliage, trying his best to see if anything was below."

"I hope you're right."

"So do I, the day is getting on so we better head back

before it gets dark."

On the way back, they stopped by the small rock pool and refilled their water bottles, both girls in brighter spirits, knowing they had food and water to sustain them until their rescue; but the fear Josh may have discovered their hideout was still at the forefront of their minds.

"Hey Jane, its Thursday."

"Yeah so?"

"It's your turn to cook."

"Okay, would you like oysters or oysters?"

"Mm let me see, I think I'll have oysters."

Both girls laughed trying to mask their fear as Jane headed towards the water and Michelle made her way to the tree house. Michelle ventured inside the tree house without waiting for her eyes to adjust to the darkness when the hairs on the back of her neck prickled.

"Great place you have here, I like what you've done with the decor."

"How did you find us?"

"Well it made sense, if you girls were dumb enough to try and swim; it was the next closest island. It took me a while to figure out how to get past those rocks, almost gave up, but I do have a reputation to uphold!"

"Why are you trying to kill us?"

"You heard the old saying, 'curiosity killed the cat' you just couldn't leave it alone could you? I wonder how Jane would feel if she knew it was because of you, her best friend, she had to take that incredibly dangerous and arduous swim, because of you, she's collateral damage?"

Michelle swallowed the lump rising in her throat; because she knew, what he said was true. Suddenly she heard Jane's voice and knew what she had to do.

"Jane run, get the hell out of here!"

Josh instinctively looked towards the door and in those few seconds he took his eyes off Michelle, she took her one and only opportunity.

Jane had heard Michelle yell out and then a commotion above, she knew instinctively Josh had found them, despite her fear she couldn't leave her friend to fight him alone and continued towards the ladder. She had barely put her foot on the first rung when she heard a gunshot, a surge of pure adrenaline caused her to turn and run, but as she thought of her friend, she stopped, torn between her urge to run and loyalty to Michelle. *Michelle wouldn't desert me, so I won't desert her!* Jane turned back towards the tree house and as she made her way to the ladder she looked for something to use as a weapon, another shot rang out stopping her instantly in her tracks. Everything around her seemed to go deadly quiet, when suddenly she heard movement above. Overcome with such terror her instincts took over and she turned to run, tripping and falling painfully to the ground.

"Run, I like nothing better than a good fox hunt!"

Jane looked up at the tree house and saw Josh bloodied, but when he lifted his gun and set his sights on her, she quickly scrambled to her feet and ran like she had never run before.

With tears streaming down her face and no sense of direction, she just knew she had to keep running. After her marathon swim and having little food to sustain her body, she was struggling to keep up the pace, finally the pain in her chest caused her to stop and catch her breath.

Leaning against a tree taking great gulps of air, another pain started to register in her brain; she looked down and saw her arm was bleeding badly, leaving a tell-tale mark on the tree and droplets of blood on the ground. Quickly ripping off her shirt, she wrapped it around trying to stem the blood flow, not only as a form of first aid, but hopefully to avoid leaving a trail for Josh to follow.

She heard the unmistakable sound of movement through the bush, sparking her to resume her run for her life. Despite her body craving rest, having no idea in which direction she had been running, it was a relief to come upon the clearing with the small rock pool, her throat now dry as parchment she knew she had to stop for a drink.

Sinking thankfully to her knees she drank greedily from the sweet clear waters, her body wanted nothing more now than to rest, the realisation dawned on her she didn't have the strength to run any further, she had to find somewhere to hide. Quickly looking around at her surroundings she noticed a rock formation to her left, it had a small opening *is it too small for me to squeeze through?*

Suddenly there was the noise of someone moving through the bushes and she knew Josh wasn't far behind. No longer worried whether she could fit through the small gap in the rocky outcrop, she lunged towards the opening and forced herself through it, ignoring the pain as the rough rock tore at her skin, momentarily frightened she was going to get stuck.

Suddenly she heard the snap of a twig and then a loud curse; her pursuer wasn't far away. With a combination of pure fear and adrenaline she managed to get inside and scrambled as far back from the opening as possible, pulling her legs up close to her chest trying to make herself very small.

Gripped by fear, her heart was pounding hard and her heavy breathing seemed to echo in the small cave, she quickly clamped her hand over her mouth in the hope she wouldn't give her hiding spot away. Seconds ticked by when suddenly the small beam of sunlight that shone through the opening disappeared and then there was the sound of someone breathing heavy, more to the point of a wheeze, *Michelle hadn't left him unscathed.*

Swallowing a sob as it rose in her throat, she screwed her eyes shut tight, waiting for him to fire random shots into the cave. Suddenly there was another noise outside that caused him to move away and once again she could see the small gap of light, she couldn't bring herself to shift her eyes from it, waiting for him to reappear, but everything had gone very quiet, almost as if the world outside was holding its breath.

After what seemed like hours and still hearing no more movement outside, she slowly turned her head and scanned her darkened hiding place, hoping there were no dangerous creatures, inhabiting the small cave. Keeping her back pressed hard against the rock surface, not game to move, watching the shadows deepen as night took hold. Her thoughts drifted to Michelle and tears slowly slid down her cheeks as she realised, her best friend had risked her life to give her a chance to escape. As the small cave sunk into a pit of blackness a distinct chill came to the air, she made a promise to her friend; she would make Josh pay for what he did, even if it took her the rest of her life!

CHAPTER FIVE

Max was checking the tracking logs on the *Talisman* and was making note of what time it had travelled and its course, when the phone rang.

"Hello."

"Ah, I was wondering if I could speak to Ann Brown."

Max's senses immediately went on alert.

"Who's calling?"

"Sorry, it's Harry Wright."

"I'm sorry but Ann hasn't had this number for several years."

"Damn, I can't believe she gave me an old number!"

"Who are you referring to, is there something I can help you with?"

"Not unless you know how to get hold of Michelle Brown, I was hoping her mother would know where she is."

Max straightened in his chair, as his instincts told him Michelle was in danger.

"Look, I might be able to get in contact with Ann, but first can you tell me why you are trying to get hold of Michelle?"

"She didn't turn up for work this morning and she is not answering her phone, she really left me in the lurch this morning to the point I had to cancel the boat trip scheduled for today."

"Oh, so your Michelle's boss, look if you give me your number I'll see if I can locate Ann and possibly the whereabouts of Michelle."

"Sure no problems and let her know if she wants to keep her job she better have a damn good excuse for the no-show today."

The call was disconnected and all previous thoughts of the *Talisman* were gone. Max knew his daughter was strong willed and managed to get herself in all sorts of sticky situations, but he knew, she wouldn't miss work without giving her boss notice, she loved her job and had worked hard to earn a position as deckhand, a position that until now had been male dominated!

He immediately walked down to the small cottage, which was a short distance from the main house. He saw her car was still parked in the drive, not bothering to knock he let himself in and it didn't take him long to see, she hadn't been home for a couple of days by the milk that was congealing around the bowl of cereal she hadn't bothered to throw out. Disgusted he tipped the contents down the garbage disposal and as he did, he noticed her mobile sitting on the bench and a sign on her fridge.

Gone camping with the gang.

He growled as he stormed out of the cottage and made his way back to the main house and his four wheel drive, he knew exactly who the gang were; a bunch of deadbeats!

He parked his vehicle on the side of the road, as it was virtually impossible to park in the driveway with the myriad of bikes, motorbikes and cars, *just how many people lived here?* As he walked up the short driveway, he could hear loud music, wondering if this was a regular occurrence and wouldn't blame the neighbours if they complained.

After pounding loudly on the door and getting no answer, he tried the doorknob and found it unlocked. Furious he stormed inside, *hadn't she listened to anything he'd told her*, the music was so loud it seemed to make the whole place vibrate. *God no wonder no one could hear me banging on the door, let alone know if an intruder came inside.* He walked up the hall and followed the music, which by now was becoming deafening, causing his anger to rise even higher. He came upon the lounge room and saw two girls calmly flipping through magazines. Without saying a word he walked over to the stereo and turned it off, causing both girls to look up and scream in fright, which immediately brought a shirtless, tattooed male running from another room.

"Who the hell are you and what are you doing in our

joint?"

"I'm looking for Michelle and if you don't want people walking in unannounced perhaps you should try locking the door; not that you'd hear anyone over that noise you call music!"

"We don't have a Michelle living here," said one of the girls.

Max stared at her noting the vacant look on her face.

"I think he means Shell. Who the hell are you and why should we tell you where she is?" Said the tattooed male.

"Because I asked you nicely and if you don't want those tattoo's rearranged I'd advise you to answer my question!"

"She's not here," replied the girl again.

Max stared at Michelle's friends and wondered what on earth possessed her to hang around with such a bunch of deadbeats. He realised he was wasting his breath trying to get an answer out of any of them and decided to take a look around.

"Hey, you can't just walk in here as if you own the place, we have rights!" Exclaimed the tattooed male.

Ignoring the protesting voices Max went from room to room, disgusted at the place; *a pigsty would be better than this*!

"Ok I'll ask the question again, where is Michelle?"

"Ah she's not here," stammered one of the girls.

"Well that's obvious, where is she?"

"Um not sure, all I know is she asked to borrow some dive gear."

"When was that?"

"Um, not yesterday the day before."

"I was under the assumption she went camping with you."

"That's news to us!" Exclaimed the tattooed male.

The girls nodded their heads in agreement, making Max realise that his daughter lied to him, but what were the reasons behind it, this only increased his concerns.

Max was filled with a mixture of anger and concern as he made a hasty exit, trying to push disturbing thoughts to the back of his mind. Not having any idea which boat she might have taken, he had no option but to go from boat to boat and ask if they had seen Michelle, who was well known down at the marina.

After a frustrating hour, the only thing Max learnt was, Michelle's best friend Jane had not turned up for work either. Whoever Michelle went with and wherever they went diving, was becoming an even greater mystery as none of the local boats were missing and the last sighting of the girls had been their last day at work before their two day break.

Max had no idea if Jane had in fact gone out with his daughter, but as the two seemed to spend a lot of time together, he assumed she was. The time had come to report his daughter and possibly Jane missing. On his way to the police station, he radioed Bob who was not only the caretaker at the local airstrip, but also a good friend and asked if he had seen Michelle Brown recently.

"No I haven't, do you know who she was flying with?"

"No I was just hoping you might have seen her."

"Why what's wrong?"

"Her mother has been trying to get hold of her, apparently she went off on a dive trip two days ago and no one knows where she is."

"Shit!"

"Exactly, can you have the chopper fuelled up and ready to go?"

"Of course, have you reported this to the police yet?"

"I'm on my way."

As Max made his way into the local police station, a sudden feeling of de`ja`vu washed over him. He had been in a similar situation a long time ago, when he had been called in to look for a missing diver, but this time it was his own daughter and no amount of training could enable him to remain detached. Trying not to let his emotions cloud his mind he pushed through the police station door and asked to speak to whoever was in charge.

"I'm Sargent Wilson, what seems to be the problem?"

"We need to organise a search party immediately, two girls are missing!"

"How about we start from the beginning, what's your name and what relation are these girls to you?"

"I'm Max Steel, I'm acting on behalf of one of the girl's mother, Ann Brown, her daughter Michelle has…"

A smile came to the Sargent's face that infuriated Max; he could almost read the guy's mind before he spoke.

"We are well familiar with Michelle, have you by chance checked with her friends?"

"Of course I've checked with her friends, what you don't understand is she went diving, not to a party or off with some guy, but diving and that was over forty-eight hours ago!"

"I see and have you checked to see if the dive boat is back in the marina?"

"Of course I have, what sort of an idiot do you think I am?"

"Now there's no need to get all riled up, I just have to see what steps you have taken to locate her before we contact Air Sea Rescue, in the mean time I will request the local radio station put out an alert for Michelle to contact the local Police Station. Then if by chance she is back on dry land, it will save wasting our time on a costly search."

Realising he was getting too emotional and could risk getting the local police Sargent offside, he took a deep breath and decided to try a different tack.

"I understand where you are coming from, if it's any help I have a helicopter at my disposal to aid in the air search."

"Do you have any idea where she went diving?"

"None whatsoever."

"That makes for a very wide search; there is a lot of ocean out there."

"I know that and despite what you think she does understand the importance of always letting someone know her destination and when she plans to return before leaving the dock!"

STEEL JUSTICE

***

"Damon, its Seth, thought you might like to know Steel has been down at the marina asking the local boaties if they know who took a couple of girls out diving day before yesterday."

Damon's face visibly paled, he had originally planned to go to Lagoon Island the previous day but had got waylaid and then it had become too late, he should have put everything aside and organised a crew yesterday; his delay could only mean things were going to get a whole lot worse.

"Damon, you still there?"

"Yeah, you got Steve there with you?"

"Yeah why?"

"Have the Van Witsen ready and whatever is required for a clean-up."

"Where we going?"

"Lagoon Island, we have to move fast before Steel organises a search party."

"She'll be ready when you get here."

Seth had no idea what was up, but he knew if it had something to do with Steel, it meant trouble. Damon deftly pulled the four-wheel drive into the car park and wasted no time getting down to where the Van Witsen was berthed. Seth started the high-powered boat as Damon jumped in the passenger seat, not wanting to draw any undue attention their way, he manoeuvred the boat slowly out of the marina, then once they were well past the marker leads he gave it full throttle.

As the wind whipped at Damon's face, he was glad Josh at least had the smarts to take the girls out via helicopter. He knew time wasn't something they had a lot of, but what was in their favour, he knew where to look for the girls; Steel had no idea where to start.

Seth eased back on the throttle of the boat as they neared Lagoon Island; Damon wanted to cruise the circumference of the island before putting down anchor, wanting to be forewarned if any other boats were anchored off the island.

As they slowly cruised around the island, Seth kept his eye out for any possible spots they could beach the boat, after seeing a few crocs in the water, anchoring off shore was definitely out of the question.

They had almost fully circumnavigated the island when a small beach came into view, the one Michelle and Jane had entered the water from on their dangerous midnight swim. Confident there were no other boats in the vicinity, Seth turned the boat back towards the small beach.

Once the boat was securely tied, all three men proceeded to walk up the beach when Damon suddenly noticed drag marks in the sand above the high tide mark. At first, he thought they were from a boat being dragged up the beach, but on closer inspection noticed bits of twigs and leaves and strange prints. He followed the trail up the beach and noted it went into the bushes and many of the branches had been broken.

"What do you think caused this?" Asked Seth.

"Got me puzzled, whatever it was, going by the width of those drag marks it was big." Said Damon as he reached for his gun.

"You think maybe a crocodile?" Asked Seth as he unholstered his gun.

"It's possible, we've seen plenty of them about today, could explain the leaves, maybe some unsuspecting animal was sleeping in the bush. I think we should fan out, Steve you search the outer perimeter while Seth and I'll split the middle, call me on the mobile if you find anything which could lead us to Josh or the two girls."

The other two men nodded and all three branched off in different directions, keeping their eyes peeled for any sign of human activity.

Damon had been walking for over an hour, the temperature was soaring and he could feel the sun burning his skin, he had thoughts of an icy cold beer when his mobile rang.

"Found a shallow grave, god, talk about sloppy work!"

Exclaimed Seth

"Shit! Where are you?"

Seth relayed the co-ordinates off his GPS and by the time Damon arrived both Steve and Seth had uncovered the body. Damon knew it was Tom before they'd even turned him over, the distinctive tattoo that covered the left arm, he'd seen it before, but when he saw the bullet hole to the centre of his forehead, he knew something had gone horribly wrong.

"I've never seen such sloppy work, the girls gear is here also and the grave was barely covered!" Exclaimed Seth.

"I've got a real bad feeling about this; Josh has never let me down before!"

"What do you want us to do?" Asked Steve

"We can't leave these things here, even if we dig a deeper hole, we can't risk the wildlife digging it up. We'll have to take everything back to the boat, Seth and I will dump it out at sea, but I need you to eliminate any signs that they were here, I know it won't be easy, but do what you can."

"What about Josh and the girls?" Asked Seth.

"Once we get rid of the body and the gear, we'll do a thorough search of the island; we need to make sure they're not here before we widen our search."

Once they had everything stowed in the boat, Damon covered the body with a tarp in the back of the boat, while Seth weighted the backpacks to ensure they sank to the ocean floor, hopefully never to be discovered.

Both men knowing they were fully exposed on the small beach, wasted no time in pushing the boat off and Damon directed Seth to a spot he knew would be a good place to dump the girls gear.

After it was thrown overboard they waited a few moments to ensure it sunk to the ocean floor and then cruised around for a while looking for a croc.

"There's one about nine o'clock," said Damon.

Seth turned the wheel and eased back on the throttle, not wanting to scare it off, when he thought he was close enough he ran to the back of the boat and helped Damon throw the body over the side. The moment the croc caught the scent, he moved swiftly through the water towards the body.

"Let's get the hell out of here!" Exclaimed Damon.

Unbeknown to Damon and Seth, a fishing trawler heavily laden with a full load of prawns after weeks at sea, was slowly making its way back to Eden Cove. As the trawler rounded the point of the island, something in the water caught the attention of a man at the bow, climbing higher for a better vantage point, signalled to another crewman for a pair of binoculars.

"What's up?" Asked the crewman.

"There's a croc in the water attacking something.

He smiled at the young man, knowing once he had travelled these waters as many times as he had, seeing a croc feasting on something that wasn't quick enough to get away was second nature.

"It's no big deal it's probably some poor unsuspecting bird," replied the crewman.

Frustrated the young man climbed down, retrieving the binoculars himself and quickly climbed back to his vantage point. The skipper watched as the young man lifted the binoculars to his eyes and then suddenly turned around and started waving his arms crazily, yelling at the skipper to change the direction of the trawler and for someone to get the rifle.

Suddenly everyone was running to the bow of the boat, wondering what all the commotion was about.

"The crocodile...in his mouth...person...got to shoot it."

The man with the rifle quickly grabbed the binoculars and felt sickened at what he saw, he knew the way the body was being flung around there was no hope for the poor bastard.

"What is it?" Asked one of the other men.

"A croc's got some poor bastard!"

"Holy mother of God, you serious?"

"Wish I wasn't, tell the skipper to get close and have the gaff ready, we need to take the body back to port to be identified."

STEEL JUSTICE

The skipper steered the trawler closer to the crocodile and his victim, he knew Gary would only have one shot, if he missed the croc would dive deep taking his victim with him, perhaps never to be seen again. As Garry took aim one of the men had a large gaff ready and as soon as the trawler was close enough, Garry took his shot and moments later the body was securely hooked and dragged aboard the boat.

Damon and Seth were just pulling the boat up on the beach to where Steve was waiting when they heard the distinctive sound of a gunshot.

"That's a rifle, Josh?"

"Not his weapon of choice, it sounded like it came from the other side of the island."

"Are you sure? We have been over the entire area with a fine tooth comb and saw no one."

Steve was about to make comment when Damon held up his hand and all men were silent as Damon strained his ears.

"Can you hear that?"

Seth was about to shake his head, when suddenly he heard something and realised it was getting louder.

"It's a boat, possibly a trawler coming this way!" Exclaimed Seth.

"Shit, we need to get out of here and fast!" Said Damon.

"But they might see us." said Steve.

"We can't afford to be seen on this island, besides if we move quickly they'll hear us but we might be lucky enough they won't get a visual."

As soon as there was enough depth to lower the motor in the water Seth pushed the throttle all the way forward, causing the powerful boat to almost bolt out of the water, throwing Damon and Steve back into their seats.

* * *

Max couldn't stand around while Sargent Wilson went through what he called procedure, he had to start his own search for his daughter and the best way he knew how was with his chopper.

On the way to the local airstrip, it suddenly dawned on Max why they could not find the boat that had taken the girls out, *they hadn't left by sea!*

"God why didn't I think of it sooner!" Max yelled as he thumped the steering wheel.

As he pulled into the local airstrip, he turned his vehicle towards a hanger where his Hughes 300C, three-seater helicopter was housed.

"Bob have you seen any unfamiliar faces or aircraft leaving the strip over the past week?"

"No why?"

"I believe that's the form of transport the girls took out to sea. Can you look into it for me; see if any aircraft are reported missing or overdue?"

"I'll get on to it right away, were you planning on going out alone?"

"Yeah why?"

"Would you like an extra pair of eyes, I can get Henry to run the show here and look into any overdue chopper for you."

"Thanks Bob I'd appreciate that."

Both men climbed into the helicopter and Max went through the usual checks before take-off. Once in the air Max steered the craft in the direction of the ocean, over the marina, past the lead markers and out to sea. As soon as Max had the chopper over the water, Bob brought the binoculars to his eyes and focused on the sea below. Max got a glimpse of white to his right and realised it was a fast moving boat, so he steered the helicopter in its direction for a closer look.

"Bob we're about to come over a boat moving fast below, see if you can get a visual on it."

Bob nodded and adjusted the lens on the binoculars, even before he saw the markings he was fairly sure he knew who's boat it was, there was only one boat that size and capable of that speed in the marina.

"It's a Van Witsen and we all know..."

"Microbe! I should have known he would somehow be involved in this!" Exclaimed Max.

"You know they were coming from the direction of Lagoon Island."

"Already on to it."

Bob kept a vigil with the binoculars, while Max tried to keep thoughts about what these guys were doing out here to the back of his mind. As the island came into view Max descended to a lower altitude and circled as low as possible looking for a possible landing site, they had almost done a full circuit when Bob got a glimpse of something.

"Max, go back I think we went over something."

Max turned the machine around, brought the chopper down to a lower altitude, and suddenly saw what had caught Bob's attention, the foliage below was different somehow and then as he flew over again he could see broken branches and a small clearing.

"Looks like someone was real desperate to land!" Exclaimed Bob

Max was holding the helicopter in a hover as he took a good look at the small clearing below.

"Whoever landed there was both an excellent pilot and an idiot!"

As the previous chopper had already cleared a landing area and Max was certain whoever did this brought his daughter here, he took the chopper down to land.

"I'm betting it's a Robinson R44 by the size of the skid marks and this guy is definitely an outsider, no local would do this!" Exclaimed Bob

"My thoughts exactly."

Max and Bob split up to conduct a search of the island, both had walkie talkies so they could keep in contact with each other, Max also had his trusty Glock 9mm secured in the waistband of his jeans, under his shirt.

The sun was high in the sky and they had been trekking

through foliage for nearly two hours and still they had found nothing, Steve had done a good job of covering any evidence of the grave or that any of them had been there. Max had made his way to the small beach and saw the visible signs of a boat recently beached, obviously they had made a hasty exit and had not had time to cover their tracks. He radioed Bob and told him the co-ordinates of the beach and while he waited for him, he looked closely at the other tracks in the sand that Damon assumed had been caused by a crocodile.

Max was inspecting the broken branches when Bob appeared on the beach; he too looked at the tracks and footprints the men had left.

"I'd say Microbe's boat pulled in here," commented Bob.

"Yeah and they left in a hurry."

"Maybe they were scared off by a croc, check out these tracks."

"I don't think they were made by a croc; take a good look at these broken branches."

Bob walked over and crouched down beside Max, looking closely at the broken foliage, on first appearance it looked as if something heavy had been resting there, but then he noticed some of the branches had slice marks, as if they had been cut by something sharp.

"What are you thinking Max?"

"I think Michelle was here, she knew she was being hunted and she had only one means of escape."

"You think they made a raft?"

"Don't think so, more like a buoyancy device, there's a lot of ocean out there and these strange tracks I'd say are from their flippers."

Max stared out at the vast expanse of water and suddenly realised he had to get back to the chopper fast, he had to contact Air Sea Rescue and let them know where to start their search; he suddenly broke into a sprint and Bob quickly followed.

As they ran back to the helicopter Max wondered how

Microbe found out Michelle was his daughter, he had gone to great lengths to ensure no one knew this. He had initially argued extensively with his daughter over it, but this was one thing he would not budge on and knew she had not gone against him. Ann was the perfect person to pose as Michelle's mother, she had been forced to retire from active duty through an injury but could not handle life behind a desk, when he had asked her to not only pose as Michelle's mother, but also offer protection; she jumped at the chance.

By the time Max and Bob reached the helicopter, the trawler was being directed into an older disused section of the marina.

CHAPTER SIX

It hadn't taken long for the news to travel through Eden Cove about the disappearance of Michelle Brown and Jane Moore. Twenty nine year old Jasmine Bronson was a pretty, petite blonde who worked for the local paper, she had been desperate for a real investigative reporting job, but found her looks a hindrance and was never taken seriously. When she overheard a conversation about the missing girls she knew this was the story she was waiting for, her one and only chance to prove herself.

Even though the Eden Cove Gazette was a small paper, Jasmine had been in the industry long enough to know a story like this was big news, it wouldn't take long before the media outside of Eden Cove got wind of it. Soon the small town would be bursting at the seams with TV crews and reporters from many of the big city papers, a story on the missing girls would become front-page news.

Jasmine's boss had no intention of letting her handle the story, but that didn't deter her in the least and she started her own investigation. Being a small town most people knew everyone else's business, it didn't take Jasmine long to discover Michelle Brown had quite a reputation about town for being bit of a hell raiser or dare devil and her best friend Jane often got herself tangled up in Michelle's hair-brained schemes. The thing that puzzled her though, despite the fact Michelle was well known, no one seemed to know anything about her family, but more so, the property where Michelle lived was considered a virtual fortress.

This intrigued Jasmine all the more, after all this was Eden Cove, why would anyone feel the need for such security, this she had to see for herself. Not knowing where this supposed house was, Jasmine thought the best place to start was with Michelle's friends. They were more than willing to divulge what they knew about Michelle and the fact she loved to party, but strangely had never thrown a party at her house, apart from Jane, no one had ever stepped foot inside the gates. Jasmine also discovered that the disappearance of Michelle first came to light when a tall stranger barged unannounced into their house looking for Michelle, it was Jasmine's belief it was this man who reported the girls missing.

After going to the address Michelle lived, Jasmine was disappointed as it was surrounded by a high fence that was covered in bougainvillea so thick one could not see what was on the other side, but also this vine though colourful, was covered in sharp thick thorns and she didn't have a hope of climbing the high gate. She decided her next best bet was to stake out the local police station and hopefully, catch sight of this mystery man and gain some information from him.

After sitting in her car for what seemed like an age, she was in desperate need of a caffeine fix; once she started thinking about coffee she could almost smell the aroma of those wonderful beans at the coffee shop down the end of the street. Eventually she gave into her cravings and quickly made her way towards the coffee shop when her phone rang and she knew instantly it would be her boss, wondering why she was not at her desk. Being of two minds to ignore him then realising it would only anger him further, she stopped suddenly and fumbled in her handbag for her phone, when she was knocked to the ground. Before she had a chance to think about what happened, a pair of strong hands pulled her to her feet. Startled and confused she looked up into an angry but handsome face.

"You know you should watch were you're going, there are more important things in life than the sound of a mobile phone ring."

Momentarily rendered speechless at his rude comment, she straightened herself to her full five feet four, about to give him an earful when he stepped past her, then broke into a run in the direction of the marina, soon followed by two police officers. Suddenly her journalistic instincts took over; all thoughts of coffee gone as she quickly kicked off her heels and shoved them in her bag as she ran off after them.

Looking ahead she could just make out a tall muscular man with military short coal black hair and two police officers in hot pursuit, she knew she was headed in the right direction. The officers were struggling to keep up with him when he suddenly made a sharp turn to the right down a side street. Jasmine was glad of not only the well-kept grass, but also the fact she ran regularly to keep herself in good physical condition. As she turned right, she realised they were headed towards the water but still a distance from the main marina, suddenly she caught sight of a trawler and noticed people were starting to gather as a police officer was trying to cordon off the area with yellow tape.

Realising this was something big and the man she thought the police were chasing, were now standing beside him as he spoke to one of the fishermen. Jasmine tried to get closer, her instincts told her this had something to do with the missing girls and the realisation she was the only reporter on the scene sent waves of excitement through her, this could be her lucky break!

Quickly scanning the area she noticed men in dark overalls with 'Forensics' printed on the back, questioning the crew. As yet she had not been spotted and managed to sneak onto the boat, knowing she might have only minutes, if not seconds before she was noticed. Looking for some form of cover, she quickly grabbed a dirty spray jacket and a rather fishy smelling cap to cover her blonde hair, keeping her eyes and ears peeled for any snippet of information as to what this was all about.

Doing her best to remain unnoticed, she saw a sudden flash and realised it was a 'Forensics' officer taking photos of something and carefully made her way towards him. *Had they finally found the girls or something that might give them some clue as to where they were and who was the tall handsome man she had run after?*

She inched her way closer to the officer taking photos, who

was so engrossed in what he was doing he hadn't noticed her approach. The excitement was building inside her, she couldn't believe she had managed to make it this far and possibly get close enough to get a photo of what had the forensic officer's full attention. Quickly reaching into her bag for her phone, she slowly inched forward in the hope to either take a photo over his shoulder or he might change his position long enough for her to get that lucky shot.

Suddenly he started to move and she pressed the button on her phone frantically hoping she managed to get something worthwhile before she was spotted, when suddenly her eyes focussed on what had caused the police to cordon off the area. She barely managed to stifle a scream before running to the back of the boat and being violently ill over the side.

She tried desperately to regain control, trying not to focus on what she had seen, but on what this was about. Despite the state of the body, one thing she knew, it was definitely not female, but her instincts told her it had something to do with the missing girls. As she stood there trying to regain her composure she heard voices close by and quickly hid behind the hanging trawler nets.

"Mr Steel I know this is not much comfort to you in finding Michelle, but trust me we are doing everything in our power to find both girls safe and well. I don't know if this person has anything to do with her disappearance, but as soon as we know his identity perhaps it may fill in some missing pieces, maybe somewhere to start."

"Please call me Max. This was no innocent swimmer; this person was dead before he hit the water, I am sure you saw the bullet hole to the head."

"Yes I did and if it hadn't been for the trawler passing by when it did, he may never have been found."

"I think that was the whole idea, my instinct tells me it is connected to the disappearance of Michelle and Jane. You might think this strange, but it gives me hope, because I know Michelle wouldn't go down without a fight!"

"If you're right, this is not just a case of two missing girls!"

"My thoughts exactly, I'm sure you'll understand why I have to start my own search. I'm sure you heard me tell your Sargent I have my own helicopter, but I could sure do with an extra pair of eyes."

"It would be a pleasure; by the way my name is Jones."

"Glad to have you on board," said Max as he shook his hand.

Jasmine heard the sound of retreating footsteps and suddenly realised, her great story was walking away. She wasted no time ridding herself of the dirty jacket and cap, as she hastened her pace after him she thought of the description of the mystery man Michelle's friends had given her and was certain it was the man she was following, but what puzzled her, *what was Michelle Brown to Max Steel?*

As she struggled to keep up, she quickly pulled her phone out of her bag and called her boss.

"Greg hold the front page, I've got a story which is going to put *The Eden Cove Gazette* on the map!"

"Jasmine, is that you?"

"Yes, I've even got a photo, although I'm not sure if you can use it, might upset the readers and all."

"What's this all about?"

"The missing girls; there could be more to it than we think and Greg, I was the only reporter there, the police are trying to keep it quiet."

"You better get here fast, if this is as good as you say it is we are going to put out a special edition."

"But I..."

"No buts get here now!"

Jasmine was about to argue further when she realised he was right, they had to get this to print as soon as possible.

She had barely stepped inside when Greg bellowed out for her to come into his office pronto and going by the looks she was getting from everyone, Greg obviously had not told them about her great scoop.

"This had better be good because I've already put a hold on the front page."

"You bet! I had been watching the Police station because I thought it strange no one knew anything about the family of Michelle Brown, I was hanging for a cup of coffee when he knocked me over and was about to..."

"Who, who knocked you over?"

"Max Steel. At first I didn't know his name but..."

"Who the hell is Max Steel and what does this have to do with the missing girls?"

"Well if you stopped interrupting me I might get a chance to explain!"

Her boss glared at her for a moment and she wondered if she had over stepped the mark, then he folded his arms and sat on the edge of the desk.

"Go on."

"At first I thought I was being mugged, but he helped me up and made a rude comment to me about my phone then ran off, followed closely by two police officers. I realised there was a story here and followed them down to the wharf, there was a trawler there and it was being taped off, also Forensics were there. I knew this had to be something big and thought it could be to do with the missing girls, so I crept aboard and grabbed someone's smelly jacket and cap so I wouldn't be recognised, that's when I saw the body."

"Was it one of the girls?"

"No it was male and I was later to find out they dragged him from the jaws of a crocodile, it was not a pretty sight."

"Jasmine this is definitely a good story, but what does this have to do with the girls and you still haven't explained who Max Steel is?"

"I don't know who he is, I've got to do some research on that one, but I overheard him talking to a police officer and apparently the dead guy was dead before he hit the water, he had been shot in the head, both believe he is involved in the girls disappearances."

"Holy shit, do you realise what this means?"

"This was no diving accident, someone tried to kill the girls."

"No, I mean yes, but if you are positive no other reporter was about, when this hits the news-stands *The Eden Cove Gazette* will be a name recognised all over the world."

"Not forgetting Jasmine Bronson was the reporter on the scene."

"Of course, now you said you had a photo."

"Like I said it's not pretty, I hope you haven't had your lunch yet."

Jasmine handed her phone to her boss and watched as his face turned a pale shade of green, he looked away then took another look at the photo.

"Your right, we wouldn't be able to publish this, but if you have the stomach to look at the photo closely enough you can see the gunshot wound to the victims forehead."

"I'll take your word for it."

"You know if we play our cards right we can spin this story out over a couple of weeks. You better start typing; I'll get the guys working on the headlines, oh and Jasmine, good work."

Finally recognition but she couldn't think of anything to say, all she could do was manage an embarrassed smile, as it was extremely rare for Greg to praise anyone, then she quickly left his office and seated herself in front of her computer. As she waited for her computer to start, she realised the office was quieter than usual and looked up to see everyone was looking at her with questioning eyes, no she wasn't going to tell them yet, she would make them wait, they will find out soon enough.

* * *

After the discovery of the body Max believed Microbe's men were obviously in clean up mode, which meant he had to get back out there and find Michelle. Finally he had got some action and the SES (State Emergency Service) were scouring

Lagoon Island, so Max flew over the surrounding waters and islands while officer Jones was his second pair of eyes with the binoculars.

Jones had been looking through the binoculars for so long his eyes were hurting and he was sure his vision was becoming blurred. He was certain there wasn't one inch of ocean they hadn't covered and apart from the odd crocodile he sighted nothing else, not so much as a small piece of flotsam and after seeing what the croc had done to the body the trawler men fished out, he believed there was very little hope of finding the girls.

The nearest island to Lagoon Island had seemed the most likely place, Max had flown over it more than once, taking the helicopter down as low as possible, but it was surrounded like a protective fortress by many sharp oyster covered rocks, even at high tide it would have been impossible to get near the small beach safely. Jones could see some of the boats making their way back to the mainland.

"I hate to say this Max but we have been over this area so many times, I think if they were anywhere near we would have seen something by now. The closest island would have been out of the question, there is no possible way a swimmer could get near it."

"I know but I had to be sure and I know we are running out of daylight, I just want to do one more low sweep over that island, then we'll head back, but I plan to come back out again at first light."

"I'm happy to accompany you tomorrow if you like."

"Thanks I appreciate that."

Max did a final sweep over the island, going so low Jones thought the skids must be touching the top of the trees and then Max took the helicopter to a higher altitude and reluctantly headed back home.

As they neared the airstrip Max made an all stations call to inform other traffic of his intentions to land, almost instantly the radio crackled back.

"Sierra-Whisky-Charlie, Eden Cove Ground, you have a welcoming committee waiting for you."

"Eden Cove Ground, Sierra-Whisky-Charlie, hi Bob anyone we know?"

"Reporters, TV crew."

Max yelled a string of expletives, and then with a deep sigh of frustration he responded to Bob.

"Copy that."

"Well you heard the man, hope you are good in front of the camera!" Max said to Jones.

The Eden Cove Gazette had put out an evening edition, something it had never done before. Greg hadn't wanted one of the other papers to get wind of Jasmine's story and had put everything else on hold, all staff had worked overtime to get this paper out, and now all the other papers, TV and radio, were trying to get in on the action.

As the airstrip came into view Jones wondered if they would even be able to land, there were vehicles and people everywhere, it was as if the entire town and all its visitors were waiting on their arrival. Max swore in disgust and started to make his descent, Jones could see his fellow officers trying to move people back. As soon as the skids touched the ground there was the constant flash of cameras and reporters following Jasmine's lead were trying to push forward, vying to be the first to interview the search party.

Jasmine was there, after gathering all her snippets of information, she decided to take a punt on the relationship between Max Steel and Michelle Brown, it was risky, but knew she had only one shot at it. She watched him as he sat in the helicopter shutting down the machine, watched as he flicked the various switches then removed his headset. *God he's good looking*, and then almost as if he could sense she was staring at him, he turned and looked directly at her, causing her stomach to suddenly fill with butterflies. She knew as soon as he made to open the door it would be safe to move forward and her heart pounded with anticipation, she could feel the adrenaline rushing through her veins and likened it to waiting on the starting block, waiting for the signal to run.

Suddenly the crowd moved forward and she was nearly pushed over, Max realised he was going to be surrounded and moved off at a fast pace towards the small office. Jasmine ran after him, holding out her small handheld recorder and yelled out to him.

"Mr Steel, have you any idea why someone would want to hurt your daughter Michelle and her friend Jane?"

Hearing the young woman mention that Michelle was his daughter shocked him, causing him to stop suddenly in his tracks and turn to look at her. Not prepared for the sudden stop, Jasmine ran into him almost dropping her recorder. She knew instantly she had played her cards right and by the look on his face, everyone present now also knew. This caused them to push forward, bombarding him with questions, but Max stepped forward and gripped her arms tightly, the anger evident in his blue eyes, instantly a hush went over the crowd and photographers had their cameras ready wondering what he would do next, then he suddenly released his grip on her and leaned forward.

"Listen very carefully, as this is the one and only statement I will ever make. In answer to your question; the person behind this, I know who you are and trust me, you will forever regret the day you tried to harm my daughter!"

CHAPTER SEVEN

Microbe was in a bad mood; everything seemed to be turning to shit, all because of Steel's daughter, which made him look like a fool in front of Savage.

"This is the very reason why you shouldn't hire incompetent fools!" Exclaimed Savage.

"One of my best men hired this bozo; he assured me he was the best!" Exclaimed Microbe.

"That's where you went wrong; you should have handled it yourself."

"Are you saying I should have been the one to pull the trigger?"

"Of course not! I am referring to the man who was commissioned for the job, you should have done a background check, palming it off on someone else is not only lazy but outright stupidity!"

Microbe bit back a retort; there was something about Savage that made him err on the side of caution.

"I suggest you sort this out and soon, because while we have all these added aircraft and search vessels in the area we haven't much hope of delivering the next shipment!"

Before Microbe could comment Savage headed out the door, causing him to grab the whiskey decanter and pour a good measure of the amber liquid into a glass. For the first time in his life, Microbe felt like he was losing control and wondered if his men realised this also, for he wasn't constantly bombarded with phone calls anymore regarding shipments or other problems they needed him to sort out. Only the other day he had questioned one of his men about a new shipment of floatation devices, when he was informed Savage had already signed off on it. Suddenly it dawned on him what Savage was doing; *God I can't believe I didn't see it before, he's slowly taking control, he's undermining my authority and he is planning to take over!*

He slammed down the glass, almost causing it to shatter and suddenly realised Burns was still in the room, but what made his blood boil was the smug smile on his face. *That little weasel I'll give him something to smile about!* Microbe walked over and backhanded Burns hard across his face, bringing tears to the man's eyes.

"This is my operation, I'm the boss not Savage; don't you ever forget that!"

Burns ran out the door like a scared rabbit clutching his hand to the side of his face. Microbe poured himself another scotch and threw it down in one gulp, as the liquid burned the back of his throat, his anger intensified. *I should have listened to my gut instinct and never joined forces with Savage. How dare he belittle and humiliate me like that, especially in front of Burns; if he thinks he can just waltz in here and take over, he's got another thing coming!*

Burns was fuming as he drove out Microbe's driveway, he would always regret the day he got involved with the man, but while Microbe had a certain folder in his safe he would always be held to ransom. Destroying that folder was always at the forefront of his mind and the sting from Microbe's backhand caused him to grind his teeth even harder.

"God I hate that man, I wish I could destroy him along with that folder!"

As he drove he thought of the most painful ways possible for Microbe to die, when suddenly he thought of Savage. The more he thought about it the more he liked the idea and the pain to the side of his face and his anger caused him to change the direction in which he was driving.

As Burns turned up the long driveway his stomach started to churn, his earlier bravado was diminishing fast and he eased his foot off the accelerator to the point the car was almost to a standstill. As he looked around him he realised there wasn't enough room to turn the car around and had no option but to continue up the driveway.

He had never been further than the front gates of Savage's

estate before and as the car rounded the bend in the drive he was surprised at the extent of the place. *He paid some serious dollars for this place!* Burns noticed a turning area that went past the front door, but to his dismay a man came outside and wanted to know who he was, he quickly apologise saying he was lost and had turned up the wrong drive when Savage appeared at the front door.

Burns could feel himself beginning to sweat and he knew there was no way he could back out now.

"It's ok Ryle, direct him to my office."

Burns nervously got out of his car and followed Ryle to Savage's office, noting how opulent the house was inside. When he stepped into the office he noticed Savage had a drink in his hand, but made no attempt to offer him one.

"Well?" Asked Savage.

"Ah um, I thought, I mean, well..."

"You seem rather nervous Burns, Microbe sent you to do his bidding?"

His comment gave Burns the courage he needed to say what was on his mind.

"I felt I needed to let you know that I had nothing to do with the contract Microbe put out on the Steel girl, but I have some information that will link Microbe to this mess!"

"Really and what might this information be?"

"First I want you to know that I could be invaluable to you, I know things about Microbe that no one else does."

"Burns you surprise me, you do have some balls after all!"

Burns got his handkerchief out of his pocket and mopped his brow.

"I doubt there is anything you could tell me that I don't already know, but that's not to say I am not interested in your proposition. So what is this information that ties Microbe to the contract on the Steel girl?"

"His helicopter was used to take the girls to Lagoon Island and both it and the man Microbe hired are missing."

A smile came to Savage's face, *this was going far better*

than he expected.

"I can't but help notice the mark to the side of your face, Microbe?"

"Yes."

"This is the real reason you are here."

When the idea had first came to Burns he thought it was a win-win situation, but now he wondered if he was only digging himself an even deeper hole.

"Well, I thought you would want to distance yourself from him as much as possible, especially because Steel is already suspicious and with all the search activity and extra police presence, it's going to make things difficult, but I think I have a solution to this problem."

"I'm listening."

"First I need to know if you will help me with my problem."

"Suppose you first tell me what I would gain out of this little transaction."

"Um well, I don't know if you are aware I own a boat yard, I buy and sell luxury boats."

"Surprisingly I was not aware of this, but you have me intrigued, go on."

Burns laid out his plan in detail, his confidence building by the interest shown on Savage's face as he walked around the room, tapping his finger to his lip in thought.

"Have you voiced these ideas to anyone else?"

"No, but I feel the only way to ensure it runs smoothly is to remove Microbe permanently!"

"What makes you think I won't go to Malcolm and tell him everything you just told me?"

For a moment Burns thought he was going to be sick, he realised his foolishness by trying to persuade Savage to rid Microbe on his behalf.

Savage suddenly threw his head back and laughed, frightening Burns all the more.

"I thought for a moment you were going to literally shit

yourself, but yes I agree one hundred percent, Microbe has become a liability and I don't like liabilities, put your proposal into action and I'll take care of Microbe."

Burns just stood there for a moment, not sure if he had done a deal with Savage or just dug his own grave.

"Well what are you waiting for, or are you having second thoughts?"

"No, ah um yeah, I'll get on to it right away."

Burns wasted no time running outside and jumping into his car, it wasn't until he drove out the estate gates that he let out a lung full of air. Suddenly the impact of the meeting he had with Savage fully dawned on him and the realisation he would finally be rid of Microbe, he felt like a massive weight had been lifted from his shoulders.

* * *

It was 2am in the morning, Max was tired but had difficulty sleeping, his instincts told him someone had deliberately targeted his daughter, *but why, was it Microbe very cleverly trying to throw him off the scent, or someone from his past who wanted to hit him where it would hurt the most?* The thing he couldn't understand was why his daughter hadn't informed anyone where she was going, despite the fact she was strong willed he knew she understood the importance of always letting someone know when and where she went diving. His daughter was well versed in martial arts and never went anywhere without her lethal dive knife, bringing him to the conclusion there had to be at least two perpetrators to get the upper hand. He was sure the body the fishermen pulled from the jaws of the croc was connected to his daughter's disappearance, *but how did he end up as croc bait, was it Michelle or Microbe's men in clean-up mode?*

Realising it was useless trying to sleep, he got up and made himself a cup of coffee and perused the map of Lagoon Island and the surrounding area for the umpteenth time. The closest neighbour was Oyster Island, but it was surrounded by a virtual fortress of oyster covered rocks, despite the fact his daughter was a strong swimmer, with the prevailing currents it would have nearly been impossible for anyone to survive the arduous swim to the next island. He realised it was time to call in a favour and quickly punched some numbers into the phone.

"Clint, Max here."

"Do you have any idea what time it is?"

"Sorry mate but my daughter's life is at stake, I need your help."

"I didn't even know you had a daughter!"

"Look it's a long story, I'm sure you've heard about the two missing girls who went out on a diving trip."

"One of them is your daughter?"

"Yes."

"Holy shit, how can I help?"

"You still with the defence signals directorate?"

"Yeah why?"

"I need you to get me ASAP, the visuals of the co-ordinates I am about to send you, I need it to be detailed enough to see if there is any possible access."

"It could take a couple of hours."

"I'll be waiting."

* * *

Despite the early hour, Max was astounded at the amount of reporters outside his property, *what's going on?* Then he remembered the young blonde who asked him about Michelle, *how did she find out?*

As he waited for the security gate to open they swarmed around the entrance like a pack of rats, he revved the engine of his powerful silver Mitsubishi four wheel drive, letting them know if anyone was stupid enough to block his way he would not hesitate to run them over. Finally the gate was open enough for him to move forward, some moved out of the way, but others tried to block his exit desperate for a story. Suddenly he was blinded by a flash from a camera pushed up against his windscreen, angry at the stupidity of such an act, he blew the horn and once again revved the engine determined to make them move out of the way.

Finally he had managed to pull out onto the road, knowing it was only a matter of time before they followed him, not caring if he was caught speeding as having a few coppers on his tail might be a good thing right now. He quickly placed a call to Bob at the airstrip and told him to have the helicopter warmed up and ready, as they would need to make a quick getaway. He wouldn't be taking his own machine today, it didn't have the specs for the job at hand and they'd be taking the EC145 as it has a winch that could be controlled by the pilot.

Twenty minutes later he was pleased to see Jones was already there, after quickly parking his car he ran to the waiting helicopter and yelled to Jones to jump in the back, knowing they had only moments to spare before the media arrived.

"You're not flying today Max?" Asked Jones as he quickly buckled his seatbelt.

"As I told you over the phone there is a safe passage to Oyster Island, but if you look at these satellite images you will see there is no possible place to land."

Max passed the photographs back to Jones.

"How the hell did you get a hold of these?"

"A friend."

"Got some pretty important friends, so how do you propose we get on the island?"

"I hope you don't have an aversion to being winched from a helicopter?"

"Ah, don't know, never done it before, how high up will we be?"

"About fifty feet, shouldn't be any problems today, hardly a breath of wind."

"If you say so."

"If you have any qualms, the winch is capable of holding 247 kilos, so we can both go down at the same time."

As the island came into view Jones became more nervous, he heard Max direct Bob to the Southwest side of the island, as there was a small beach he thought would be the safest place for winching down. Max un-clipped his seatbelt and climbed into the back with Jones, he could tell he was nervous and thought it best if they both exited together. He explained to Jones the procedure for winching, firstly they would both put on a harness, and then he would open the door and retrieve the winch hook, which would be clipped to both harnesses. They will then need to step out on the skid step and stabilise themselves tensioning the cable, once they had done so Bob will extend the winch arm and winch them down.

When Max had the cable clipped to them both he gave the signal to move to the skid step and Jones was praying his legs that were now visibly shaking, would not fail him.

The noise of the rotor blades above them was deafening and Jones had never been so frightened in his life and was hoping he would not embarrass himself. Suddenly he heard a noise and felt himself moving, realising Bob had commenced winching and they were descending to the small beach below. Within a matter of minutes his feet finally came in contact with terra firma, he was so relieved he almost felt like kissing the ground beneath him and did not want to contemplate doing that exercise in reverse. As soon as Max had unhooked the winch cable from their harnesses he gave the all clear to Bob.

"Bob is going to find a safe landing spot as close by as possible and wait for my call. First we need to check the area surrounding the beach and see if there is any sign of the girls being here."

Both men freed themselves of their harness and started a search in and around the foliage near the beach. Max knew if Michelle was here she would have left him some kind of sign close to the beach, but she would have ensured it was not easily visible. Max realised the foliage was well rooted and not easy to pull from the sandy soil and started pulling at the tufts of grass for any signs of it being replanted recently. Suddenly a handful pulled easily from the sand and he immediately started digging.

"Jones I think I've found something."

He came running over just as Max started pulling something long and blue from the sandy soil, it was a flipper.

"She's here!"

"How can you be sure, flippers get washed up on the beach all the time?"

"It's hers, look inside."

Jones took the flipper from Max; inside was written in bold black marker the word 'Shell'. Before he could comment Max was on the handheld to Bob, asking him to do some low flyovers as they had confirmation of his daughter being here.

"We'll separate but not too far, call me if you see anything, a broken branch, twig, anything," said Max

"Gotcha."

They had been walking for only about fifteen minutes when Max paused again to look at the thick bush in front of him, something he had been doing about every five minutes after concentrating on the ground as he walked. As he stood there and stretched his back, he realised there was something odd about the tree in front of him. He moved slowly forward, focusing on the tree and as he neared he realised that it was not just a tree, he could make out a ladder that was well camouflaged by a thick vine. He called out to Jones before making his way up the ladder and it wasn't until he was half way up he realised his hands were wet with a sticky substance, pausing he look at his hand, it was dark red and he knew instantly it was blood that had not completely dried.

He turned and signalled to Jones below to remain silent, then he un-clipped his Maglite from his belt and clipped it to the bottom of the barrel of his Glock pistol and cautiously went up the remainder of the ladder and shone the bright light into the darkness of the shack. Apart from a kit bag and the scurry of a small furry animal, the shack appeared empty.

As he climbed inside the bright beam of his torch shone on a dark pool of blood to his left, a sudden sick feeling came to his stomach, *am I too late?* He bent down, looked at the dried outer edges and figured it had been there for less than twenty-four hours.

"Is it blood?" Asked Jones.

"Yeah, not enough to have been fatal, but still not a good sign."

"Why do you think they left here, it would have been the safest place to wait for help?"

Max walked over to the bag in the corner of the room and examined the contents.

"Obviously their hideout was discovered."

"How can you be so sure?"

"They left in a hurry, Michelle's waterproof bag is still here, there's bottled water and their jackets, they wouldn't last too long without water and the nights out here can get very cold."

"Max shine the torch over here, I think there is more blood."

Max shone the torch at Jones's feet; it was definitely blood.

"I think there was a struggle, see how it's smudged and there's a partial hand print, we need to get moving, because if this blood is from one of the girls, they don't have a lot of time without medical treatment."

Max quickly grabbed Michelle's bag, if the girls had been holed up in the bush somewhere, they could be suffering from not only dehydration but also hypothermia. Max immediately called Bob to give him the latest update, while Jones put a call through to his Sargent; both men knew it was imperative a medical crew were ready.

As they walked through the bush Max noticed markings on some of the branches and trees and knew immediately Michelle had left these, but also he noticed branches and small shrubs were broken and trampled and then he saw the blood.

"Jones, I've got blood over here and by the looks of this foliage, someone was in a hurry, possibly running for their life!"

Jones quickly came over, noticed a few droplets of blood on the ground, and wondered if it was from one of the girls or perhaps their hunter. After a short time Max noticed more blood on and at the base of a tree and as he inspected the ground cover he could see a slight shoe impression in the sand, it was small.

"Either this guy is small or its one of the girls," said Jones.

"It's too small for my daughter, it has to be Jane, but what I don't understand, is there's no sign of any other prints here."

"You're thinking Jane was alone?"

"Yeah, but that doesn't make sense."

After doing a quick check on the surrounding area Max picked up the pace and followed the bloody trail. When they came upon the small spring Max noted the many prints in the sand and also there was a lot more blood.

"I can make out three different sets of prints here and by the looks of these impressions someone has a leg injury."

Both men followed the footprints for a few minutes when Max realised there was only two sets of prints leading away from the spring. He backtracked a bit and tried to find out where the third set of prints ended.

"Max what are you looking for, shouldn't we be following the trail?"

"Someone is still here!" Exclaimed Max.

"You sure?"

Max ignored Jones and searched around the rocky outcrop when he noticed a small opening and what appeared to be a bloody hand smear. He quickly grabbed his Maglite and shone it in the opening, its powerful beam shining on something in the back corner of the small cave and as his eyes focused he realised it was someone huddled in a small ball.

"Jane its Max Steel!"

There was no movement or response and Max wasn't sure

if she was asleep, or that perhaps they were too late. He picked up a small rock and threw it gently at her, still no movement, he then threw another rock but this time a little harder and to his relief she started to move.

"Jane its Max Steel, your safe now, you can come out."

Jane sat up and held her hand over her eyes to shield them from the bright light, but made no attempt to move towards the opening of the cave and Max realised she had no idea who was behind the bright beam, so he turned the light so it shone on his face.

"Come on, I have a helicopter waiting to take you back to Eden Cove."

Jane still didn't move and Max wondered if she had heard him.

"Jane?"

"It's your fault!" She sobbed.

"Sorry?"

"You, you're the reason she is dead!"

Max was thrown by her outburst and wasn't sure how to respond, when Jones stepped forward.

"Give me your Maglite."

"What?"

"Just give it to me!"

Max wasn't sure what he intended to do, but handed the Maglite to him.

"Jane, there's no need to be afraid, I'm a policeman, my name is Jones. Now I am going to throw in the Maglite and my ID so you can see for yourself."

He quickly unclipped his police ID from his belt and threw it in with the Maglite, both Max and Jones watched as she picked up the torch and shone it on the ID before shinning the light onto Jones' face.

"Jane, like I said we are here to help you, but what makes you think Michelle is dead?" Asked Max.

"I heard the gun shots, I know she is dead!"

"We found the tree house and saw the blood, but there was

no sign of Michelle.

"You mean she is alive?"

"I hope so!"

Realising she was probably very dehydrated he quickly got a water bottle out of the backpack and held it out to her. She hesitated for a moment and then crawled across and reached out through the opening and Max noticed the bloodied shirt tied around her arm. She wasted no time draining the contents of the bottle, making Max realise despite the fact there was fresh water close by, she had been too afraid to leave her hiding place. The opening was so narrow Max had to help pull her out, making him wonder how she had gotten through it in the first place.

After being confined in such a small place for so long, Jane struggled to stand.

"Jane, why do you think this is my fault, do you know who tried to hurt you?"

"Michelle told me who you are; she told me why she had to keep it a secret, that's why he tried to kill us, to get back at you!"

"Who, who tried to kill you?"

"His name is Josh, although Michelle didn't believe that was his real name."

"Can you tell me what happened, how did you and Michelle get separated?"

As she looked up at Max the sound of Michelle's scream to run followed by two gunshots came flooding back, causing her to burst into tears.

"Please Jane; I need to know what happened."

"I was going to get some oysters off the rocks when I realised I forgot the knife, I called out to Michelle…"

Jane started sobbing uncontrollably, Max realised she had been through a terrible ordeal but he had to know what happened to his daughter.

"Jane!"

"She was in the tree house, she screamed at me to run, I

didn't know what to do and then I heard the gunshot."

"Keep going."

"I was scared, I started to run I wasn't sure what to do, then I heard another shot, I just kept running till I came here!"

Jane was so overcome with emotion she sunk to the ground, crying at the realisation her nightmare was now finally over, but also with shame as her friend had risked her life for hers and she had not been able to help her.

"I saw the blood in the tree house."

"You're sure Michelle wasn't there, she's still alive?"

"The tree house was empty, but there was a lot of blood, whoever it was from won't last long without medical treatment!"

"I know Josh was following me and I am sure it was him who looked into the cave trying to see if I was hiding there, but I also heard something else, perhaps it was Michelle?"

"Have you any idea how many others there are on the island?"

"As far as I know there was only Josh and Tom, but I think Tom is dead, we overheard Josh talking to someone on the phone, he said we would be dead by morning, that's when Michelle decided we had to swim to Oyster Island, I was so scared I thought we were going to die!"

"Well you're safe now. Jones take Jane to the chopper and organise a search party to come to Oyster Island as soon as possible, I'm going to go ahead and look for Michelle."

Without waiting for a response Max headed off through the bush, following the other two sets of prints, leaving Jones nervous at the thought of being winched back up into the helicopter with a jittery and frightened girl; without Max's aid.

CHAPTER EIGHT

Despite a thorough search of Oyster Island, no sign of Michelle or the gunman could be found, it was proven there were two blood types in the tree house, one from Michelle and the other presumed to be that of her male assailant, known only as Josh. The real identity of this man was a mystery, Jane had gone through countless mug shots to no avail and the blood sample alone was not enough to match him with any offenders they had listed with CODIS (Combined DNA Index System). An identity kit photo was posted in all the papers and TV channels, but to date no one had come forward with any information.

After The Eden Cove Gazette ran a series of stories, regarding the missing girls and theories as to why they were targeted; Eden Cove soon became a place of interest. The small town was suddenly a hive of activity with not only the ongoing search for Michelle, but also the media and tourists wanting to see the dangerous crocodile infested waters, through which the girls had swum for their lives. The editor had encouraged Jasmine to stretch the story out for as long as possible. In her bid to do so, she managed to unearth some information on Max Steel, not only was he highly decorated, but his actual position in the army was a closely guarded secret, making her believe that perhaps the real intended target was Max Steel himself; an idea she put forward to her readers.

This infuriated Max even further as he could no longer blend into the background, she had given him celebrity status, but more so exposing his daughter to further danger; as it was his belief she was still alive. He had questioned Jane extensively about everything that had transpired. Despite the fact she had not seen the boat Michelle had viewed through his night vision binoculars, she believed it was a yacht as it was so quiet; there was no engine noise to be heard despite it moving swiftly past the island, it was only a small light that gave them away. Instantly Max thought of the *Talisman and rechecked the date and time on the tracking log of its last voyage;* this only confirmed his suspicions Microbe was involved.

Max decided to voice his opinion to the local police.

"I'm telling you Microbe is your man, have you even had him in for questioning?"

"On what grounds?"

"Well the fact both Bob and I saw his Van Witsen making a hasty retreat from Lagoon Island."

"I hardly think that warrants calling the man in for questioning."

"Come on, don't you think it's rather a coincidence only moments after we saw the Van Witsen from the air, a trawler found one of the supposed perpetrators fed to the crocs?"

"Still nothing to warrant bringing in Microbe for questioning, but before you blow a fuse I did have a chat with the man."

"Chat!"

"As I was about to say, he said they had been having some maintenance issues with the Van Witsen and had to run the motor hard to sort out the problem."

"That's bullshit and you know it!"

"Unless you have anything concrete against the man, I suggest you focus more on those from your past, according to Jasmine Bronson you…"

"So you're going to believe her trumped up story over what's right under your nose?"

"Mr Steel I understand you are upset, but if you continue to be abusive and aggressive when you come into my station, I may be forced to lay charges against you."

"You can't do that, it's not a chargeable offence."

"Good day Mr Steel, I think in future you should deal with our head office in the city regarding your daughter's disappearance."

Before Max could make any further comment, the Senior Sargent turned and walked back into the connecting office and closed the door. Max knew it was pointless involving the local police any further as he was now sure they believed she was dead, he also had his suspicions Microbe was contributing to the local Sargent's pay packet.

Angry and frustrated, Max headed straight for Microbe's office. Microbe had just signed another property deal for another complex he had bought cheap, if he played his cards right he would really make a bundle on this one and what sweetened the pot, Savage had no involvement, he had gone to great lengths to keep him out of this one. Suddenly he heard the office door open and the smile immediately disappeared when he saw it was Steel.

"Get the hell out of my office!"

"Not before I deliver something!"

Microbe didn't get a chance to respond, as Max delivered a nose breaking punch that slammed Microbe up against the wall, knocking him out cold.

"I don't know why the hell I didn't do that a long time ago!"

Max made a hasty retreat, on one hand glad there were no witnesses, but on the other he couldn't care less. He had almost reached his four-wheel drive when he heard his name called and turned around to see Jasmine Bronson, making his simmering temper boil.

The look on Max Steel's face caused Jasmine to falter in her step, but she was on a roll with her story and knew she could not let the sight of an angry face come between her and a good story.

"Mr Steel I was wondering what you believed happened to your daughter?"

"You're like a vulture, how do you sleep at night?"

"Pardon?"

"Do you have any idea what danger your trumped up story has put my daughter in?"

"So you still believe she is alive?"

"Your pathetic and you have my permission to print that!"

He quickly turned on his heel and wasted no time getting into his vehicle and driving off, leaving a speechless Jasmine standing in the middle of the road. Suddenly a car horn tooted shaking her senses and she quickly ran back to the safety of the footpath. Max Steel's comment made her feel a mixture of hurt and anger, angry that he had been so rude, but a part of her was upset that he likened her to a vulture, had she really gone too far for the sake of a story. Suddenly her phone rang and as she looked at the screen she didn't recognise the number.

"Hello," she said hesitantly.

"Jasmine Bronson?"

"Yes."

"My name is Jodi Major, you recently submitted your resume to Frontline News; I was wondering if we could arrange a time for an interview?"

Jasmine was so excited she could barely contain herself.

"Whatever time suits you."

"How about one o'clock tomorrow down at the Marina, I heard great things about a little seafood restaurant there?"

"You're in Eden Cove?"

"I had to come and see the place Jasmine Bronson has the world talking about."

"Really? Um yes one o'clock will be fine."

"Look forward to meeting you."

Before Jasmine could respond the line was disconnected, she was so excited she wanted to tell all of Eden Cove she had an interview with Jodi Major, then suddenly she wondered if it was all a cruel prank, *would Max Steel stoop that low?*

* * *

The Diners were vying for the best water front table at the popular seafood restaurant on the marina, Jasmine was glad she had booked to ensure they had a good table. The weather couldn't have been better if she had planned it herself and despite her nerves she liked Jodi the moment she introduced herself. They had just put in their lunch order when a splendid sixty-five-foot yacht glided past and many diners rushed over to the railing to get a photo as it unfurled it sails and within minutes the wind billowed them out to their full extent, gliding the yacht quickly on its way.

"You sure you want to give up all this for a life, where at times you will be living out of a suitcase?"

"I can always come back here on my breaks."

"True, but…"

Suddenly there was a loud explosion that seemed to rock the entire marina and people looked around in fear, someone stood and pointed in the direction of the beautiful yacht and both women turned to see it was now engulfed in flames. The plumes of thick, black smoke rising so high it was visible kilometres away, suddenly the wind changed direction and ash from the intense fire began raining down on the diners.

It was as if time stood still, everyone momentarily froze as if their minds were trying to register what just happened, when suddenly thoughts of 9/11 still fresh in their minds sent everyone into a state of panic. As the black ash stained the white tablecloths an instant fear blanketed the crowd, people started running for cover, trying to get as far away from the marina as possible, for fear of another attack.

Jasmine instinctively grabbed her phone and started taking photos, ignoring the thick smoke as it threatened to engulf the marina in its entirety. Despite the sound of breaking glass and chairs being knocked over as patrons and staff tried to flee the marina, Jasmine climbed up onto her chair with her small recorder in one hand and her phone in the other, trying to get photos of not only the burning yacht but also of the chaos around her.

There was the sound of sirens off in the distance and within a matter of minutes the busy restaurant and marina were deserted and without even thinking Jasmine quickly jumped to the ground and ran towards the car park, taking more photos all the while speaking into her recorder about what she saw. She noted the sound of blaring horns and raised voices, as everyone was trying to leave the car park at once, causing more problems. The exit road from the marina had become congested, the sound of car horns was now deafening, tempers flared; frustration and fear causing some to leave their vehicle where it stood and flee on foot.

Suddenly Jasmine turned and saw Jodi and realised to her horror she had possibly screwed up her one chance to gain a position with a coveted News reporting programme and quickly ran over towards her.

"Jodi I'm so sorry I didn't think, its…"

"The job is yours!"

"Pardon?"

"You just proved to me better than any interview could, you live and breathe a news story, you didn't once consider you could be in danger, your first thought was getting the story; welcome to the team!"

Jodi held out her hand and Jasmine shook it, still trying to absorb the fact she had just scored the job of her dreams. Suddenly her phone rang and she looked down at the number on the screen.

"It's my boss at the paper."

"You mean your old boss; this is one scoop he is going to miss out on!"

"But…"

"The decision is yours, the reason we are number one is we have the story first, what better way to start than with a feature story from your home town."

Jasmine let her phone go to message bank and put her phone back in her bag, smiling at Jodi.

"Good choice, now we'd better get moving if we are going to get that story to air!"

Moments later a man wearing a baseball cap and dark glasses placed a call at the phone box down the end of the street.

"It's done."

"And the device?"

"Somewhere not too conspicuous, but where they will find it."

"Good!"

The man hung up the phone and walked off in the direction of his car.

At the time of the explosion, Burns had also been at the marina, Savage had given him no indication as to where or when he would deal with Microbe; in fact he had wondered if he had any intentions of disposing of him. He had been talking to one of his employees about a new shipment of boats when he heard the explosion that shook the marina. His immediate reaction was to run and as he did he heard someone yell out that the *Talisman* had blown up, instantly changing his direction, he hastened towards the inlet.

By the time he found a good vantage point there wasn't much remaining of the luxury yacht, apart from what was below the water line. After taking a photo with his phone he quickly made his way to his car, finally he could destroy what Microbe had in his office safe!

He had no qualms about opening the safe, as he had come across the combination a long time ago, but had never had the opportunity to gain access. He was just about to move the picture that covered the wall safe when he heard the storeroom door open, instantly causing his heart to race.

"What the hell are you doing here?" Yelled Damon.

"I was just going to call you, the battery on my phone died, Microbe's dead!" Rushed Burns in one breath.

"What?"

"Didn't you hear the explosion?"

"No I've been in the storeroom; you know you can't hear anything when you're inside! What's this about Microbe and an explosion?"

"His boat just blew up; it's total chaos down at the marina."

"Shit! Are you sure?"

"Yep."

"Does Savage know?"

"I have no idea; do you want me to call him?"

Burns knew Damon was extremely loyal to Microbe, which meant he did not like dealing with Savage.

"Yeah, I'm going to check things out for myself, perhaps he had prior warning and had time to jump ship."

"Ok, I'll lock up as soon as I've rung Savage."

Damon didn't bother to respond and Burns waited till he saw him drive off before he locked the door and pulled down the blinds and then quickly removed the picture from the wall. He tried to still his shaking hands as he nervously spun the dial on the safe, hoping Microbe hadn't had the smarts to change the combination. As he spun the dial after the last number his heart was racing, he grasped the handle holding his breath hoping it would turn, releasing a lung full of air as it moved and the door opened. In a matter of seconds his excitement took a nosedive, as the safe was empty, sending him into another state of panic.

How could this be, did Microbe take the contents with him on the boat, had he grown suspicious and kept them on his person at all times? If Microbe had in fact taken the folder with him on the boat he had no worries, but it was the uncertainty of not knowing that raised his stress levels even higher, *what if it has fallen into the hands of someone far more dangerous than Microbe?*

Greg the Editor of *The Eden Cove Gazette* was seething, he had tried calling Jasmine countless times but her phone kept going to message bank, he had a paper to print and his star reporter was missing. He opened the door to his office and noticed the majority of his staff had gathered around one of the desks looking at something on the computer.

"What the hell is going on, we have a paper to print and speaking of which has anyone heard from Jasmine Bronson?"

"She's on the news."

"What?"

"Well actually she is reporting the news!"

Greg quickly walked over, looked at the screen, and seethed in anger as he saw footage of the explosion and the chaos that happened thereafter. Then the camera was directed to Jasmine who had a headset on and was obviously reporting from the air.

"It's not yet confirmed, but it is believed the owner and his wife, a well-known and respected local couple were the only ones on board the luxury yacht called the *Talisman*. As you can see there is not much hope for any survivors, the fire crew have almost extinguished the fire and from our bird's eye view all that remains of that magnificent yacht is the charred hull and a massive oil slick, which poses a problem in itself! Tune in tomorrow night for part two, 'The End of an Era', for the small town of Eden Cove and also coverage of the impending environmental disaster caused by the oil slick to the Great Barrier Reef. I'm Jasmine Bronson from Frontline News, bringing you the story first, goodnight!"

"That little turncoat, after all I did for her!" Exclaimed Greg.

Everyone in the room knew his comment was a load of bullshit, Jasmine had been begging him for years to do something other than births and obituaries, it was only through her persistence she managed to get the scoop of the century and put the *Eden Cove Gazette* on the map. Later that evening everyone gathered at the local pub and drank to Jasmine's success.

Max Steel had his own quiet celebratory drink, his nemesis Microbe, was dead!

STEEL JUSTICE

CHAPTER NINE

The search for Michelle Brown had been scaled down, it was well into the second week and still no sign of her or her assailant could be found. Lagoon and Oyster Island had been extensively searched, including the surrounding waters, most now believed her body had been dumped at sea and with the amount of crocodiles in the area, many believed there was very little hope of finding any remains. This frustrated Max immensely, so he put a call through to an old army friend.

"Geoff, Max Steel. Do you still get an adrenaline rush from diving in dangerous waters?"

"Max, good to hear from you, what've you got in mind?"

"The waters near Oyster Island, its crocodile territory and not far from a place called Eden Cove?"

"Sounds interesting, but this is no pleasure trip is it?"

"I'm assuming you've been following the latest story the media has been circling like vultures?"

"Kind of hard not to, so the reports one of the girls is your daughter is true?"

"Yeah."

"I assumed it was more media bullshit!"

"I only found out myself a couple of years back, it was something I was trying to keep under-wraps; I am sure you can understand why."

"Totally, so do you have a specific area you wish to go diving?"

"I thought the North-western side of Oyster Island would be a good place to start."

"You know it's funny you called me, because I had just been contemplating my next dive trip. I don't suppose Eden Cove has such a thing as an airport?"

"It does have a local airstrip, but you can't get a direct flight here, call me when you have secured a flight to the closest commercial airport and I'll pick you up from there in my chopper."

"Will do."

Max knew there was no point going back onto the island, it had been extensively searched by himself and the police with the aid of tracker dogs, who led them to the North-western side of the island, and this is where her trail went cold. The thing that baffled Max, Michelle never went anywhere without her knife and she knew how to use it, *how did Josh manage to overpower her when he had sustained an injury, but more so, why did Josh take her with him when his intention was to kill her?*

Max voiced these questions to Geoff on their flight to Eden Cove the following afternoon.

"Perhaps he used her as a hostage," commented Geoff.

"Why, when it was supposed to be a hit?"

"Well we know he was injured, he knew he had screwed things up and was running out of time, perhaps to the point he might need a hostage."

"You don't know my daughter; I can't see how he managed to get off this island with her?"

"Remember she was injured."

"So was he."

"Perhaps her injury was much worse?"

After an uncomfortable pause, Geoff realised he knew he had to get Max's mind off any thoughts of the worst case scenario, so changed his questioning.

"You said this guy took the girls to the island via helicopter, have they unearthed whose it is or its whereabouts?

"No, but the description Jane gave me, I'll bet my last dollar it was Microbe's and not surprisingly it appears to be missing."

"Bit of a coincidence."

"Yes rather."

STEEL JUSTICE

* * *

As Eden Cove's main focus is the reef and fishing, Max had no trouble hiring a boat, he opted to be passenger while Geoff took the helm and expertly manoeuvred the boat around the sharp rocks. Max knew despite the fact the hired guns had risked life and limb to land on Lagoon Island, Oyster Island was so densely vegetated it was virtually impossible to land on the island itself. Max believed Josh had used the floats, which Jane said the chopper was equipped with. As he looked at the mass of rocks with their covering of razor sharp oysters, he concluded, it would have been insanity to swim across them, so his only other option to gain access to the island would have been the life raft all helicopters are required to carry.

Suddenly he noticed a small splash of colour on one of the black rocks and asked Geoff to get as close to the rock as possible. As they got closer Max could see a small piece of bright orange fabric had been snared on one of the sharp oyster shells, he immediately grabbed the gaff, hoping to snare it with the hook.

"Ok, we've got a wave coming, on my say so, grab it," said Geoff

Max braced himself, not taking his eyes off the intended target.

"Now!" Yelled Geoff.

In one fluid motion Max hooked the fabric and brought the gaff back into the boat and Geoff quickly steered the boat away from the rocks before the next wave came upon them. As Max pulled the fabric from the hook he could make out the letters Zo.

"As I suspected, it's from a Zodiac life raft."

"So now we know how they got off the island, I wonder which direction he took and was his injury enough to warrant medical help?" Asked Geoff.

"Well according to Jane, she doesn't remember seeing any extra fuel on board, which doesn't mean there wasn't any. Bob and I did the calculations of fuel consumption from the place they originally left the mainland to Lagoon Island, taking into account this guy searched the area before landing here; I have searched all possible places he could have flown to and have come up with zilch!"

"Is it possible one of the locals were paid to keep quiet?"

"Unfortunately yes."

"You have another theory don't you?"

"Yeah, one I don't want to think about, but can't rule out; they never made it to land."

"The very reason you asked me if I was interested in a spot of dangerous diving?"

"Yeah."

"So where do you want to start?"

"Going by the ocean currents, I think we need to head a bit further due-west."

Both men knew encountering a croc in the water was a whole different ball game to encountering a shark, so both men worked on the buddy system and ensured they remained within a reasonable distance of each other. A diver is most vulnerable of being attacked by a croc while exiting and entering the water, as a croc needs to be on the surface to eat, but the larger male crocs have been known to attack a diver down deep, before bringing them to the surface to eat.

After going out virtually every day diving, over the past week, covering a large radius of the waters off the northern side of Oyster Island, Max made a discovery; he found the helicopter he believed to be owned by Microbe.

Because of the strong currents, the depth of the water and one particularly large male croc, it took the men several attempts before they could get down to the actual cabin of the helicopter; still strapped in the pilot's seat was a male Max believed to be the elusive Josh, but the passenger seat was empty.

Max's first thought was the large croc, which had been hampering their efforts to get close enough to the cabin of the chopper, but then immediately pushed such thoughts to the back of his mind.

"Perhaps she never got back in the helicopter," suggested Geoff.

"Well then where is she?"

"I don't know, perhaps when ATSB (Australian Transport Safety Bureau) get the chopper on dry land they might uncover a clue."

"I can only hope, but in the meantime I can't sit back and wait, I have to keep looking!"

"I wouldn't have expected anything different."

It was equally difficult for ATSB to retrieve Microbe's helicopter from the ocean floor. Max believed the Senior Sargent from Eden Cove, was merely there to protect Microbe and his illegal activities, but what puzzled Max was why, *Microbe was dead, did he have a vested interest in whatever Microbe was involved in, or had someone else stepped into his shoes?*

Max was concerned the local police Sargent would do his best to sweep the disappearance of his daughter under the carpet, directing any heat away from Microbe. To avoid this from happening he first had to view what the ATSB uncover, as it could be his only link to finding his daughter; this meant he would need to call in another favour.

The ATSB preliminary report stated; the helicopter was missing one life jacket, but then there was the possibility Microbe hadn't followed emergency procedure by having the required amount of life jackets on board, but it was a glimmer of hope, one Max clung to.

Geoff and Max widened their search area and uncovered the girls weighted backpacks, confirming Max's suspicions that the day he had seen the Van Witsen speeding from Lagoon Island; they were in clean up mode.

Not surprisingly after it was confirmed the helicopter was in fact registered to a Malcolm Microbe, the local police Sargent was able to pull a report stating the helicopter had been stolen. Max knew he was fast running out of favours, but he had to know what caused the chopper to crash. Knowing it would possibly take months before the ATSB had completed their investigation, his instincts told him the crash was pilot error and the only way of confirming his suspicions was to view the autopsy report.

Fortunately he had some loyal friends in high places, so he was currently seated in the Medical Examiner's office.

"Mr Steel I believe you are hoping my findings on our John Doe will offer you an insight as to where your missing daughter maybe?" Asked the M.E.

"Yes, I am hoping your report will be able to determine whether the victim was alive, dead, conscious, or unconscious before the helicopter hit the water."

"I am afraid I cannot answer that question, as there are so many variables, but I can tell you the victim sustained multiple knife wounds prior to entering the water, one which I find rather baffling."

"Why?"

"According to the information given to me by the police, there were only two people in the tree house when a struggle ensured, one your daughter and the other our John Doe."

"Yes that is correct."

"I believe there was another person in the tree house."

"Why?"

"Our John Doe suffered injuries to the right armpit, the left side of the neck close to the carotid artery, also the upper thigh, although I must admit there appears to be some hesitation with the blade."

"I don't see how these injuries would make you think there was a third person in the tree house."

"All these injuries are not immediately fatal, but could have been if the blade had continued further or deeper, for instance the one to the upper thigh I believe the perineum was the intended target. These injuries show all the traits of a form of martial arts called Sa…"

"Sayoc Kali, my daughter is well versed in the use of a knife."

The female M.E. looked stunned at Max and wasn't quite sure how to respond.

"My daughter wasn't your normal nineteen year old girl."

"Obviously! As I said, if the blade had continued further, or deeper, the victim would have died within seconds. No offence but perhaps the age of your daughter and the fact it is not a female's normal instinct to kill, is why she hesitated with the blade?"

"It's possible, thinking it and actually committing the act are two entirely different scenarios."

"Yes, I am sure you are well aware of the fact."

There was a pregnant pause and the M.E. looked back down at her papers.

"I can read you like an open book, so I will answer the question, yes Michelle was comfortable with a knife, in fact she carried her knife like most girls their mobile phone. It was a; Military Predator SQR 50 HRC titanium, blade length 125mm, or in basic layman's terms; a dive knife, does that fit the description of the one that caused the injuries to your John Doe?" Commented Max

"Ah yeah, but I must say as a parent, I am surprised you allowed her to have such a thing in her possession, especially if she used it for more than the purpose it was designed for!"

"I bought it for her."

"Oh!"

"If you knew my daughter you would understand why. Now getting back to the John Doe, how long before you know his identity now you have his DNA?"

"Unfortunately these things take time."

"Something my daughter doesn't have a lot of!"

"I don't see how…"

"If I know who he is, it might give me some idea as to where she is, I believe she was in that chopper when it went down, what if your John Doe had time to prepare for a crash landing, what if he had time to contact someone?"

"I don't see how that would give you any clues as to where your daughter might be."

"It will explain the missing life jacket."

"Meaning, giving you an element of hope?"

"Exactly!"

"I wish I could give you the answers you seek, but really only the ATSB can determine whether it was the aircraft or pilot error that caused the crash and whether your daughter had enough time to prepare for the crash."

It wasn't the answer Max wanted, but he had to concede she was right and hounding her for an answer wasn't going to bring him any closer to finding Michelle. He thanked her for the information she had given him and made his way out to the car park and climbed in behind the wheel of his four-wheel drive, but he couldn't seem to bring himself to go through the motions of putting the key in the ignition and making the drive back home. He couldn't stop the niggling questions that kept bouncing around in his head, *he could understand her not going for the kill shot, he always remembered the first time he killed someone, but she had the upper hand, she remembered her training, how the hell did he overpower her and get her off the island; where the hell was she?*

While Max asked himself these questions, forensics who were working on the charred hull and surrounding debris of the *Talisman* had uncovered evidence proving the explosion was no accident, but also found remnants of a tracking device attached to the hull, the investigation was now listed as a homicide.

STEEL JUSTICE

CHAPTER TEN

As the cab pulled up to the curb Deanne's excitement plummeted into a heap as she looked out the window.

"Are you sure this is the place?" She asked the driver.

"Number twenty five, Victoria Street?"

"Yeah."

"Well this is the place."

When Deanne had learnt she'd inherited a house in Queensland, she wasted no time handing in her notice at the cafe and packed up her few possessions to start a new life. As she looked at the ramshackle timber house she realised in hindsight she should have come and looked at the place first, before making any rash decisions.

"Well I was told it needed a little TLC."

"More like a bulldozer!"

"Well maybe it isn't so bad inside." She said as she opened the cab door.

As the cab driver looked at the small petite girl, her long dark brown hair tied back in a simple ponytail, he thought she couldn't be much older than his daughter of seventeen and felt guilty about leaving her here on her own.

"Do you want me to wait in case you change your mind?"

"No, thanks anyway."

The driver got her suitcases out of the trunk while Deanne struggled to open the gate that was half hanging on one hinge. As she walked up to the crumbling front steps she wondered whether she should even try navigating them.

"Perhaps you should see if the back entrance is any better," suggested the cab driver

"I was thinking the same thing. Look I appreciate your help, but really I'll be fine, just leave the suitcases here.

Deanne paid the cab driver and then tentatively tried one of the stairs, after feeling movement and hearing the distinct sound of splintering wood, she decided to investigate the back entrance.

To her relief the back stairs were made of brick and looked structurally sound, she opened the door with trepidation, preparing herself for the worst. Expecting her nostrils to be hit with the smell of mould and decay, but was pleasantly surprised to find there was none.

As she walked from room to room she found the house was clean but spartanly furnished. Deanne remembered the lawyer had said someone came once a week to mow the lawn, but never mentioned anything about the inside of the house.

It had come as a shock when Deanne learnt her father had bequeathed a house to her, a man she had never met; a man her mother had refused to speak of.

Deanne had quizzed Mr Dobson from the law firm, for as much detail about her father as possible and was surprised to discover he was a well-respected surgeon who had died five years previous of a heart attack and his only other living relative was his sister.

Suddenly there was a knock at the back door and Deanne wondered if it was the cab driver coming back to check up on her. She had to smile to herself; life in the country was going to be far different to living in the city, where one would be hard pressed just to get the driver to assist with the luggage. She opened the door and was surprised to see a heavily set woman with greying hair pulled back into a matronly bun, who she guessed to be in her early sixties.

"Hello dear, I hope you had been forewarned about the front steps?"

"No I hadn't, do you live next door?"

"Oh silly me I should have introduced myself, my name is Jan Thomas, Robert Shoal was my brother, so I suppose that makes me your aunt, you know you are the spitting image of your grandmother."

Deanne stood momentarily lost for words.

"Ah, do you mind if I come in, I'd like to put this in the oven before it gets cold?"

Deanne suddenly noticed the woman was holding a casserole dish in her hands.

"Yes of course, sorry, Mr Dobson had told me my father had a sister, but I didn't know you lived close by."

"No need to apologise dear, I'm sure you're still coming to grips with the news of your father."

Deanne followed her newfound aunt into the kitchen and noted she seemed to know her way around the house and surmised she was the one responsible for keeping it reasonably clean.

"I know the house needs a little work, but your father loved this place, he used to come here every chance he had."

"So he didn't live here?"

"No he spent most of his time in the city; his first priority was his patients, oh and of course finding you and your mother."

"Yes, Mr Dobson said that, the thing I found strange though, he said it was the obituary notice I put in the paper about my mother that led them to me, surely I couldn't have been that hard to find?"

"It is if you are looking for a Mary Denver."

"I don't understand."

"How about we put on the kettle and I'll tell you all I know?"

Once they had both settled in the kitchen over a cup of coffee Jan started to talk.

"You know your mother and your father were once engaged to be married."

"Really?"

"Yes, I still remember the last day I saw your mother, she was so excited about the wedding, she had already picked out a dress and the invitations had been sent out and she hinted to me she had a special surprise to tell Robert."

"What was it?"

"I believe she was going to tell him she was carrying his child, but she never got a chance to tell him what her surprise was, because by the time he came home your mother was gone."

"What happened?"

"Salina."

"Who's Salina?"

"An evil conniving woman who would resort to anything to get what she wanted and unfortunately she had set her sights on your father!"

"What happened?"

"At the time your father was studying to become a plastic surgeon and his future prospects were looking bright and that was how he met Salina, she was studying at the same university."

"That doesn't explain why my mother suddenly disappeared."

"Robert believed she threatened your mother, but by the time he discovered this he had married Salina."

"Ok, firstly, if my mother was so in love with my father, how could a threat from this woman make her run away and secondly, why the hell did he marry Salina if he was so in love with my mother?"

"He was so devastated when your mother left, he searched for her everywhere, but it was looking more and more like she had run off with another man; Salina took advantage of that!"

"So he sought solace in another woman!"

"Please don't think badly of Robert, Salina had done her homework, she made Robert vulnerable, and she attacked his Achilles heel."

"What do you mean?"

"Salina knew just making your mother leave would not be enough, she knew your father would never give up on your mother unless she hurt him in the cruellest of ways. Salina very cleverly planted evidence that made your mother's disappearance look like she had run off with another man."

"What a bitch! I'm sure my mother would have seen this. She might have been upset and run off, because of whatever this woman said to her, but what I don't understand, is all my life we only lived in two places; why was it so difficult for my father to find us, maybe that is what my mother was waiting for?"

"Your mother changed her name."

"What?"

"Your mother's real name is Mary Denver."

"No that can't be, her name is Marianne Jones, it's on my Birth Certificate and I saw her driver's licence, obviously this has all been one big mistake; I'm not the daughter Robert Shoal was looking for!"

"I know it is a shock to you, but it is the truth, your mother changed her name through the Registry of Births Deaths and Marriages, Robert found evidence to prove this and Dobson and Dobson Lawyers have copies of this documentation if you wish to see them."

"Why didn't Mr Dobson tell me this?"

"He thought it best that I should tell you."

"Why would my mother do that, why would she change her name?"

"So Salina wouldn't find her."

"Why?"

"Robert discovered Salina had not only threatened your mother's life, but also the life of her unborn child."

"My god! Well then why the hell did he marry her?"

"He had no idea at the time, in fact he didn't even know your mother was carrying his child, you would have been about two when he discovered this."

"Why would Salina do this, why did she hate my mother so much?"

"She was what was standing between her and Robert."

"My god to love someone that much you would resort to killing someone!"

"She didn't love him; she wanted what he could give her!"

"Which was?"

"Money, prestige, a place in society, only she hadn't

factored in that Robert had a heart."

"What do you mean?"

"Your father could have made a lot of money as a cosmetic surgeon, but he believed he had been given a gift for a reason and that was to help those who really needed it; those who had suffered disfigurement through an accident or even victims of a violent crime."

"So how would that change things, I was told he was well-respected?"

"Firstly the money, in some instances these victims could not pay him much or any at all. If he had been a cosmetic surgeon purely for the vanity of some, he could have been a very rich man. Secondly he found most people that moved in those circles to be shallow and self-centred; he wanted nothing to do with that kind of life, something that angered Salina greatly!"

"The reason they got divorced?"

"Yes."

"Was he still married to her when he found out why my mother disappeared?"

"No, but I believe when he unearthed this knowledge this is what got him killed."

"Killed, I was told he died of a heart attack?"

"That's what the autopsy report states, but I don't believe that for one minute!"

"Why?"

"He was as strong as an ox and I know there was nothing wrong with his heart, besides not long before he died he told me he was forced to do something that went against all his beliefs!"

"Did he tell you what that was?"

"No and that is the reason I have kept all his files, I believe the answer is in there somewhere."

"Would you mind if I looked through them?"

"I was hoping you would ask me that, perhaps a young mind can get a better grasp on them."

STEEL JUSTICE

* * *

Deanne managed to gain employment at the local boatyard working in the office and after speaking to her aunt she decided she would use the small amount of funds she had saved to start repairs on the house her father loved. She also planned to peruse his files and see what she could uncover about her father and his death.

Deanne arrived early for her first day at work feeling rather nervous, as there was something about Sam, her new boss, which made her uncomfortable. She pulled on the door and realised it was locked and noticed the *Closed* sign; she wasn't sure whether to knock or wait the fifteen minutes till she was supposed to start.

She knew someone was inside because she could hear them talking, suddenly the blind moved at the window and she got a glimpse of Sam's face, before the talking resumed. Assuming he was talking on the phone she waited patiently for him to end his call and open the door.

After a further ten minutes and he still hadn't opened the door she wondered if he had forgotten she was standing outside and knocked firmly on the door.

"We're closed; we don't open till 8am."

"Um, I'm Deanne your new receptionist, we spoke yesterday."

He stared at her for a moment and she was hoping her job hadn't ended before it had even begun.

"Your early, in future don't come before 8am."

"Okay sorry, I'm just a bit nervous, first day and all."

Deanne was surprised at his attitude; she thought being early would score her some brownie points. She followed Sam inside and tried to quell any second thoughts she had about the job, as Sam ran through the list of things she was required to do.

"Now Deanne, you should have everything you require in the office here, there is a lunch room and a bathroom through that door, but it is imperative you do not go any further, the shed is definitely out of bounds."

"Ah, ok."

"Look I'm not trying to scare you, it is a health and safety issue, we had a situation in the past and I definitely don't want a repeat episode of that!"

"Yes Sam, I promise I won't come out to the shed, if I need you I will buzz through to you."

"Good, I think you will work out well here. Now there is already a pile of invoices for you to type up, the previous girl had got quite lax in that department, if you have any questions, just buzz through to me."

Sam gave a quick nod and walked out the back door in the direction of the shed. Deanne took a deep breath, sat down at the desk, and started sorting through the invoices.

* * *

Despite the fact Microbe was no longer a threat to Burns, the missing folder was always at the forefront of his mind, had Microbe for some reason taken them on the boat that day, or had they fallen into the hands of someone else. Admittedly he was much better off financially since he had proposed his idea to Michael Savage, but the man made him extremely nervous, more so than Microbe could.

Burns decided to do something he hadn't done in a very long time, he first made sure the door to his office was securely locked then sat down in front of his computer

After going through many encrypted channels he keyed in his password and instantly the chat icon flashed on his screen.

Where've you been Felix, its Top Cat?
I've been away.
You missed out on a meeting.
Was it good?
Extremely! Planning another, are you interested?

Sure! When and where?
The usual place, Friday next week. Can you make it?
What time?
Midnight.
I'll be there.
See you then.

Burns quickly signed out; his heart was racing with a mixture of fear and excitement, then suddenly an awful fear came over him, *what if it's a trap?* He sat there and thought about the missing folder, then he realised the venue hadn't been mentioned and no one but Top Cat would know where this place was. Suddenly the phone rang causing him to jump and he sat and stared at it for a moment before finally picking it up.

"Hello," he said hesitantly.
"Burns?"
"Is that you Sam?"
"Yeah, what's up you sound strange?"
"Nothing, my mind was just on something else, why the call?"
"I need you to come down to the boatyard."
"Why?"
"We're having a bit of a problem and I would rather not discuss it over the phone."
"Alright, but I can't make it till tomorrow night."
"This needs to be sorted out now!"
"There is absolutely no possible way I can make it before then."
"Tomorrow night will be too late, make it during the day."
"I can't risk being seen."
"Like I said tomorrow night will be too late, unless you'd prefer Savage on your back?"
"Alright! I'll be there about midday."

The call was disconnected and Burns reached for his bottle of Zantac, all this stress was not good for his ulcer.

* * *

Max knew the only way he was going to find any more answers regarding his daughter's whereabouts was to keep searching the waters off Oyster Island. Geoff and himself decided to make an early start as the water would be much calmer and more favourable. As he drove down his long drive towards the front gates he was annoyed to see the local police Sargent blocking his exit.

"God what now?"

"Perhaps he has an update on Microbe's chopper," suggested Geoff.

"I doubt it; even if he did he wouldn't divulge that information to me!"

Max pushed the buzzer for the gate to open and then got out of his four-wheel drive and walked towards Sargent Wilson.

"Sargent, it must be important to get you out of bed so early."

As Max stepped through the gate he noticed Sargent Wilson wasn't alone, there were three other police vehicles and a tow-truck parked along the curb.

"What the hell…"

"Max Steel, I have a warrant to impound your vehicle and a warrant to search your premises."

Sargent Wilson handed him the two warrants and Max quickly scanned them.

"This is bullshit! On what grounds?"

"On the basis there is evidence someone put a remotely controlled bomb on the *Talisman,* also remnants of a tracking device attached to the boat's hull; army issue."

The colour drained from Max's face, he had been so focused on trying to find his daughter he had totally forgotten the tracking device.

"Max Steel, I am placing you under arrest for the murders of Malcolm and Charlene Microbe. You have the right to remain silent, anything you say or do can and will be used against you in a court of law. Do you understand these rights' as they have been stated to you?"

"This is bullshit!" Exclaimed Max.

Geoff immediately got out of the car as he saw Sargent Wilson try to handcuff Max.

"Max, what's going on?"

"Rent a cop seems to think I killed Microbe and his wife, they're impounding the four-wheel drive and have a warrant to search the house!"

"Sargent you can't be serious?" Asked Geoff.

"Deadly! You know a lot of people respected Malcolm Microbe, he had done a lot for this town."

"The guy was a lowlife scumbag, a slimy crook and his supposed generosity was only to buy off the town so people would turn a blind eye to his illegal activities. I wouldn't be surprised if he was paying your wage!" Exclaimed Max

"If you're suggesting police corruption, I would tread very carefully if I was you!"

"Is that a threat?"

Geoff knew Max was at snapping point and trying to goad the Sargent into a fight, his emotions were strung so tight he was afraid Max would do something he would later regret.

"Max cut it! I'll make a few calls; you'll be out in a couple of hour's tops."

Geoff stood between Max and the Sargent, giving him a chance to get his emotions in check, as Max looked at him he could see he was regaining control and stepped aside so the Sargent could handcuff him.

As Max climbed into the back of the police car he was annoyed at himself for losing control, he hadn't gained the nickname *Mr Cool* for no reason, but back then he didn't know he had a daughter, one who was out there somewhere; waiting for him to bring her back home!

While Max was seething behind bars, others believed they had good cause for a celebration. After expertly popping the cork from the bottle of champagne, he poured two glasses before handing one across to the woman, admiring her long slender fingers as they wrapped around the stem of the glass, her nails were blood red, his favourite colour. He looked out over the water and admired the view, then turned back to clink his glass against hers.

"To Microbe!"

STEEL JUSTICE

CHAPTER ELEVEN

When 5 o'clock finally came around Deanne wasted no time shutting down her computer and locking the office door behind her. On the walk home she couldn't shake the feeling she was being watched and kept looking over her shoulder, but saw no one. *Perhaps it's the combination of Sam's strange behaviour and being in the office alone all day that has me paranoid.*

After living most her life in a small apartment where the walls were paper-thin and with the constant noise of the city, she figured the quite life of Fig Tree Grove was going to take some getting used to. One thing that puzzled her was why Sam chose Fig Tree Grove to set up a boat yard, the closest body of water was miles away, a place called Eden Cove.

As she walked around the back of the house, she saw movement at the window and a wave of fear swept over her. Keeping her eyes focused on the window she slowly moved forward and suddenly realised it was just breeze blowing the curtain through the open window. Smiling to herself at her ridiculous paranoia, she made her way up the few short steps and inserted the key in the lock, when suddenly she realised she had ensured all windows and doors were locked before she left in the morning. Despite the fact her aunt had told her most people of Fig Tree Grove didn't feel the need to lock their doors or windows, it was a habit she couldn't get used to, not after having her apartment in the city broken into on more than one occasion.

She paused with the key still in the lock not sure what to do, *what if someone is still in there, should I go ask my neighbour to come inside with me?* She withdrew the key and started to make her way back down the stairs when she realised the neighbour wouldn't be much help; he was almost eighty.

After going back up the steps and unlocking the door, she held her keys in one hand as a weapon and had her handbag in the other; ready to clout someone over the head if necessary. Once inside she quickly ran to the kitchen, grabbed a large sharp knife from the drawer, and then cautiously checked each room. She had the knife gripped so tightly her fingernails dug into her palms and her throat was so dry, she doubted she'd be able to scream for help if she had to.

After doing a thorough search of every room, including looking under the beds and in the cupboards and finding nothing, she started to relax thinking that perhaps she had left the window open after all; she had been nervous about her first day at her new job.

In desperate need of a drink of water, she made her way back to the kitchen and wasted no time filling a glass and draining its contents. As she leaned against the sink, she looked at the walls, they were sorely in need of a coat of paint and then her eyes drifted to the floor and realised the floorcoverings would need replacing as well. She then noticed the boxes of files her aunt had left for her and instantly the hairs on the back of her neck prickled. She hadn't had a chance to go through them, but when her aunt had delivered them they were all securely taped closed; someone had sliced the tape and it looked as if the contents of one box had been hurriedly shoved back in. *Why would someone want to go through my father's files, what were they looking for?*

Deanne went and inspected the open window and despite the peeling paint she could see slight marks in the timber as if someone has used some sort of tool to open it. She inspected the lock and realised it wouldn't have taken much to jimmy it open, overcome with a sudden panic she raced around the house and inspected all the other windows and the front and back doors, both doors had deadlocks, but the windows were really only a latch; *they would have to be replaced.*

Deanne couldn't sleep, every time she started to nod off she would hear a noise, causing her to get out of bed and recheck all the windows and doors. Realising sleep was virtually hopeless, she decided to go through her father's files and perhaps uncover what someone felt was worth breaking into her house for.

She read countless pages of medical jargon that didn't make an ounce of sense, but all files contained before and after photos, so graphic they started to make her stomach churn. Despite feeling queasy, she had to admit her father was not only talented, but he had given these people a life, some of their injuries so horrific, they could not go out in public without a veil to cover their face. *If my aunt is right and someone killed him, why, when he gave these people a life?*

Getting little to no sleep and knowing the hardware store opened at 6am, Deanne was there when the doors opened, much to the surprise of the storeowner when he unlocked the doors.

"You're rather early girly, usually at this hour I only see scruffy tradesman who look like they're sorely in need of a good breakfast and a cup of coffee!"

"I want to get some window locks and was hoping I could install them before I have to go to work."

"You're new to these parts aren't you?"

"Why yes, how did you know?"

"None of the locals would bother with window locks; as a matter of fact most don't even lock their doors."

"Well I'm from the city and until I'm classed as a 'local', if I want to be able to sleep at night, I need locks on my windows. Do you have such a thing?"

"Matter of fact I do."

Deanne followed him to the back of the store and he showed her the window locks, they were covered in dust and looked like they'd been there for years. He picked one up, blew off the dust and handed it to her.

"I'm not sure, they look rather old."

"Well like I said, most folks of Fig Tree Grove don't even bother to lock their doors, so haven't had much call for window locks. I can assure you, despite the dust on the packet, they are still as good as new, and in fact if you decide to purchase them

I'll even install them for you for a small charge."

Deanne had a feeling the old guy was trying to con her, but then it was obvious they had been in his shop for a long time, but then perhaps his offer to install them was prompted by the doubt he would ever sell them otherwise.

"I'll take them if you can install them now, free of charge."

"Ah, I only just opened the shop and the time and effort it would take for me to install them."

"Well the condition on me buying them is if you can install them now and free of charge, otherwise no deal."

Deanne could almost hear the wheels ticking over in his head as she suddenly realised she had the upper hand, he'd had these locks for years, thought he would never shift them; she might be his only chance.

"Well, do we have a deal?" She asked.

"I can't very well leave the shop just after I've opened it and as I said my time and labour."

"No problems, I know I can order the same thing online, in fact there is a good chance I will get them cheaper and probably a much more updated item."

"That's possible, but you won't get them installed this morning, in fact you'll probably have to wait days, even weeks before they arrive."

"At least I will know they haven't been sitting in some hardware store for years and probably don't even work."

Deanne desperately wanted those locks today, but she stood her ground and she knew by the look on his face he was desperate to off-load them.

"You drive a hard bargain girly, looks like we have a deal. I just have to make a phone call and get someone to mind the shop."

Deanne waited patiently as she knew she still had plenty of time before starting work, after all, Sam did not appreciate her arriving early.

By the time Deanne arrived at the boatyard she was tired, but felt confident she would not have any intruders breaking into her house, whoever did on the previous day would be in for a surprise.

She wasn't sure if it was the lack of sleep, or the fact someone had broken into her house, but she had trouble concentrating on typing up the invoices Sam had requested. Her mind kept drifting to the conversation she'd had with her aunt about her father's death, causing her to make countless typing mistakes. She decided to take a break from what she was supposed to be doing and do some research that might answer some of the questions that kept running through her mind, she wanted to know more about Salina, the woman her mother feared so much it gave her cause to change her name.

She Googled Salina Shoal and was disappointed when nothing came up, so decided to type in Robert Shoal and was pleasantly surprised how many articles came up about her father and as her aunt had stated he was a well-respected surgeon, so much so a wing in a Brisbane hospital had been named after him. As she scrolled through the article she came upon of photo of a man and a woman, Robert and Salina Shoal.

"So that's what you look like." Deanne said out loud as she looked at the woman.

Suddenly the door leading from the shed to the office closed causing Deanne to jump and she barely had time to close out of the program and resume typing the invoices before Sam walked in.

"Deanne, I'm going to be very busy for the rest of the afternoon and I don't want to be disturbed. That means no phone calls, no visitors, just take down messages and leave them for me on your desk and finish at five o'clock sharp and lock the door on your way out."

"Okay, no problems."

When Sam left she waited till she was sure he had gone out both doors and quickly went back into the web program, to the photo of her father and Salina and decided to print it.

The printer seemed to take an age to print, she was so paranoid Sam would come back in she stood by the window to keep lookout.

She heard a car pull up in the driveway and started to panic, the page had only half printed, *what if they come through the front door and then Sam happens to come in and see what's sitting in the printer?* She ran towards her computer and was about to cancel the printing when she heard the car move slowly up the side entrance that was only a footpath, *what the hell is this idiot doing?* Forgetting about the printer she ran back to the window and was surprised to see an expensive looking car with very dark windows trying to squeeze between the building and the fence. *Can't he read the sign for the entrance to the shed; it's on the other side and has a wide driveway!* She stood on tiptoe trying to get a look at the driver who must be so dumb he can't read a sign and would risk scratching an expensive car.

Suddenly the car door opened and a small man in his fifties stepped out with thick wavy hair fashioned in a way that would have done Elvis proud. She thought he appeared nervous as he looked in every direction, almost as if he was expecting to be ambushed at any moment. Suddenly he looked her way and her heart seemed to jump into her throat, instinct more than anything made her run over to the printer, grab the photo and quickly shove it in her desk drawer before closing out of the program and resuming her typing. Minutes later Sam burst through the door, her heart was pounding so hard she was sure he could see the movement beneath her blouse and she struggled to stop her fingers shaking as she held them over the keyboard.

"You gave me a fright; I wasn't expecting to see you again today."

Sam stared at her for a moment, almost as if deciding what to say.

"Has anyone come in since I last spoke to you?"

"No, were you expecting someone? I thought you were tied up for the rest of the afternoon; remember you said no calls or visitors?"

"Yes I am! I just thought I heard someone pull up."

"Well either I'm going deaf or you're hearing things, because I haven't seen or heard anything, but then I have been madly typing trying to get through as much of this work as I can before five o'clock. Some of this handwriting is really hard to read, I am hoping once I get a better understanding about boats it will make it easier."

He stared at her for a moment and she was wondering if he could see the beads of sweat she could feel starting to form on her brow.

"Yeah your right, some of the guys handwriting is pretty bad, I'll tell them to take a bit more time in future and write more clearly," said Sam smiling.

"That would be a great help!"

Sam walked back out the door, Deanne leaned back in her chair, and let out a lung full of air, amazed she had been able to answer his questions so casually to the extent he believed her, normally she would have cried or done something to give herself away. She decided that was the last time she did any personal stuff at work; next time she would use the computer at the local library. Then she thought about the mystery man who pulled up, *who was he and why all the secrecy, was Sam involved in something illegal, hence the strange behaviour?*

She decided to set the alarm on her mobile for five minutes to five, she wanted to make sure she was out of this place on the dot of five!

Burns was sure the girl had seen him, but Sam told him he was being paranoid and assured him she had been busy in the office when he walked in and on questioning her if she had seen or heard anyone or a vehicle, she had said no.

"I'm sure I saw someone."

"Why would she lie?"

"I don't know; it's just..."

"You've got to stop being so jumpy, or you WILL make someone suspicious!"

"It's Savage, he makes me nervous."

"Look you're not the only one, but look at the money we're making."

"I suppose you're right."

Burns realised he was becoming more paranoid by the minute; he wouldn't relax until he found the missing file from Microbe's office, which made him even more nervous about the meeting tonight.

Sometimes he wondered if it had been smart to put forth his idea to Savage, just so he could be rid of Microbe. He realised now he should have taken more time to consider the consequences of joining forces with such a man. He was becoming a major pain with his constant demand to increase the size of the shipments, posing a headache to both himself and Sam; he had no idea of the dynamics of a boat!

Deanne once again had the feeling of being watched on her walk home and after the strange visitor they had at work this afternoon, plus the discovery someone had broken into her house, it made her reassess her first impression of Fig Tree Grove as a sleepy little town.

As she walked home her heels seemed to echo loudly on the footpath and suddenly it dawned on her how quiet the street was; *where were the kids who were usually playing in the street and the friendly wave from those normally leaning over the neighbouring fence, catching up on the latest gossip?* The place appeared deserted, which only added to her paranoia. As she rounded the corner and her house came into view, she broke into a run, desperate to feel the safety of being inside her own four walls.

STEEL JUSTICE

CHAPTER TWELVE

Burns had caught a series of buses and then alighted a block from the designated meeting place, normally by now he would have trouble containing his excitement at the thought of meeting up with Top Cat, but thoughts of the missing folder from Microbe's safe were still at the forefront of his mind.

The moment the building came into view his anxiety increased, causing him to quickly hide in the shadows of a large tree. He scanned the street for any suspicious looking vehicles or any sign he had been followed; he just couldn't shake this feeling of impending dread. He was now sweating so much he had to mop his face with his handkerchief and noticed that his hands were beginning to shake; his inner voice was telling him to leave now, before it was too late, but then a compelling urge dispelled such thoughts.

A cool breeze suddenly whipped past, causing a cold shiver to run up his spine, he looked towards the house and could see a faint glow coming from the windows *Top Cat is here!* After taking another cursory look up the street, he made his way towards the front door, *collected the key from its usual place,* and quickly let himself inside. He noticed the soft glow seemed to flicker and assumed Top Cat had lit some candles, but also he could hear the murmur of voices coming from the other room. He paused and took a deep breath, pushing all previous paranoid thoughts to the back of his mind and allowed the excitement to finally build and think about the reason he was here tonight.

He quickly opened the door to the other room and soon realised the flickering light was not from candles but the television. Suddenly overcome with a mixture of disappointment and irritation, as it had been a long time since their last meeting, he had expected a bit more effort from Top Cat than sitting in front of the TV.

"Top Cat it's me, what's going on?" Asked Burns.

After receiving no answer the hairs on the back of his neck began to prickle and that old fear started to blanket his body as he made his way over towards the chair.

"Top Cat, did you hear me?"

By now he had reached the back of the chair and he noticed Top Cat's arm was hanging over the side and a wine glass had dropped to the floor. *Has he fallen asleep, surely I'm not that late?* As he rounded the chair, light from the TV momentarily lit up Top Cat's face and Burns felt sick to the stomach, his friend had a large red spot to the centre of his forehead that was oozing blood; he was dead.

Burns quickly backed away from the chair and suddenly the lights came on, temporarily blinding him, he looked up to see who was responsible when he noticed the walls, they were plastered with photos, *oh my god!* He turned to run, but before he made it to the doorway a hooded figure suddenly blocked his exit.

"Who are you?" Burns blurted in a fit of fear.

Burns knew he was next on the list, but was desperately trying to delay the inevitable, suddenly the hood was pushed back and Burns gasped as he saw the face.

"I don't understand?"

"I can't believe you would ask such a thing!"

"Why kill Top Cat if it was me you were after?"

"I knew you couldn't orchestrate such a thing on your own, I had to get the King Pin or the Top Cat so to speak!"

"But why?" Asked Burns

"You are not only a sick bastard, but a dumb one at that! Now go and say your goodbyes to your 'friend' and make sure you look at my handiwork under the bright lights!"

"Please, I can give you money!" Exclaimed Burns

"I don't want your filthy money, you disgust me!"

Burns started to cry; he didn't want to see what he'd done to Top Cat, because then he would know what was going to happen to him!

"I think you've pissed your pants."

"Please, I don't want to die!"
Suddenly a gun was raised to Burns head.
"Move!"
Burns walked over and looked at his friend and the sight of all the blood made him gag, he wished he hadn't looked; he should have stood his ground and taken the bullet to the head. Simultaneously he heard a noise and then felt the most excruciating pain, causing him to drop to his knees, he opened his mouth to scream, but no sound came out.

"I wish I could prolong your pain like I did for your 'friend', but time is something I don't have!"

He raised his gun, pulled the trigger, and drew great satisfaction seeing Burns brain matter hit the wall behind. He dropped the gun at his feet and calmly walked out the door and made his way across the street to a pay phone.

"Police, Fire or ambulance, what is your emergency?" Asked the operator

"I want to report a shooting at the residence on 52 Palm Street."

"Do you know how many people are involved and the extent of any injuries?" Asked the operator.

"They're both dead."

"Sir your name, is the shooter still at large?"

All she heard was the dial tone as the line was disconnected.

A smile came to his face as he made his way up the street and pulled out a cigarette from his top pocket and paused momentarily to light it. Suddenly he heard the sound of sirens off in the distance and he continued on his way.

When the police arrived the first thing they noticed was the front door was slightly ajar and there was the soft sound of voices.

"Go and see if there is a back entrance, I'll go in the front," said the senior officer.

As the young officer ran around the back, his senior partner drew his gun and cautiously kicked open the door.

"Police."

Receiving no answer he slowly stepped inside the door and as he moved forward he heard the murmur of voices became louder and headed in their direction.

"Police, we received a report someone was shot."

Still no answer and the realisation the voices were coming from the TV and then he saw the photos plastered over the walls, alerting him this was no random hit.

"Holy shit!" Exclaimed the young constable behind him.

"It doesn't matter how many times you see this sort of thing it will always kick you in the gut!"

The Senior Sargent scanned the room, he knew this was not going to be pretty; the perpetrator wanted his victim to suffer. He saw the dark stain on the carpet before he found the first victim on the floor and as he came closer he saw the other in the chair.

"Sargent, we have a gun, it could be the murder weapon."

"Bag it and tag it, I hope you have a strong stomach son, because whoever did this was making their point clear!"

* * *

Michael Savage had just unfolded the morning paper when the phone rang.

"Boss, just thought you should know the cops are asking questions at Burns's office."

"Do you know what it's about?"

"No, they aren't saying much."

Savage was about to comment when he looked down at the paper and saw the headlines. *Two men believed to be involved in child sex ring gunned down!*

"Shit! Are they still there?"

"No, but I get the feeling they'll be back!"

"You know what needs to be done."

"Gotcha."

The line was disconnected and Savage looked down at the

paper, they weren't naming any names at present but he was certain one of the men was Burns; he had known about Burns and his sick little secret. He had always made a point of knowing everything there was to know about those he did business with, as much as it disgusted him, he had planned to use it to his advantage, just as Microbe had. He quickly snatched up the phone and punched in some numbers.

"Sam's boat yard," said the female voice.

"Switch me through to Sam."

"May I say who...?"

"Just do it!"

Deanne was about to comment further but thought better of it and quickly buzzed Sam.

"Ah Sam there is a man on the other line, he is refusing to state his name but he wants to speak to you."

"Switch him through."

She did as requested and wondered who the rude man was and if by chance he was the weird guy who drove around the back the other day.

"Is there any way the police can tie Burns to the boat yard?"

"Savage?"

"Of course you fool; now answer the question!"

"We mostly spoke over the phone, he was paranoid as hell about coming here and when he did it was never during opening hours. Why?"

"You read the paper this morning?"

"Not as yet no, look what's going on?"

"You might want to buy the morning paper and you better make damn sure the cops can't make the connection between the boat yard and Burns!"

Before Sam could respond, the line was disconnected, as he stood there and wondered what the hell was going on he realised his answer had something to do with the morning paper. He walked quickly from the shed to the office and Deanne turned quickly in her chair.

"Who was that rude man?"

"Nothing you need to concern yourself with, I just need to duck out for a few minutes."

Before Deanne could comment he was out the door, confirming her belief that there was definitely something strange going on and felt sure it had something do to with the man who came the other day.

Later when Sam came back into the office Deanne noticed he had a newspaper under his arm and he seemed distracted. She kept on typing up the invoices, but felt a bit nervous as he didn't leave the office but started pacing the room as if he was trying to make a decision.

"Sam is there something I can help you with?"

He stopped and looked at her for a moment as though he had totally forgotten who she was and what she was doing in the office.

"Sam, you ok?"

"Ah look, I've just received some disturbing news and I think it best if I close up shop for a few days."

"Do you still want me to come in and finish all these invoices?"

"Ah no, ah you see there's been a death in the family."

"Oh Sam, I am so sorry, is there anything I can do?"

"No, but thanks anyway, I think it best if you pack up your things and go now, I'll call you when I need you."

He waited while Deanne gathered her things and the moment she walked out the front door she heard him lock it shut, she had the distinct feeling there was no 'death in the family' but felt sure it had something to do with the morning paper, so decided to go via the newsagent on her way home.

After reading the headlines she was not only shocked but surprised that the shooting had taken place only a few hours away from Fig Tree Grove and her thoughts were along the lines of many others, the gunman should be rewarded not persecuted for such a crime. Feeling at a loose end, she decided now was the time to tackle a job she had been putting off, painting the inside of her father's beloved cottage.

When Deanne got home she made herself a cup of coffee and read the paper from front to back, trying to find some clue why Sam had closed up shop, her gut instinct told her it had nothing to do with a death in the family but more to do with the phone call. The only deaths listed in the paper apart from the two men gunned down, was one person who was well into their nineties.

The following day she decided to start the painting in the lounge and as she began preparing the walls for paint, her mind wandered to Sam's behaviour and the two men gunned down, *is that why Sam is acting so strangely, is he also involved in paedophilia?* She had to find out for her own peace of mind; *what was Sam up to, what was going on in the back shed?*

Being a small town not much happened after 10 o'clock, after putting on some dark clothes she quietly slipped out the back door, this made her nervous in more ways than one, she still couldn't shake the feeling she was being watched.

Keeping to the shadows as best as she could, she made her way to the little side road that led to the boat yard. She hadn't gone very far when she tripped and her tension heightened, this road was totally devoid of lights and her mind conjured up all sorts of scary scenarios to the point she started having second thoughts about going any further. After tripping for a second time she decided to turn back when she suddenly noticed a soft glow off in the distance and in the direction of the boat shed, confirming her suspicion something was going on.

She continued forward slowly, despite the light off in the distance it was difficult to see the road in front of her. Her eyes had adjusted to the darkness by the time she neared the boatyard, she could make out the shape of the front office up ahead and realised the faint glow of light was coming from the shed behind.

Noticing the yard gates had been left slightly ajar, she cautiously stepped through and made her way around the back to the shed. Never having been around the back, she had no idea if she was going to be suddenly exposed.

To her disappointment the shed was closed and any windows were so high up she would need to stand on a ladder to look in. *I can't believe I came all this way for nothing!* As she stood there trying to decide what to do, she heard voices and movement inside the shed; *I've got to find out what he is up to!* Scanning the area around her she noticed an old 44 gallon drum and after testing to see if she could move it, discovered it was empty, but possibly too rusty to hold her weight. After testing its stability, she rolled it on its edge over towards the window and it made a crunching sound as it moved over the dirt and rocks and on a still quiet night like tonight she was sure those in the shed would hear it.

After pausing momentarily, she was confident those inside hadn't heard her as the noise inside remained unchanged and there were no approaching footfalls in the dirt.

Once the drum was up against the wall she now had the job of climbing onto it without tipping the thing over, there was nothing for her to grasp onto to stop herself and the drum from tipping.

As she climbed onto the drum it rocked on the uneven ground and she tried her best to cling to the side of the building. Finally she stabilised herself with her feet spread apart when she realised the night had suddenly become silent *God did I make that much noise?* As the seconds ticked past she could feel herself beginning to sweat and was debating whether to stay put, or make a run for it while she had the chance, then to her relief the activity inside resumed.

Stretching on tiptoes she peered inside the window, only to discover there was paper taped over it. *Bloody hell why didn't I check this out first?*

Suddenly there was movement at the window and she quickly ducked down hoping she hadn't displayed a silhouette, but as she looked up she realised the movement was the paper flapping from a draft inside the shed, which had caused the tape to come unstuck.

More conscious now than ever of making a noise, she slowly pulled herself back up, managed to get a grip on the windowsill, and cautiously looked in through the small gap. She didn't know what to expect, but certainly hadn't expected to see men in overalls working on three possibly four boats. *Why all the secrecy if their just working on the boats?*

Deanne carefully climbed back down, slowly putting the drum back where it had been and did her best to smooth over the drag marks the drum had made in the dirt. Suddenly she heard voices and then saw the beam of a torch light being waved around as someone came around the side of the shed, she quickly looked around for somewhere to hide and realised her only hope was a big oak tree!

With her heart in her throat she climbed up and hid amongst the thick foliage; so fast the neighbourhood boys would have been impressed. Despite the exertion she wasn't game to take a deep lung full of air, as the torchlight was now moving around below the tree and she realised someone was looking for something.

"I'm telling you I heard something."

Deanne put her hand over her mouth as she realised it was Sam and he was directly below her, her lungs were screaming out for air and the lack of oxygen was making her feel faint. Suddenly there was an awful screech that almost made her fall out of the tree.

"Well looks like we found your intruder Sam, it's just that old ally-cat, maybe you should stop feeding it and then it will stop hanging around making us all jumpy."

"Okay guys back to work, we're already behind schedule," said Sam.

As the men walked off Deanne took a slow deep breath and waited a further five minutes to calm her jangled nerves but also to ensure all the men had gone back inside the shed.

On the walk back home Deanne pondered over the secrecy of the back shed, it didn't make sense, *perhaps he's cutting corners to make more money, but then I know nothing about boat building so what's the big secret?* Once back home and after a long hot shower Deanne decided to resume going through her father's files, *what was in there that caused someone to break into her house, perhaps there is something that would confirm her aunt's suspicions about his death?*

After reading well into the night, she suddenly realised there was one handwritten word *Camino* which was in the top right corner of all, but one file. She quickly grabbed her dictionary and looked it up, but there was no such word listed.

"I wonder what it means," she said out loud.

The following day Deanne called the boat yard to see if Sam wanted her to come back to work, after what she had seen last night he obviously wasn't mourning his lost relative for too long. After countless rings the phone went to the message service, stating that the place was closed until the following week, *that's strange, why are you working at night and keeping the placed closed during the day?*

Deanne thought it was about time she visited her aunt, perhaps she knew what the word *Camino* meant.

"Deanne, how lovely to see you!"

"I'm sorry I haven't been around sooner, but with the new job and painting, I've been rather busy."

"No need to apologise, I knew it would take you a little while to settle in and what's this painting?"

"I've started painting inside the house."

"Oh that's wonderful, he would be so pleased, so have you got the day off or are you just on a break?"

"Actually I've got a few days off; apparently there has been a death in Sam's family so the boat yard is closed."

"Really, that's odd; I never saw anything in the paper and usually being a small town everyone would know about that by now."

"Well that's the excuse he gave me."

"Hmm, well I suppose I can't complain, after all I get to see my favourite niece!"

"I do have another reason for coming here, you see I have

been going through my father's files and one word keeps cropping up and for some reason I don't feel it has anything to do with an actual patient."

"Why is that?"

"Well its written in the top right corner of most files, yes most of the files have his handwritten notes in them, but my gut tells me this was written long after, I even tried looking up the word in the dictionary, but it's not listed there. The word is *Camino*; does this mean anything to you?"

"Wasn't there a car called something like that?"

"Yeah but that was El Camino, this is just *Camino*, did my father by chance speak any other language?"

"Why yes, Italian, our mother, your grandmother was Italian. It's been a long time since I have spoken the language, both Robert and I were quite fluent when our mother was alive, but that was years ago so I'm rather rusty, I'll have to think about that one."

"Well at least you have given me somewhere to start; I might go down to the library later and use one of the computers there, saves you trying to stretch your memory."

"That's a good idea, at least then you know you have the correct translation."

Deanne stayed and chatted with her aunt a while longer and promised not to let so much time lapse between visits and then made her way off to the library.

With shaky hands Deanne typed in Google for the English translation of the Italian word *Camino* and held her breath as she waited for her answer: *Fireplace*. She looked at it for a moment and felt she must have typed it in wrong, *why would her father repeatedly write the word Fireplace on his files, it didn't make sense.* So she typed it again and came up with the same answer, one thing it confirmed her belief that the word had nothing to do with a patients file, *but what on earth did a Fireplace have to do with anything, why did he keep writing this?*

She left the library feeling slightly deflated and decided to go home and once again peruse the files and see if she could somehow make a connection.

STEEL JUSTICE

CHAPTER THIRTEEN

Max was now certain someone was trying to frame him, as the remote device that had detonated the bomb on Microbe's boat, was found hidden in his four-wheel drive; he was now the prime suspect in the murder of Microbe and his wife. Forensics also linked the tracking log found in his house to the device, remnants of which, they discovered attached to the hull of the *Talisman*. He was out on bail, not only for the fact his lawyer was good, but he was also a friend.

"Ok so I attached a tracking device to the *Talisman* because I wanted to see what this guy was up to, but surely you don't think I would be stupid enough to hide the remote that was used to detonate the bomb, in my own vehicle!" Exclaimed Max.

"Look buddy I believe you, it's just not looking good for you at the moment," stated Rob, Max's lawyer.

"Someone is trying to set me up, my first thought was the local Sargent, but then I don't think he is that smart."

"You have someone in mind?"

"I don't know who, but I think it is someone who has stepped into Microbe's shoes, I think that was the plan all along."

"What do you mean?"

"I'm almost certain Microbe was using his boat somehow to smuggle drugs, a very lucrative operation that someone wanted to takeover. I think this person used me as the scapegoat."

"How so?"

"Well for starters the whole town knew how I felt about Microbe, god I virtually announced to a bunch of reporters I knew Microbe was behind Michelle's disappearance and I was out for blood!"

"Are you serious?"

"Look I know it wasn't the smartest thing to do, but

Microbe managed to discover my Achilles heel; Michelle. I had no idea someone else was gunning for him as well!"

"So your saying with the finger pointed at you, this guy can take over the operation without anyone questioning his motives?"

"Exactly, but that is where he made his big mistake."

"How so?"

"I plan to find him!"

"Well as your lawyer and your friend, I have to warn you to tread very carefully, I may not be so lucky in getting you out next time!"

"Don't worry, now I know there are other players involved, I won't be letting my guard down and just so you know, my number one priority is to find Michelle!"

"Max, I'm going to have to say what others are not game to, it's been too long, and it's time to lay her to rest."

"No!"

Max jumped up out of his chair and for a moment Rob thought he was going to hit him.

"Rob, I know you mean well, but you don't know my daughter, she's a fighter and I will not give up on her, I will not believe she is dead until I see her body! Do I make myself clear?"

"I understand, just watch your back?"

"Thanks Rob, you're a good friend!"

* * *

The unit complex was surrounded by a high steel picket fence and the gate was always manned by a guard, Jasmine had to devise a way to gain entry.

She had been watching the coming and goings of not only the occupants of the complex, but also deliveries and one of these gave her an idea. Every second day a linen service arrived, dropping off the bags of clean linen and taking the dirty ones away for cleaning. She knew it was risky and wasn't sure if she could pull it off, but she was to the point where desperate times called for desperate actions.

After following the linen service to its depot, she watched for a couple of days until she was confident of their routine and had now devised a plan how to use them to enter the complex. Since Jasmine had been given the plum role with Frontline News, she had gained an adversary who was not too pleased about her placement and would resort to anything to gain the position. She had only hinted at her new story to Jodi, giving her only minimal details. She trusted Jodi implicitly, after all she had been the one who offered her the position, but the problem was, Jodi liked to talk.

Jasmine knew despite all her research, she needed help to gain access to the complex, *but who could she trust not to expose her idea, someone who would do anything she asked.*

She sat at her desk and looked around at all her colleagues and suddenly her eyes fell on Nigel's desk, a young pimple faced photographer. She knew he had a crush on her, in fact the entire office knew and she often got a ribbing about it, *he would be perfect.*

Despite his young age of nineteen, he was actually a good photographer and passionate about his work, at least when he wasn't devising ways to follow Jasmine out on the job. Knowing what the gossip was like in the office, she had to pick her moment to speak to him. Suddenly spotting him coming out of the development room, she quickly scribbled a note before deliberately bumping into him and causing her to drop the papers she was carrying.

"Ah I'm sorry, ah really I am," he stammered as he gathered the papers and handed them to her.

"That's okay, no harm done," she said and pushed the note into his hand.

He looked at her and she winked at him before walking away, hoping he would keep the note to himself.

A few hours later she was sitting on a park bench, sharing the remnants of her sandwich with the seagulls when he arrived promptly at one thirty. He was nervously holding a paper bag in his hands, not sure whether to sit or stand.

"Why don't you sit down and eat your lunch."

He sat down next to her and she watched as he took his sandwich out of the paper bag and nervously picked at it before turning towards her.

"Why did you ask me to meet you here?"

"Straight to the point, I like that. I need your help, but you can't mention a word of it to anyone, can I trust you?"

"Um depends, would we be breaking the law?"

"Not really."

"Hmm what do you mean not really?"

"Well it's not actually, break and enter; you'll just be helping me gain access."

"How?"

"By hiding me in a bag of linen, the linen service will be the ones taking me inside."

"Inside where?"

"A particular unit complex that is well guarded, because they don't want the outside world to know what the complex is used for."

"Sounds dangerous."

"Danger is my middle name, so will you help me?"

"Ok, but can I ask why you picked me?"

"I'm sure you are aware there are some who are not happy about me joining the team at Frontline News; you are the only person I could think of that doesn't have designs on my job!"

"Fair enough, so what exactly are you planning to do?"

"The complex has a linen service which arrives every second day, it's the perfect cover, as I said the place is heavily guarded and the only way I can see me getting inside is by hiding inside one of those linen bags and that is where I need your help."

"What do you want me to do?"

"Well I have actually managed to get a bag similar to the ones they use, I need you to wrap me in a duvet then put me inside the bag and the tricky part will be getting me in the back of the delivery van undetected."

"It sounds dangerous, you could suffocate!"

"I'm prepared to take the risk, besides if you are careful how you wrap me in the duvet, I should be able to get enough air until I'm inside the building."

"What about when you get inside, how do you plan to get out of the bag undetected?"

"Well I have noticed the van does not stay long, only long enough to unload and reload, and then they leave. I plan to take a small pocket knife with me so I can quickly cut myself out, or at least make myself an air hole if necessary."

Jasmine watched as Nigel pondered over her plan and she could see by the look on his face, he had serious doubts about her plan. She madly racked her brain trying to think of a way to change his mind, when he turned to her and smiled.

"Ok I'll do it."

"Nigel you're a legend, I owe you one!"

She leaned forward and kissed him on the cheek, causing him to go bright red.

"The next delivery is tomorrow morning."

The following morning she parked the car a short distance from the industrial Laundromat and quickly popped the boot of the car.

"Okay, we don't have a lot of time, as soon as you get me wrapped and inside the bag, you'll need to park as close to the delivery van as possible, then as soon as the coast is clear, dump me in the back."

She could see Nigel was nervous as he was starting to sweat and she was worried he was going to change his mind.

"Come on hurry up," she said as she quickly climbed into the boot of the car.

Thankfully her hurried movement sparked Nigel into action and he deftly wrapped the cover around her, ensuring she could still breathe before struggling to slide her cocooned body into the bag. Once Jasmine heard the boot slam shut and the engine of her car start up, her heart started pumping, she was feeling a mixture of excitement and fear, hoping they could pull this off.

Adjusting her position as best she could inside her cocoon, making sure she had the small pocketknife firmly in her grasp, she knew once she was moved from her car to the van, it was imperative she remain still.

Within moments the car came to a halt and she strained her ears, waiting for any sound, trying to relax her body as much as possible and slow down her breathing. *What was taking him so long; he should have lifted her out of the car by now?*

Her frustration and her cocoon were making her hot and her irritation started to rise when suddenly she heard a noise and then felt herself being roughly lifted from the car. Suddenly a terrible thought went through her head, as she realised even though she was small, *what if I'm too heavy for him?* Suddenly she felt herself being dropped and rolled and then there was the sound of voices. *God we should have done a practise run, what now.* Not game to move, but also trying to hear what was being said, she almost jumped when she heard a loud bang and then she felt the vibration of an engine beneath her before rolling up against something. As she tried to figure out what was happening, she felt another jolt and suddenly realised Nigel had managed to dump her in the back of the van that was now moving.

After feeling the motion of the van for about five minutes, it momentarily came to a halt before moving again. Not sure if they had stopped for traffic or in fact had reached the gates of the complex. Desperately hoping it was the latter, she heard what she hoped was the van door open and within moments felt herself being lifted up, then painfully dumped on the ground, only just stopping herself from crying out, as a searing pain went through her shoulder.

Waiting for the pain to subside and the men to leave, she cautiously cut a small slit in the bag so she could take a peek at her surroundings, it appeared she was alone. Very slowly she moved her hand up towards the string pull of the bag and proceeded to cut it with her pocketknife, once the string was cut the bag was loose enough for her to wriggle out of her cocoon.

Jasmine had barely stretched her cramped limbs and hidden the remnants of her means of entry, when she heard a door open, and quickly scanned the room for somewhere to hide.

"What the hell do you think you are doing?"

Jasmine turned and saw a mean looking muscular heavy, causing her heart to jump into her throat.

"Thought you could escape through the linen service?" Growled the guard.

"I, ah…"

"Get back upstairs where you belong!"

Jasmine suddenly realised this could be a good thing, because she had no idea of the layout of the complex and this bozo might take her right where she wanted to go.

"Come on, get moving!"

Jasmine quickly made her way to the door, but then hesitated; she didn't know whether she was supposed to go left or right.

"Still thinking of making a run for it, well think again girlie!"

Jasmine felt her upper arm grabbed in a vice-like grip before being almost dragged to a stairway, realising it made sense to keep the girls upstairs, she quickly grasped her Cross necklace, which was in fact an 8GB digital spy audio/video recorder. She knew if she managed to get inside she couldn't very well wave around a camera to expose what was going on. She was amazed at the gadgetry you could buy on the Internet and decided the Cross necklace would not only appear innocent, but would be situated in the best position to film what was really going on here.

After tripping countless times up the stairs, she was sure her shins would be black and blue by tomorrow. She estimated they must have walked up at least three levels and wondered why they didn't have an elevator, *or were the stairs used exclusively for the girls, was there a legitimate side of the complex also?* Finally he paused at a door and knocked loudly, moments later the door was opened by a woman.

"I caught this one down in the linen room trying to escape."

Jasmine was shocked at the sight of the woman; she didn't fit the profile she'd envisioned to be running this sort of operation. Everything about her looked expensive, from her stylish blonde hair, to the expensive cut of her dress that screamed Chanel and her shoes had to be Prada. Jasmine guessed she was in her early forties, but then as she looked at her hands thought she could be older, *perhaps she has a good plastic surgeon!*

Suddenly Jasmine realised the woman had also been summing her up and for an awful moment wondered if the woman knew the faces of all her girls.

"You said you found her in the linen room trying to escape?"

"Yeah."

"Hmm, I try to make a point of knowing all my girls, but her face is unfamiliar."

Jasmine's mind was going a million miles an hour, she couldn't lose out after getting this close, but also she doubted the woman would just let her go, she had seen and heard too much!

"I'm pretty sure she was with the lot that came in last night," said the muscled heavy.

Jasmine realised this guy had unknowingly saved her bacon, but also she needed to act the part to back up his theory.

"You might have managed to bully the other girls, but there is no way in hell some old sleazebag is getting anywhere near me!"

"Ah, we've got a fighter, you're going to be real popular my dear."

"Over my dead body!"

"Be careful what you wish for!"

Jasmine stared at the woman and realised she was serious,

oh my god this is worse than I thought! The woman suddenly smiled at Jasmine, almost as if she had read her thoughts.

"Take her to Maliha and tell her to get her out of those ridiculous clothes!"

The woman stood aside as the heavy pushed her through the doorway and into a long hallway, which had many doors leading from it. Jasmine slowly moved forward and wondered if the doors were no different to a prison cell. Suddenly she was pulled to a stop as the heavy grasped a handful of her hair and then she heard the sound of a key turning in a lock.

"Get inside!"

Not wanting to argue with the guy she did as directed and was surprised to see the room was full of stuffed toys and in the centre was a bed with a pretty frilly pink cover and lots of frilly pink pillows.

"Maliha!"

Suddenly a girl appeared clutching a soft toy, she was dressed in pink pyjamas that had teddy bears all over them; Jasmine figured she couldn't be more than fifteen.

"The Mistress wants you to give her some decent clothes, you know the deal."

Before either she or the young girl could respond, he left the room and locked the door behind him. Both Maliha and Jasmine stared at each other for a moment, when the girl spoke.

"I say you be eight, yes?"

"Pardon?"

"Must dress you for Mistress, eight be your size."

"Yes but…"

"First have bath, must clean properly."

"Maliha, how old are you?"

"Why?"

"Well to me you don't look a day over fifteen and that takes everything wrong about this place to a whole new level!"

"I not so young, but men like to think so."

"Who?"

"No more questions; must have bath, take off clothes."

"What if I don't want to?"

"Mistress become angry, you make trouble for me."

"I don't want to get you into trouble, but I need to ask you some questions, how about we help each other?"

"How will questions help me?"

"Don't you want to get out of here?"

"Your questions stupid, now take off clothes!"

"I will if you promise to answer my questions."

"First you get in bath!"

Jasmine wasn't sure if she was being conned, but she had to take the risk, as Maliha turned on the bath Jasmine touched her cross necklace and switched it to only audio, she didn't want people seeing more than they should. She quickly undressed and stepped into the bath, hoping that Maliha would now live up to her side of the bargain.

"Maliha, your accent sounds Indian, but your eyes are green and your skin is almost as fair as mine."

"You right, I Indian; my sister twin, we have blood of distant ancestors, Aryans."

"I have heard stories about that but there is much controversy as to whether it is true."

"I your proof."

"How did you end up here?"

"My family very poor, my sister twin, men like how we look."

"Are you saying your parents sold you?"

"It is not what you think, my father have no choice."

"Explain it to me?"

"Man came to village, he say rich lady need maid, she offer food and medicine for sick brother, in exchange for me and sister twin."

"When you say maid of the rich lady, that's the Mistress isn't it?"

"Yes, but father think she mean clean, not this, not ever!"

"How did you get here?"

"Many days we travel on boat with little food and water,

there were many others, we had no window, we see no light, many sick, some die; I wish I had too!"

"So you were smuggled here illegally?"

"Yes."

"Have you ever tried to escape?"

"Yes, but Mistress, she beat me, then for long time I have no food."

"What about your sister; is she here with you or did they take her somewhere else?"

"Not anymore."

Maliha walked away and grabbed a towel, but not before Jasmine saw the tears in her eyes.

"Maliha, what happened to your sister?"

"I think she dead."

"Why?"

"We escape together, but I never see her again, I think Mistress beat her worse than me."

"Maybe she managed to escape."

"No, she would not leave me behind."

"What is your sister's name?"

"Madhulekha, it means beautiful," she said tearfully.

"That is a hard name to pronounce; did they by chance call her something else, or perhaps shorten it to Maddy?"

Maliha gasped and Jasmine noticed the colour drain from her face.

"You trick me, you here to spy on me!"

"That's not true; I came here to help you."

"You lie; you not come with new girls!"

"Maliha, I'm not lying, honestly I am here to help you!"

"How you know Maddy?"

"A lucky guess."

"Tell me truth, last night; you not come with girls."

"No."

"If you not here to spy on me, why you come to this?"

Maliha swept her arms wide and glared at her, Jasmine knew now was the time to tell her the truth, but a small part of her was afraid Maliha would expose her to the Mistress in a misguided sense of loyalty.

"I have not lied to you, I came here in the hope I could help you and expose what is really going on here. My name is Jasmine Bronson, I am with Frontline News, I received a letter about a month ago, it detailed everything that goes on here, at first I found it hard to believe, surely not in my own country, so I did a bit of investigating, and I was shocked to discover the letter could in fact be genuine. The letter stated she had escaped, but her sister was still held prisoner, the letter was signed 'Maddy'."

Jasmine could see Maliha was still hesitant about trusting her, but also saw behind the tears a glimmer of hope.

"She also said in the letter that if I found you, to ask you a question."

"What is question?"

Jasmine grabbed the towel from Maliha and wrapped it around herself and then walked around the room and started looking for something.

"What you doing?"

"Looking for something, I have to find it before I ask the question."

Jasmine was starting to panic, because she couldn't find what she was looking for, *god what if she has thrown it out.*

"Stop, no one touches things!" Maliha said as she grabbed Jasmine's arm.

"She told me to."

"Tell me question, what she want you do?"

"She wanted to know if Humphrey missed her, she told me Humphrey was a toy hedgehog."

Maliha ran to her bed, pulled from beneath the pillows a well-worn toy hedgehog, clutching it to her as she cried tears of joy. Suddenly there was a loud pounding on the door, instantly stopping her tears.

"What's going on in there?" Yelled a rough male voice.

"I just putting new girl in her place," replied Maliha.

"Do you want me to come in there and sort her out?"

"No! I make her behave."

"Ok."

Both girls stared at the door for a few moments and then Maliha led Jasmine to the far corner of the room away from the door.

"You speak truth, only Madhulekha knows about Humphrey. I happy she safe, but why you come here to tell me, you are now prisoner?"

"I have a plan to get all of you out of here, but first I have to expose what is going on here, I need proof, is there some way I can film what is happening in here?"

"I show you, but you not film it, we always watched, often searched."

"For cameras?"

"For weapons."

"Weapons?"

"Some men like inflict pain, sometimes we fight back."

"Oh my god, the sooner I get you out of here the better!"

"I think you now prisoner like us!"

"See this cross I wear around my neck, this is what is going to get us out of here."

"God not help here!"

"It is more than a cross, it is a camera and a listening device, I have a good friend in the police force who is listening right now to everything we say, but before she and her team can get us out of here she needs proof for them to gain access to the building."

"Why risk danger for us, we nothing, we not important?"

"I know some cultures don't regard the female race worthy, but where I come from we are equal to any man and besides what they are forcing you to do goes against everything I stand for!"

"You a good person, I hope one day I repay you."

"Getting you out of here safely is all the payment I need, now how do we go about getting this proof?"

"First we must dress you to please Mistress."

Jasmine followed Maliha over to a wardrobe, when she opened the door, Jasmine's mouth dropped opened at what it contained.

"Oh my god, that is what you are expected to wear?"

"After time, no longer bother you, you see."

"I doubt it!"

Maliha started moving the garments that virtually consisted of scraps of fabric a quarter of the size of a handkerchief with strips of leather, ribbon or cording that wasn't much different to a shoelace.

"Is there something with a little more covering, surely not all the guys are into this stuff?"

Maliha turned and looked at Jasmine for a moment, as if sizing her up for something.

"Very uncomfortable."

"As long as it has more coverage than this!"

Jasmine followed Maliha over to another cupboard and saw that everything inside was black and looked as if it was made out of leather.

"Most girls only wear once."

She handed her a leather look corset that Jasmine thought looked awfully small and had severe doubts she would even get into it.

"It look small, but you see, first put on panties then I lace you up."

After Jasmine pulled on the very brief and very uncomfortable vinyl panties, Maliha proceeded to lace her into the corset. The tighter she pulled it the less Jasmine could breathe and as she looked at herself in the mirror she noticed her breasts were almost pushed up under her chin.

"Now boots."

She handed a pair of thigh-high, black boots to Jasmine who tried her best to bend down and pull them on.

"This thing is so tight I can't bend down to put them on!"

"I try tell you, you want me take it off?"

"Yes, but no, it's preferable to that other stuff!"

Maliha smiled at her, bent down, and helped Jasmine into the boots and once she had zipped them up Jasmine realised they also had very high heels, adding inches to her height. As Jasmine looked at her image in the mirror, thankful she hadn't yet turned on the small camera; she would never live this one down if anyone saw her.

"No one ever look good as you in this."

"God, I can hardly breathe, I now understand why women fainted so much in the days when the corset was part of their undergarments, I just hope I can pull this off before I faint or crack a rib!"

"We must go."

"What about you, aren't you getting changed?"

"Not tonight, tonight I show new girl."

"Show me what?"

"What you must do."

As Jasmine followed Maliha to the door she realised she might have to add a broken ankle or leg to the list as she tried to walk in the boots. Maliha banged on the door and called out to the heavy outside and Jasmine quickly turned on the camera on her pendant. As she heard the key turn in the lock she was suddenly overcome with a mixture of fear and nerves.

When the door was opened the muscled heavy took in Jasmine's appearance and gave her a leering look.

"This one's going to be popular tonight; perhaps I should give her a test run first."

"Touch her and I tell Mistress!" Yelled Maliha.

He looked at her and instantly stepped back, making Jasmine realise the Mistress at least kept her safe from this creep.

"I make sure she behave."

She turned and looked at Jasmine and gave her a wink before saying gruffly.

"Come, we waste time!"

Jasmine followed her cue knowing she had to play the part

of being submissive, but also afraid, which that part wasn't too hard.

STEEL JUSTICE

CHAPTER FOURTEEN

The ATSB had found no mechanical faults to Microbe's helicopter and listed the crash as pilot error, making Max believe Michelle was forewarned they were going to crash and the reason the chopper was minus one lifejacket. The mystery still remained as to his daughter's whereabouts, he knew all had given her up for dead, most believed she had become croc bait, the reason he could find no sign of her body; this he would not accept.

He decided to re-visit the island even though he had gone over it countless times, after the recent week of monsoonal rain he thought perhaps a clue he had missed might have been uncovered. Now he knew how the girls had managed to gain access to the island, he moored his boat a safe distance from the island and used the boat's small dinghy to get onto the beach. He decided to start his search where it had all begun, in the tree house.

This time he took a larger and more powerful flashlight, which almost lit up the tree house in its entirety, but there was nothing, nothing that hadn't been there for years. Disappointed and despondent he turned off his flashlight and sat down on the floor, willing Michelle to keep fighting, but also leave him some sort of clue. As he looked around at his surroundings he once again thought of the incredible feat the girls had gone through to make it to this bush shelter, to think after risking not only being croc bait, but being run over by a tanker, only to lose…suddenly a glint caught his eye between the cracks in the rough flooring.

He quickly lay on his stomach and tried to look between the cracks, knowing whatever was reflective on the sunrays had not been here for years. Suddenly there was another gust of breeze and as it moved through the bush below, Max once again saw the reflective glint and he was almost certain he knew what it was.

Barely touching the rungs of the ladder as he clambered down and proceeded to cut through the bush with his Dewey combat/utility knife, designed especially for the Australian Army. Unlike Michelle's knife his 9-3/4 inch blade has a flat finish that is relatively non-reflective and the grip is made of Australian hardwood.

Finally he reached his target, caught amongst the bramble of the thick bush was Michelle's dive knife, now he knew how Josh managed to get her off the island, not only was she injured, but also without a weapon.

Max knew there was no point in searching the island further, the knife was the only personal effects of Michelle's they had not found, he also knew he had exhausted his search of the ocean, he now had to look at other possibilities.

* * *

It was almost two weeks now since Sam had told Deanne he was closing shop for a few days due to a death in the family, something she doubted was true. She was in two minds about even going back there, but after checking her finances and the limited job opportunities in the small town, she had no other choice but to call him, but the call went straight to message bank. After countless calls and messages she came to the conclusion she was now officially on the unemployed list.

She had come to love living in her father's ramshackle little house that she was slowly trying to restore, but knew if she didn't find another form of employment soon she would have no other choice but to sell up and move back to the city, something she voiced to her aunt.

"Deanne you can't, your father loved that house, it is all we have left of him and besides we are only just getting to know each other, please reconsider this!"

"The thought of selling my father's house pains me greatly, but Aunty Jan you don't understand, I have bills mounting up and have almost exhausted my savings."

"I have a little nest egg I have been saving for a rainy day, which…"

"No absolutely not and don't try to sway me otherwise."

"Well can you at least for the time being look on it as a well-deserved holiday, finish the painting and enjoy what Fig Tree Grove has to offer, who knows you might meet some nice boy?"

"I doubt it, but yes I won't make any rash decisions, but if I haven't found employment by the end of the month, I'm afraid I will have no other choice but to sell up and leave."

"Let's cross that bridge when we come to it, in the meantime you can save on your grocery bill and have your meals here, it is so much more enjoyable to cook when you have company."

"Only if it's not too much trouble."

"Of course not, now that's settled, tell me have you had a chance to go to the library and find out the translation of the word Robert wrote on his files?"

"Yes, but it just doesn't make sense; *Camino* means *Fireplace*."

"Hmm, yes I see what you mean, but then wouldn't that be the whole idea, if he was trying to relay a message to someone it would have to be something that would stand out."

"Yeah, I suppose you're right, but how the hell am I supposed to figure out what it means, I mean if there was such a thing in the house at least I would know where to look."

"Oh my goodness, I had totally forgotten all about it, when Robert first bought the house it had a fireplace!"

"Really, but how is that going to help me now if he had it removed?"

"He didn't, he had it boarded up."

"Are you sure, I have looked at that roof over a hundred times and it definitely doesn't have a chimney?"

"Oh he had that removed, it was dangerous and would have been far too costly to have it repaired, but also the roof had issues, so he decided the cheapest option was to remove the chimney, replace the roof and board up the fireplace inside."

"We need to find the fireplace, it is the clue!"

"Lucky I remember where it was; in fact I'm sure I've got some old photos of it."

"Perfect, Aunt Jan you're the best!"

"I'm glad you think so, now how about some dinner and then I'll drag out those old photos?"

The following day Deanne was expecting some questions about her purchases at the hardware store, a sledgehammer, crow bar, handsaw and a box cutter, but the old guy was more interested in the horse race that was blaring over the radio.

As she walked through the gate to her house she noticed a white envelope sticking out of her mailbox and thought it strange, apart from some advertising material she had never received any actual mail. Struggling with the weight of her purchases she grasped the letter from the box and made her way to the front door, glad that the steps had been replaced and she no longer needed to gain access to her house via the back door.

Once inside, she dumped the heavy bags on the floor and looked at the envelope, apart from her name and address, there was nothing to say who or where it had come from. As she walked over to the old armchair she realised the type on the front of the envelope was strange, the letters were uneven, she hadn't seen type like this before, she tried to decipher the post mark but it was too hard to read. Plonking herself down in the chair she quickly ripped it open, her curiosity fully aroused, it was a single piece of paper, and she had to read it twice before it fully registered.

If you value your life you'll pack your bags and go back where you came from!

A cold fear came over Deanne, causing her to quickly check the front door and ensure it was securely locked, she lifted the curtain from the window and saw the children playing their usual cricket match on the street out front, and then she ran and checked that the back door and all other windows were also locked. She was scared and didn't know what to do, a phone still hadn't been connected and her mobile had died days ago, but then who would she call, certainly not her aunt and she hadn't yet established any friends. Her nerves were so tightly strung she jumped at the slightest noise, finally making her way to the fridge and pouring herself a good measure of wine.

Once again, sitting back in the old armchair she reread the letter, trying to figure out who would have sent it to her. She remembered coming home from work one day and finding the window open and her father's files had been disturbed and then there was Sam, with his strange behaviour and sudden closure of the boatshed after the headlines in the newspaper of an execution style killing. Her only option was to wait till morning and walk to the local police station.

Early the following morning after little sleep, Deanne made her way to town, constantly looking over her shoulder, still not being able to shake the feeling of being watched. By the time she walked into the small police station she was a babbling mess.

"Miss, calm down, take a deep breath and tell me what has got you so upset."

Quickly pulling the letter from her bag she held it out to the officer.

"Someone wants to kill me!"

The officer frowned and quickly scanned the letter.

"Do you have any idea who would have sent this to you?" Asked the officer.

"Not really."

"Either you do or you don't."

"Well since I came to town I've felt as if I'm being watched, then there was the open window and finding my father's files jumbled, then Sam's strange behaviour."

"Who's Sam?"

"He runs the local boatyard, but then it's closed at the moment."

"Sam, I know Sam, he's a good bloke; surely you're not

insinuating he would send this to you?"

Deanne knew by the look on the officer's face she had already got him off side by mentioning his name.

"Ah no, but then what about the window to my house being open when I know I closed it before I went to work and the fact someone had been going through my father's files?"

"Ok, who was your father and why would someone want to break into your house to go through his files?"

"Dr Robert Shoal, he…"

"Hang on, I knew Dr Shoal, he died of a heart attack years ago."

"Well that's what the autopsy report says, but I don't think he did."

The officer let out a deep sigh and looked at Deanne.

"Girly…"

"Deanne."

"Deanne, if I remember rightly your father died a good few years ago…"

"Five."

"It appears to me you are still coming to terms with his death, have you considered counselling?"

"I don't need counselling!" She said through gritted teeth.

"The reason an autopsy is usually performed is to rule out any foul play and confirm cause of death."

"I know that, but what if his killer was very clever and knew how to make it look like he died of a heart attack?"

The officer let out another deep sigh before leaning in towards Deanne.

"Why did you wait till now to decide he had been murdered?" Asked the officer.

"I only found out about my father a few months ago, and some things don't add up. So I decided to do my own research."

"Really, how lucky for me."

"I beg your pardon?"

The officer straightened and looked stone faced at Deanne.

"I know what you're thinking, but how do you explain this letter?"

"I will have one of my officers look into it, in the meantime I suggest you ensure all your doors and windows are secure."

"I already have."

Deanne left the police station feeling even more depressed than when she walked in, she had a strong impression the officer thought she was some kind of nutter and doubted he would seriously look into who sent her the letter.

By the time Deanne walked in her front door her depression had turned to anger, that letter she had handed to the police officer was evidence someone in town meant her harm and yet he seemed to brush it aside as nothing! She slammed the front door behind her and turned the deadlock with such force it bit at her fingers. Turning sharply she surveyed the room; she wanted to hit something or someone and then noticed her purchases from the hardware store.

"I think now is as good a time as any to smash in a wall!"

She picked up the photos her aunt had given her and stood back and held them up and looked at the room in front of her, it looked as if the fireplace had been behind the wall where the armchair was now positioned. Remembering a time, when her mother had called in a handyman, watching him knock on the walls to find the hollow spots and where the framework was. She immediately started knocking on the wall until there was a distinct change in the sound, quickly marking the spot with a felt pen, then stepped back and looked from the photo to the mark on the wall.

"Well, either I'm going to wreck a perfectly good wall for nothing, or I'm on the mark!"

After looking out the window and seeing the kids getting ready to set up their usual afternoon cricket match in the street, she picked up the heavy sledgehammer, focusing on the spot on the wall and thinking of the arrogant police officer, hitting the wall with such force it left a deep hole. She put her hand through the wall and smiled, she could feel nothing but empty space, excitedly grabbing the torch and shinning it inside to see blackened brickwork; she had found the fireplace!

Her excitement now in full swing she alternated between the sledgehammer, handsaw and box cutter, until finally the fireplace was fully exposed. She felt like yelling at the top of her lungs, but then realised she had been going at it 'hell for leather' and someone may have wondered what was going on. Quickly running to the front window and cautiously moving the blinds, she was pleased to see the cricket match was now in full swing and her efforts hadn't drawn any attention.

After most of the rubbish had been carefully sifted through and put in garbage bags, her excitement started to plummet, there was nothing but rubble.

Looking despondently at the gaping hole, she suddenly realised if her father had gone to this much trouble he wouldn't make it easy to find. Grabbing the torch she stepped into the opening and shone the light up into the dark hole.

She waved the beam around amongst the black soot and dust, hoping no rodents still resided in the chimney, when suddenly she saw something reflective high up. Excitedly she ran and grabbed the small stepladder and after stretching on tiptoes managed to grab the object, it was a thick envelope and had the words *daughter* written on the front of it in reflective pen.

Clutching it reverently in her hands she slowly stepped back down, *my father left this for me, he had faith I would uncover his clue!* With shaky hands she opened the envelope and as she unfolded the pages, a photo fell out, it was a photo of a man, she turned it over, and on the back, were some numbers. Not sure what the photo or the numbers meant she unfolded the letter and noticed it was the same beautiful handwriting that was on his files, confirming he had left this for her.

My dearest darling daughter, the only reason you have discovered this clue, is because I am dead, a death that will be disguised as natural causes. I should never have done what they demanded, but I was left with no choice, the life of my daughter was at stake! At least with my passing Mary will no longer live in fear. Tell your mother I forgive her, I understand, it was Salina, she was the reason we could not be together as a family, she is the reason I must play a part in her evil scheme!

Darling daughter, if it is in fact you reading these pages, remember this. I loved you from the moment I discovered I was a father. I tried my best to find you, but unfortunately that wasn't meant to be!

Despite all my caution I can never be sure my daughter will be the one who reads these pages, so I have left a riddle that only she will understand.

Beware of the Black sheep,
He is a chameleon, one who purges forth white,
Look closely, because all is not as it seems,
Day can become night and night become day.
Follow the numbers they hold the key.
However, remember the eyes don't always see.
Find someone you trust,
So before you choose,
Look deep in your heart,
For the brain can confuse.
Your friend could be your foe.
Only your heart will truly know!

As her first tear hit the page she carefully put down the letter and paced the room, *if only I could have met him, if only Salina hadn't ruined our chance to be a family!* Feeling despondent she poured herself a good measure of wine and after drinking half the glass she looked down at the photo her father had enclosed in the letter.

"Who the hell are you and what is your connection with my father?"

She turned over the photo and looked at the numbers and

remembered his letter; *follow the numbers!*

"How do I follow them if I don't know what they mean?"

She reread the letter many times over and was still no closer to uncovering what her father wanted her to do, but one thing rang out loud and clear, he wanted her to get someone to help her, but she had to be very careful who that person was, it had to be someone she trusted implicitly!

STEEL JUSTICE

CHAPTER FIFTEEN

The police had gone through Burns' office with a fine-tooth comb, but found nothing, although there were signs the original hard-drive had been swapped out. There was not enough relevant data on the computer of a flourishing business to warrant it being the original. Sergeant Wilson could smell a rat and hoped whoever removed the computer files hadn't tampered with the security cameras.

It was not surprising the camera covering the office had been moved the day after Burns was murdered, but what did surprise the sergeant was the appearance of Microbe and on more than one occasion. Even though there was no sound, Wilson got a strong impression Burns was afraid of Microbe and as he scanned all the tapes there was one occasion he appeared to be very angry with Burns, which got Wilson wondering, *was there a connection between the two deaths?*

* * *

Deanne was in the process of cleaning the black soot from the brickwork of the fireplace when there was a knock at the door. Her only visitor to date had been her aunt and was not expecting her to drop by today. Cautiously making her way over to the window, she moved the curtain aside and was surprised to see two police officers, one being the Sargent she had spoken to days prior.

She quickly opened the door and judging by the look on both men's faces she must have looked a sight.

"Ah, doing some renovations," she explained nervously.

"May we come in?"

"Yes of course, is this in regards to that letter?"

"Correct, Miss Jones do you have an old typewriter in your possession?"

"What, why?"

"Just answer the question."

"Um, well there is an old one in the bottom of the linen cupboard; I dare say it was my father's."

"Is it an Olivetti Lexikon 80?" Asked the other officer.

"I wouldn't have a clue, why?"

"We would like to see it," commented the Sargent.

"Yeah sure, I'll go get it."

As Deanne dragged the old typewriter out of the cupboard, she wondered what the interest was and what it had to do with the threatening letter.

"God its heavy!" She commented nervously.

The young officer took it from her and placed it on a table nearby, then he opened the file he had been holding and pulled out a sheet of paper and fed it through the roller and to Deanne's surprise proceeded to type.

"Will someone tell me what's going on?" Asked Deanne impatiently.

"They're the same sarg," said the officer, as he pulled the paper from the typewriter.

As the Sargent compared what the officer had just typed to what was in the file, Deanne suddenly recognised the envelope and letter she had received in the mail, realising her troubles were going to get a whole lot worse.

"You think this is some sort of game do you?" Asked the Sargent.

"I don't…I can't…"

"I had a word with Sam; he said he had to lay you off because he caught you stealing from the petty cash."

"That's not true, he…"

"He has decided not to press charges; that's not to say I won't be keeping my eye on you, if you so much as litter in the street I will slap a fine on you so fast your head will spin!"

"You have to believe me, I didn't type that letter, I didn't even know that old thing worked, let alone how to use it!"

"A word of advice, we are a quiet little country town and don't take too kindly to trouble makers!"

STEEL JUSTICE

Deanne knew it was pointless arguing with him any further, she knew she had got him off side the other day when she had suggested Sam was the author of the letter. She stood at the open door and watched as the two men walked out the front gate and climbed into the police vehicle, wondering how many of her neighbours had been watching, sure that by the afternoon she would be the focus of local gossip.

Feeling more alone than ever, she closed the door and turned the deadlock; thankful that she had at least had the sense to install those weeks ago.

* * *

As Jasmine went from room to room she was burdened with feelings of horror and anger, most of the girls were under the age of fifteen. She desperately wanted to call Tracey and her team in now, but she knew they needed hard evidence that would prove, beyond a doubt what was going on here.

Suddenly the air was pierced with screams from another room; Jasmine headed quickly towards it and instructed Maliha to open the door. Nothing could prepare Jasmine for the sight of a young girl who couldn't be more than eight being held down by one man, while being raped by another. Both men were unaware of her presence and as she surveyed the room for a weapon she noticed a third man was filming the assault.

Anger boiled up inside her and using all her strength she kicked out at the one assaulting the young girl, catching him painfully in the kidneys with her spiked heel, then she charged at the one holding the camera, smashing it to the ground, screaming out at Tracey.

"Is that evidence enough for you?"

Moments later Jasmine could hear screams, raised voices, and all hell seemed to break loose, young girls were crying and running in all directions, not sure what was going on, naked men were trying to dress as they ran, trying to avoid arrest. Jasmine tried her best to use her small camera to capture everything that was unfolding around her, men wearing heavy body armour carrying entry shields and assault rifles. Jasmine knew it was Tracey and the police tactical unit, but the sight of them would have been frightening to the young girls.

Much later after the police vehicles and ambulances had departed, Jasmine walked over towards Tracey and despite having planned a lot of this together, they had only been able to converse over the phone.

"Tracey, its Jasmine. Long-time no see."

"Jasmine, how are you going?"

Both girls hugged and Tracey flicked open the oversized jacket Jasmine had covering her scanty outfit and laughed.

"All the guys have been asking me for your phone number, especially after seeing you in that little number."

"Very funny. You know it was the only way I could get in there, it was part of my cover."

"It didn't cover much."

"Yeah well, it was better than my other choices! I can't wait to get it off, I am sure my ribs are going to be black and blue tomorrow and it is only by a sheer miracle that I haven't broken an ankle in these boots."

"You know Jas that was good work you did in there, it took some guts to do what you did!"

"Thanks, but I can't take all the credit, I couldn't have done it without your help!"

"All part of the job, speaking of which I have to go, got to make sure these bastards don't weasel out of this one, we'll have to catch up sometime!"

"Definitely, somewhere that has good cocktails and great seafood."

"Sounds good."

The following day Jasmine was going through the video with Nigel, it was sickening to watch and she knew they would have to heavily edit it, she knew they had to be very careful how they used the video in their exposé, Jasmine didn't want to jeopardise any future trial of those involved. Some of the video moved around the room so fast it made Jasmine's stomach queasy.

"I didn't realise I was swinging the camera around so much."

"It's understandable, everything was moving so fast you were trying to cover everything."

"Thanks, but…just a minute, back it up a bit."

Nigel did as she requested and then hit the play button again.

"God, there it goes again, is there any way you can move this thing really slow?"

"Sure."

Nigel once again wound the video back a bit and then moved it forward frame by frame.

"Stop!"

Jasmine got up and pointed to an image on the screen.

"Is there any way you can get a print of that and possibly make it clearer?"

"I can definitely get a print, as to getting a clearer view, I can't promise you anything."

"Thanks Nigel, let me know as soon as you have something."

* * *

Deanne was dog tired, she had barely slept a wink; wondering if whoever sent the letter was watching her every move and if she should tell her aunt, or whether that would put her life in danger. She kept the letter and photo from her father with her at all times, not wanting to risk losing the only vital piece of information she had, that could help her uncover not only who killed her father but why?

Deciding not to tell her aunt about the threatening letter, she felt it only fair that she now show her what she had found in the chimney.

"This is our proof Deanne, proof your father was murdered!

We have to take it to the police."

"No!"

Deanne hadn't meant to say the word with such force, but the thought of taking her father's letter to the rude police Sargent was unthinkable.

"Sorry I didn't mean to yell, but just think about it, dad wrote his letter to me in a riddle, he is warning me to be careful who I trust. *Your friend could be your foe. Only your heart will truly know!* My gut and my heart tell me I can't trust our local police."

"Deanne, is there something you're not telling me?"

"I wasn't going to tell you, because I knew you would worry, but also I was worried you would march down to the police station and say something we might both regret!"

"Now you're going to have to tell me!"

"Someone sent me a letter basically threatening me if I don't leave town…"

"Oh my god!"

"I took it to the police station; firstly I hinted it could have come from Sam…"

"Those two are old fishing buddies."

"Yeah well that for starters got the Sargent's back up, then it turns out the letter was typed on dad's old typewriter which is sitting of the bottom of my linen cupboard."

"Deanne, this is serious!"

"I know, but I don't know what else to do."

"Move in with me, at least till we get this sorted out."

"Thanks for the offer, but I won't be bullied out of my own home, besides whoever sent the letter wants me to leave town, I don't think moving in with you will change things."

Her aunt rose from her chair and left the room, only to come back moments later carrying her handbag.

"Come on, let's go," she said as she stood in front of Deanne.

"Where?"

"To town, if you won't move in with me at least let me buy

you a new phone, I will feel much better if I know you are only a phone call away, or if you need me to call the police!"

* * *

Jasmine looked at the enlarged photo Nigel had handed to her, the image was slightly blurred as the camera had caught her face as she was running from the room and her face was slightly turned from the camera, *could it be?*

"I'm sorry, but I couldn't get it any clearer than that. I thought you might also be interested in this one, I'm assuming she is the one the girls referred to as the 'Mistress'?"

As Jasmine looked at the photo she could see it was a zoomed out image of what she had asked him to print for her, there were two people in the photo, something she hadn't realised before as she had been focusing on the other face. The girl who she thought had been running from the room was actually being pushed, her hands were handcuffed and a gun was held to her back, the one holding the gun was the Mistress.

"I have to speak to Maliha!"

* * *

As Deanne made her way to her front gate she noticed a white envelope sticking out of her letterbox, she stopped instantly and surveyed the area around her, the street was deserted. She cautiously lifted the lid of the box and pulled out the letter, her name and address was in type print, but to her relief it was not the same as the other one.

She waited until she was inside and ensured the door was locked securely behind her before opening the letter.

You think you are clever going to the police, but they won't help you!

Deanne's skin instantly prickled with fear, causing the letter to fall to the ground, her heart started to pound in her chest and her mouth went dry. She quickly checked all the doors and windows, reassuring herself they were still locked, and then looked for any signs of someone having been in her house.

She didn't know what to do, she could call her aunt, but then how would that help her and then she thought about her father's letter and the fact someone had initially broken into her house and typed on her father's old typewriter and then there was evidence someone had gone through her father's files.

"What if this is about my father and not Sam, what if someone is worried about what I will find?"

She paced the room; more for the need of a distraction than anything else, she turned on the TV and flicked randomly through the channels when a programme caught her attention. The camera footage was all over the place and she could hear a distinct hint of fear in the commentator's voice. As the camera roamed the room there was glimpses of young scantily clad girls and their faces portrayed a mixture of fear and despair.

"I have been smuggled in here, posing as one of these girls. The girls, mostly from very poor countries are falsely lured here with the prospect of a respectable job to help provide for their families, none of them have passports, they are smuggled illegally into the country and forced into a life of prostitution. Many have tried to escape, but the security is tight and their punishment severe. One brave girl managed against all odds to escape from this living hell and despite further risk to herself, her one thought was to free her sister still trapped inside and to expose what this building was really used for."

The camera started moving forward up a hall and to the many doors leading off it, Deanne was horrified, *where was this place?*

"Now for the real shocker, I am sure you all have your assumptions what country would allow such a thing, well folks, I'm in Sydney Australia, this has been happening right under our noses! There are many more of these places, all over the world. Unfortunately I cannot help them all, but at least I can help these girls here today and reunite one brave girl with her sister!" Exclaimed the female voice.

Suddenly the doors burst open, the camera vision was going all over the place. Deanne leaned forward wondering what was happening. She could hear the sound of running feet and the heavy breathing and realised it was the reporter running with the camera, there were flashes of men and young girls running past the camera, then suddenly there were heavily armed men with the word *Police* emblazed on the back of their Kevlar vests.

The scene suddenly changed and there was a pretty young reporter standing in front of the camera wearing an oversized coat and in the background the viewer could see the flashing lights of ambulances and police vehicles.

"Well we can only hope, that the justice system does its job and those involved are severely punished for the injustices dealt to these poor girls. Despite the girls being rescued from a living hell, it is not yet over for them, they have a long road of counselling ahead, they will also have to relive this nightmare in court, something that will take a lot of courage to do. If you have a story that you think needs to be exposed, you can send an email to the address at the bottom of the screen or visit our website. Until next time, bringing you the real story, I'm Jasmine Bronson with Frontline News."

The station then went to a commercial and Deanne turned off the TV and mulled over what she had just seen, *would Jasmine Bronson help her and more importantly, could she trust her?*

The following morning Deanne used one of the computers at the local library and was astounded at all the stories Jasmine Bronson had covered. Deciding she had no one else to turn to, Deanne logged into a free e-mail site. She thought for a moment, realising she had only one crack at this, it had to be something that would get Jasmine's attention!

***

Jasmine was looking at the photos she had splayed out on her desk, when she heard the distinct ding on her computer alerting her she had mail. In two minds about checking her 'in box' as she had more pressing things on her mind, she decided to at least view what the subject was and decide from there.
Life in danger, needing your help!
"Mm, this sounds interesting!"

To Jasmine Bronson,

You are my last hope. I believe my father was murdered, but covered up. I also witnessed something strange going on at the boatyard where I used to work and I believe Sam is somehow connected with the recent double murder that happened only a few hours from here! Someone has not only broken into my house but also made a threat on my life. I have been to the police but they won't help me. Please can you help!

Deanne Jones
Fig Tree Grove

Jasmine was certainly interested, *but where was Fig Tree Grove.* She went online to search maps and was surprised to discover it was about an hour and a half from Eden Cove, her old stomping ground. She had been working on her story about the young girls being forced into prostitution when the double murder had hit the headlines; she remembered wondering if there was any connection between that and her exposé. She was curious about Deanne's father, *what had he been involved in that would cause someone to threaten his daughter, could this be a follow-on from her other story?*

The following day Deanne sat in front of the computer, mentally crossing her fingers as she logged in to her e-mail, there was a message in her 'Inbox'. She was almost too afraid to open it; worried it was only an automated response, or worse still, a refusal to help.

Miss Deanne Jones

You certainly have my curiosity, but I need more details. Where is this boat yard and who is Sam, why do you think he is connected with the double murder that was reported in the paper? In addition, who was your father and why do you believe he was murdered? Are you comfortable divulging your phone number, or would you prefer to respond via e-mail only? Looking forward to hearing from you.

Jasmine Bronson

Deanne was relieved Jasmine was interested and hopefully would help her. She quickly began her response to Jasmine, but hesitated about giving her phone number and then her father's words came to her *follow your heart*. She thought about what Jasmine had done for those girls, she had put her life on the line for them. She quickly typed in the numbers and her father's name, deciding to refrain from mentioning anything further about the boatyard and Sam's strange behaviour. After quickly hitting the send button she logged out of the computer and hurriedly made her way home. Now all she could do was wait.

CHAPTER SIXTEEN

Maliha was a key witness in exposing the illegal smuggling of young girls into the country for prostitution and was now in protective custody with her sister. This made it very difficult for Jasmine to speak to her. Jasmine knew the 'Mistress' had managed to evade the authorities, so came up with the ploy she had a lead that could be vital in tracking down the woman's whereabouts, but needed to first speak to Maliha; she was allowed one brief visit.

"Hello Maliha, how are you doing?"

"A little scared, but happy I with Madhulekha again, thank you from us both!"

"I'm just glad I was able to help, but now it is I who needs your help."

"Me help you, how?"

"Do you remember I told you my necklace was a tiny camera?"

"Yes."

"As you know people were running everywhere, everything happened very fast, but later when I looked at the photos there was one of a girl I don't remember seeing, unfortunately the Mistress took her with her when she escaped, and I'm hoping you might know who this girl is."

"Rusalka."

"Pardon?"

"The girl in photo, she Rusalka."

"How do you know, I haven't even shown you the photo yet?"

"Rusalka is only one Mistress would take, she make her very rich!"

"Did you speak to her; did she tell you where she came from?"

"No, she always guarded, no girls allow near her, but I saw her once, she looked sad, but when she look at me I feel scared."

"Why?"

"Mistress say she mermaid, but others say she very dangerous, has special power!

"Why does the Mistress say she is a mermaid?"

"She come from bottom of ocean, was in fisherman's net."

"Oh my god, do you know where this was?"

"No, why Rusalka so important?"

"I believe she is a girl who disappeared a long time ago."

"Then she now dead."

"Why do you say that?"

"Legend of Rusalka?"

"What legend?"

"Beautiful girl murdered at sea, no one find her because she is now ghost, she haunt ocean to avenge her death; she fight the fight of many knives!"

"Maliha, there's no such thing as ghosts, they are just stories to scare people."

"You not look in her eyes; you not see what I see."

"You said she fights the fight of many knives, what do you mean?"

"She not put in room with men like we do, men must fight for Rusalka."

"So you're saying men fight each other with knives and the winner claims Rusalka as his prize?"

"No, men fight Rusalka."

"Oh my god, this is terrible, that poor girl!"

"I heard guard talking, she kill many men, she very dangerous!"

"This all sounds a little far-fetched; I understand the Mistress is involved in illegal smuggling, and prostitution, but men actually paying moncy to bc involvcd in a knife fight against a girl, just so they can have sex with her!"

"Tis true, I not lie!"

"Ok, I can see talking about Rusalka is making you nervous, so I won't bother you with any more questions about her, you have been very helpful."

"I not help much."

"More than you realise. Well I must go I don't know if I will see you again, I am sure they have explained how the witness protection program works."

"Yes."

"Take care and I hope there is a bright and happy future ahead for you and Maddy."

"Thank you."

Both girls hugged and moments later Maliha was whisked away to a destination unknown. Jasmine's mind was going a million miles an hour, firstly after speaking to Maliha her suspicions about the girl in the photo being Max Steel's daughter appeared to be correct. Even though she had left Eden Cove to join the team at Frontline News, she had still followed closely the search for the missing girls and knew Max Steel believed his daughter was in the helicopter that crashed into the ocean, even though her body was never found. She knew those waters were frequented by many large vessels from all over the world, *could it be one such vessel was illegally fishing and happened to snare Michelle in their net?*

The thought of Max Steel immediately caused her pulse to quicken, she knew he hadn't given up the search for his daughter and believed this could be a vital clue, but also there was Deanne, she desperately needed her help, her life could depend on it; she was undecided what to do.

As she sat at traffic lights mulling the situation over in her mind, she remembered looking up Fig Tree Grove and was surprised to discover it was about an hour and a half from Eden Cove, *perhaps she could check out the situation with Deanne and then travel on to Eden Cove and see Max Steel?*

"Who are you kidding girl, you haven't got a chance in hell of getting past the gates of Max Steel's home, let alone getting him to speak to you!"

Suddenly a car horn beeped and she realised the lights had turned green. Once back at her office she checked her emails hoping not only for a response from Deanne, but that she trusted her enough to give a phone number, it would make everything so much easier.

The moment Jasmine read Deanne's response; she wasted no time placing the call.

"Hello."

"Deanne Jones?"

"Ah, who's speaking?"

"Jasmine Bronson, from Frontline News."

"Oh, thank god!"

Jasmine heard crying on the other end and realised Deanne was not only upset, but also frightened.

"Deanne, where are you?"

"I'm at home; I'm too scared to leave the house."

"Can you tell me why you don't think the police will help you?"

"Firstly I thought Sam might have sent the letter…"

"Who is Sam?"

"He was my boss at the boatyard."

"You said was, what happened and why do you think he would make a threat on your life?"

"Firstly he scared me and made a point on more than one occasion that I was never allowed past the office, then a man came around acting really strange, I know he saw me looking out the window and then there was that murder and Sam closed up the boatyard saying someone died in the family…"

"Deanne slow down, you're not making sense."

"Ah, sorry."

"Firstly, who was this man you saw through the window, was he at your house?"

"No, it was at the boatyard, I was using the work computer to do some research on my father, I didn't want Sam to know I was slacking off, that's when I saw this car trying to sneak up the side of the building."

"So you think this man was trying to steal something?"

"I didn't know what to think, I couldn't understand why he

didn't come in the main entrance and then Sam came rushing in the office and wanted to know if I saw anyone or heard a car."

"Did you tell him what you saw?"

"No, I was too scared to!"

"Why?"

"Well for one, Sam saw him and the way the guy was acting I felt sure he was trying to avoid being seen, my gut instinct told me it was safer to lie."

"Ok, but I still don't understand why the police won't help you and why you think Sam sent you a threatening letter?"

"Firstly it turns out Sam is a mate of the local Sargent, but worse still, the letter was done on my dad's old typewriter which was in the bottom of my linen cupboard and I think Sam found out I was snooping around the yard one night."

"Why did you do that?"

"Well days after seeing that man act strangely, there was that double murder, after Sam read about it in the paper he closed up shop, saying there had been a death in the family, which I don't believe was true."

"Why?"

"Well for one my aunt knows him and his family and said she hadn't heard anything, but also that day, Sam received a phone call which caused him to buy the newspaper, the one with the headlines about the murder and then later he closed up the shop. I was worried he was also involved in that paedophile ring, so I went to the boatyard that night hoping to see what he was up to."

"That was a very dangerous thing to do, but did you see anything?"

"Only men working on the boats, which is what really puzzles me, because it is a boatyard after all, why all the secrecy?"

"Why do you think he was being secretive?"

"Well for one, the place was closed up during the day, the phone always went to message bank and when I went to the shed that night all the windows were covered up, why would you go to this trouble if everything was above board?"

"Hmm, that does sound a little strange."

"Sam also lied to the police Sargent, he told him I was sacked because he caught me stealing which is not true, in fact he didn't actually sack me, he told me he was closing up shop for a couple of days and I never heard from him again."

"Hmm, you said you had been doing some research about your father on the work computer did Sam catch you doing this?"

"No, but I was so scared after that, I only used the one at the library."

"Deanne, who was your father?"

"Dr Robert Shoal, they say he died of a heart attack, but I believe he was murdered."

"What would make you think that?"

"Well for one, he left me a cryptic letter hidden in the fireplace, in it he says he was forced to do something he didn't want to do, but did it to protect me and my mother."

"Do you know what that was?"

"I have no idea, you see he wasn't sure if I would be the one to find the letter, so he wrote it in the form of a riddle that only I would understand, only thing is, it doesn't make any sense to me, and also there was a photo of a man enclosed."

"Do you know who it is?"

"No, but I think it has something to do with his work."

"How?"

"My father was a plastic surgeon."

"Hmm I see, the thing I don't understand is, why would your father leave the letter in the fireplace where anyone could find it?"

"I doubt it, you see the fireplace had been covered up, I didn't know it was there until I started reading his files, there was the word *Camino* that was handwritten in the corner of all but one of his files, it is Italian, meaning *fireplace*."

"Well it looks like you have definitely stumbled upon

something; I would definitely like to have a look at these files and the letter he left you."

"The files are mostly medical stuff, but your welcome to read them. So, does this mean you will help me?"

"Of course, but as we don't know who we are dealing with, or what Sam is involved in, we have to be very careful. Tell me, is your mother living close by, do you have any siblings?"

"No my mother died a few years ago, I was an only child, but I do have an aunt living close by, why?"

"Your aunt, does she know about your father's letter?"

"Yes, in fact she was the one who gave me my father's files, she didn't believe he died of a heart attack, she was hoping I would find something in his files to prove that."

"Ok good, have you told her that you contacted me?"

"Not yet, I was waiting to see if you would or could help first."

"Well I will do my best, but to avoid suspicion I will need to be incognito, I will pose as your sister, but obviously you will have to let your aunt know about this and I'll need a photo of you so I can do my best to pass as a sibling of Deanne Jones."

"I can do that now, I'll take a photo with my phone and send it to you."

"Ok, good."

Deanne quickly held her phone out in front of her and pushed the snapshot button then sent the photo to Jasmine. Moments later Jasmine looked at the image of Deanne and the first thing she noticed was Deanne was not only young, but the fear was evident on her face. As she studied the image she noted her small pale almost pixie-like face, with green eyes that seemed far too large for her little face and her dark brown hair was tied back.

"I think with a dark wig I could pass as your sister."

"Really?"

"Sure, now I have to organise a few things here and check on available flights, once that's all sorted I'll give you a call."

"Oh thank you so much Jasmine, you have no idea how much this means to me."

"Don't thank me yet, I can't promise you anything, but it might be a good idea if you stay with your aunt until I arrive."

"No, I won't be bullied out of my own home, besides I don't want to put my aunt in any danger."

"Fair enough, I'll call you later."

Once the call was ended Jasmine decided to call her friend Tracey and see if she could prize even the smallest amount of information from her regarding the double murder, believed to be in connection with a paedophile ring.

"Tracey, Jasmine here, you got a minute?"

"Well that depends, I'm guessing your after information?"

"Yeah, it's about that double murder that was…"

"Sorry, can't help you there."

"Oh come on, can't you tell me something?"

"No can do."

"Look, it doesn't have to be crucial evidence, just something, like who were these guys, did they have families, and were they married?"

"Jas, you know I can't discuss this with you."

"Not even a teeny weeny hint?"

"Nope."

"Look, my help could be invaluable, look how I helped you with the illegal smuggling of those young girls."

"Have you been given a tip off?"

"Not really, I got an email from a young girl who lives in Fig Tree Grove, you ever heard of the place?"

"Can't say I have."

"Well it's about an hour and a half from Eden Cove, anyway this young girl received some death threats and apparently the local Sargent won't take it seriously."

"He must have a reason, what do you know about this girl?"

"Well we haven't met face to face yet, but my gut instinct tells me she's legit."

"How about you tell me what you know about this girl."

"Her name is Deanne Jones, apparently the daughter of the now deceased Dr Robert Shoal, who by the way she believes was murdered. She used to work in the office of the local boatyard until her boss received a phone call that caused him to buy a newspaper featuring the double murder; he suddenly closed up shop claiming a family member died, but…"

"Did you say boatyard?"

"Yeah why?"

"One of the victims was a boat dealer, he sold luxury boats."

"My god, so Deanne could be right about a connection with her old boss and the victims?"

"It's possible, what else can you tell me?"

"Well apparently she paid a visit to the boatyard one night and discovered it was still operational, which she thought was strange, firstly because all the windows were covered, but from what she could see everything was above board, just men in overalls working on the boats."

"Hmm, does sound strange."

"Apparently, a few days after that she received her first death threat."

"So you think her old Boss saw her snooping around?"

"Possibly, but where it gets tricky is her old boss is good mates with the local Sargent and apparently the letters where typed on her father's old typewriter which sits in the bottom of her linen cupboard."

"Did she mention if her house had been broken into?"

"Yes, and she said she found a cryptic letter from her father hidden in a fireplace that had been boarded up."

"What did it say?"

"Basically he was forced to do something to protect is wife and child, she believes this person was responsible for his death."

"I can see why you're interested, this one's really got you intrigued hasn't it?"

"Hell yeah, but don't you think it is a bit too much of a coincidence that her old boss owned a boatyard and one of the murder victims sold luxury boats?"

"I agree."

"Any chance I could get a photo of this guy?"

"Why?"

"Deanne said she saw a guy she believed was trying to avoid being seen, she could possibly be our only witness linking this murder victim to her boss."

"I've got a better idea, get her to describe him to you and..."

"How is that going to help?"

"Trust me, if this particular victim was the man she saw that day, I will know."

"Ok, I'll get back to you on that one, now it's my turn to give you a snippet of information."

"Has this got something to do with your visit to a particular person who is now with the witness protection program?"

"Yes, you see when Nigel and I were going through all the images I captured on my little camera, there was one person that really caught my attention, one Maliha said went by the name of Rusalka, I believe she is Max Steel's daughter, Michelle Brown."

"No, most of the girls were smuggled in from India!"

"You haven't seen the photo, besides Maliha said the 'Mistress' was passing her off as a mermaid, who was making her a lot of money, apparently she was pulled up in a fisherman's net. Just think about it, her tracks ended at the water, what if Max Steel is right; she was forced into the helicopter, but managed to bail out before the crash and survived. The area is not far from the shipping channel, vessels from all over the world pass near there..."

"You're thinking illegal fishing vessel?"

"Yeah, or I just had another thought, what if the vessel was also involved in people smuggling?"

"Hmm, looks like you might have stumbled upon

something here; get back to me the moment you get a description from Deanne."

"Will do."

The moment the call ended Jasmine checked available fights; her excitement building, she sensed this was going to be big.

STEEL JUSTICE

CHAPTER SEVENTEEN

Leaving the airport and after three and a half hours of driving, Jasmine finally reached Fig Tree Grove, ignoring the GPS directions to Deanne's house, she wanted to first take in the small village and its surroundings, as it could be anyone in this sleepy little town who was threatening Deanne. After a short tour Jasmine came upon Deanne's street, noting the house numbers until a quaint little house came into view that was sorely in need of a coat of paint and going by Deanne's description she knew she had reached her destination.

Jasmine parked near the front gate and turned off the engine, noting the gardens and lawn were neat, and well tendered, but also the front steps appeared to be new. Suddenly she saw a curtain move in the window and realised Deanne wasn't taking any chances by coming outside, with the dark windows of the car Jasmine knew she was waiting to see who was inside. Quickly gathering her handbag she exited the car and made a point of smiling and waving towards the window before collecting her luggage from the boot of the car.

Reassured that her visitor was in fact Jasmine, Deanne made her way outside to greet her, nervous about meeting for the first time, but also conscious of the fact anyone of her neighbours could be behind the threat and could be watching her house at this very moment.

"Hi sis, long time no see!" Said Jasmine, as she stepped forward and gave her a hug.

"Try to act natural, pretend I'm a best friend you haven't seen in ages," Jasmine whispered.

Deanne stepped back and put her hands to her face.

"You know I still can't believe you're actually here, I never thought I would be able to drag you away from the city!"

"I know, I've been slack, but after that last lot of photo's you sent me I just had to check out your new digs for myself."

Deanne grabbed one of Jasmine's bags and as they both

walked to the front door she explained what repairs had been done so far and what was next on the list. Once inside Jasmine could not help but notice the damaged wall and the now exposed fireplace.

"So it really was walled up."

"Yes, he even had the chimney removed, so unless you knew otherwise, one would never have known there was a fireplace hidden behind this wall."

"Very clever!"

"Yes, although if my aunt hadn't kept dad's files and given them to me, or I hadn't been interested enough to read them, that letter may never have been discovered."

"Obviously your father knew you both well enough to know you would."

"That's the strange thing, I never met my father, in fact I had no idea who my father was until his lawyers managed to track me down and inform me I had inherited this house."

"This is getting more interesting by the minute, how about you show me where I can put my luggage and then you can fill me in over a cup of coffee?"

Both girls made themselves comfortable in the lounge room and Deanne explained her parent's relationship, how her mother fled and changed her name making it difficult for anyone to find them.

"So how did they track you down?"

"It was through my mother's obituary notice I put in the paper, it wasn't until I met my aunt that I discovered my mother had changed her name, it was also my aunt's belief that my father had been murdered, that was why she had kept his files and passed them onto me."

"Why did your mother leave your father and change her name?"

"Firstly let me tell you when my mother ran off, my father had no idea my mother was pregnant, it was by sheer accident he found out, this made him more determined to find us. My aunt said he believed Salina was the reason my mother disappeared, she also believes she is responsible for his death."

"Who is Salina and why does your aunt feel she was the reason your mother ran off?"

"My father's ex-wife."

"Now I'm confused!"

"Sorry, let me explain, Salina had designs on my father when he was studying at university, she knew the only way to get him to turn his attention to her was to make it look like my mother had run off with another man, but my father discovered years later that Salina threatened my mother."

"Do you think she is responsible for your father's death?"

"I don't know, his letter was so cryptic and there was a photo of a man attached and on the back is a list of numbers."

"Can I see this?"

"Sure."

Deanne reached for her handbag and retrieved her one and only letter from her father and handed it to Jasmine who quickly read it before looking at the photo.

"Well according to this letter your father believed he was going to be murdered, as for who this man is or the meaning of the numbers, do you have any idea?"

"No."

"Now you said it was your father's files that led you to uncovering the fireplace, perhaps they also contain a clue to the identity of this man?"

"It's possible, you can read them if you like, I tried but it's all medical mumbo jumbo to me."

"The other thing I wanted to ask you was, I remember you mentioning that these letters that were sent to you were written on your father's typewriter which you have in your cupboard, is that correct?"

"Yes, but it was only the first letter, you see I changed my locks because I came home one day to find the window open and discovered my father's files had been disturbed, so I had new locks installed. I can't show you the first letter because the police have that, but I can show you the second one and the type is definitely different."

Deanne once again rummaged through her handbag and passed the letter to Jasmine.

"Well if the police believe the first letter was done on your father's typewriter, which means whoever broke in typed the letter at the same time."

"I was thinking the same thing, but why did they wait so long then before they sent it, it was weeks after I changed my locks?"

"Perhaps they were watching to see what you were doing here first, see if you were any kind of threat?"

"Of what?"

"I don't know, as for whoever broke into your house, what did the police say?"

"Nothing, because I didn't report it."

"Why on earth not?"

"Well at the time I wasn't sure, I thought perhaps I hadn't closed the window properly and that maybe I accidently broken the seal on the files when I moved the boxes, as the tape had been on there for years. It wasn't until the police said the letter had been typed on my dad's old typewriter I knew for sure someone had broken in."

"Why didn't you mention this to the police?"

"I don't think the Sargent was prepared to listen to anything else I had to say, not after I had suggested Sam, his good mate, had been the one who sent the letter and lied about me getting the sack for stealing."

"Fair enough, so why do you think Sam lied about you no longer being employed at the boatyard?"

"I have no idea, but as I told you on the phone he scared me, I got the feeling he was up to something and then there was that weird guy that came around one day and then Sam suddenly closing up shop after reading about the double murder."

"Speaking of which, can you describe that guy you saw, was there anything about him that stood out, or did he just look like your ordinary everyday kind of Joe?"

"I suppose it depends whether you live in Memphis or not," laughed Deanne.

"Why do you say that?"

"Picture a guy in his fifties, about five three, small build with a hairdo that looked as though he had just stepped off the stage after singing 'Jail house rock!"

"Are you serious?" Laughed Jasmine.

"Of course, I remember I was about to laugh when I saw him, but then he turned around and it was as if he looked right at me. I panicked and quickly grabbed what was in the printer and closed out of the programme I was in, I don't know how I managed to stay calm when Sam came bursting in the office!"

"What were you printing?"

"It was a picture of my father and Salina; I wanted to know what she looked like."

"Do you still have it?"

"Yeah, it's with all my father's files."

Jasmine followed Deanne to the linen cupboard and gasped when she saw how many boxes there were.

"Oh my god, are they all his files?"

"Yes."

"Looks like I've got a lot of reading to do!"

Deanne crouched down and rummaged through the box before pulling out a file.

"I don't know if it's any help, but I have gone through quite a few of them and trust me some of the photos are pretty horrendous, but so far this is the only file that doesn't appear to have any photos at all, I thought that was strange."

Before handing the file to Jasmine, Deanne opened it and removed a single sheet of paper.

"This is the only picture I could find of Salina, judging by how my father looks I'd say this was taken quite a few years back."

Jasmine looked at the grainy black and white photo and quickly made her way back out into the lounge room and turned on the reading lamp.

"Well I'll be!"

"What?"

"I'm not one hundred percent sure, but I think you just helped uncover the identity of the 'Mistress'!"

"Who?"

"The exposé I did about those innocent young girls being smuggled into the country for prostitution, the woman whom we believe is behind it escaped, she was known as the 'Mistress'!"

Deanne's eyes widened as she gasped and Jasmine realised her gut instinct about a connection between her story and Deanne had been correct, but not in the way she had thought. She had to contact Tracey as soon as possible, not only with the evidence she had in her hand, but also the description she had been given, of the man acting suspiciously at the boatyard that day.

After trying to reach Tracey throughout the afternoon and leaving countless messages, Jasmine came to the conclusion she was most likely on another undercover job and realised it could be days, even weeks before she got back to her, she would just have to carry on with what she knew so far.

"Deanne, I was wondering if you would like to go for a drive, show me where this boatyard is."

"Sure, but why?"

"Maybe with my nose for snooping I might be able to uncover what old Sam is up to."

It didn't take long to drive the short distance and from what Jasmine could see the place looked deserted, she got out and tried the gate and wasn't surprised to find it locked; so climbed back in the car.

"I could easily pick that lock, but not in broad daylight."

"If you're planning on coming back here tonight, I'm coming with you."

"I don't think that's a good idea, I'm used to this sort of stuff, how do you think I get some of my stories?"

"You can't make me stay at home, besides I know the layout of this place, you don't."

"Good point."

Later that night the girls donned dark clothes and Deanne warned Jasmine that the road leading to the yard had no streetlight, so Jasmine brought her small torch, which she assured Deanne would not give them away. As they walked along the uneven dirt road, Deanne kept glancing up ahead for any sign of light coming from the direction of the shed; suddenly Jasmine stopped causing Deanne to trip.

"Careful, we've reached the front gates," Jasmine stated.

Deanne looked up and noted there was still no light and wondered if they had covered the windows with something heavier or perhaps no one was here. She turned to see Jasmine had the small torch between her teeth, shining it down on the padlock and was wiggling two pieces of wire in the lock, when suddenly it fell away from the chain.

"You'd be amazed at the things I've picked up through my travels."

After letting themselves through the gate, Jasmine looped the chain and padlock back into position, so if anyone happened to drive past, all would look as it should. Deanne directed Jasmine around the side of the shed and noticed the old drum she had used previously was still there, both girls carried it and placed it under a window, Jasmine carefully climbed up while Deanne held it steady for her.

"The place looks deserted; I'm going to take a look inside." Whispered Jasmine.

Deanne nodded her response and waited while Jasmine once again picked the lock and eased the door open, just enough so both girls could squeeze through. Once she had closed the door behind them, she turned the end of her torch and it shone a much brighter beam, waving it in a wide arc around the shed; but the place was empty, even the shelves were bare.

Jasmine walked the perimeter of the shed looking for

anything that might have been left behind, but it was looking like Sam had done a thorough clean-up job when she got a glimpse of something amongst the dirt and dust that had been swept in a pile, but not removed. She crouched down and prodded at it with her finger, then pulled a sealable plastic bag from her back pocket.

"Have you found something?" Asked Deanne

"Perhaps, I'll know for sure when we get back to the house."

"How?"

"Another little trick I learnt in my travels, actually I have a friend in the police force that is probably regretting showing me."

"So does that mean we can get the hell out of here?"

"I think we have found all there is to find."

Deanne was pleased they kept a fast pace back home and by the time they snuck around to her back door her heart seemed to be beating at one hundred miles an hour.

She watched in amazement as Jasmine carefully put some of the white substance in a little cylinder, then added a clear liquid before replacing its lid and shook the vial.

"If this is cocaine as I suspect, it will turn brown," said Jasmine

Deanne could see it start to change colour and sure enough it turned the colour of coffee.

"Now we know what Sam was up to, he was using the boats to distribute his drugs, but the question is how?" Commented Jasmine.

"Well we obviously can't go to the local police about this, because that rude Sargent is mates with Sam. Oh my god, do you think he could be in on this as well?"

"I don't know, one thing's for sure, I don't think it's safe for you to stay here…"

"I'm not leaving!"

"Deanne I'm serious, we still don't know if Sam is behind those death threats or if it has something to do with your father's alleged murder. Look let's get out of these hot clothes and pour ourselves a glass of wine, because there is something else I should tell you."

Once both girls had changed and settled themselves in the lounge room, Jasmine told Deanne about the story that kick started her career with Frontline News.

"I remember seeing that on television, they never found one of the girls did they?"

"No, her name was Michelle Brown, but her father never gave up on her, in fact he still believes she is alive and as far as I know has not stopped his search to find her."

"He sounds a bit like my father."

"Well there is a strange twist to this story, you see when I did that exposé on those poor young girls, I had a small camera disguised as a pendant that hung around my neck, it filmed everything that was going on around me, and it captured something I myself didn't see at the time."

Jasmine opened her briefcase and pulled out two A4 sized photos and handed them to Deanne.

"Oh my god, that's Salina and that girl, her hands are handcuffed behind her back!"

"I know it's a bit blurry, but Salina isn't just grabbing the girls arm, she is holding a gun."

"Oh, that poor girl, but why are you showing me this?"

"Look at the other photo, now look at this paper clipping about the two missing girls from Eden Cove."

"Ah, you think this is Michelle Brown don't you?"

"Yes."

"You have to show this to her father!"

"Easier said than done."

"Why?"

"Long story, but what I propose we do is pack up some of your things, including the entirety of your father's files and we pay a visit to Eden Cove."

"I understand you wanting to go there to show this to Michelle's father, but why do you want me to go and take all dad's files?"

"Firstly let me tell you Michelle's father is Max Steel, before retirement, if he is in fact really retired, was in the army, Special Forces Division, not the sort of person you would want to get on the wrong side of, but also I wouldn't be surprised if this guy has a lot of powerful connections. Secondly I think we have stumbled on something that calls for someone who can not only offer better protection than the police, but has the trained skills that can help us unravel the meaning of the riddle your father left you."

"Ah, I see where you're going with this, because I think Salina has something to do with my father's death, the same woman you believe has Michelle, he has the muscle and the connections, but we have the information."

"Exactly, so now how do you feel about taking a trip to Eden Cove?"

"Ok, but first I have to tell my aunt."

"We can load up the car in the morning and then stop by her house on the way."

STEEL JUSTICE

CHAPTER EIGHTEEN

Jasmine gave Deanne a quick tour of Eden Cove and then took her to her favourite restaurant at the marina.

"My god this place is paradise, how the hell could you give this up for the city?"

"It wasn't easy, I always told myself I could come back here anytime for a visit, but unfortunately I have been so busy I haven't had a chance until now."

"I noticed you're still wearing the dark wig and those big sunglasses, something I should know about?"

"I don't want to sound vain, but I am trying to avoid being noticed, more from Max Steel than anyone else."

"Why, he's the reason we're here?"

"Trust me, if he gets wind Jasmine Bronson is back in town, I won't have a hope in hell of getting anywhere near him!"

"Why?"

"At the time of his daughter's disappearance I was working for the local newspaper, I managed to unearth that Michelle Brown was his daughter, he believes I endangered her further by making it public knowledge."

"Did you?"

"Possibly and for that reason I could never put that story behind me, you see it was never unearthed why someone tried to harm these girls. My belief is Michelle was the main target, the other girl just happened to be in the wrong place at the wrong time."

"Hmm, well if that's the case, how the hell are you going to get Max Steel to listen to you?"

"That's where you come in."

"Me, how?"

"His place is like a fortress, the only entry is through the high gates at the entrance of his property where he has a security camera and an intercom, you're going to be the one to get out of the car and tell him you have information about his daughter, but can only give it to him in person."

"Now I feel scared, what if he doesn't believe me?"

"He will."

Once the girls had finished their lunch, Jasmine drove the short distance to the entrance of Max Steel's home and Deanne gasped at the sight of the high fence and looming gates that were topped with razor wire.

"He's a bit over the top with his security, especially for such a small little fishing village!"

"Apparently he is paranoid about security."

"Bit of an over-kill if you ask me!"

"Now if you look at the main pillar on your left you will see there is a buzzer for the intercom and above it is a camera, make sure you let him see your face."

"Ok."

Jasmine watched as Deanne got out of the car and walked towards the gate, she looked nervously back at the car before pressing the buzzer and looked up at the camera. After a few moments Jasmine heard a response, but could not understand what was being said and saw Deanne lean in towards the intercom to speak. There was another response and Deanne looked hesitantly at the car before walking towards the driver's side door.

"What's wrong?" Asked Jasmine.

"He wants to see who else is in the car."

"Did you tell him you were alone?"

"Yes, but he doesn't believe me, he said he saw me get out of the passenger side door."

"Bloody hell, does he have a bell that goes off every time a car pulls up? He must have cameras covering every angle of the entrance!"

"What are you going to do?"

"I don't have any other choice; I'll have to get out of the car."

"He wants to see your face."

"Shit!"

"He mightn't recognise you; after all you still have on the dark wig."

"Trust me, he will!"

Jasmine waited till she was standing directly in front of the camera before pulling the wig from her head and Deanne put her hands over her ears as a loud string of expletives came from the intercom.

"Despite what you think Mr Steel, Deanne is telling the truth, we really do have some evidence that proves your daughter is still alive."

"If that's true, why come to me, why not go to the police, or is this one of your ploys to get a story?"

"Touché, as for going to the police, that's kind of a tricky situation, you see Deanne managed to stumble across something that not only has put her life in danger, but has managed to get the authorities off side."

Before Max Steel could respond, Deanne leaned towards the intercom.

"Please Mr Steel, Jasmine has photos to prove she is telling the truth and I believe the woman who killed my father has your daughter!"

There was a pregnant pause and then suddenly there was a loud noise and Jasmine realised the front gates were opening.

"Quick, get in the car."

Jasmine wasted no time starting up the engine and as soon as the gates were open enough she drove the car between them and made her way up the long winding drive.

"Wow, his property must be huge!"

"I told you he would listen to you."

"Have you been here before?"

"No, very few people have."

As Jasmine steered the car around the bend in the road, a large low set house came into view and Deanne noted there was a narrow road that went down off to the right, she could just make out the roof of a smaller dwelling. She heard Jasmine mumble something to herself as she pulled the car to a halt and turned off the ignition. About to question what she said; her eyes were suddenly drawn to a man walking down the front steps and towards them.

"Oh my god, who is the hunk?"

"Max Steel."

"Are you serious, I was expecting someone old, like you know, old enough to be a father?"

Deanne looked across at Jasmine and noted the look on her face and laughed.

"Jasmine you're blushing!"

"Shh, he'll hear you."

Both girls climbed out of the car, ignoring Jasmine, Max walked towards Deanne and held out his hand.

"Deanne, Max Steel."

"Please to meet you, you have such a lovely place here," she said nervously.

"I think so; now where are these photos?"

"Right to the point, mind if we come inside first?" Asked Jasmine.

"I do."

He looked pointedly at Jasmine and her cheeks began to burn, she quickly looked down at her briefcase and tried to open the latch as her hand shook, annoyed at herself for acting like a silly school girl and annoyed at Max Steel for making her feel this way.

Finally with the briefcase open she pulled out the two A4 photos and handed them to him. He studied them for a few moments and then looked up at her.

"Who took these and who is this woman?"

"I took the photos, but at the time I didn't realise I had, or that Michelle was even there."

"Where?"

"Look, do you mind if we stand in the shade, it's really hot out here and I can feel my skin burning already."

"Come inside, I suppose you would both like a cool drink."

Jasmine looked across a Deanne and rolled her eyes, causing a smile to come to her face.

"That would be nice." Jasmine said with a hint of sarcasm.

The moment both girls stepped inside the front door they felt the temperature drop a good ten degrees. Taking a moment for their eyes to adjust, after being outside in the bright sunlight, they followed Max as he led them through the house to a long veranda. It fronted onto a long pool that was surrounded by palms and beautiful tropical plants, the place had a Balinese feel about it, with the overtones of the Australian north, with a large BBQ and an outdoor bar. Jasmine could just imagine Max turning a couple of steaks on the hot grill with a cool beer in hand, or gliding effortlessly through the water with his powerful arms and legs.

"Jasmine, you ok."

Jasmine turned and looked at Deanne and to her horror Max Steel was standing next to her placing some frosty tall glasses on the table.

"Jeez, its hot isn't it." Jasmine said as she reached for a glass.

"Apparently some of us seem to feel it more than others."

Jasmine noted the undertone in Max's voice and wondered if he was able to read her mind.

"You were going to explain these photos."

"Yes well, I don't know if you ever watch Frontline News, or happened to see the one about the young girls being smuggled into the country for prostitution."

Jasmine paused and waited for Max to respond, but realised he wasn't going to.

"Ah well, at the time of the filming it was pretty chaotic and it wasn't until I was going through the video the next day that I noticed this scene in the background, I got Nigel our cameraman to make these stills. I know they are not real clear, but I believe the girl is Michelle, what do you think?"

"What can you tell me about this photo?"

"The woman was known only as 'Mistress', according to

one of the girls who was held prisoner, the girl in the photo is known as Rusalka. Apparently the 'Mistress' was using the spiel that she was a mermaid, because she was brought up from the bottom of the ocean in a fishing net."

"I'd like to know everything about this girl they call Rusalka, in fact I would like to speak to whoever gave you this information."

"Her name was Maliha; she is now in the witness protection program, so I don't see any possible way you could speak to her."

"You managed to."

"It wasn't easy, trust me!"

"I don't care how you do it, I want you to organise another meeting and this time I would like to be present!"

"I'm telling you it's not going to happen, besides I doubt Maliha could tell you anything else, she told me Rusalka was kept away from the other girls and she was heavily guarded."

Max got up angrily and paced the room, before coming back and leaning on the table towards Jasmine, making it very difficult for her to look anywhere but directly into his eyes.

"Are you sure there wasn't anything else Maliha told you, anything at all that would confirm this girl is Michelle?"

"Well she did say one other thing, but I'm finding it a bit hard to believe."

"Well spit it out woman, what did she say?"

The look on Max's face was menacing and Jasmine leaned away from him.

"She said the men must fight Rusalka to claim her, they fight the fight of knives."

"Sayoc Kali." Max said quietly.

"What?"

"It's a form a martial art using knives, Michelle was well versed in the sport."

"You're kidding me right?"

"I'm serious."

"How did you feel about your daughter doing such a

thing?"

"You don't know my daughter, that's why I couldn't understand how that guy managed to overpower her, she never went anywhere without her knife. I later found it amongst the foliage under the tree house; it must have fallen through the cracks.

"Then you agree with me, the girl in the photo is Michelle?"

"I wasn't sure until you mentioned the knife fighting, my daughter is a fighter in every sense of the word and this 'Mistress' decided to use it in the most despicable way to make money! Have you any idea who this woman is?

"Yes, that's where Deanne comes into the picture; you see she contacted me because she received two death threats in the mail. The police were of no help; it was after watching my program she thought I might be able to help her."

"Hang on, if she received two death threats, why wouldn't the police help her?"

"Because the first one was done on my dad's old typewriter, which just happened to be in the bottom of my linen cupboard and also I hinted that Sam had sent them," explained Deanne.

"Your confusing me, what does this have to do with the woman in the photo?"

"It doesn't, Deanne contacted me because of a culmination of things, firstly she felt her boss, who by the way is good friends with the local police Sargent, was up to something and upon reading about the double murder involving a paedophile ring, he suddenly closes up shop and she gets a death threat that she thinks her boss sent. In addition, she uncovered evidence that could prove her father was murdered, possibly by his ex-wife Salina, who happens to be the woman in the photo known as the 'Mistress'."

"Don't forget the cocaine we found in Sam's shed!" Exclaimed Deanne.

"Who's Sam?"

"Deanne's boss."

"My god, it sounds like you've opened a can of worms," stated Max

"My thoughts exactly," said Jasmine.

"Deanne, who was your father and why do you think he was murdered by this woman Salina?"

"My father was Dr Robert Shoal, his death was listed as a heart attack, but my aunt never believed that, even though the autopsy proved otherwise. It wasn't until I was going through his files that I found a letter he left me."

She pulled the letter from her handbag and handed it to Max to read.

"You said he left you this letter and yet it states he doesn't know if you will be the one who actually reads it."

"Ok, firstly I never met my father; in fact I never knew who he was until his lawyers tracked me down and told me he had bequeathed a house to me. When I was going through my father's files there was this one handwritten word *Camino* in the margin of most of the files, turns out its Italian for *fireplace*, which he had walled up in the house he left to me, that letter was hidden inside."

"Is this your father?" Max held up the photo.

"No, I don't know who that man is, but if you look on the back there is a series of numbers and in the riddle he says to follow the numbers."

"Hmm, I wouldn't mind taking a look at these files."

"I thought you would, that's why we brought them with us," commented Jasmine.

"There's a lot of them and there are some pretty gory photos, you see my father was a plastic surgeon, his focus was victims that had suffered a terrible injury, but then I suppose you being in the army you would have seen a lot of that sort of thing…"

Deanne realised by the look on Max Steel's face she'd touched on a subject he would probably rather forget.

"There is one file though that doesn't have any photos, it

could be significant," suggested Jasmine.

"It's a good place to start, so where are you girls staying?"

"Ah, we hadn't got that far yet, our first priority was to tell you about Michelle."

"Well you won't get anywhere this time of year."

"Why, it's only the beginning of November, the busy season hasn't started yet."

"You've got to be kidding, you're the top reporter for Frontline News and you don't know about the solar eclipse!"

"Oh my god, I totally forgot! Come on Deanne we better get going."

"Where?"

"Looks like it's back to your place."

"But you said…"

"You can stay here."

"What?" Both girls said in unison.

"I've got plenty of room and I'm figuring Deanne is not going to leave her father's files with me and they could be my only link to finding Michelle."

"Ah, ok if you're sure," said Jasmine.

"I'm not, but it's the only solution we have at the moment."

Jasmine knew that was aimed directly at her and wondered if he would ever get past the fact she exposed to the world Michelle was his daughter. Max collected Deanne's luggage, but made no offer to assist Jasmine, she wondered how the hell she was going to manage living under the same roof as him, with his obvious dislike towards her and the way her crazy hormones reacted every time he was in close proximity.

Hours later after all three had been going through the files of Dr Robert Shoal, trying to find any clue that would help solve the riddle he had written for his daughter.

"Everything seems to point to this one file that has no patient name or contains any photos, I think we should all focus on this one file, so I have made copies, maybe three pair of eyes might pick up something one might have missed," said Max.

"What would be really helpful is someone with medical knowledge who might be able to explain in layman's terms what this file says," commented Jasmine.

"Already ahead of you on that one, I have scanned a copy and sent it off to a friend who might be able to translate it for me," stated Max.

After about another two hours when Jasmine's eyes had begun to burn, her neck and shoulders were sore from hunching over countless pages and she was about to suggest they take a break when she noticed Deanne was madly highlighting sections on various pages of the file.

"Have you found something?"

"I think so, I didn't notice it before, but after looking at page after page about a zillion times, I realised there is a tiny number on certain lines, then I realised there was a system to it."

Both Jasmine and Max moved over towards Deanne to see what she was doing.

"I use to do this stuff at school, it just took me a while to work out the sequence, but look, these numbers I have highlighted, match the ones on the back of the photo; my guess is this photo belongs to this file!"

"Good work!" Exclaimed Jasmine.

"I kind of expected it might be the case, simply for the fact it had no photos, very clever though, it ensured you connected the two together, so whatever he was trying to tell you is in this file," commented Max.

"The thing is what? I followed the numbers to the file, but where do they take us after that?"

"Good question, perhaps when we know more about this file, we might have a better understanding of where to go next. In the meantime I suggest we take a break, I don't know about you two, but I need some sustenance."

"I am rather hungry," said Deanne.

"I hope neither of you are vegetarians, cause I was thinking of throwing some thick juicy steaks on the BBQ?"

"Sounds good," said Jasmine and Deanne nodded in agreement.

The following morning Jasmine rose early, she'd hardly slept a wink, her mind switching from trying to solve the mystery of the riddle, to the abruptness of Max Steel. He was a perfect host to Deanne, they both could talk for hours, whereas she felt like the uninvited guest and wished to god she'd had the forethought to ring ahead and book some accommodation. She decided to go for a run, it always managed to clear her head, her only choice was to go around the perimeter of the property and just hoped he didn't have any booby-traps or vicious dogs silently waiting to pounce.

Jasmine was amazed at the expanse of the property, she had been running for a good forty-five minutes and there was still no sign of the house coming into view, thick dense foliage surrounded it, making it impossible to see what was beyond the boundary line, something she was sure was his reason for purchasing the place.

Suddenly a rooftop came into view, but as she drew nearer she realised it was not the main house, but a small cottage. Curiosity getting the better of her, Jasmine decided to take a closer look and slowed her pace to a walk, tentatively looking in the windows as she made her way around the house.

The place appeared deserted and wondered why Max hadn't housed herself and Deanne here instead of the main house; she for one would have felt much more comfortable not having to be under the same roof as Max Steel. As she rounded the house a vehicle came into view, causing her to stop in her tracks, it was a Jeep Wrangler Sport, just the sort of vehicle an ex-army man would drive, only thing it was fire engine red, not exactly a colour to make one inconspicuous, then she noticed the number plate *Shell 01. This must be where Michelle lived, that explains why she could find no evidence of her up at the house.*

Her curiosity now in full swing, Jasmine walked up the few steps to the front door and turned the handle, surprised to find it was unlocked, but then realised with the property being virtually impenetrable to intruders, there was no need to lock any doors or windows.

She paused as she stepped inside, listening for any signs of someone about, mainly Max Steel. The place was dead quiet, reassured with this, she moved silently forward, taking in her surroundings. There was a sideboard that held varying picture frames with images of Michelle, which mainly consisted of her and another girl, whom she recognised as her best friend Jane. There were few photos of Michelle with her father, but the images before her told her one thing, despite her father following a strict army regime, his daughter wasn't having a bar of it!

She noted all the photos were of her early teens up until, she presumed, the time of her disappearance and thought it strange there were none of her early childhood years. There were posters on the walls, as to be expected of a girl Michelle's age, but then she saw the wakeboard leaning against one wall and on the other was a large picture box that housed varying shapes and sizes of knives and the caption '*All the blade, all the time*'. These were definitely not of the kitchen variety, but more like dangerous weapons.

Below was a trophy cabinet that held many gold fighting figurines and on closer inspection they all had an inscription, *Sayoc Kali, Michele Brown* and the varying levels she had reached.

"What the hell do you think you are doing?"

Jasmine screamed in fright and turned to see Max Steel with a menacing look on his face and fists clenched at his side.

"Um, I was just, ah…"

"Snooping, I knew it was a mistake to let you set foot on my property!"

"It's not what you think."

"Really?"

Max took a step closer and folded his arms across his chest; Jasmine knew she had to do some quick talking before she found herself booted from his property.

"Yes I was curious; I wanted to know more about your daughter…"

"For part two of your story!"

"No, that's not true; I swear to god I am not here to write a story, least not about your daughter!"

Jasmine knew by the look on his face he didn't believe her.

"Look, after I did that story on those poor girls, so young they should be still playing with dolls, not exploited to such atrocious acts for the financial gain of one and the sick minds of others. After seeing what I saw I made a promise to myself and those girls I would do everything in my power to make those responsible pay. Yes I was curious about Michelle, initially I couldn't understand why the Mistress or should I say Salina had a girl her age there, she didn't fit in with the woman's M.O. After hearing what both you and Maliha told me, even though brief, about Michelle, I got to thinking about the plight your daughter is in. I know it's no consolation, but this room alone, has told me a lot about her. She has a stubborn streak, something she no doubt inherited from her father, Salina might be holding Michelle against her will, forcing her to fight for her honour, but Salina will never be able to break her, she will never have full control over her; she is far too strong for that!"

Jasmine noticed Max's stance relax a little and his face softened as he picked up one of the framed photos of his daughter.

"It's the one thing that keeps me sane, the one thing that helps me stay focused so I can find her and bring her home; she would always say to me *'Dad, chill out, I can take care of myself'*!"

Jasmine realised Max had revealed more to her than he had intended and tried to make light of his comment.

"Well I supposed we'd better get back to those files, because I believe Deanne's father knew his days were numbered, but also who his killer would be. If Deanne's assumption is correct, it will lead us to Salina and when we find her we will find Michelle."

Max looked at her intently for a moment as if choosing his next words.

"By the way, I received word this morning about that file we all believe is connected to the photo; the procedure was purely cosmetic surgery, not a reconstruction from a birth defect or an accident, which is what Dr Shoal specialised in."

"That's really strange, because Deanne told me the main reason behind the divorce between her father and Salina, was because he opted to help injured people over the far more lucrative profession of cosmetic surgery."

"Well it gets even more interesting, everyone who assisted in that operation is now dead!"

"Oh my god! With no witnesses, that's going to make our job a whole lot harder!"

"I believe Dr Shoal knew this, that's why he left that cryptic letter to Deanne, we just have to unravel what he was trying to tell her."

"Ok, so the man in the photo had this cosmetic surgery, it's a pity Dr Shoal didn't leave a photo of what he looks like now!"

"Perhaps he didn't live long enough to see the final result."

"Good point."

Max and Jasmine walked the rest of the way to the main house in silence, she for one felt that they had come to a mutual understanding, for the time being at least.

Hours later after many cups of coffee and discussions, trying to nut out the answer, Jasmine finally tweaked to something that had been niggling at the back of her brain.

"You know that line where it says *'Beware of the Black sheep, he is a chameleon who purges forth white'*, he uses a capital for the word black."

"So?" Said Max.

"I was always taught that a capital is used only, at the beginning of a sentence or for a noun."

"Where are you going with this?" Asked Max

"Perhaps Dr Shoal used a capital for the word black because it is a noun, as in Mr Black?"

"Yes, the man in the photo is Mr Black," said Deanne excitedly.

"You could be right, but it still doesn't get us anywhere," commented Max.

"I could call Aunt Jan, you never know, she might know of someone my father knew by that name?"

"I suppose it's worth a try, you can use the phone in the office."

The moment Deanne left the room Jasmine could feel the tension rising, *was it just her and the fact she was once again alone with Max, or did he really despise her that much and Deanne was the only reason he wasn't blatantly rude to her?* She got up and walked over towards the window and looked longingly out towards the pool.

"I think the numbers are co-ordinates for something," commented Max.

"What?"

"You know, longitude and latitude, it pinpoints a place on the map."

"Ah yeah, I never thought of that."

Max quickly typed on the keypad of his laptop and she watched the changing expression on his face.

"Did you find something?"

"It could be a coincidence, but it leads us to an address in the city, namely the Commonwealth Bank."

"Are you sure?"

"Yes, providing those numbers are in fact co-ordinates."

"Why would Dr Shoal leave co-ordinates for a bank?"

"What better place to keep something sccurc, than a Security Box."

"If that's the case why didn't his lawyers inform Deanne of this?"

"Perhaps they are unaware of its existence."

Before Jasmine could comment any further, Deanne came bursting into the room.

"You'll never guess who Mr Black is?"

"Who?" Both Max and Jasmine said in unison.

"He was the man Salina left my father for!"

"Really!" Exclaimed Jasmine.

"Yes, but unfortunately there's a problem."

"Which is?" Asked Max.

"He's dead; he died in a house fire!"

"Sounds a bit too convenient if you ask me, did your aunt say when this fire happened to take place?" Asked Max.

"Apparently it was about a year before my father died."

"Well that rules out my theory about the black sheep being someone's name," commented Jasmine.

"I wouldn't rule it out just yet."

"Deanne, did your father's lawyers ever mention anything about a Security Box held at a bank somewhere?" Asked Max.

"No why?"

"I thought perhaps the numbers could be the co-ordinates for an address, the internet search brought it up as being the address of a bank in the city."

"Really?"

"I was thinking I'd give them a call, posing as your lawyer with the spiel that after your father's death it was discovered he had a security box, but as he had so many accounts with varying institutions, it is unsure which one actually has the box in safe keeping."

"Ok."

Max went into the office to place the call and Deanne nervously paced the room.

"Why did dad have to make everything so hard, I feel like we are just banging our heads against a brick wall, I don't think we're ever going to figure this out?"

"Perhaps he had something so incriminating he knew he had to be extremely careful that it didn't fall into the wrong hands, perhaps he had faith that his daughter would not give up."

"I just hope I can live up to his expectations!"

"You already have."

At that moment Max walked back into the room.

"Please tell me the bank has a Security Box for my father!"

"They don't."

"Damn, this is…"

"They do have one for a Deanne Jones." Max said with a smile on his face.

"Really!" Exclaimed Deanne.

"It's about a three hour drive from here, obviously it is too late in the day to go today; we can leave first thing in the morning," stated Jasmine.

"Unfortunately it's not that simple, apart from Deanne showing proof of ID, she needs to know the unique security code to be able to access the box."

"Oh my god, not more numbers!" Exclaimed Deanne.

"Well your father did say, follow the numbers," commented Jasmine.

"I suggest we all take a break from this, it's a hot day and I certainly could do with a cold beer and a swim in the pool!" Suggested Max.

"Ok for you, but I didn't bring my bathing suit," lamented Jasmine.

"You mean to tell me, you came to Eden Cove, your home town and you didn't even think about packing a bathing suit!" Exclaimed Max.

"Well I…"

"I brought mine," smiled Deanne.

"Yeah well your mind wasn't totally focused on getting the scoop of the century!"

"I resent that, I had no idea I was coming here; initially I was only supposed to be away for a few days. In fact my boss…"

"Allowed you to extend your trip to do a follow up story on Max Steel!"

"Ahh!"

Jasmine was so angry she stormed out of the room and Deanne quickly followed her.

"What is it with you two; you're like a pair of squabbling kids?"

"I told you this all before; he won't forgive me for exposing Michelle Brown as his daughter!"

"Have you actually apologised to him for doing that?"

"What's the point; it wouldn't make an ounce of difference!"

"How do you know?"

"God the sooner we can figure out your father's message the sooner I can get away from Max Steel!"

"I think you need to calm down and cool down, haven't you got a bra and knickers that will pass as a bikini?"

"Oh, I don't know."

Deanne started rummaging through Jasmine's suitcase and pulled out a pair of yellow gingham knickers and matching bra.

"This looks cute, I've seen bikini's that look similar to these."

"Yeah, only problem is there's a good chance that fabric will become transparent when wet."

"I'll let you know as soon as you get in the water, you can keep your towel on the pools edge, besides it's a long pool, swim up the opposite end to Max."

Jasmine sighed, it was rather hot and the pool did look inviting.

"Ok, but promise you'll tell me if they become see-through?"

"I promise."

The girls quickly changed and Jasmine feeling self-conscious wrapped a towel around her before walking outside.

"Oh man, I always thought speedos should be banned, but man oh man I've totally changed my mind," said Deanne just loud enough so Jasmine could hear.

Jasmine looked up to see Max walk over to one of the sun

lounges, he was wearing a pair of brief black speedos and his body was dripping with water, obviously from being in the pool.

"You know I went to a male strip show once and none of them looked as good as Max does, do you reckon he works out?" Asked Deanne.

Suddenly Max turned as though he knew he was the object of conversation and wrapped the towel around himself before sitting down and taking a long swig of his beer.

"I think we just got sprung," giggled Deanne.

"God it's hot, let's go up the other end and stop staring at Max like you've never seen a man before!"

"Ah, I wasn't the only one."

Jasmine didn't want to continue with the conversation any further and quickly walked to the other end of the pool, dropping her towel and diving into the cooling water. Forgetting her earlier conversation with Deanne, she quickly swam out using clean graceful strokes, up and down the length of the pool until she felt the tension ease from her body.

She neared the shallow end of the pool and suddenly noticed something dangle in the water in front of her. As she wiped the water from her eyes she realised it was an icy cold beer held by a large tanned hand.

"Thanks."

Jasmine waded over to the steps and sat up to her waist in the water before taking a long swig of the ice-cold amber liquid. She wondered if this was a form of a peace offering and thought about what Deanne had said to her earlier.

"I'm sorry."

Max sat down on the edge of the pool and stared across at her.

"About what?"

"For revealing to the world Michelle Brown was your daughter, I should have delved deeper into why this was not common knowledge."

Max looked down at her and his eyes bored into her so

intently she felt uncomfortable, unable to keep up the stance, she looked away and noticed Deanne signally frantically to her. Jasmine frowned and mouthed the word *what.*

"She's trying to tell you that the water has made your bra completely transparent."

Jasmine felt her cheeks go red as she noted the smile on Max's face and tried to cover her breasts.

"I suppose I should tell you, your knickers are also transparent."

Jasmine scraped her side on the step as she hurriedly tried to place the beer on the side of the pool before swimming towards the other end and the safety of her towel. To add further to her embarrassment, she could hear Max laughing as she swam off and by the time she reached the other end Deanne was holding her towel out for her.

"You swam off before I could tell you!"

"It's ok, I'm not mad at you." Jasmine said as she climbed out of the pool.

Jasmine quickly wrapped the towel around her and hastily made her way inside the house, *why did she always manage to look like an idiot when Max Steel was around?*

Later that evening Deanne sat alone in the lounge room and watched TV, Jasmine was hiding in the bedroom hunched over her laptop and Max had retreated to his office. She had read and reread her father's letter so many times she knew it off by heart and the thought of looking at those files one more time tonight would send her round the twist!

As she flicked through the channels she came to a program about the solar eclipse, an event that many had come to Eden Cove to witness in two days' time. The commentator was going to great lengths to explain the difference between a Lunar eclipse and a Solar eclipse, she vaguely remembered doing an assignment on such a thing at school, when suddenly something jarred her memory.

"Jasmine, Max, come here quick!"

Max immediately came out of the office.

"What's wrong?"

"I think I've figured out part of the riddle, *'Day can become night and night become day.'* This program is about an eclipse, there are two basic types, Lunar, which is when there is always a full moon present and Solar, where daytime briefly turns to darkness. I think dad was referring to a Solar eclipse!"

Just at that moment Jasmine came into the room carrying her laptop.

"I think you could be on to something there," stated Max.

"Yes, but what does an eclipse have to do with numbers?" Asked Jasmine.

"That's what this guy on TV was explaining, I started writing it down, but I couldn't keep up with him, but I'm sure we can look it up on the computer."

Jasmine sat down and typed Solar eclipse into the search field.

"It says here a total Solar eclipse can be up to 200 miles wide and never covers more than 1.5% of the Earth's surface, with fewer than 70 total eclipses per century, it goes on further, but there is no other mention of numbers."

"I get 200, 1.5% and 70. Do you think it might be another co-ordinate?" Asked Deanne.

"I think you've just figured out your access code at the bank." Stated Max.

"What makes you think that?" Asked Jasmine.

"Well he has already given us the co-ordinates for the bank that hold a Security box for Deanne, which requires an access code that I think is 200.1.5.70."

"Of course!" Exclaimed Jasmine.

"What if it's wrong, what will happen if I give them these numbers and they're incorrect?"

"Don't panic, I'm sure they have had situations where people have forgotten their access code before, people forget their pin code on their ATM cards all the time. If the number is wrong, just tell them your father gave it to you so long ago you must have got it mixed up. They will have already viewed your

ID to know you are in fact Deanne Jones. Just tell them you'll have to have a rethink and come back another time," said Max.

"Now I'm scared."

"Deanne relax, you'll be fine," reassured Jasmine.

STEEL JUSTICE

CHAPTER NINETEEN

Max had to drive around the block a few times before he could find a parking space close to the bank and by now Deanne was starting to feel sick to her stomach, her palms were sweating and she felt faint. Jasmine looked towards her as they walked through the bank entrance and noticed not only her pale pallor, but she was notably shaking.

"Deanne it's ok, there's no need to be nervous."

"I can't help it, what if I was wrong and the numbers are incorrect?"

"Remember we discussed this last night, people forget their pin codes all the time. Look there's the Enquiry desk, just take a deep breath and please try not to look so nervous!"

They waited in line and by the time the woman called them up to the desk Jasmine could see Deanne was incapable of speech, so she explained that her friend was here to view her security box. The woman smiled at Deanne and asked for her name and proof of identity. The woman quickly scanned the documentation before typing on her computer keyboard; Jasmine quickly turned to see where Max had gone and was annoyed to see he had taken a seat near the entrance. The woman seemed to take an age, staring at the computer and down at the papers Deanne had given her, a faint flicker of panic washed over her, causing her to reach out and squeeze Deanne's hand.

"Right then, everything appears to be in order, if you'll just follow me I will take you to a private room," said the woman.

Both girls moved in the direction she indicated, when the woman suddenly turned and looked at Jasmine.

"I'm afraid you'll have to wait for your friend here, only the owner of the box is allowed beyond this point."

By now Deanne was sure she was going to be physically sick and nervously followed the woman into an anteroom and over towards a door that had a keypad.

"Just enter your five digit pass code and press enter, this will take you into a private room where another Bank Officer will look after you."

Deanne immediately panicked, she had figured on there being seven numbers, not five *oh god what do I do now?* Stalling for time she stepped up close to the keypad, momentarily closing her eyes trying to decide what to do, then grit her teeth and quickly punched five numbers into the keypad and hit the enter button, holding her breath expecting alarms to sound at any moment. Suddenly there was a loud beep that caused her to jump and then the sound of the door clicking open. Deanne barely contained herself from exclaiming a sigh of relief before walking inside the room, moments later the door closed behind her.

The room consisted of merely a single table and chair, making Deanne wonder if she had been led to some sort of interrogation room. Too nervous to sit, she stood with her arms folded tightly across her chest and when she heard the sound of an adjoining door to the room open, she backed up hard against the wall.

To her relief a woman walked through the door carrying a shallow metal box that was about thirty centimetres long and fifteen centimetres wide and smiled at Deanne as she placed it on the table.

"To open the box, you'll need to enter your two-digit code, take as long as you like to view the contents or add any other items, or perhaps you may wish to take them with you. If you decide to keep them lodged here, just push the buzzer and I'll put the box back into secure holding."

"Do I need another pass code to exit the room?"

"No, you only need a code upon entry."

"Thank you."

Deanne waited until the woman left the room and then keyed in the remaining two numbers she had memorised, she let out a great sigh of relief when she heard a loud click as the lid unlocked. With shaky hands she opened the lid to its full extent, inside were three envelopes, one contained old newspaper clippings, the second contained copies of bank statements and the third held a single sheet of paper that had a number written on it.

She leaned back in her chair feeling a sense of disappointment, she had pinned her hopes on this box containing all the answers to her questions, but felt her father had just left her another series of riddles to solve. Realising that Jasmine and Max were waiting outside, she quickly slipped the envelopes inside her bag and relocked the box, even though it was empty. With all that had happened to date she decided to keep the pretence that its contents were still held in the security of the bank.

It seemed like mere seconds after pushing the buzzer the woman returned to the room, making Deanne wonder if she had been waiting the whole time on the other side of the door and hoping she had not been able to view what she had done with the contents. As soon as the woman left the room, Deanne quickly opened the secure door and made her way towards Max and Jasmine, who upon seeing her, rose anxiously from her chair.

"How did you go?" Asked Jasmine.

"Not sure, can we get out of here?"

"Ah, ok." Jasmine sensed something was wrong.

All three walked out into the hot sun and made their way towards the car park; no one said a word until they were in the safe confines of the car. Max quickly turned on the car and boosted up the air-conditioning, before turning around to Deanne.

"I'm guessing you didn't find what you were looking for?"

"How did you know?"

"Facial expressions and body language can tell a lot."

"God I hope the woman in the bank couldn't read me like you did!"

"Why?" Asked Jasmine.

"Because I gave her an empty box to place back into secure

holding!"

Both Jasmine and Max laughed.

"Clever girl, what made you decide to do that?" Asked Max.

"I don't know, gut instinct I suppose."

"Did you have any trouble with the pass-code?" Asked Jasmine.

"Oh god I was so scared when the woman told me I had to enter a five digit code to enter the room, I thought my heart was going to jump out of my throat, because I had calculated seven. I began to panic and then I remembered you said people forget their pin codes all the time, so I thought I would try leaving off the last two digits and it worked."

"Good girl!" Jasmine and Max said in unison.

"I was waiting for an alarm to go off, I was so scared and then, while I was waiting for the box to be brought through to me, I wondered what the other two numbers where for, I soon found out I needed a two digit code to open the box."

"Well don't keep us in suspense, what was inside?" Asked Max.

Deanne pulled the envelopes out of her bag and handed them across to him, both girls waited in silence while he scanned the contents of all three envelopes.

"Well the old paper clippings are death notices and from what I can gather all these people were elderly, as for the bank statements they show large deposits were made, which makes me wonder if there is a connection between the deaths and this bank account. As for this number written on this piece of paper, I'm guessing it is a phone number."

"Wow that was quick; I stared at it for ages and couldn't make head nor tale of it. Should we try the phone number?" Asked Deanne.

"Not yet, I'd like to delve more into these death notices and bank accounts first before I make any phone calls, I would like to have some idea of who the person is on the other end."

When they arrived back at Max's house he suggested they

start with the paper clippings and divided them between them.

"Deanne as you don't have a computer you can use my laptop." Max stated.

"How do you propose we go about this?" Asked Jasmine.

"Simple, start with an internet search, see if we get any hits."

Jasmine was wishing she hadn't asked the question, because she knew by the way he was looking at her he was questioning her ability as an investigative reporter. Ignoring his pointed gaze, she quickly logged into her laptop and typed in the name Edwina Mary Dolton and was surprised at how many entries there were and proceeded to read through each one.

She was almost to the bottom of page five and was starting to think it was a waste of time, her neck and shoulders were sore from hunching over the laptop sitting low in her lap, when she found something on the bottom of the page. She quickly read it and made a few notes, then decided to try a new search.

"I might have found something here."

"God I hope so, I'm not having any luck so far!" Exclaimed Deanne.

"Ok, first of all I found this, *Seeking Leanne Mary Dolton, daughter of Edwina Mary Dolton, please contact Everglades Nursing Home.* It was an advert placed in the Sydney Morning Herald. Now I know that doesn't mean much, but I decided to do a search on Leanne Mary Dolton and came across this article. *Leanne Mary Dolton loses court battle to claim her inheritance*; it goes on to say that her mother Edwina Mary Dolton left her entire Estate to a nurse at the Everglades nursing home."

"Does it state how much the inheritance was worth?" Asked Max.

"Not on that particular one, I'll try the other papers, hopefully we'll get a more in-depth story."

"Actually I didn't think it was much at the time, but when I looked up Reymont Skinner, it also stated he left his entire fortune to a nurse."

"I think we have just found our connection to these paper clippings, I'll bet all of them read along the same line. Let's try cross referencing the death notices with when the large deposits were made." Max suggested.

"Ah that's not going to work, as in the instance of Edwina Mary Dolton, her daughter contested the will, there's no telling how long that went for!" Stated Jasmine.

"What about the date of the article where it states she lost everything to the nurse?"

"Ah, let me see. November twenty eight, nineteen ninety two."

"There was a large deposit made on the thirty first of March nineteen ninety four, I suppose with such a large inheritance its possible it took that long," suggested Max.

"You could be right; after all you have to admit it is rather a coincidence that these two elderly people left their entire Estate to a nurse. Deanne could you find anything else on Reymont Skinner, was there any mention of the nurse's name or if the Will was contested?" Asked Jasmine.

"Not that I could find."

"Is there a date on that article?" Asked Max.

"Ah, twenty seventh of January, nineteen ninety."

"There was a large deposit made six months later."

"I just thought of something else, Reymont Skinner left his Estate, presumably to the same nurse, why was that not mentioned in the court case regarding the Estate of Edwina Mary Dolton?" Asked Deanne.

"Good point, perhaps our nurse was using a fake identity," commented Max.

"Well while you two were talking I checked the other two names, they pretty much all read the same, apart from the Will being contested, looks like Edwina's was the only one," stated Jasmine.

"I think we all agree these bank statements, belong to our mystery nurse and I bet she is connected with the guy in the photo, which was enclosed in the letter your father left in the fireplace," said Max.

"I have no idea who the man is, but there is only one woman's name that comes to my mind that was devious enough to be the nurse!" Exclaimed Deanne.

"You're thinking of Salina, aren't you?" Asked Jasmine.

"Well she was studying at the same university as my father, my father's death was made to look like a heart attack, so I'm guessing she had medical knowledge. Who's to say she didn't actually kill off these old people for their money, all of them were quite elderly, perhaps they didn't bother with an autopsy because of their age?"

"You could be onto something there," said Max.

"Is there any way we can find out who owned these bank accounts?" Asked Deanne.

"There probably is, but I doubt it would do us any good, especially if she was using assumed names," said Max.

"So what do we do now?" Asked Deanne.

"I'm going to follow my hunch and dial that number that was in the third envelope."

Both girls sat silently as Max dialled the number, Deanne crossed her fingers for good luck, but moments later her shoulders slumped when she heard Max speak into the phone.

"Sorry, I must have called the wrong number."

"Did they say a name?" Asked Jasmine.

"Yes as a matter of fact, it was a receptionist by the name of Debbie for a Dr Cook."

This immediately got Deanne's attention.

"If he was a doctor, he had to have known my father!"

"It's possible."

"Why did you hang up, why not ask to speak to him?" Asked Jasmine.

"I thought it would be better if you did; the face of Frontline News!"

Jasmine wasn't sure if he was being sarcastic, but she had to agree he did have a point, her name and face were well known, what better way to ensure the man gave them an audience.

"Ok, give me that number."

Jasmine quickly dialled the number, which was answered on the third ring.

"Good afternoon, Dr Cook's surgery, Debbie speaking."

"Hello Debbie, I was wondering if it was possible to speak to the doctor."

"He is rather busy, what is the nature of your call?"

"It's kind of complicated, look my name is Jasmine Bronson and I was hoping…"

"Did you say Jasmine Bronson?"

"Yes, of Frontline News…"

"Oh my god, I can't believe I'm actually talking to you on the phone, I watch your show all the time…"

"I don't want to be rude but is it possible to speak to the doctor?"

"Oh yes of course, I'll just switch you through."

"Dr Cook speaking."

Jasmine could tell by his voice he was getting on in years and was surprised he was still practicing. She didn't bother introducing herself, as she was sure his excited receptionist had already done so.

"Dr Cook, I am working on a case regarding Dr Robert Shoal, did you by chance know him?" Asked Jasmine

"Yes I did, he was a good friend as a matter of fact?"

"I was wondering if I could meet with you. It is very important."

"You said case, what is this all about?"

"I don't want to say too much over the phone, but it's in regards Dr Shoal's daughter, I'm not sure if he mentioned her to you at all."

"How about you come to my office, the day after tomorrow," suggested Doctor Cook

"Thank you, but just where is your office located exactly, I'm currently in North Queensland?"

"Have you ever heard of a country town called Cowra?"

"It's outside Sydney?"

"A good four hours' drive from Sydney, I'm assuming you would be flying out of Cairns."

"Yes."

"I suggest you get a direct flight from there to Orange, you can hire a car from there; it's a lovely drive, less than ninety km away."

"So you're saying there aren't any direct flights to Cowra?"

"We do have a local airstrip but flights are limited, your best bet would be via Orange."

"I'll check the available fights and get back to you."

"If I'm with a patient you can leave the details with my receptionist Debbie."

"I shall."

As Jasmine disconnected the call, she realised Max was already checking the flights from Cairns to Orange.

"Did he know my father?"

"Yes he did as a matter of fact; he said he was a good friend."

"Finally we can speak to a person, no more riddles!" Exclaimed Deanne.

"Don't get your hopes up just yet, he might just have another clue to steer us in the right direction."

Before Deanne could comment her phone rang, almost causing her to jump out of her skin, the only person she spoke to on it was her aunt and Deanne always called her.

"Hello," she said hesitantly.

"Yes it is."

"Oh my god, is she ok?"

Both Max and Jasmine looked towards Deanne and they could see she was visibly upset.

"Can I speak to her?"

Deanne started to cry and had trouble speaking into the phone, so Jasmine put her arm around her and took the phone from her.

"Hello Jasmine here, I'm a friend of Deanne's, she's too

upset to talk at the moment, can I help."

"My name is Rita, I'm a nurse at the local hospital in Fig Tree Grove, her aunt was involved in a house fire and is suffering from severe smoke inhalation and is currently unable to talk, she was quite distressed and we couldn't calm her down until I made this call to ensure her niece was safe and well."

"Apart from being upset by the news, she is fine. Do you know if there was much damage to her aunt's house?"

"The fire wasn't at her aunt's house, it was her house, apparently her aunt was there checking up on things for her while she was away."

"Oh my god, do you have any idea how it started?" Jasmine looked from Deanne to Max.

"I probably shouldn't be saying this, but being a small town, people talk. Apparently the fire started in the front of the house and she was rescued, thanks to the quick thinking of a neighbour."

"Was she caught in the front section where the fire was?"

"No, she was trying to get out via the back door, but apparently someone had wedged something in the handle from the outside so it wouldn't open."

"Oh my god! Did you tell Deanne this?"

"No, I didn't want to distress her too much; the main reason for the call was her aunt would not calm down until I made the call."

"Is she still awake?"

"Yes, but the sedative is starting to take effect."

"Can you hold the phone to her ear?"

"Ok, give me a moment. You can speak now."

"Jan it's me Jasmine, I promise you Deanne is safe and well, so you rest up and do as the doctor says. We'll call you tomorrow."

"She's nodding her head and smiling, so I'll let you go now," said the nurse.

"Thank you Rita, we'll call for an update tomorrow morning."

Jasmine hung up and paced the room.

"You care to fill me in?" Asked Max.

Jasmine looked across at Deanne and wondered if she should explain the full extent of what happened in front of her, but then realised she would find out soon enough.

"Deanne's aunt is in hospital suffering smoke inhalation from a house fire, but it wasn't her house."

"What!" Deanne quickly jumped to her feet.

"I'm sorry to tell you this, but the fire was at your house, your aunt was keeping an eye on things for you while you were away. According to the nurse, the fire was deliberately lit."

"What makes her think that?" Asked Max.

"Apparently the fire happened in the front of the house, her aunt could have got out via the back door, only thing; someone had wedged the handle so she couldn't open the door."

"Oh my god, someone tried to murder her!" Exclaimed Deanne.

"I think your aunt believes you were the intended target, no one knows you have left town."

Deanne's face visibly paled, causing Jasmine to walk over and put her arm around her.

"Ok change of plans, we might have to put off a visit to Dr Cook for a day or so…"

"Why?" Both girls asked in unison.

"To go and collect Deanne's aunt, I think the safest place for both Deanne and her aunt is here. I for one cannot focus on the job at hand if I have to take on the role of a babysitter. No offense Deanne, but my main focus is finding my daughter and to find her I need to find Salina, I believe your father is the key."

Jasmine looked at Max in a state of shock, she couldn't believe he had been so callous in his comments, especially after the news she had just received about her aunt and the fact someone had tried to kill her believing it was Deanne inside.

"It's ok Jasmine, don't get angry at Max, he's right, I'm not cut out for this sort of stuff. Yes I want to solve my father's riddle and uncover what he was trying to tell me, but I know I would be more of a hindrance than help, besides, my aunt, my only remaining family member needs me. I would like to take up your offer Max, providing you're really ok with this!"

"My home is yours, under one condition."

"Which is?"

"While I am away you do not set foot off the property, you only answer the phone that I will leave with you and most definitely do not venture near the front gate."

"What if we need to go to the store for food?"

"Follow me."

Both girls followed Max, Jasmine was really curious because she hadn't been game to explore the house for fear of being kicked out with his large size ten's. He took them through a door that led off the kitchen and both girls jaws dropped at what they saw. It was as if he had his own supermarket built into his house, one half of the large area consisted of shelves full of dry goods, everything from food products to toiletry items, even certain items that a woman would require. Jasmine surprisingly felt a stab of jealousy and then remembered his daughter had lived here also. The other half of the area consisted of glass doors that held all the freezer and cold goods and just when they though it couldn't get any better, he led them through another door that was stocked full of beer and wine.

"God you could live here for a year without venturing outside the front gates!" Exclaimed Deanne.

"That's the whole idea."

"Ah but your forgetting something," stated Jasmine.

Max looked at her pointedly.

"Medical supplies, what if you get sick or suffer an injury?"

"Follow me."

Jasmine looked at Deanne who shrugged her shoulders and both quickly followed him. He opened a door to what appeared to be a large linen cupboard, but inside were neatly stacked shelves of a miniature chemist.

"How the hell did you get this much medication in here without having the drug squad busting down your doors?" Asked Jasmine.

"Don't ask, which brings me to the question, Deanne, I need to know of any medications you or your aunt take and I won't take kindly to you leaving anything out. I don't care if it is treatment for herpes, or the contraceptive pill, if it is something that you can't live without in the next twelve months I need to know!"

"Are you planning on keeping her prisoner here for the next twelve months?" Jasmine asked incredulously.

"She will not be a prisoner and I certainly hope it won't take twelve months to solve this, but we have to be prepared for the worst case scenario."

Both Jasmine and Deanne looked at Max and wondered if this was what it was like to be one of the men in his platoon and then Jasmine's mind wandered to Michelle, *no wonder she pushed the boundaries!*

CHAPTER TWENTY

After Max dropped Jasmine and Deanne off at the small hospital in Fig Tree Grove, he drove the short distance to Deanne's house, as he wanted to assess the damage for himself, hoping to gain some idea of the type of people they were dealing with. As the house came into view he could see a large blackened hole in the front section of the house, doubting any chance of restoration.

He walked through the small front gate, looking for signs of accelerant, he noticed a large red blob of melted plastic amongst the charred remains of what was once the front porch, on closer examination he was almost certain it was a jerry can and he could smell the distinct odour of petrol.

"Can I ask what you are doing?"

Max turned to see a man wearing overalls and knew instantly he was a fire investigator; he rose quickly to his feet and held out his hand.

"My name's Max, I'm a good friend of Deanne Jones, this is, or should I say was her house."

"John."

Both men shook hands and then Max handed him the remnants of the jerry can.

"This is not the work of a pro," commented Max.

"You in this line of work?"

"No, but I've seen it often enough."

"So you're a cop."

"Retired."

"Half your luck, I've got a few years to go yet."

"What are your thoughts on what happened here?"

"Well I'll have to admit this one has me concerned, the M.O. clearly points to the work of juveniles, but never while the place is occupied, let alone deliberately trapping aunt Jan inside."

"I was under the impression Deanne is her only living

relative," Max said in surprise.

"She is, but everyone calls her Aunt Jan. When I was a young tacker I used to play cricket in the street with all the other kids, she would always bring out homemade lemonade and cookies. I'll tell you the whole town is reeling that someone tried to kill her!"

"I don't think she was the intended target."

"Then who?"

"Her niece, after all this is her house."

"You any idea why?"

"None whatsoever!"

Max wasn't about to voice what he knew to John, or anyone else in this town, least not until he had more of an idea who they were dealing with.

"By the way, how is Jan doing?"

"She's a tough old bird, speaking of which, I'm supposed to be taking her and her niece on a little vacation to rest and recuperate."

"Good for you and tell her John wishes her a speedy recovery."

"Will do."

Max headed back towards his car, he had learnt all he was going to here. He called Jasmine to let her know he would be outside the hospital entrance shortly; he wanted to ensure Deanne's aunt was well and truly settled in the security of his home, before he and Jasmine left early the following morning.

Max had barely pulled the car to a halt, when Jasmine and Deanne walked out the entrance, pushing Aunt Jan in a wheelchair. He quickly got out of the car and offered his assistance to the woman, as he gently took hold of her arm she surprised him, by giving him an all-embracing hug.

"Thank you," she said hoarsely with tears in her eyes.

"The pleasure is all mine," he said with a dazzling smile.

Jasmine looked at him and realised it was the first time she had actually seen him smile, but what surprised her was how aunt Jan managed to have him wrapped around her little finger so easily.

The following morning on the drive to Cairns Airport, the conversation was stilted, Jasmine asked him about the state of Deanne's house and whether he had found any clues that would lead to the perpetrator.

"I'm guessing it's going to be condemned, as for clues, it looks like kids."

"You're joking!"

"You really think I would joke about this?"

"I didn't mean…oh forget it!"

Jasmine was angry, it didn't matter what she said or did, Max always managed to turn it against her. *God how many times does a girl have to say sorry?*

The rest of the journey was spent in silence and neither said a word to each other until Max loaded their luggage into the hire car at Orange Airport.

"I don't know how long this is going to take, so I've booked us a motel room at Cowra for a couple of nights."

"Separate rooms I hope!"

"Need you ask?"

To Jasmine's annoyance, she felt her cheeks go hot and angrily slammed the car door as she got in, swearing to herself she was not going to speak to him again unless it was absolutely necessary.

Dr Cook's house was a quaint little low set, white weatherboard house, surrounded by the most beautiful garden and as Max turned the car into the driveway, Jasmine saw a man with a head of thick white hair, pruning a rosebush; he looked to be in his late sixties. He looked across at them and smiled, but continued with what he was doing. Not sure if this gentleman was in fact Dr Cook, she smiled at him as she got out of the car.

"You have such a lovely garden."

"Yes, it was a favourite pastime of my wife, I'm afraid I just don't have the green thumb she did, she's been gone nearly a year now."

"I'm sorry to hear that, ah I suppose I should introduce myself, I'm Jasmine Bro..."

"Bronson, yes I would recognise your face anywhere and I suppose the handsome chap is your husband?"

Jasmine nearly choked at his comment and before she could reply, Max stepped forward.

"No, I'm here on behalf of Deanne who is nursing her sick aunt at the moment. My name's Max."

"Pleased to meet you Max, now when you say sick aunt, are you referring to Jan?"

"Oh, so you know her."

"I only met her once, but Robert talked fondly of her, I hope it's nothing serious."

"No she's fine, currently enjoying the spoils of Far North Queensland," replied Max.

"Good for her, would either of you like a cup of coffee? I know I need one."

"Sounds great, what they serve you on the plane is totally undrinkable!" Said Max

"I don't fly too often, but on the few occasions I have, I would have to agree with you."

Even though he hadn't officially introduced himself, both Max and Jasmine assumed him to be Dr Cook, especially after his reference to Jan and Robert. He directed them to the lounge room and then disappeared to make the coffee.

He later walked back in carrying a tray of coffee and biscuits, after pouring the steaming hot liquid into three cups, Jasmine watched as he sat down in his chair and took a long appreciative drink of the hot brew, before placing his cup back on the table.

"Ah, that's better, now we can get down to business. Miss Bronson..."

"Please, call me Jasmine."

"Jasmine, I was wondering what led you to call me?"

"It was actually Deanne, to cut a long story short, she found a letter her father had hidden in the fireplace of the house he'd bequeathed her, or should I say riddle, which led her to a security box at the bank. It contained three envelopes, one had your phone number."

Both Jasmine and Max watched as he mulled this over for a few minutes before he spoke.

"It's such a shame he died before he could meet her, he never gave up on her. After Mary disappeared, that's Deanne's mother…"

"Disappeared?" Asked Max.

"I'll explain later, carry on Dr Cook," she said quickly.

"Robert just fell to pieces, he couldn't understand what he had done wrong, he took solace from the bottom of a bottle and then Salina came along. Both myself and my wife were relieved, she pulled him from the pits of despair and got him back on the straight and narrow, unfortunately she was a wolf in sheep's clothing."

"So we've heard!" Commented Max.

"Yes well, when Robert discovered he had a daughter, he hired a private detective to find her, but Mary had gone to great lengths to keep their whereabouts unknown. It wasn't long before his death he told me he was almost certain Salina was the reason Mary fled."

"Dr Cook, do you believe Robert Shoal died of a heart attack?" Asked Jasmine.

"No, but then the autopsy report proved otherwise."

"What about the possibility of it being fudged to make it look like a heart attack?" Asked Max.

"I'm afraid not, I myself read the report, but also I knew the doctor who performed the autopsy, he was also a good friend of Robert's, in fact he insisted on doing the procedure, he needed to see with his own eyes there was no foul play."

"Ok so it was proven beyond a doubt what caused his death, why do I get the impression you don't believe it?" Asked Max.

"Will you just excuse me a moment?"

Before either Jasmine or Max could respond, Dr Cook rose

from his chair and left the room, only to return moments later carrying a leather satchel. Both waited for him to speak, but he calmly sat down and took another long drink from his coffee, Jasmine's curiosity was almost getting the better of her and she had to restrain herself from asking him what the satchel contained.

"Nothing like a good coffee. Now where were we?"

"I asked you why you don't believe the autopsy report," stated Max.

"Firstly he was as fit as a fiddle, but more so the last conversation I had with him, it was the day he gave me this," he said as he pointed to the leather satchel.

"What did he say?" Both Max and Jasmine asked in unison.

"Firstly he told me he did something that went against all his beliefs, but he did it to protect his daughter."

"Did you ask him what it was?" Asked Jasmine.

"Yes, but he said he would be endangering my life if he told me, so to this day I don't know what it was. He also told me that he felt he was living on borrowed time and his only priority was to ensure his daughter's future was taken care of, financially, but also her safety."

"He actually said that to you?" Asked Max.

"Yes, he warned me a very dangerous woman seeks what the satchel contains, so I must be careful who I pass it on to."

"How do you know I'm not that woman, yes everyone knows my face, but how do you know I am working for the benefit of Deanne?" Asked Jasmine.

"You mentioned the letter in the fireplace, he told me this, but also that fireplace was expertly hidden behind a wall and he had left subtle clues for his daughter to find it."

"Are you aware that there was recently a fire in that house, the reason aunt Jan was in hospital?" Asked Max.

The doctor physically paled and Jasmine glared at him.

"I'm sorry to hit you with the news this way doc, but I learnt a long time ago to trust no one!"

"Young man I can see you have a lot of hurt and hate pent

up inside you, but I follow a different rule, my instincts have never proven me wrong and my instincts tell me I can trust Jasmine. I have a lot of years on you and despite the façade she shows the world, underneath she's not as tough as she would like us to think, she genuinely cares about people. By the way Jasmine I watched that programme you did exposing the prostitution ring, involving innocent young girls; that really took a lot of guts!"

"Thank you."

"Now Max if you've finished interrupting, we can continue our discussion."

Jasmine wanted to kiss the old man, but resorted to putting her hand over her mouth to cover her smile. Suddenly she realised Dr Cook was looking at her expectantly and quickly regained composure and resumed her questioning.

"Why did you agree to safeguard the satchel, when it meant putting not only your life but your wife's in jeopardy?" Asked Jasmine.

"I assure you, I didn't take his request lightly, I told him I needed time to think, but also I had to discuss it with Edith, my wife."

"How did he take this?"

"He understood."

"Dr Cook, can I just ask you, what's in the satchel that made you, even consider putting your wife and yourself in danger?" Asked Jasmine.

"I don't know."

"You're kidding me, how could you even consider what he was asking without knowing what was inside?" Asked Max incredulously.

"Despite Robert being a good friend, I am not a fool, I knew there was a difference between guarding the satchel and actually seeing its contents; I simply asked him what was inside."

"What did he say?" Both Max and Jasmine asked in unison.

"He said it was his daughter's life."

"That could mean so many things," said Max.

"Exactly what I said to him, he then said and I quote. *The contents of this satchel are the surety that Justice is served and my daughter lives another day.* A comment I could not take lightly."

"If the contents of this satchel are so damning, why didn't he just go to the police?" Asked Jasmine.

"From the little Robert told me, I don't think it was that simple, they managed to coerce him to do something that could possibly incriminate himself, also he said these people were not only very dangerous but clever."

Dr Cook handed the leather satchel to Jasmine.

"Do you have any qualms about me opening it in front of you, or would you prefer I wait till I get back to my motel room?"

"I am no longer threatened by what it contains, my dear Edith is now passed and to be honest I am a little curious."

She smiled at him before untying the satchel and pulling out the contents, which consisted of a magazine, a newspaper clipping and Doctor's Reports. Jasmine spread them all out on the table, so they could all view them.

"Doctor with your expertise could you explain what these reports mean?"

"Certainly."

Max picked up the magazine and flicked through it, while Jasmine read the newspaper clipping.

"Oh my god!"

"What is it?" Asked Max.

"I think we have found our nurse, listen to this. Alison Grady, a former nurse of the Everglades Nursing home, was released from Long Bay Woman's Detention Centre today. All charges against her for the death of Edwina Mary Dolton, a former patient at the Everglades nursing home, have been quashed."

"I'll bet my last dollar she was also responsible for those other deaths!" Exclaimed Max.

"Jasmine these reports you gave me are actually autopsy reports, all the patients were elderly and surprisingly they all died of a heart attack." He said as he placed the documents back on the table.

"Is it normal, to conduct an autopsy on an elderly patient, who was in a nursing home?" Asked Max

"Not unless it is specifically requested by a relative, or there are signs of foul play," said Dr Cook

Jasmine suddenly had a thought and quickly pulled her note pad out of her briefcase; she flicked through the pages until she found what she was looking for and then cross-referenced her notes with the reports.

"The names on the reports are a match to the newspaper clippings that were in the security box. Is this what Dr Shoal was involved in, is this why he was murdered?"

"Robert would never agree to such a thing, I refuse to believe it!" Exclaimed the doctor.

"You yourself said he was involved in something that went against his beliefs," stated Jasmine.

"I know, but not this, he would never be a party to murder!"

"I tend to agree with the doctor, firstly look at the dates, this was years before he died, secondly one of those deaths was already questioned and all charges quashed, I think it was something else and somehow this nurse was involved," commented Max.

"God if only he had left us a photo like he did with that first letter!" Exclaimed Jasmine.

"I think he did."

Max handed her the magazine he had been flipping through and pointed to a particular page.

"It's an article about the opening of the Everglades Nursing home, including a photo of the staff at the time, take note of the name underlined," he said as he handed her the magazine.

"Oh my god, its Salina!"

"May I have a look?" Asked the doctor.

Jasmine handed the magazine across to him and upon scanning the photo he nodded his head.

"I met Salina on more than one occasion and yes Jasmine is right, Alison Grady is the woman I knew as Salina."

"So somehow the death of Dr Shoal and your missing daughter are connected," commented Jasmine.

"It appears so," replied Max.

"Would someone care to fill me in?" Asked the doctor.

"The program I did about the young girls, there was a woman the girls referred to as the 'Mistress'. I had a small camera disguised as a pendant, later on viewing the photos there was an out of focus image of a girl that wasn't amongst those rescued, both Max and I believe this girl is his missing daughter Michelle, also in the photo was the 'Mistress'; Deanne identified her as Salina."

"May I see this photo?"

Jasmine opened her briefcase and handed the photo to the doctor. On viewing it he shook his head and sighed.

"Now I understand why you two are working together and yes, I agree with Deanne, this is Salina."

"Ok so we know Dr Shoal is trying to tell us Salina has a dark side, these reports state all the people who bequeathed their Estate to her and died of a heart attack, including Dr Shoal, so how does a heart attack become murder? Asked Jasmine

"I might be able to help you there, years ago there was an experimental drug, it was believed to be a cure for arthritis, unfortunately it had severe side effects, and one of them being cardiac arrest, the program was scrapped."

"Perhaps he was involved in this program and it played on his conscience," suggested Jasmine.

"As far as I know, Robert was never involved in any experimental drug; it was not his field of medicine. Besides he said he was forced to do something to protect his daughter, this program was legal and above board."

"Ok if these people were given this drug, why wasn't it

detected in the autopsies?" Asked Max

"The drug is virtually undetectable, unless one was specifically tested for it, it won't show up in the normal tox screen. As it was only in the experimental stages, it was not available on the market, many didn't even know of its existence," explained Dr Cook

"I wonder if it is possible to find out who was involved in this program," asked Max.

"It wouldn't be easy and I doubt I would have any sway, I'm just your everyday GP."

"More up your alley Max," commented Jasmine.

Max looked across at Jasmine, something the doctor noticed, making him wonder who this Max character was and if in fact that was his real name.

"What if we have the bodies exhumed and tested for this drug?" Asked Jasmine.

"Firstly you would need a court order and secondly they would need the drug to cross reference with, there is a good chance it was all destroyed," commented the doctor.

"Hmm, I suppose you're right."

"Well I think we have taken up enough of the good doctor's time and we do have an early flight in the morning," said Max as he rose from his chair.

Jasmine looked at Max with a puzzled look on her face, she was sure the return flight wasn't until the day after the next. He stared pointedly at her for a moment and she knew he didn't want to be questioned on this, especially in front of the doctor. She quickly replaced the contents of the leather satchel and was about to place it in her briefcase when she looked up at the doctor.

"Is it ok if I take this?"

"It's all yours; I was just safeguarding it for Robert until the rightful owner came along."

"Thank you for your hospitality and I'm sure Deanne would like me to pass on her thanks for all you have done," said Jasmine.

He walked them out to the car and Jasmine waited until his house was out of sight before she spoke.

"What's with the dark looks and the lie about us leaving early tomorrow?"

"Firstly I think we had used up enough of the good doctor's time and secondly I always stick to the rule of keeping my future plans close to my chest, its saved my bacon on more than one occasion."

"As I am also involved in the equation, are we leaving tomorrow, or do we leave the following day as originally planned?"

"We'll see."

"This is ridiculous, why can't you tell me?"

"Because I haven't decided yet."

Jasmine closed her eyes in frustration, *god this man can be so infuriating!* She mentally went over everything they had uncovered so far and was certain beyond any doubt, Salina was involved in the deaths of the elderly people. According to the bank statements, she had amassed a small fortune from their Estates. The more she thought about Salina the more puzzled she became, *with all this money, why the need to resort to the prostitution of young girls, was this what she threatened Dr Shoal would happen to his young daughter and who was the man in the photo, how did he fit in?* Jasmine had been so deep in thought she hadn't realised Max had stopped the vehicle.

"You obviously find all this tiring; perhaps you should take a nap."

Jasmine quickly opened her eyes and realised they were parked in the parking lot of the local motel.

"I am not tired, I was thinking!"

"Whatever you say, here's your key, and I hope you're not superstitious."

"Why?"

"Thirteen, your room number."

Jasmine looked at the key in her hand for a moment.

"Why is there a B after the number, what does that mean?"

"I don't know, just be thankful we got the last two rooms available, if it is any consolation, mine has an A after it."

Yeah and I can think of a couple of things that would stand for! Jasmine decided she needed to clear her head and the only thing for that was a run, as soon as she put her things in her room; she changed into her running gear.

Jasmine had no idea of the layout of the town, but felt sure she wouldn't get lost; the worst-case scenario was she could always ask someone for directions back to her motel. As always, she ran with her phone which doubled as an iPod, clipped to the waistband of her shorts, the music helped her keep her pace, but also her boss expected her to be contactable at all times.

After about an hour, she came to realise the town of Cowra was full of very friendly people, she couldn't believe how many perfect strangers smiled and waved at her, she had tied her hair in a ponytail and was wearing dark glasses, so she knew no one recognised her face. Feeling she had released the tension from her body, she slowed down to a walk and made her way back to the motel, when her phone rang.

"Jasmine, long time - no hear. Care to fill me in?"

"Jodi, sorry, it's been kind of crazy, when I said this one was going to be big, I was wrong. It's going to be huge!"

"Really, what did you find out?"

"Well I'm walking back to my motel room at the moment, so I'll have to be careful what I say, but firstly, we can definitely do a follow up on my last story, oh my god this woman, I've uncovered stuff that goes back years!"

"Are you referring to the elusive 'Mistress'?"

"Yes, it's going to blow your mind!"

"Really, do you think we could get a couple of shows from it?"

"A couple, the more I dig the more I find, like I said this is huge, there could be enough stuff here to run a whole season!"

Jasmine had made it back to her motel room and fumbled in her pocket for her key, once inside she quickly removed her shoes and socks while trying to end the call to Jodi, her body now in a lather of sweat and in desperate need of a shower.

"Jodi…"

"Are you referring to the illegal prostitution ring, or are there other aspects of the story?"

Jasmine pushed open the bathroom door and was surprised to hear the sound of running water and turned towards the shower.

"Jas, are you still there?"

Jasmine now understood why there was an A on her key and a B on Max's, the rooms were separated by an adjoining bathroom, which was currently occupied by Max. He was unaware of her presence and she knew she should politely leave, but she could not take her eyes off the scene before her, mesmerized by the way the muscles moved across his back and in his arms as he shampooed his hair. Jasmine barely noticed Jodi's voice in her ear; she was more intent on looking at Max's perfect form, apart from a nasty scar to his left shoulder.

Aware of another presence in the room, Max suddenly turned and looked directly at her.

"Oh my god!" She said under her breath.

"Jasmine, what's going on, is everything ok?"

"Ah yeah, I'll have to call you back," she said before disconnecting the call.

She knew she should leave the room, but it was as if her feet were rooted to the floor.

"Either you get in, or get out!" Max exclaimed.

It was as if she no longer had control over her body, she slowly undressed while a distant voice screamed at her she had lost her mind. Now fully naked she walked as if in a trance towards the shower, Max taking an appreciated look at her as he opened the shower door.

The moment the stream of water hit her in the face, she came to her senses, but before she could exit the shower she felt a pair of large hands push her towards the shower wall. She was about to protest when those hands started to lather soap up and down her back, releasing all the knots and tension in her body.

She leaned willingly against the cool tiles and let out a soft moan, causing his hands to go lower, down over her hips and buttocks and then slowly down one leg. He never touched her in places a legit masseuse wouldn't, but the feel of his hands on her body caused her temperature to rise. Suddenly his hands worked their way back up her leg and she tensed in anticipation, but to her disappointment as he neared the uppermost of her inner thigh, he moved his hands across to her other leg and repeated what he had done on the other.

"Now my turn."

"What?" She said hoarsely.

"For a massage."

She stood and stared at his bare back for a few moments and then lathered her hands before placing them on his back, starting out very clinically, but soon the feel on his broad muscled back beneath her hands caused her movements to become more sensuous, moving down over his firm buttocks, making Max release a deep moan of pleasure.

Jasmine was so aroused she leaned into his body, moving her hands up over his shoulders, across his broad chest and travelled down his firm stomach, until she felt thick tight curls of hair, before she could go any lower his hand grabbed hold of her wrist.

By now her arousal and frustration were so great, her chest was heaving, and he turned quickly, taking her with him so that now her back was against the wall. Without taking his eyes off of hers, he lathered his hands with soap and then placed his hands just below her breasts, he moved his hands everywhere but where she wanted them, it was like a form of torture and she wondered if he had done this to his female prisoners.

When she thought she could take it no more, he suddenly lowered his head and sucked at the nipple of her left breast while massaging the other. The sheer pleasure caused her legs to buckle, making her grab his shoulders for support. She could feel his arousal pressed up against her, causing the heat to rise between her legs.

Suddenly his hand moved from her left breast, travelling down to the core of her arousal, causing her to climax immediately, she could barely breathe and was seeing spots before her eyes. Before she realised what was happening, Max had wrapped her in a towel and carried her through to her room and laid her down on the bed.

"I think it best if you get some rest."

"What?" She asked hoarsely.

"I don't know if you have a heart condition, but you nearly passed out on me just now."

"I can assure you I don't have a heart condition, maybe I overdid my run."

"Either way, I think it best we don't take things any further."

She watched his retreating back as he left the room and heard the adjoining bathroom door close softly.

"Rest he says, yeah right!"

She got up from the bed and threw on a pair of knickers and cotton camisole, feeling hunger pains as she had barely eaten all day, *no wonder I nearly passed out!* She looked at the selection of chips and nuts in the mini bar, but felt like something more substantial and looked through the list of local eateries that management had left in the room. She decided on ordering a pizza, not feeling like going out.

Once she placed her order, she opened her briefcase and proceeded to go through everything they had so far, trying to see what pieces of information fitted in with the riddle Dr Shoal had left Deanne.

Suddenly there was a knock and Jasmine instinctively looked towards the bathroom door.

"Is that you Max?"

"Ah, it's the pizza delivery."

"Just a minute."

Jasmine quickly pulled on a pair of shorts and t-shirt and as an afterthought, tied her hair in a ponytail before opening the door. She handed across a tip as she took hold of the pizza box and realised the young boy was staring at her.

"Is there something else?"

"You're not that girl off that TV show are you?"

"Really, who?"

"Um, Jasmine, Burns I think."

"Oh, you mean Jasmine Bronson, god if I got a dollar for every time someone asked me that, I'd be a millionaire by now!"

"God, you so look like her!"

"Here's another five bucks for the compliment."

"Jeez thanks!"

Jasmine quickly closed the door, not wanting the conversation to go any further and the smell of the pizza made her stomach rumble.

Hours later she looked at her watch and realised, it was almost one o'clock in the morning. She'd made countless notes, they'd already established Salina's involvement, but Jasmine also believed, Salina had somehow obtained the experimental drug Dr Cook had spoken of, using it not only for financial gain, but to silence Deanne's father. *What was Dr Shoal involved in that was worth killing for and who is the man in the photo?* Jasmine realised her brain was no longer capable of functioning without some sleep; she carefully placed all her notes and the contents of the leather satchel back in her briefcase.

It seemed like she had only just closed her eyes, when she was woken by the sound of her phone ringing, reaching for it in the darkness, she notice the bedside clock glowed 3am.

"Hello," said Jasmine sleepily.

"Sorry, did I wake you?"

"Tracey?"

"Yeah, I got your string of messages, sorry I've been undercover and I didn't realise the time."

Jasmine was now wide-awake and sat up in bed.

"So does the description of the guy Deanne described, match one of the murder victims?"

"Yeah."

"I knew it, but I don't think the link between Deanne's boss and the dead guy was paedophilia, I not sure if I told you, but we went to the shed and found evidence of drugs."

"Yeah you did."

"I kept the evidence I found and I'm sure your team would be able to find more evidence than I did."

"Already done."

"So have you arrested this guy?"

"I'm assuming you're talking about Deanne's boss Sam?"

"Of course."

"He's dead, apparently died of a massive overdose."

"Meaning he didn't really."

"Well let's just say, there was no evidence of him ever being a drug user, but we do believe he was using his shed to cut some very high grade cocaine."

"Holy shit! Any idea why someone wanted him dead?"

"I can't say too much, but I can tell you the Elvis looking dude Deanne described, he was somehow connected with Microbe, you know the guy…"

"Yeah I know; that story was my big break!"

"So where are you now?"

"Have you heard of a place called Cowra?"

"What the hell are you doing there?"

"Following a story and my god is this one a doozie!"

"Care to enlighten me?"

"I'm still trying to fit all the pieces together, but I am almost certain Michelle Brown is still alive."

"Why does that name ring a bell?"

"Her and her friend Jane, went missing off Eden Cove, they never found Michelle, Max Steel always blamed Malcolm Microbe. Well, it looks like this woman who was running that prostitution ring you and your guys busted, is holding her against her will."

"How the hell is that possible?"

"Apparently some illegal fishing boat caught her in their net, that's why it was never reported."

"Makes sense. Well I've got to go, keep me in the loop won't you?"

"Likewise."

The call was disconnected and Jasmine lay back against her pillows, but she was far from sleep, her mind was going over the things Tracey told her. She quickly jotted down a few things on her notepad, when suddenly another thought came to her mind and she wondered why she hadn't made the connection sooner.

Without thinking she ran through the adjoining bathroom door that led to Max's room and across to his bed, she barely touched his shoulder, when she felt herself being thrown through the air, landing on her back on the bed and simultaneously felt a gun pressed to her forehead and the safety released.

"Max it's me Jasmine," fear obvious in her voice.

Instantly the bedside lamp was turned on and Jasmine was temporarily blinded.

"You were very close to getting yourself killed!"

Jasmine looked up at him and as hard as she tried, she couldn't help the tears forming in her eyes. He stared down at her and she tried desperately to swallow the lump that had formed in her throat, not able to look at his angry gaze she closed her eyes and moments later felt his lips upon hers.

The fear she had just experience and pent-up sexual tension caused her to return his kiss, Max's earlier restrain was gone, she heard and felt the straps to her camisole tear and moments later his hands and lips were on her breasts. Her nails raked his shoulders and then he moved lower and virtually ripped her brief panties from her, their desire so great they were both beyond the slow dance of foreplay, Max straddled her, but paused and pulled back.

Jasmine was so angry she thought she would explode, *how*

could he do this to me again? As he got up from the bed, she looked towards his gun on the pillow beside her and made a reach for it, but stopped when she heard him mumbling in frustration and looked towards him, realising he was trying to put on a condom.

The realisation that her frustration had been so great all her sensibilities had gone out the window, causing her to nearly shoot the man who was the main focus of her plight. She knelt on the bed beside him and took the condom from his hands, first kissing him passionately on the lips then letting her hands move sensuously down his chest, tormenting him like he had done her earlier, until finally grasping his arousal and shakily pulling the condom over it.

He pushed her back against the bed and grabbed her hips, entering her with a hard thrust, Jasmine let out a primal moan and raked her nails across his back, wrapping her legs around him, ensuring he couldn't tease her any further.

Her sexual spring had been wound so tight, it didn't take long to reach the height of her climax, her body quivering at the sheer pleasure and Max followed not long after. He lay down beside her and turned off the bedside lamp, before gathering her in his arms and both instantly fell into a deep sleep.

Jasmine woke the following morning to the smell of coffee, she lay there for a few moments and smiled as she remember what had happened the night before, then realised it had actually been early that morning, she turned her head and saw the time on the bedside clock was 9.30 am.

"If I remember correctly, you have your coffee black with one sugar."

Jasmine sat up and looked towards Max and was disappointed to see he was fully dressed.

"Thank you."

"The coffee's very hot, so you've got time for a quick shower."

Jasmine knew him well enough now to know it wasn't a

suggestion; it was a command and wasted no time getting under the hot spray of water. As she quickly washed herself, she was overcome with mixed feelings of regret and content, it was all business as usual with Max and she wasn't sure if that was how she wanted things to be. After quickly dressing she walked back into Max's room.

"While you were sleeping I was going through some of your notes, when were you planning on telling me about Microbe's connection with Deanne's boss, who by the way is dead?"

Jasmine could see he was angry and this really annoyed her, because this was the reason she had tried to wake him and nearly got her head blown off.

"Well for your information I only found this out last night! I tried to wake you but having a gun held to my head made it slip from my mind!"

She was pleased to see her comment had knocked him down a peg and waited for an apology.

"A word of advice, never surprise a man whose only trusted friend is his gun."

Jasmine stared at him for a moment and realised she had more chance of winning the lottery than getting an apology from Max Steel.

"As you have already read my notes there is no point going over them, but something else came to me that you won't find there, something that has been in front of our face all along!"

"What is that?"

"The man in the photo and Mr Black, what if they are one and the same?"

"Deanne already asked her aunt about Mr Black..."

"Yes, she said he died, but we haven't shown her the photo, if she can identify him as Mr Black..."

"Who is apparently dead, but what if that is just a ruse and he had Dr Shoal perform cosmetic surgery to change his appearance? My god, how the hell did we miss this? It's just as well I changed our flights, if you're all packed we can grab

something to eat at the airport."
"And when did you do this?"
"Yesterday."
"Jeez, thanks for the advanced notice!"

CHAPTER TWENTY-ONE

Aunt Jan confirmed Jasmine's suspicion that the unknown man in the photo was in fact Graham Black, the man Salina had left Robert Shoal for, all four were currently sitting in the lounge room trying to piece all the information together.

"I think Dr Shoal was killed because he knew Graham Black was still alive, whom by the way was wanted for murder and drug trafficking."

"Yes I remember that, it made all the news headlines; there was much speculation about his death. Many thought he was killed by another drug lord, but others thought his death was a bit too convenient; DNA test of the remains proved beyond doubt, Graham Black had perished in the fire," said aunt Jan.

"I wouldn't mind betting someone was paid generously to ensure that was how the report read!" Exclaimed Max.

"You know I just had another thought, you believed Microbe was using his yacht for transporting drugs, what if someone wanted to move in on the action; so they bumped off Microbe and set up Max to direct any heat from themselves," said Jasmine.

"I voiced that to the police when I was arrested for Microbe's murder, but the local copper didn't take too kindly to any slurs against the Microbe name!" Exclaimed Max.

"I had a similar experience with the copper in Fig Tree Grove, when I suggested Sam was the one who sent me the death threats," said Deanne.

"Who is now dead!" Stated Jasmine.

"He's dead?" Asked Deanne with a look of shock.

"Sorry, I shouldn't have told you that way," apologised Jasmine.

"I've known Sam since he was a little tacker, when Deanne told me about his behaviour as an employer, I thought she must have been confusing him with someone else, but then when he accused her of stealing, that really got me riled up, so I went and spoke to his mother. Poor thing, she was a mess, she told me he hardly came to see her anymore and had snubbed all his mates, reckoned he was moving on to bigger and better things in the city," said Aunt Jan.

"The one thing that confuses me is the murder of the strange looking guy Deanne saw, who by the way was connected to both Microbe and Sam; it doesn't fit the M.O. of how the others were killed," said Jasmine.

"Perhaps because his murder was unrelated to Microbe and Sam, the way he was killed, all the photos that were plastered to the walls and then there was the mystery caller who dialled 000. I think this one was personal," commented Max.

Before anyone could comment further Max's phone rang and he left the room to answer it, only to return moments later.

"There's been a development on the arsonist who set fire to Deanne's house, a blue 2000 model Ford Falcon sedan was seen rushing from the scene, an observant neighbour got a partial on the number plate, its registered to an Alex Benton, ring any bells?"

"No," said Deanne.

"Oh my goodness what's happening to Fig Tree Grove?" Asked Aunt Jan.

"Another one of the boys you used to give lemonade and cookies to?" Asked Max.

"Yes, he was a lovely boy, very quiet, poor Mabel."

"Who's Mabel?" Asked Max.

"She's the boy's grandmother, doted on him terribly."

"I know it's a big ask Jan, but is there any chance you could give her a call and ask if she'd mind if we pay her a visit?" Asked Max.

"Of course dear, anything to help. Now when you say 'we', do you mean all of us?"

Max walked over and sat on the couch beside her and patted her hand.

"Actually I was just referring to Jasmine and myself, Mabel mightn't have any information of value, but then she might, which could mean we mightn't come directly back here. I would rest much easier if I knew both yourself and Deanne were in a safe and secure environment."

"Oh you're a charmer, but if that is what you would prefer, you will get no argument from Deanne or me, we are just so thankful for all you have done!" She said as she squeezed his hand.

Jasmine looked across at Deanne and they both smiled at each other, both knowing Aunt Jan was quite content to stay behind and mind the fort.

"Aunt Jan I'd been meaning to ask, obviously you were keeping an eye on Deanne's house, but how often did you go there and was it always about the same time of day?" Asked Jasmine.

"I made a point of going every day, usually midmorning to lunch, but the day of the fire I had a doctor's appointment and then I took some scones around to my dear friend Molly who recently lost her husband, by the time I got home it was coming on sunset."

Jasmine looked across at Max and she knew he was thinking the same thing, *someone had been watching the house, it was late and possibly dark inside, aunt Jan would have turned on the lights, they thought Deanne had returned home.*

Max and Jasmine left soon after breakfast the following morning, for Fig Tree Grove, Jan had said Mabel was expecting them for morning tea. On the drive both avoided the subject of what happened in Cowra and discussed all the aspects of what information they had so far.

"What puzzles me, I know Salina is one mean bitch, but if Graham Black is still alive and behind the demise of Microbe and god knows how many others, how the hell does a country kid like Alex Benton fit into the equation?"

"Good question, let's just hope Mabel can enlighten us."

"My concern is, Aunt Jan said she doted on Alex, what if she clams up to protect him?"

"I'm sure Jasmine Bronson, cutting edge reporter of Frontline News will be able to prize it out of her."

Jasmine looked across at him, but he didn't take his eyes off the road, she wasn't sure if he was being sarcastic, or if he was actually giving her a compliment for a change.

"This looks like the place," commented Max.

Jasmine looked ahead and saw a low-set brick house come into view; it was surrounded by a colourful garden and had a white picket fence out front. Suddenly the front door opened and a buxom woman of about seventy stepped out onto the front step.

"Looks like Mabel has been waiting, I wonder what Aunt Jan said to her," commented Jasmine.

"I'm sure we'll soon find out."

As they walked up the front path, Jasmine noticed Mabel's hair was neatly set and was sure she was wearing her best dress, *was this why she was specific about the time because she had other plans?*

"Hello Mabel, I'm Jas…"

"Oh, my-gosh, when Jan said I should wear my best dress because someone special was coming today, I never thought in a million years it would be Jasmine Bronson!"

"She didn't tell you who was coming?" Asked Jasmine.

"No, she said it was a surprise, I've been watching the window all morning!"

"Well obviously you know who I am, this is Max…"

"The chauffeur," said Max.

"Oh how wonderful and so handsome too!"

"Do you mind if we come inside?" Asked Jasmine.

"Oh sorry, where are my manners!"

Mabel led them into a cosy lounge room, there was a table covered in photo frames, which Max walked towards and intently looked at. As Jasmine surveyed the room she could see Mable loved to crochet, there were crocheted doilies everywhere, under every lamp, ornament, even the arms of the chairs and there was a beautiful crochet rug thrown across the back of the couch.

Mabel came back in carrying a tray laden with a coffee pot, cups, cakes and biscuits.

"Harold will be disappointed that he wasn't here, but he is down at the local R.S.L. with a few of his friends. It has been a tradition every Friday since he retired," said Mabel.

"Well we can't interfere with tradition," commented Max

"Mabel I have to compliment you on your crochet, its exquisite!" Exclaimed Jasmine.

"Why thank you, I won first prize in the local show this year!"

"I can see why," said Jasmine with a smile

"So is that why you have come to Fig Tree Grove, because you heard about my crochet?"

"Sadly no, we have come here on another matter; it is about your grandson Alex."

Mabel instantly pulled a handkerchief from the sleeve of her dress and dabbed at her eyes.

"He's in trouble isn't he?"

"I'm afraid so, that recent house fire…"

"You mean Dr Shoal's house?"

"Yes, they believe Alex…"

"He would never do that to Jan!"

"Of course, we think he thought Deanne was in the house, Jan's niece."

"Alex wouldn't do that, he's a good boy, he's just a little lost at the moment."

"When you say lost, what do you mean?"

"My daughter wasn't able to have children of her own, Alex was adopted as a baby, she loved him so much she was always afraid his mother would try to find him, so she never told him he was adopted. I told her many times this was wrong, but it was not my place to go against her wishes. He was always a very shy boy; he didn't always fit in with others his age. I remember he said to me one day, 'grandma I'm going to join the army, I'm going to make you proud and people will respect me' I hugged him and told him I was already proud of him. I didn't realise he hadn't told his mother of this…"

"He would have needed his birth certificate," commented Max.

"Yes. He came to me first, wanted to know why I never told him. I'll never forget the look in his eyes; he felt I had betrayed him."

"Did he try to find her?" Asked Jasmine

"Yes."

"And did he?"

"Yes, that's when I noticed the change in him."

"How did he change?" Asked Jasmine

"He became dark and sullen, he would fly into fits of rage for no reason and then he would disappear for days on end. He refused to talk to my daughter; it was as if he hated her for keeping his adoption from him."

"With these mood swings and the fits of rage, do you think it possible, he was taking drugs?" Asked Jasmine, cautiously

"The thought had crossed everyone's mind; to the point my daughter went through his things, which he found out, that was when he told her he never wanted to see her again. He said he had a new job and was leaving this backward town for good."

"Mabel, it is obvious to me you love Alex as much as if he was your biological grandson, have you had any contact with him, are you helping him financially?" Asked Jasmine.

"Yes, but please don't tell Harold!"

"I promise you this stays between you and me, but can you tell me, does he call and ask for money?"

"Yes."

"So when he does, how do you give it to him?"

"I have his bank account number, I have an account of my own; I draw out the cash and deposit it into his account."

"Mabel, would you like me to help you bring the old Alex back, the boy who wanted to save his country and make you proud?"

"Would you do that?"

"Yes, but I would need your help."

"Will he go to jail?"

"If he agrees to tell us who coerced him to light that fire, because both you and I know it wasn't something he really wanted to do; I will do my utmost to help him!"

"What do you want me to do?"

"Next time he asks you for money, tell him you need to see him, you need to know he is ok and if he wants the money he will agree to meet you at a place of your choosing."

"What if he doesn't agree to it?"

"He will, not at first, but if you stand firm, he will agree to your terms. I know this is hard, but we are looking out for Alex's best interest, I can't help him if you're not prepared to be strong. He will try to wear you down, but just keep telling yourself this is for his own good, because if you buckle he could be looking at spending a very long time behind bars. I'm sorry to be so blunt with you, but this is a young boy's life we are talking about, your grandson!"

Mabel broke down and cried, which did not surprise Jasmine, but she was surprised that Max had remained silent, as she leant across and hugged Mabel.

"I'm so sorry I've upset you, aunt Jan speaks so highly of you, perhaps when this is all over Aunt Jan and I can come around for coffee and scones and you can show me your latest entry in the local show," suggested Jasmine.

"Would you really do that?"

"Of course, I'll even go as far as to say, providing it fits in with my schedule at the time, I'll be a guest judge at the show."

"Can I ask one favour?"

"Yes, but no promises."

"Can you call me Aunt Mabel?"

"Of course, Fig Tree Grove, the home of my two favourite aunts, Mabel and Jan?"

"Thank you Jasmine!"

"Here's my card, call me as soon as Alex contacts you."

"I will and once again thank you."

"The pleasure is all mine, now I must be going, but thank you for all your help."

"Before we go, Mabel I was wondering if you know the name of Alex's biological mother?" Asked Max.

"Why yes, her name is Alison Grady."

Max and Jasmine looked at each other, both now knew who was behind the death threats made on Deanne's life and why. Jasmine rose and hugged Mabel and reassured her everything would be ok, before following Max out to the car. Neither said a word until Max started up the car.

"Oh my god, everything is starting to make sense!" Exclaimed Jasmine.

"Obviously Salina knows Deanne has the contents of the leather satchel."

"I'm guessing she wasn't sure in the beginning, that's why Deanne's house was broken into and someone went through the files, probably Alex," said Jasmine.

"That's where Salina slipped up, if she had sent in a pro to search the house, instead of playing on the emotions of a teenager, those files would have gone missing and that fireplace would have never been discovered and we would have no clue as to who the woman is that has Michelle," said Max.

"We'll find her Max; we're one step closer to finding out where Salina is."

"I know; you did well," commented Max.

"Pardon."

"The way you made Mabel trust you, I can see why Frontline News plucked you from the little town of Eden Cove."

"Thank you."

"Well it looks like we're hanging around here for a while; I think we should find a place to stay."

"Sure."

"Then perhaps have a pub meal, or would you prefer to eat in?"

"I'm easy." Jasmine immediately regretted her choice of words.

They found a motel that had an eatery attached to it and Max assured Jasmine there was no connecting bathroom separating the rooms. The sign outside the eatery stated they made the best burgers in town, so both Max and Jasmine decided to put them to the test. They sat at a table far enough away from the other diners, so they could talk without being overheard.

"How do you think Microbe was using his boat to traffic drugs, without drawing suspicion from the authorities?" Asked Jasmine.

"I believe he was using tourists as his cover, I attached a tracking device to the bottom of the *Talisman*, which unfortunately didn't look too favourably towards me when they found the remnants of it, or the tracking log in my office..."

"That wasn't very smart," commented Jasmine.

"Yeah well, I had other things on my mind at the time, anyway I logged him doing a trip late one night, in an area where there was the likelihood of him being run over by a tanker. Jane, Michelle's friend said they saw a boat the night they embarked on their dangerous swim, she said it wasn't displaying any lights and even though it was moving she said there was no engine noise, so it had to be a yacht, I'm guessing the *Talisman*."

"Why?"

"Well firstly the time factor matched the tracking log, but also Jane said Michelle saw them throw a box or crate overboard, I'm guessing it was loaded with drugs."

"I know that area is very deep and the currents strong, they would have needed to have some sort of floatation on it, how could they be sure the right people collected it?"

"You're right about the floatation, it was probably fitted with a remote control floatation device, the box sinks to the ocean floor, when someone wants to retrieve it, they enable the floats by remote control, the box probably also had a tracking device so they could exactly pinpoint where it was going to surface."

"Very clever, so if you are right and a bigger fish wanted to takeover Microbe's operation, why blow up his boat, it was his only way of moving the drugs?"

"Michelle's disappearance and greed."

"How so?"

"To this day I believe Microbe instigated the hit on Michelle, his first big mistake was getting someone to take her on a 'supposed diving trip', near the area of his drop off point. Suddenly the area is swarming with aircraft and search boats, making it impossible to deliver any more goods, something his customers wouldn't have taken too kindly to. Secondly I think whoever had Microbe bumped off, wanted to increase the supply, cover a wider area and I think that is where Sam's boatyard came into play."

"You know, Deanne told me she was worried Sam was involved in that paedophile ring, the reason she went to the shed one night was to see what he was up to. All she could see was a bunch of guys working on some luxury boats and strangely enough, the following day everything was quiet and the place appeared to be closed."

"How long after this did you find evidence of drugs?"

"About a week and a half, possibly two and by the way the place was empty, no boats, equipment; not so much as a single bolt."

"Now Deanne went there after the shifty looking guy was murdered?" Asked Max.

"Yeah."

"He was linked to Sam; they couldn't afford the police making the connection, what Deanne saw were the guys getting ready to move."

"I've got a friend in the police force, I told her I had found evidence of drugs, she had her guys do a thorough sweep of the place; she believed Sam was using the shed to cut some very high grade cocaine," said Jasmine.

"Of course, that's what Deanne saw, the guys were altering the boats to store the drugs ready for transport, that's how he was moving them!" Exclaimed Max.

"Clever, but to where and how does he pass the drugs on to his customers?"

"Something I intend to find out, but first I have to find Michelle!"

"Of course."

They started to rise from the table when Jasmine's phone rang, upon looking at the number she signalled to Max to sit back down.

"Hello Mabel."

"How did you know it was me?"

"I have your number keyed in my phone so I know who's calling."

"Oh, can you do that?"

"Yes it's amazing what they can do with phones nowadays. Did you get a call from Alex?"

"Yes, but he was angry at me when I told him I wouldn't give him any money unless he agreed to see me."

"I know it's hard, but it's for his own good, I'm sure he'll ring back, just remember what we discussed, ok, bye."

"Well I'm sure you got the gist of that," said Jasmine.

"Do you think she'll buckle?"

"No, as hard as it is for her, she understands what the consequences will be if she does."

"I don't know about you, but I could do with a beer, fancy a drink at the local pub?"

"Sure, but do you mind if we walk, my legs could do with a stretch."

Later, Max was thinking a drink at the local hadn't been such a good idea. After years of working undercover on many covert operations, he had always gone by the rule of blending in; avoiding anything that would draw attention to oneself, but Jasmine had managed to attract a crowd of admirers all wanting an autograph, or their picture taken with the famous

Jasmine Bronson.

To his relief her phone rang and she had to walk outside to be able to hear, using the opportunity to his advantage, he grabbed hold of her elbow to keep her moving and steered her in the direction of their motel. Moments later she disconnected the call and smiled at Max.

"It worked; Mabel is meeting Alex in the park tomorrow morning."

"What time?"

"Ten."

CHAPTER TWENTY-TWO

Max and Jasmine were dressed in jogging gear, not wanting to give Alex any cause for suspicion as to why they were in the park. It had been decided when they approached the park bench Mabel and Alex were sitting at, Jasmine would feint a stitch and stop for a rest, something Mabel was also aware of. She had been given strict instructions not to hand over any money before they had a chance to talk to him.

Jasmine looked across at Max as they approached the park bench and moments later he gave her a slight nod, causing her to instantly stop and bend over, making noises as if she was in pain and out of breath.

"Darling, you ok," said Max, as he put his hand on her back.

"Uh, I've got a terrible stitch in my side."

"Take a deep breath."

"Is she alright?" Asked Mabel.

"Pushing herself too hard, as usual," commented Max.

"Perhaps she should sit down, it is rather hot out today and she does look rather flushed," suggested Mable.

Max looked across and he could tell by the look on Alex's face he wanted to bolt, but Mabel had a firm hold of his hand.

"As long as you don't mind us sharing your seat?" Asked Max.

"We don't mind, do we Alex."

He instantly gave his grandmother a dark look, but did not say anything. Max helped Jasmine to the park bench, but remained standing.

"So Alex, I hear you've managed to get yourself in a bit of strife," said Max.

Alex looked bewilderedly at Max for a moment and then at his grandmother.

"You set me up!"

Alex jumped to his feet, but Max was prepared for him, he

put his hand on his shoulder and squeezed a certain pressure point that caused Alex to immediately sit back down.

"Grandma, how could you do this to me?"

"I'm sorry Alex, but these people are here to help you."

"Bullshit!"

"Alex!" Said Mable in shock.

"Your grandmother is right, we know you set fire to Dr Shoal's house and we know you tried to trap Deanne inside," said Max.

"I had nothing to do with that!"

"I know you did," said Max.

"You can't prove anything!"

"That's where you're wrong, we found your fingerprints on the jerry can that was used to light the fire, they were also on the handle of the back door and the metal bar you used to wedge the door shut!" Max bluffed.

Alex instantly broke down and cried, causing Mabel to put her arm around him.

"Am I going to jail?"

"Depends whether you're prepared to help us or not," replied Max.

"Honest, I didn't know it was aunt Jan inside!"

"I know, you thought it was Deanne, that's attempted murder."

"I didn't want to do it, I didn't want to hurt anyone," he sobbed.

"Then why did you do it?"

"They were going to hurt grandma if I didn't."

"Oh Alex, why didn't you come to me?" Said Mabel

"You couldn't help me grandma, no one could!"

"If you help us now, tell us everything you know, it will look favourably upon you and I promise I will do everything in my power to keep you from a jail sentence," said Max.

Alex looked at his grandmother, who shook her head in encouragement.

"What do you want to know?" Asked Alex.

"Did you break into Deanne's house and use the old typewriter she had in the cupboard and type a threatening letter?"

"Yes, I also did another one on my computer."

"Why?" Asked Max.

"Because she told me to."

"You're referring to your mother Alison Grady, aren't you?"

"Uh, how did you know?"

"Let's just say I know a lot more about her than she thinks, which brings me to the question, how did you find her?"

"I didn't, she found me."

"How so?" Asked Max.

"Well I first went through the adoption board trying to find her, but had no luck, apparently both parties have to be listed as wanting to be contacted for us to meet, she wasn't, which is why it surprised me she contacted me!"

"Really, did she say why?"

"Not really, I was just so happy she wanted to get to know me."

"So what did you think the first time you met her?" Asked Max.

"She was nice at first, had her chauffeur pick me up in the limo, I wasn't sure if she was trying to impress me by going to the expense, but then when we pulled up at this really fancy place, I thought she's got to be loaded!"

"Do you know where this place is?"

"No, you see the windows in the limo were so dark I couldn't see a thing, there was this huge big screen TV that was behind the driver, it was playing the latest movie that hadn't even been released at the cinemas yet."

"Where did the limo pick you up from?"

"Brisbane airport."

"How on earth did you afford that?" Asked Mabel.

"Alison paid for my airfare."

"Did you get to see the end of the movie before you

reached her house?" Asked Max.

"Yeah, it was really good, you should go see it..."

"How long did the movie go for, two, two and a half hours."

"About two hours."

"Did you see anyone else at the house, apart from the staff?"

"No."

"Are you sure?"

"Yeah why?"

"I'm trying to locate a young girl, she's a bit older than you, tall, blonde..."

"You mean Rusalka?"

"So you did see her?" Max asked excitedly.

"No, but I know she works for Alison."

"How do you know this?"

"There was a big picture of her hanging up on the wall and she had this stack of brochures, I was going to keep one, but Alison wouldn't let me, she said they were only for clients."

"So what makes you think she works for Alison?"

"Well the brochures..."

"Can you remember what the brochures contained?"

"Well of course Rusalka was on the front, she was dressed a bit like Xena the Warrior Princess, only ten times hotter. I'm guessing it was some kind of show or something, because I didn't get a chance to read what it said inside."

"Why the interest?"

Max looked at Alex and wondered if he should be upfront with the boy, for so many years he had thought he was protecting Michelle, by maintaining the secret he was her father, now he was not so sure.

"She's my daughter."

"Holy shit!" Exclaimed Alex.

"She went missing almost a year ago, Alison is holding her against her will."

"Oh my goodness, Alex if you know anything, you have to

tell him!" Exclaimed Mable

"Honestly I have no idea where she is, apart from what I saw at Alison's house, the only other time I've seen anything about her is on a website."

"What website?"

"I came across it when I was thinking about learning martial Arts, I can't remember what the site was called; I just remember the guy's name was Blade and brags about being the only man to fight Rusalka and live to tell the tale."

"Did you sign up with him?"

"Hell no, no offence but if his great achievement is beating a girl, he wasn't going to teach me anything I didn't already know!"

"A word of advice, don't let gender fool you, because you might be in for one hell of a surprise!" Said Max.

"So what happens now?" Asked Alex.

"Firstly, I want you to stop giving your grandmother grief, move back to Fig Tree Grove and keep your nose clean. I'm going to make a few calls, which could put you under house arrest."

"What!" Exclaimed Alex.

"Under your grandmother's care, which is far better than a jail cell. If you manage to keep your nose clean, I might be able to pull a few strings to get you the army career you always wanted."

Alex looked at his grandmother who was dabbing at the tears in her eyes and back at Max.

"No joshing, you'd really do that for me?"

"Yes, but don't get your hopes up, you have some pretty serious charges hanging over your head, but I am sure I can at least convince Deanne and her aunt to drop any charges against you, especially when I explain the circumstances."

"What do you say Alex?" Prompted Mable.

"Thank you."

"Now take your grandmother home and ignore any further contact with Alison. If you think of anything else, or Alison gives you grief, you can call me on this number any time, day or night!" Said Max has he handed Mable a card.

"I knew you were more than a chauffeur," she said as she patted his hand.

"Speaking of which, would you like a lift back to your house?" Asked Max.

"Actually I was thinking if it was alright with grandma, perhaps we could go and get an ice-cream and catch the bus home, like we used to do when you picked me up from school?"

"I was thinking exactly the same thing, I had a sudden craving for rum and raisin ice-cream." Mabel said with a laugh.

After saying their goodbyes, Max and Jasmine headed back to their motel room, Max wanted to locate the website Alex had told him about, he was a step closer to locating Michelle.

After about an hour of scanning every possible website about Sayoc Kali, Max finally found the one Alex had been talking about, after quickly reading the contents he looked up at Jasmine.

"Blade runs a school for Sayoc Kali, it's located in Brisbane, I plan to book the next available flight, it's up to you whether you come or not."

"Does that mean you would rather I didn't?"

"No, it means the decision is yours whether you come with me or go back to wherever."

"I'd like to follow this through, who knows, you might need me to disguise myself as a hooker, so I can get into the building," she said with a laugh.

He looked at her for a moment and then checked the flight schedule.

"Unfortunately we wouldn't reach the airport in time to catch the last flight today, so I'll book us on the first flight tomorrow morning, it'll mean we'll need to leave at 4am to reach the airport in time."

"That's fine by me."

"Oh and Jasmine, as far as I can ascertain, Blade only

knows Michelle as Rusalka, let's keep it that way shall we."

"Sure, but why?"

"I still don't know for sure Microbe was the one who ordered the hit on Michelle, until I do, I think she will be a lot safer if the world believes she perished at sea."

"Ok."

Once Max had organised the flights, both of them looked intently at their laptops, searching for any possible information on Rusalka. Jasmine came across a site on YouTube and quickly plugged in her earphones, on the chance the content would be too upsetting for Max.

The scene started out with a large circular stage, which was surrounded with rows of seats that were occupied with both men and women, but their faces were all obscure. Suddenly the voice of the ringside announcer came on, giving the spiel about the Legend of Rusalka who became a mermaid to avenge her death, but when she was ensnared in a fisherman's net and pulled from the water, her caudal fin became a deadly knife and her tail became legs.

Jasmine rolled her eyes at the bullshit and was tempted to fast-forward the footage, but was afraid she might miss something vital. Suddenly she heard loud cheering and the lights dimmed until the stage was the only thing lit, then a cage came down from above and she could see someone was inside, the camera zoomed in, there was a girl dressed as Alex had described.

When the cage door opened the girl stepped out and walked around the stage with her arms raised in the air, holding two very dangerous looking knives, the crowd cheered, as she turned Jasmine saw her face; it was Michelle.

Another cage then came down and when the door opened, a large muscled man stepped out, he also had a knife in each hand and walked around the stage as Michelle had done. Both cages were removed and suddenly the room became very quiet, then Michelle let out a loud primal scream and advanced on the muscle man with her knives moving so fast they were a blur.

The man followed suit and the battle was on, there was the sound of chinking blades and grunts as both opponents were using all their force behind each swing of the blade. To Jasmine's surprise she could see Michelle had the upper hand, her action with the knife was much faster than her opponent, who started moving backwards to the edge of the stage. Just when Jasmine thought he was going to fall off and into the audience below, he came up hard against an invisible wall and she realised the stage was surrounded with glass.

Suddenly Michelle moved backwards, well out of reach from her opponent's blades and Jasmine could see blood oozing from him. The crowd cheered and she assumed this was the end of the fight, but she was wrong. Michelle's movements appeared to be even faster, but she could see her opponent was weakening. His upper torso was covered in blood and there were splatter marks on the glass, from where Michelle flicked his blood from her knife. The crowd was going crazy, despite the guy's injuries he still kept fighting, until Michelle did one final swish of her blade and suddenly blood spurted from his neck, she had sliced his carotid artery; he staggered for a moment and then dropped to the ground like a stone.

Michelle stood with her arms raised in the air and the crowd went berserk, Jasmine felt sickened, as she knew the guy was either dead or not far off.

"Where's the medic?"

"There won't be one," stated Max.

Jasmine didn't realise she had spoken out loud, or the fact Max had been watching over her shoulder. She looked back at the screen and saw the cage had descended from above and Michelle climbed in and was slowly taken back up out of camera view. Moments later the stage became dark and the footage ended.

"Did you see all of it?" Asked Jasmine.

"I saw enough."

"I don't understand how she can do that," stated Jasmine.

"It's called survival."

"What I don't understand is, she has these weapons, why hasn't she used them to escape?"

"I don't know, hopefully Blade will be able to give us some answers."

STEEL JUSTICE

CHAPTER TWENTY-THREE

Max was a mixture of emotions when he walked through the front door of Blade's establishment, there was currently a class in progress, a tall, muscled guy with tattoos and a shaved head was giving instruction, Max presumed him to be Blade. He noticed him glance his way briefly, but continued on with the class, which made Max clench his fists. To date he had managed to keep his emotions in check, even when everything pointed to Michelle having perished at sea and then Jasmine gave him a glimmer of hope. Now, sitting in this room, waiting to speak to the man who not only knows of her whereabouts, but uses her to boost his career, Max wanted nothing more than to knock his head off!

Finally the class had finished and the last student had walked out the door.

"Looking at joining the class?" Asked the instructor.

"Are you Blade?" Asked Max.

"That's what the name says on the door."

"I'm wondering what sort of a man would use the defeat of a young girl to boost his career," commented Max.

"Excuse me?"

Jasmine was surprised at Max's line of questioning; it was definitely going to get the guy offside.

"Rusalka," replied Max.

"Ah, we have a fan! Look I paid big dollars for her, I think it only fair I get my money's worth!"

Max responded with a right hook to Blade's jaw, causing the big guy to stagger back a few feet.

"Max!" Yelled Jasmine as she grabbed at his shirt.

"Looks like your boyfriend has it real bad for Rusalka!"

"He's not my boyfriend and Rusalka is his daughter!"

The guy looked shocked and looked questioningly at Max.

"This true?"

"Yes and you still haven't answered my question."

"She asked me to."

"What?" Both Max and Jasmine said in unison.

"She asked me to post the fight on my site."

"Are you trying to tell me she is proud of her new status?"

"No she asked me to post it to gain your attention and it obviously worked."

"Why didn't you just contact me?"

"Because I didn't know who you were, she never mentioned a name; she just said she needed to get a message to her father and posting that spiel on my site was the only safe way to do it."

"Ok, how about we start at the beginning, how did you come to meet Rusalka?"

"I'd heard rumours about this girl who was undefeated at Sayoc Kali, no offence to the female gender, but I found this hard to believe, especially as it is a male dominated sport. So I did a bit of research and found a site that showed footage of her in action; I'll admit I was blown away!"

"Was it on YouTube?" Asked Jasmine.

"Yeah, it got me real curious, because the fight was like a modern day gladiator and I wondered how come the authorities hadn't canned it, I mean this is a fight to the death. Well actually I'll rephrase that, if you overpower Rusalka, you both live, if she overpowers you, you die!"

"So obviously, you thought you were good enough to defeat her, what did you have to do to get into the ring with her?" Asked Max.

"Firstly you have to prove your level of skill in Sayoc Kali, people pay a lot of money to see the fight, they don't want any amateurs in the ring, if you pass that test, it comes down to money."

"How much?" Asked Max.

"One hundred thousand Australian dollars."

"Oh my god!" Exclaimed Jasmine.

"So if you lose, you lose one hundred thousand and your life, what do you get if you win?" Asked Max.

"Rusalka."

Even though Jasmine had said Maliha told her this, Max struggled with the fact he was standing in front of a man who paid a lot of money to not only fight his daughter, but to have sex with her.

"You were obviously very confident of winning," said Jasmine.

"Initially I was."

"What changed your mind?" Asked Max.

"First let me explain how the whole process works, you have to pay half the money up front, that then entitles you to videos of her fights, it was after viewing these I started to doubt my chances."

"Then why didn't you pull out?" Asked Max.

"My fifty thou was non-refundable."

"So you figured you'd already thrown away a lot of money, you might as well see it to the end," commented Max.

"Yeah, but it wasn't the main factor, Rusalka intrigued me, she was beautiful, her technique with the blade was like none I'd ever seen before, also I wondered what made her tick, what kind of girl with looks like hers, would choose to fight to the death!"

"And did you get your answer?" Asked Max.

"Yes, she told me about this woman called the 'Mistress' who is holding her prisoner."

"You've seen my daughter's fighting skills, she has these dangerous weapons at her disposal, what is keeping her from escaping?" Asked Max.

"She nearly did once, come here I'll show you something," said Blade.

Both Max and Jasmine followed him into another room, presumably his office, he got a brochure out of the desk drawer and handed it to Max; it was the same as the one Alex had described.

"Look at her wrists and ankles, looks like part of her costume, but these are on her at all times, they are devices that will deliver a debilitating shock if she tries to remove them, or steps outside her restricted area, like being tasered."

"Ok so you won the fight against my daughter, what did you say to make her trust you enough, to ask for your help?"

"Firstly, let me tell you she had the upper hand in the fight, I thought she was coming in for the kill shot and I swung my blade to divert it, causing it to knock cleanly out of her hand. I knew by the look in her eyes, she had allowed this to happen, I was now the one in control, I had her on the backward step, she looked like she was tiring, which surprised me. I told her I didn't want to hurt her and that's when she tripped and fell to the ground, losing her final blade in the process."

"What makes you so sure she allowed you to win?" Asked Jasmine.

"She told me so."

"Did you ask her why?" Asked Max.

"Of course, first she said she liked what she saw and then later she asked me if I would get a message to her father."

"That was a big risk on her part, she's not usually so trusting of people," commented Max.

"Probably the fact I told her I'd never met anyone like her and would do whatever it takes, to get her out of there."

"Possibly. Obviously the devices she is wearing are going to pose a problem, can you tell me exactly where this place is?"

"I don't know."

"What do you mean, you don't know, you were there?" Asked Max.

"Firstly I was blindfolded before being taken to the airport and assisted onto a private jet, it wasn't until we were in the air my blindfold was removed, it was later replaced before we landed and I was then escorted to a helicopter, it wasn't removed again until I was inside the stadium."

"Contact them, tell them you are up for another challenge," said Max.

"No can do."

"I'll pay the one hundred grand."

"It's not the money, the rules state a contender can only compete once, one of the reasons the asking price is so high, also she had remained undefeated until I came along. How about yourself, how good are your skills at Sayoc Kali?"

"Unfortunately not to a competitive level, surely you could recommend someone," stated Max.

"I could rattle off any number of names of guys, but I certainly wouldn't trust them with Rusalka, nor to aid in her escape!"

"Hmm, this aircraft you were taken in, can you describe it?" Asked Max.

"The aircraft was very plush, I noted no more than six leather seats and the bulkheads, cupboards and tables were all wood-grain panelling. I was told I wasn't allowed to leave my seat, but the flight was only about forty-five minutes."

"Possibly a Gulfstream 150, what about the helicopter flight to the stadium, how long did that take?"

"I'd say about half an hour."

"Blade did you see this woman the 'Mistress'?" Asked Jasmine.

"No, I didn't even know of her existence until Rusalka told me about her, the only people I had any direct dealings with, were the hired heavies. My first initial contact was through email, I had to first send a demo of myself in action and then I had to compete with some guy I'd never heard of before, he was pretty good, but not as good as me."

"Meaning you past the final test?"

"Yeah, perhaps I could ask around, see if anyone has heard of this woman," suggested Blade.

"It's worth a try, but I doubt it will do you any good, more likely get yourself killed," said Max.

"I'm prepared to take that risk."

"Thanks, here's my number, call me if you come up with anything."

"Will do."

While Max had been trying to establish where Michelle

was, Jasmine had been taking notes, she was guessing Max would try to establish a radius from the airport to Michelle's location; using the type of aircraft and estimated time, travelled to the stadium.

* * *

A week had past and Max was no closer to finding Michelle than on the day he first spoke to Blade, he had poured over numerous maps and tried countless scenarios, going by the estimated times Blade had given him, but all had turned out fruitless, there was just no possible place for a fixed wing aircraft to land. Both he and Jasmine had remained in Brisbane, as it was the closest base to where Michelle was being held. Jasmine was currently following up on a couple of possible leads, from interviews she'd had with the girls Salina had smuggled into the country. He was about to ring her, when he suddenly got a text message from Blade to meet him in forty-five minutes when his class ended.

Max arrived ten minutes early and was surprised to find the place deserted, his instincts telling him something was wrong. Cautiously making his way towards the office, the door was closed, without standing directly inline of the door, he quickly turned the handle and kicked it open and immediately saw Blade sitting behind his desk, but the look on his face alerted him he was not alone. Looking intently at Blade, he noticed his eyes move slightly to the left, but before he could make a move the other occupant spoke.

"Be warned, my gun is pointed at your pretty girlfriend's head."

Max looked at Blade, who acknowledged with a nod, that what had been said was true.

"What do you want?" Asked Max, without entering the room.

"I want to do a deal."

"About what?"

"First come into the room nice and slow, I don't like talking through a door."

Max did as he requested, still holding his gun at the ready and saw Jasmine was being used as a human shield and a gun was held to her temple. Max was sure if it hadn't been for the gun, Jasmine could have easily overpowered the man, his build was about on par with her, but also the man's face was vaguely familiar.

"As you can see I have the upper hand, now put your gun down on the floor nice and slow and kick it over towards me."

"Why do I feel we have met before?" Asked Max.

"Maybe we have, maybe we haven't, that's not important, what is, is whether I put a bullet in her pretty little head!"

Max slowly bent down and put his gun on the floor, but instead of kicking it towards the gunman; he kicked it across the other side of the room.

"Clever, but not really smart."

"Let the girl go," said Max.

The man looked from Max to Blade, who was still seated.

"Let her go, I'm unarmed, you said you wanted to talk, so let's talk!" Demanded Max.

The gunman hesitated for a moment and then released his hold on Jasmine.

"Word has it that you have been trying to locate the 'Mistress'."

"So?"

"I'll tell you where she is, but first you have to help me."

"How?"

"Bring down Michael Savage."

"Who the hell is Michael Savage?" Asked Max.

"The man who killed my brother!"

"Who was your brother?"

"Sam Hendy."

Jasmine gasped.

"Did he by chance manage a boatyard in Fig Tree Grove?"

"You knew him?"

"No, but…"

"How do I know this isn't just some ploy to get me to help you?" Asked Max, as he looked at Jasmine, warning her not to say too much.

"What if I told you the 'Mistress's real name is Salina, and she has your daughter."

Blade immediately jumped to his feet and lunged towards the gunman.

"You bastard, tell us where she is!"

Max immediately dropped Blade to the floor; he knew Blade's idea of questioning was not going to get him any answers.

"Try that again and I'll put a bullet in your head myself!" Exclaimed Max to Blade.

"I'd say he's got the hots for your daughter, like just about every other man on the planet."

"Let's get one thing clear; you want my help bringing your brother's killer down, no more smutting remarks about my daughter!" Said Max through clenched teeth.

"Gotcha."

"What can you tell me about Michael Savage, apart from the fact he killed your brother?" Asked Max.

"He's virtually untouchable, he's uses people as stepping stones to build his empire and once they've reached their extent of usefulness, they suddenly wind up dead."

"This empire, I'm guessing it's based on drugs," said Max.

"Clever boy."

"If he's as big as you say, how come I have never heard of him?"

"Because he is paranoid about his privacy, he goes to great lengths to ensure no one knows his identity."

"Sounds a bit hard to believe, I'm sure if his empire is based on drugs, the authorities would know of him," stated Max.

"Ah, but that's because they don't know, he's very cleverly hidden it behind a legitimate business, luxury yachts."

"How does it work?"

"His boats aren't available to just anyone, he's very selective with his clients, he deals in appointments only, once an appointment is secured, the client can inspect the yacht, if the client is interested, the deal is done on board."

"So your saying, the client has to buy the boat to get the drugs?" Asked Max.

"Yes, but he does also sell boats that don't have that added extra, after all there is a great demand amongst the rich to own one of these luxury yachts."

"I don't see how that could work, the client wanting the added extras would have to buy a lot of boats to gain this supply of drugs." Asked Max.

"Ah, but you see once he has established that client, they then deal in a trade-up process, like many people do with their cars, after a certain period they upgrade to a newer model."

"Hmm, very clever. So did your brother Sam tell you all this?"

"No, I am Michael Savage's front man; all deals are done through me."

"You introduced Sam to Savage didn't you?"

"Yes."

"So what's stopping Savage from killing you, surely he can't trust his front man after he ordered the death of your brother?"

"Firstly he doesn't know I'm his brother, it wasn't common knowledge, I'm actually his half-brother, our mother got knocked up when she was a kid, I got adopted out. Secondly Savage has kept me as his front man, because I helped him take over from Microbe."

"You planted the device in my car, now I know why your face is familiar!"

"Hey, before you start jumping to conclusions, I had nothing to do with that, or the hit on your daughter, I was just part of the clean-up crew!"

Max stood with his fists clenched and glared at him, trying

to bring himself back to an element of control.

"Now it's my turn to ask you some questions, what's your name and why was a hit put out on my daughter?"

"Seth, apparently she snuck on board the *Talisman* and saw what was in the secure room, it was all captured on the security surveillance cameras on the boat."

"Who did Microbe get to do his dirty work?"

"He left it up to Damon, his head of security; he hired some guy that insisted on bringing along an amateur, partly why your daughter is still alive."

"I'll help you with Savage on the condition you tell me where I can find Damon."

"I know what you're thinking, but you're wasting your time, he's already dead. I'm the only one of Microbe's crew left standing, that's why I need your help."

"How do you know so much about Salina?" Asked Max.

"She's Savage's girlfriend."

"Shit!" Exclaimed Max.

"Do we have a deal?" Asked Seth.

"How do I know you're not just trying to set me up, that in fact you're one of Salina's men?" Asked Max.

"I figured you'd want some proof."

Seth pulled a disk from his back pocket and handed it across to Max.

"What's this?" Asked Max.

"Security video of how things work."

"Blade put this in your computer and let's see this proof," said Max

Max and Jasmine stood either side of Blade and moments later they could see what appeared to be the inside of a luxury boat, suddenly there were voices and two men came into view, one of them being Seth.

"Where's Savage?" Asked Max.

"He watches the proceedings from another boat close by, like I said no one has ever done face to face dealings with him."

"Shh, they're talking," said Jasmine.

"Would you like to view the layout of the boat?" Asked Seth

"Yes, I want to make sure everything is of high quality," said the other man.

"As you will see, we have very high standards, everything has been catered for," said Seth

"We shall see."

The video showed the men's movements progressively throughout the boat, while the prospective buyer asked Seth many questions about the actual running of the boat, making Max wonder if and when they were going to get their 'proof', when suddenly the conversation turned.

"I believe this boat has an added extra, one that makes it standout from all the others," said the other man.

"Yes, Mr Savage would have emailed you all that information," replied Seth

"Of course, but I would like to view what I am paying such a high price for."

"Most certainly, how about we take a seat in the main lounge," suggested Seth.

Once the prospective buyer was seated, Seth walked over and unlocked a low cupboard and pulled out a briefcase, which he placed on the table and quickly spun the combination locks. When it was opened Max and Jasmine could see a plastic bag that contained a white substance, moments later the briefcase was turned and pushed towards the buyer, who clicked his fingers and suddenly a third man appeared and placed a briefcase on the table and pulled out a series of tubes and bottles.

He first added the contents of two tubes to a small bottle of liquid and instantly a greenish upper layer formed, then using a paper knife, he removed a small portion of white powder from the plastic bag placing it into the bottle and sealed it. He quickly shook the bottle for a few seconds, before placing the bottle on the table in front of the buyer. All three watched the colour change until it became dark and resembled the colour of coffee.

"Cocaine," stated Max.

"Five star, ninety percent pure!"

The buyer rose from the chair and smiled at Seth.

"It will be a pleasure doing business with you!"

The screen then went black and Blade ejected the disk and handed it back to Seth.

"We need to set up a deal, but I want Michael Savage to do the deal, not you," said Max.

"He won't go for it," replied Seth.

"He will, if we make him an offer he can't refuse," replied Max.

STEEL JUSTICE

CHAPTER TWENTY-FOUR

Max had used a fake identity many times in the past, whether it be to expose an arms dealer, or infiltrate the enemy, he was well aware of the background checks Michael Savage would insist upon, before he even considered doing business with a new buyer, one he had never heard of before.

Seth stepped into the lift and noticed his hand shook as he pressed the button that would take him to the top floor, Savage's office. He looked at his face in the reflective wall of the lift and noticed not only could he see the fear in his eyes, but also his face was beaded in sweat. He had tried to convince Max to email the man directly, but he had insisted the only way to convince Savage this new buyer was legit, was if he, his front man, put forth the proposal himself.

The lift made a loud ding, notifying Seth he had reached the top floor, as the doors opened, Savage's secretary, whose desk was a short distance from the lift, was looking directly at him with a stern look on her face.

"I hope you're not here to see Mr Savage, I have no appointment marked in the book and you know he will not see anyone unless an appointment has been made."

Suddenly Seth began to panic, he hadn't thought to make an appointment, in fact he had never needed to before, the few occasions he set foot in Savage's office, was because Savage had summoned him.

"Oh Shit!"

"I'll have none of that language around here, now if you wish to make an appointment; he is free 10am Wednesday next week."

"No, I have to see him now."

"I've already told you that is impossible, now shall I slot you in for 10am…"

"No, I have to see him now!" Seth's nerves were quickly turning to anger.

"Don't you raise your voice to me!"

Before Seth could comment, the door to Savage's office opened.

"What the hell is going on out here?"

"Oh, Mr Savage, I was just trying to explain to this man the need to make an appoint…"

"It's important; it won't wait till next week," explained Seth.

"Is there a problem with the show?" Asked Savage.

"No, but…"

"Make an appointment," he said as he started to close the door.

"It's in regards to a buyer!" Seth rushed.

Savaged looked from his secretary to Seth and then opened the door wider, motioning for him to enter.

"What seems to be the problem?" Asked Savage, once the door was closed.

"It's not actually a problem; well I mean it could be a problem…"

"You're babbling, get straight to the point."

"Victor Seminov…"

"Never heard of him," said Savage as he sat behind his desk.

"Really, um, well he's heard of you and is interested in doing business."

Seth was so nervous he thought he was going to be sick and the way Savage stared at him was only heightening his nerves.

"He said he is prepared to pay double the asking price," said Seth, hoping he hadn't blown it.

Savage got up from his chair and looked out the vast window to the right of his desk, before turning towards Seth.

"Why would this Victor, what was his name?"

"Seminov."

"Victor Seminov, a man I have never done business with, in fact never heard of, suddenly wants to do business with me and is prepared to pay double the asking price?"

"He's after quality; he'd heard you only supply the best."

"Hmm, so he's heard I only deal in the finest, it still doesn't explain why he is prepared to offer me double the going price."

"Probably because I told him you were very selective with your buyers and there was no guarantee you would have any dealings with him."

"Tell me, apart from the fact he wants a quality product, why did he approach you?"

"He, like you, is very cautious, he knows me from when I worked for Microbe."

"Is that so, I thought I had secured all of Microbe's clients!" Exclaimed Savage.

Seth knew he was treading a fine line between making Savage believe him, or winding up like his brother Sam.

"To be honest, Microbe lost him as a client; he didn't deliver the required shipment of goods as promised."

"Microbe had no idea about running a successful business; in fact I'm surprised he lasted as long as he did."

"So what do you want me to tell Victor?" Asked Seth.

"Nothing, at least not yet, I want to know all there is to know about Victor Seminov."

"He was hoping he'd be able to inspect one or your boats at the next show," said Seth nervously.

"He is keen isn't he?" Said Savage as he turned back towards the window.

"That's why I had to see you today."

Seth stood there nervously, staring at Savage's large frame, which by no means was overweight. Seth had no idea how old the man was, he could be anywhere between fifty and seventy. His well-kept black hair was so dark, he was sure he had it dyed, there was nothing about his face that would make him standout in a crowd, apart from the fact it was virtually line free. He appeared incapable of showing any form of expression; his eyes were so dark the iris's blended with the pupils, giving the appearance of two black soulless eyes of a shark. Seth was sure if he ever came face to face with the devil, his eyes would be identical to Savage's.

"Sir?"

"I'll let you know when I've made my decision, ensure the door is closed on your way out."

Savage remained looking out the window and Seth wasted no time leaving the room, ignoring Savage's indignant secretary as he walked past and quickly pressed the button to the elevator, stepping in as the doors opened.

Seth headed straight back to Blade's office; the only place all four felt it was safe to meet.

"Well, how did it go?" Asked Blade.

"I was shitting myself!" Exclaimed Seth.

"Yeah, but did he go for it?" Asked Blade anxiously.

"He wouldn't have given Seth an answer yet, he'll want to check out who Victor Seminov is first," said Max.

"Like Max said, but at least he didn't rule it out altogether," replied Seth.

"Did you tell him Victor wants to deal with him personally?" Asked Blade.

"Hell no, I wasn't stupid enough to hit him with that yet!"

"Smart man, Savage would have definitely become suspicious if you had mentioned that upfront, we have to wait till he feels he needs Victor Seminov as a client," said Max.

"So what do we do now?" Asked Blade.

"Work on the other half of our plan, ensuring Savage is accountable for every shady deal he has been involved in," said Max.

"Which is?" Asked Seth and Blade in unison.

"Gaining access to Savage's computer," said Max.

"You mean hack into it?" Asked Seth.

"In a sense, by placing a Trojan on his computer."

"Max, a man like Savage would have every possible firewall on his computer, it would take even the best hacker, weeks, possibly months to hack into his system," stated Jasmine

"Ah, but if we upload it via a USB stick…"

"Are you crazy, how the hell do you think you are going to get into his office to do that?" Asked Seth.

"I'm not, you are."

"What! Firstly I have no idea when he is, or is not in his office, secondly I wouldn't have a hope in hell of getting past his Gestapo secretary and if by a mere miracle she was not there... "

"You'd be doing this at night, when you know everyone has left the building," replied Max.

"How am I supposed to get into the building, your forgetting the security guards?"

"You'll go in from the roof," replied Max.

"You've already come up with a plan, haven't you?" Asked Jasmine.

"I've got something in mind, but it all depends on where Savage's office is situated and the layout."

"His office is on the top floor, as for layout, it's big, plush, has a magnificent view," said Seth sarcastically.

"Perfect, but we'll still need to get hold of the plans, I'm sure that's right up your alley Jasmine."

"Sure."

"What do you have in mind?" Asked Blade.

"We gain access via the rooftop fire door; every high rise has a roof top exit."

"If you're thinking of landing a helicopter there, forget it, it would draw too much attention, the guards that patrol the building would be on the phone to Savage within minutes," stated Seth.

"Ah, but we're not actually going to land on the rooftop; you'll be winched down from the helicopter."

"Me, are you crazy!" Exclaimed Seth.

"It makes perfect sense, you're small enough to fit through tight spaces, besides I'm sure all the guards are aware of who you are, if by chance they see you, I'm sure you can come up with a plausible excuse as to why you're in the building at that hour," commented Max.

"Max, you're forgetting the fact a helicopter flying in the city, whether it be day or night, will draw too much attention and then there is the factor of clearance from Air Traffic Control," stated Jasmine.

"You're going to contact your boss and tell her you need not only the station's helicopter, but to lodge a flight plan with the Air Traffic Control and be granted clearance to fly in the city and over a particular building."

"How do you propose I get her to agree to this?"

"Tell her if she wants an exclusive with Max Steel, she will do as you ask."

"Would you really do that?"

"If it means getting my daughter back and ensuring these bastards are locked away for good, then yes!"

"I'll see what I can do, but I can't make any promises."

"I think it sounds like a good plan," stated Blade.

"Easy for you to say, you're not the one risking your life for this hair brain scheme of his!"

"I thought you wanted to avenge your brother's death," replied Blade.

"Yeah, but not if it means getting myself killed in the process."

"What if I offered you an incentive that would make it worth your while?" Asked Max.

"I'm listening."

"First of all, if you were given the opportunity to start life over and money wasn't an object, what would you do?"

Seth thought about it for a moment and then a smile came to his face.

"I'd buy one of Savage's luxury yachts, without the extras of course and live out my days sailing around the world."

"What if I had the power to do that, plus a new identity?"

"If you could do that, which I doubt it, we have a deal."

"Then we have a deal." Max smiled as he held out his hand.

Seth shook his hand, wondering if he had just been conned, or did Max Steel really have the power to do as he said. He knew Microbe had regretted the day he scammed Max Steel, he also knew the more he tried to find out about the man, the more worried he became. Seth had never seen Microbe show any signs of fear, least not until Max Steel became a resident of Eden Cove.

"So explain this plan to me?" Asked Seth.

"I'm sure Savage has movement sensors on the floor of his office, one of the reasons you will enter the office via the ceiling, you'll lower yourself down to the desk with a mini winch."

"How the hell am I supposed to get into the ceiling?"

"Most offices now have what's called a suspended ceiling, it is hung from the structure above with ceiling joists with a metal grid, which consist of a series of metal channels in the shape of an upside down T, it was designed to cover pipes and air-conditioning, but also for acoustic control, movable tile panelling sits in this frame. So basically all you need to do is move one of these tiles, attach your mini winch to the bar above and haul yourself up. In your kit bag there will be two adhesive handles so you can put the tile back in place once you are inside the cavity, but also so you can remove the one above Savage's desk."

"Too easy!" Exclaimed Blade.

Seth didn't bother to comment; he just gave Blade a dark look.

"Our biggest hurdle is going to be the password to Savage's computer," stated Max.

"Well there goes that plan!" Exclaimed Seth.

"There is a way around that, I'll give you a CD to insert into the computer, when you have done that, hit the reset button, this process is called 'Brute Forcing', the password will then flash momentarily on the screen. Providing it's a relatively simple one, you remove the CD and re-boot the computer. Now you know the password, you type it in before attaching the USB stick. We can then upload a Trojan to allow us remote access, when we're assured of that, you'll remove the USB stick and shut down the computer, Savage will be none the wiser, "said Max.

"How the hell am I supposed to remember all this?"

"You don't have to; you'll be fitted with an earpiece and will be told, step by step, what you have to do."

"Piece of cake," said Blade.

"Easy for you to say, you're not the one going into the lion's den!" Exclaimed Seth.

"Max, were you planning on flying the helicopter, because if you were, I don't know how you can concentrate on that as well as work on hacking into Savage's computer," asked Jasmine.

"Before I answer that, would your boss be willing to let us use the station's chopper, as well as let me fly it?"

"Ah, no."

"Can we trust the pilot to keep his mouth shut about what we're doing?" Asked Max.

"I think so, but to be on the safe side, I'll stress to Jodi if word of this leaks out, she loses her exclusive and you'll go to another station, namely the opposition."

"That should work."

"So what do you want me to do and don't say sit back and twiddle my thumbs?" Asked Blade.

"I'll need you to man the winch, but also you'll be our dummy camera man, this whole scenario has to look legit, which brings me to the use of your building. I hope that Jasmine can get a hold of the plans of Savage's office within the next day or so, which will give me time to get everything required to carry out this operation. I want to recreate the layout of the office, using Seth's memory of where the desk is located; the best case scenario would be Savage calling him back into the office and planting one of these little babies on his desk."

"What is it?" Asked Blade.

"It's a little tracking beacon so I can direct Seth exactly over Savage's desk," replied Max.

"You know I've been trying to figure you out, Rusalka wouldn't say much, but this operation you've got planned, I'm guessing you've got something to do with National Security, or something of that nature," said Blade.

Max just looked at Blade, he had no intention of discussing with him, or anyone else for that matter about his past. Despite him telling Jasmine he would give them an exclusive interview, he hadn't gone so far as to tell her what he was prepared to say in the interview. Wanting to change the subject he looked at Seth, he had to ask him about something that had been niggling at the back of his brain.

"Seth, you said you were the only one of Microbe's men left alive, we've established what kind of man Savage is, but what I don't understand is the murder of Burns, it was as if his killer went out of his way to draw attention to it, which possibly put some heat in Savage's direction."

Max noticed the colour drain from Seth's face and then shrugged his shoulders and looked anywhere but at the three faces that were looking at him.

"You said you were Sam's half-brother, your mother was very young when she had you, what happened, who raised you?"

"I'd rather not talk about it."

"It was you, wasn't it?" Asked Max.

"Damon and I were in Microbe's office the day of the explosion, both of us knew Savage was moving in on Microbe's operation, Microbe was so focussed on you and eliminating your daughter he couldn't see what was going on. Damon had actually been talking to Microbe on the phone when the bomb went off; we both knew it was the *Talisman*. Damon was loyal as hell to Microbe, his instincts kicked in before mine; he opened the safe, which I had no idea he knew the combination for. We heard someone coming, Damon assumed it was Savage, so we quickly went into the storeroom, he kept the door ajar just enough to see who it was, it was Burns; he was after something in the safe. Damon never liked him, he always got great pleasure scaring the shit out of him, he went out to confront him and I stayed in the storeroom, while I waited, I looked through the stuff from the safe. I discovered what Burns was after, Microbe had a file on him; it made me sick!"

"The photos that were plastered all over the walls of the room Burns was killed in?" Asked Max.

"Yes."

"I can understand why you did it the way you did, but why did you wait so long?" Asked Max.

"It wasn't easy, but I knew how these sick bastards operate, I knew they had their own disgusting club, but there was one particular person I was after, I was waiting to see if Burns made contact with him, finally he did."

"How did you discover this?" Asked Max.

"I attached a little spy camera to the picture that hung on the wall behind where he sat, once I had his passwords and read their disgusting conversations, I was able to set them up."

"Very clever, not only did you get revenge, but you exposed a paedophile ring, many of whom are now behind bars," said Max.

"Yeah, with all the comforts of the world!" Said Seth Sarcastically.

"Unfortunately yes," replied Max.

"So what happens now?"

"About what?" Asked Max.

"The murder of Burns," replied Seth.

"I don't know anything about it, Jasmine, Blade, do you know anything?"

"No." They both said in unison.

"Well it looks like we're all clueless on that one, so let's concentrate on the job at hand. I've got some supplies to organise, Jasmine the plans of Savage's office, also contact your boss, Blade carry on with business as usual till I get back to you and Seth, you better get back to whatever, before Savage becomes suspicious."

STEEL JUSTICE

As soon as Jasmine got in the car, she put a call through to her boss. Max listened to the one sided conversation and knew her boss wasn't liking the idea, then she took a deep breath and informed her boss that the opposition had already approached Max for an interview and he was strongly considering it, moments later she hung up and Max looked across at her.

"Well, don't keep me in suspense?"

"She didn't say no, but then she didn't say yes either, give her some time to think things over. I think my comment about you giving an interview to the opposition will work in our favour."

"I hope so, everything is riding on the use of Frontline News's helicopter."

Jasmine just nodded her head and both sat in silence for a while, going over the events of the day.

"Max, I've been going over and over that riddle Deanne's father wrote, so much so, I know it off by heart;

Beware of the Black sheep,
His is a chameleon, one who purges forth white,
Look closely, because all is not as it seems.
Day can become night and night become day.
Follow the numbers they hold the key.
However, remember the eyes don't always see.
Find someone you trust,
So before you choose,
Look deep in your heart,
For the brain can confuse.
Your friend could be your foe.
Only your heart will know.

"The end part was easy, she decided she could trust me, the reason she contacted me. The eclipse was the night and day, which gave us the numbers that led us to the security box at the bank. We've established the Black sheep is Graham Black, I think Graham Black is Michael Savage. He is the chameleon and the part that says, *one who purges forth white, look closely, because all is not as it seems*, I think he was trying to tell us he is selling cocaine and is using a legitimate business as a front to do so!" Exclaimed Jasmine.

"You know you could be right, Seth said Savage is paranoid about his privacy, he doesn't even deal directly with any of his customers, as far as we know, Seth is possibly the only person who knows what Savage looks like."

"Don't forget the secretary."

"If I was Seth, I would be feeling decidedly nervous right now," stated Max.

"You know I just had another thought, we're fairly sure Salina used this experimental drug to kill Dr Shoal, after he performed cosmetic surgery on Graham Black. What if Dr Shoal knew these two people well enough to know, they would sell each other out if it came to it. What if the reason they are still together after all these years is because, she is the only person alive who knows the true identity of Michael Savage and he in inturn knows about her using an experimental drug to kill all those people?"

"I think you just hit the nail on the head, meaning we can also use this knowledge to our advantage to entrap them both!"

CHAPTER TWENTY-FIVE

Max was busily formulating a boot disk to brute-force the password from the computer, it was essential to loading the Trojan horse via the USB stick. When that was completed he focussed all his attention on creating a Trojan that would be so well hidden, it would be undetectable.

Jasmine had managed to secure the plans to Savage's office, it hadn't been an easy matter, she'd had to resort to flirting with the clerk down at Town Planning, even having to go as far as having a coffee with him. Jodi still hadn't got back to her about the use of the station's helicopter, but Jasmine wasn't overly concerned, at least not yet, they still had a lot to do in the lead-up to what Max proposed.

As anxious as Max was to put his plans into action, he didn't want to be seen publicly with Blade, he didn't want to risk any possible chance of one of the parents recognising his face, not after his identity had been exposed in Eden Cove. He couldn't risk Salina making the link between Blade and himself, so he placed a call to ensure his classes were finished for the day.

"Blade, Max here, I have the plans to Savage's office in hand, is everything finished for the day?"

"Yes, in fact for the year, classes don't start up again till early February."

"Finished for the year?"

"Yeah man, it's only a few weeks till Christmas."

Max looked out the window of the apartment and noticed for the first time the streets were decorated with Christmas decorations and as he looked to the windows of other buildings close by, he could see the occasional flashing lights of a Christmas tree inside.

"Max, you still there?"

"Ah yeah sorry, my mind was on something else, I'll be over shortly."

Jasmine had been standing close by, she hadn't wanted to mention the 25th of December wasn't far off, nor the fact her mother had been trying to convince her she should be home for Christmas. Jasmine knew if she had brought up the matter with Max he would have insisted she go home, but she hadn't come this far to back out now, she had to see this to the end. As if reading her thoughts, he turned towards her.

"Why didn't you tell me?"

"To be honest, apart from my mother's constant reminders, it kind of snuck up on me as well."

"You should be home with your family; I can take care of things from here."

"When I told you I wanted to follow this through to the end, I meant it, besides you need me here."

"I told you, I…"

"Ah, your forgetting about a certain helicopter, one that only through my clever art of persuasion, will you be allowed the use of."

"What about your mother?"

"She'll get over it, especially when she discovers I assisted in the downfall of the elusive Mistress!"

"Ok, then we better get a move on."

With plans in hand, Max transformed the hall to resemble the layout of Savage's office, including the fire door exit from the rooftop and an elevated bar that represented the framework of the suspended ceiling so Seth could practice using the mini winch.

Max had various gadgets spread out on a table, a personal communicator, which consisted of an earpiece, a belt clip radio and a wristwatch videophone and a strange looking gun.

"Now we each have personal communicators, so we can be in contact we each other, but Jasmine there should be no need for you to say anything, just thought you would like to hear what is going on, so let's give them a test run shall we? Everyone spread out, I will ask each of you a question and I want you to respond softly," said Max.

All three did as Max requested and after a few adjustments he was confident all were operating correctly.

"Blade, as you'll be manning the winch, you'll need to clip the helicopter cable to the front of Seth's harness, like so, this way he will be able to remove it without difficulty once he is safely on the rooftop. Now I know you're all wondering what this contraption is and no it is not a gun, it's a mini winch, you will need this to haul yourself up into the ceiling and lower yourself over Savage's desk to gain access to his computer; I'll explain how it works in a moment."

"Max, if by chance the security guards see Seth, won't they get suspicious seeing him wearing that harness?" Asked Jasmine.

"Not if he is wearing a jacket over the top, once he's unclipped the cable, he'll do up the jacket..."

"What about security cameras?" Asked Jasmine.

"I'll be checking that out when I do the fire inspection," replied Max.

They all looked at him with a blank stare, wondering what on earth he was talking about.

"All high-rise buildings have to have regular fire safety inspections, making sure there are adequate fire extinguishers and they are operational, but also, ensuring all fire doors meet the required standards, many people have perished because they could not open the fire door, I need to ensure Seth can open the two fire doors."

"Max, you're forgetting fire exits are designed to open into the stairwell, not the other way around, how will Seth be able to gain access through them?" Asked Jasmine.

"Yeah, I didn't think of that!" Exclaimed Seth.

"Ah, but he will have a key," said Max.

"How?" All three asked in unison.

"I'll make one, which is why I need to check the fire doors."

"How are you going to make a key, without the original key?" Asked Seth.

"Easy, it's called impressing, I insert a blank key into the lock and turn it to bind the pins, when the pins are binding, I wiggle the key to produce the pin marks on the blank, once I've got those I know where to file the key and voila; you have a key to the door."

"You make it sound so easy, but something like that would take a while, I can guarantee Savage's secretary will be timing you, she is suspicious of anyone who steps on the top floor, if she thinks you're taking too long, she'll check up on you!" Said Seth.

"I've done this sort of thing so many times I could do it with my eyes closed, it would take me five minutes tops. So if you are finished asking questions about getting into the building, can we get on with the actual process of gaining access to Savage's office and his computer?" Asked Max.

Max wanted the test run to be as realistic as possible, so when the time came Seth would go through the steps automatically, he helped him into the harness and checked all the clips and straps.

"Ok, first we'll practice you unclipping yourself from the helicopter cable and getting yourself through both the fire door exits and into the ceiling. This odd looking gun, is a mini winch, you pull the trigger like so and it will clamp on the bar above you, flick the switch and it will haul you up into the ceiling."

"How am I supposed to move one of those tiles so I can do this?" Asked Seth.

"With this extendable rod that will be in your pack, ok let's give this a run through."

Blade and Seth went through the motions of clipping and unclipping the helicopter cable to the harness and then Seth went through the two fire doors, before removing the ceiling panel and attaching the winch to the bar above, dubious as to whether the thing was strong enough to hold his weight as he was hauled up.

"Good, now winch yourself back down," said Max

Seth did as Max requested; the little winch hummed happily and showed no signs of straining with his weight.

"Okay, now when you need to suspend yourself over Savage's desk, obviously you will need your hands to be free, so once you are inside the ceiling and have replaced the panel, clip the winch to your harness like so. Blade, when Seth has winched himself back into the ceiling, give me a hand moving the desk and computer underneath him."

"Okay Seth, this time, lower yourself slowly so that you are within reach of the computer."

All three watched as he did this smoothly.

"Good, now first, manually eject the CD tray by inserting the end of a paperclip into the manual override hole, now insert the disk and press the reset button and the moment you see the password flash on the screen, say it so I can hear, then remove the disk and re-boot the computer. Assuming you have the password type it in and wait till it logs in. When you see that has happened, attach the USB stick, wait for the 'load programme' prompt and hit 'enter', wait for my all clear before you remove the stick and shutdown the computer. We'll run through this till you can go through the process with your eyes closed," stated Max.

"Are you saying, I'm gunna have to do this in the dark?" Asked Seth.

"No, you will have a small headlamp; I just want you to go over and over it, till you feel you could do it with your eyes closed."

After a few practice runs, Max was confident he didn't have to give Seth step-by-step instructions, so he began timing him to see how quickly he could go through the whole process. Suddenly Seth's phone rang, as he was suspended mid-air.

"Shit, it's Savage."

All remained quiet while he retrieved the phone from his pocket and answered it.

"Yep, no problems, I'll be there shortly."

Seth quickly winched himself back to the ground and Max

helped him remove the harness.

"I'm hoping the meeting is in his office," said Max.

"Yep."

"Good, you need to attach this to his desk."

"Shit, I never usually walk that far into the room."

"Well this time you'll have to make an exception, because it will make our job a hell of a lot easier later on!" Exclaimed Max.

Seth took the tiny device that was no larger than a small button and put it in the pocket of his trousers, before nervously walking out the door. No sooner had he left, when Jasmine's phone rang, it was her boss Jodi.

"Hello… ah-huh… really, ok… not sure yet…will do, thanks."

"Well?" Asked Max.

"She'll agree to let us have use of the helicopter and clear it with Air Traffic Control, on one condition."

"And what is that?"

"Your daughter is also present at the interview."

"I'm sorry, but I can't answer you on that one."

"Jodi won't agree to it unless I give her a yes."

"Max, you have to say yes, we need that helicopter!" Exclaimed Blade.

"My daughter is an adult, she is almost twenty years old and therefore I cannot speak for her."

"If you won't speak for her, then I will. Jasmine ring back your boss and give her the ok," said Blade.

"You have no idea what you are getting yourself into," replied Max.

Jasmine could see Blade was getting angry, but she also understood what Max was saying, she hadn't met Michelle personally, but she believed she knew enough about her to know she was definitely her own person and no one would tell her what she could or could not do!

"Look, how about I call her and tell her she is going to have her interview…"

"I told you…," said Max.

"You have already agreed to give an interview, I'll just let her think it includes your daughter. I won't be lying to my boss, I'm just ensuring we get that helicopter, which brings me to when are you planning on doing this so she can get clearance from Air Traffic Control."

"Give me three days, it will give me time to fine tune my Trojan horse and make a key for the fire doors."

"Ok."

"In the meantime Blade, we need to keep running through the process of Seth accessing Savage's office."

"Gotcha."

Meanwhile Seth was waiting nervously outside Savage's office, waiting for his secretary to buzz him through.

"Mr Savage is ready to see you now."

When Seth entered the office he noticed Savage had his back to him and was standing over by the window, giving him the cue to walk quickly over by his desk and plant the small device Max had given him.

"What do you think you are doing?"

Seth looked up to see Savage walking across the room towards him, madly trying to think of something to say, he quickly dropped his phone to the floor and bent down and picked it up.

"Um I was just picking up my phone, bloody pocket, must have a hole in it. It gave me a fright, I felt something moving down my leg and I must have kicked it across the room."

Savage came up close to him and Seth could feel his legs shake as he looked into the eyes of the devil.

"Show me your pockets."

"What?" Asked Seth nervously.

"You heard me."

Seth removed his car keys from one of his pockets before pulling it out, then slowly pulled out the other pocket and to his relief it actually had a hole in it. Savage just stared at him for a moment longer and then walked over to the liquor cabinet and placed a few ice cubes into a glass, before pouring a measure of whiskey from the decanter.

"Make sure Victor Seminov receives an invitation to the boat show."

"Yeah sure."

Seth tried to respond as casually as possible; he didn't want to give Savage any cause for suspicion.

"Well, what are you waiting for?" Demanded Savage.

"Ah, yeah ok, I'm on to it."

Seth nearly tripped over himself trying to get out the door and wasted no time getting over to the lift. He waited till he was safely in his car before he put the call to Max telling him the homing device was planted on Savage's desk and he had taken the bait.

* * *

Jasmine had explained to the helicopter pilot, that Frontline News had been given the rare opportunity to be involved in a stunt for a movie. Because of his excellent flying skills, the director had agreed to let him fly the helicopter, but he had to swear to secrecy he wouldn't mention a word of this, otherwise the whole scene would be scrapped. The pilot agreed to this, as it was an opportunity of a lifetime, she introduced Max as the director, Blade the cameraman, also stunt assistant and Seth was the stuntman.

As the building came into view, Blade helped Seth attach the winch cable to his harness and slid open the helicopter door. Under Max's instructions, the pilot decreased the altitude until they were about ten metres above the building. As soon as Max gave Seth the signal, he was out of the helicopter and on the rooftop within sixty seconds. Seth immediately released the winch from his harness and gave Blade the all clear, who then hit the switch to reel in the winch and the helicopter flew off.

Seth wasted no time unlocking the first fire door and was running down the stairs to the second; he knew he had a fifteen-minute window, before a guard would do a patrol.

By the time he stepped through the second door, adrenaline was coursing through his veins, as practised; he lifted one of the tile panels with the extendable rod and successfully anchored the winch to one of the steel beams and within seconds was in the ceiling and had replaced the tile panel. He quickly turned on his head torch and proceeded forward until Max told him he was directly over Savage's desk.

He attached an adhesive handle and removed the tile panel and looked down through the opening to ensure he was actually above his mark. After ensuring the winch was securely attached to a supporting beam, he then clipped it to his harness and made the slow decent down towards Savage's computer. He had travelled about a metre when the winch jammed suddenly.

"Shit!"

"What's wrong? Asked Max.

"The winch has jammed!"

Max could tell by his voice he was starting to panic.

"It's ok; just flick the switch to go back up a bit, then trying coming down again."

Seth did as he said and was relieved that it didn't jam this time.

"It worked!"

"Ok, now use your paperclip to open the tray and insert the disc into the computer, then hit the reset button and keep your eyes on the screen."

After inserting the disc, he held his finger over the reset button, focussing his eyes on the screen, he hit the button but nothing happened.

"Nothing, nothing is coming up."

"Give it time."

Suddenly the word MONEY flashed on the screen and Seth laughed, he should have known. He quickly removed the disc and then re-booted the computer and typed in the password, not bothering to converse with Max; he had gone through the motions so many times, he was confident he knew what he was doing.

"Seth, what's happening?" Asked Max.

"I've just typed in the password, just waiting for the screen to come up, so I can attach the USB stick."

"Good."

"Okay, I'm attaching the USB stick now."

"Gotcha, this should only take about a minute," replied Max.

While Seth waited he strained his ears for any sounds of movement coming from the outer office.

"Okay Seth I'm in, take out the USB stick, shutdown the computer and get the hell out of there."

Seth didn't have to be told twice, within seconds everything was back in the pack and he winched himself back up inside the ceiling, quickly replacing the tile and with Max's directions made it back to his starting point.

"Get moving the lift is on its way up!" Urged Max.

Seth wished Max hadn't said that, it immediately put him into a panic, he fumbled trying to attach the winch to the beam, then decided against it and awkwardly pulled the tile panel across as he held onto the beam with one hand, before he let himself fall to the floor, jarring his ankle as he did so. He had just placed his hand on the fire exit door, when he heard the ding of the lift.

As soon as he was safely on the other side he paused to catch his breath and whispered to Max he had made it through the first door.

"Okay, we'll give him five minutes before we fly back over, just on the off chance he can see us from one of the windows," replied Max

Seth slowly made his way up the stairs, not only because of his injured ankle, but being careful not to make any sound. He waited on the top step until he could hear the vibrating thump of the approaching helicopter, before exiting the final door.

Blade lowered the winch and the moment it was low

enough Seth hobbled across to it and securely attached it to his harness, before giving him the signal to haul him up.

"I'd say that's a cut, great work," said Max.

"Just another day at the office," replied Seth.

"Thanks guys, thank you so much for letting Frontline News, be a part of this movie," said Jasmine; for the benefit of the pilot.

"The pleasure was all ours, wouldn't you say boys," said Max.

"Yeah, I just hope we don't have to do another take on that one!" Exclaimed Seth

CHAPTER TWENTY-SIX

Max sifted through the data from Savage's computer, he could see the man was not only very clever, but also extremely paranoid, given he had so many firewalls to break through before he could even view any data. He uncovered the crisscross pattern of funds being transferred to many different companies, which appeared to be legit and above board, it wasn't until he delved deeper he found something of interest. There was a pattern of regular trades for certain entities, which paid exorbitant prices for the sale of a luxury yacht, but one off customers paid a much lesser amount for the exact, same item, which was more suited to the market value of such a boat.

Despite the fact Max could see Savage was doing some shady deals, it still didn't prove he was dealing in drugs, evidence that was required to put Savage away for a very long time. With Seth's help he had managed to get Savage to take the bait, he just hoped Seth's nerves and determination to avenge his brother's death stood fast, everything hinged on him following this to the end.

Max had convinced Jasmine to fly home for Christmas, as he had barely scratched the surface of the data on Savage's computer, something he was focussing all his efforts on at the present and as the proposed boat show wasn't until the New Year, it was pointless her hanging around waiting for something to happen.

Seth hadn't as yet put to Savage that Seminov would only do a deal with the man himself. After much discussion it had been agreed they would wait till the day of the boat show, it was a big risk, but Max thought the best tactic was to put Savage on the spot, as he had ensured Seminov's offer was so attractive, his immediate reaction would be to agree.

STEEL JUSTICE

* * *

It was the day of the boat show and Seth had done many test runs with the camera so he knew exactly where to stand, they wanted only two people visible on the security cameras and he wasn't one of them. Seth's nerves were strung so tight, he had one final message to relay to Savage, he just hoped he could pull it off; so much was riding on it.

As he stood in the elevator watching the numbers count-up to the top floor, Seth suddenly wished he had drunk a good measure of Dutch courage, but then realised that probably would tip off Savage that something was up. Suddenly there was a ding announcing the lift had reached its destination, Seth braced himself as the doors opened, knowing he would be looking directly at the scowling face of Savage's secretary. He immediately stepped out of the lift and strode purposefully towards her desk.

"Before you make comment, no, I don't have an appointment, but this is an urgent matter. If you will just buzz through to him and tell him we have a problem with the new client."

"Now look here…"

"Just do it!"

Seth shocked both himself and the secretary by his forceful demand, but it had its desired effect, as she immediately pushed the intercom through to Savage's office. Moments later the door was opened by the man himself, who without uttering a word, motioned to Seth to come into his office and closed the door firmly behind him. Seth could feel the man's cold hard eyes boring into his back, instantly causing him to breakout into a sweat, with the stealth of a leopard eyeing off its prey, Savage suddenly appeared in front of him.

"You seem rather nervous, I wonder why?"

Seth struggled to look into those cold black eyes.

"It's about Seminov; he's suddenly got jumpy and is considering pulling out."

"What!" Exploded Savage.

"He's worried he's being setup."

"You can't be serious?"

"Deadly sir."

Seth felt a trickle of perspiration run down the centre of his back, as he watched Savage's face darken with rage and hoped that he couldn't see his legs quake.

"This man who came to me, begging to become one of my clients and finally when everything is set in place; he decides to get cold feet!"

"Ah, it's because you're not actually handling the deal."

"What do you mean?"

"He wants to deal with you personally, else the deal is off."

"You know I don't deal directly with my clients, that's what I pay you for."

"Yeah well that's what bothers him, he said the only way he would be assured this deal is legit, is if you deal with him personally."

"I don't see how that will reassure him, he doesn't even know what I look like and that's how I wish it to remain."

"I told him this, in fact I even lied and told him I don't even know what you look like, but he stands firm, either you do a face to face with him today, or the deal is off. He also said he will know if you send someone in your place."

"How?"

"I don't know, he could be bluffing, but do you want to risk losing him, no one has ever put in such a large order before, nor have they been prepared to pay such a high price."

As Seth watched Savage's eyes narrow, he realised he had possibly signed his own death warrant, but figured if he couldn't convince Savage to do the deal, he was probably a dead man anyway.

"Very well," said Savage as he made his way towards the window.

"Wwwhat?" Asked Seth nervously.

"You heard me, but mark my words, this is a one off!"

Seth just nodded and not waiting to be dismissed bolted from the office. By the time the doors on the lift closed, he had to restrain himself from smiling, he was well aware Savage had cameras everywhere, but by the time he reached the safety of his car he could barely contain himself and quickly placed a call to Max.

"Yes?"

"He took the bait."

"Good work, see you in two hours."

The call was disconnected and Seth headed straight for the marina, he wanted to check everything over again, this would be a onetime only show, one that was hopefully the ticket to his new life!

* * *

Michelle looked at herself in the mirror, noting her pale pasty skin, which she had learnt to expertly cover in make-up before she entered the arena. Suddenly a slow tear ran down her face as she remembered a time when her skin was the colour of warm honey, a time when she was carefree with the world at her feet. Angrily she wiped the tear from her face and marched over to her desk, yanking out one of the drawers, feeling underneath for her diary that was hidden there; since she had been fitted with her deadly bracelets, her room was no longer searched and it was no longer necessary for her to hide her diary, but she still did anyway.

Since being incarcerated her diary had been her only friend, not only someone to talk to, but a way of keeping track of time. Today was her birthday, she had now been incarcerated for ten months and it had been six weeks since she had asked Blade to deliver a message to her father. She angrily marked another day in her book and wrote in bold letters **'Men you can't trust them, you can't rely on them!'**

She taped her diary back into its hiding place and paced about her lavish room, which in reality was nothing more than a cage. Her only solace was Sayoc Kali, a source to vent not only her anger and frustrations, but also her despair. The irony of it was, after years of searching for that big adrenaline hit, nothing gave her a bigger rush, not until she was forced to fight for her virtue, but also her life!

* * *

Seth was standing on the deck of the luxury yacht and focussed his eyes on a man with a briefcase as he approached the boat. He knew Max would be coming in disguise, but the way the man carried his body, the way he walked, he wondered if this was him or just a stranger wanting a closer look.

Not once did the man look at him as he came up beside the yacht, he rubbed his hand along the boat's sleek lines, admiring the gleaming stainless steel railings. He suddenly turned and started to make his way up the few short steps.

"I'm sorry sir, but its appointment only," said Seth

"Well it's lucky I have an appointment," he said, as he held out a card.

Seth looked at the card, raising his eyebrows in surprise, as the name Victor Seminov was clearly printed. He looked at the man more intently and still found it hard to believe it was Max.

"My apologies Mr Seminov, if you would like to follow me, I will show you what this magnificent yacht has to offer."

Max followed Seth inside and looked around, noting they were alone.

"There must be some misunderstanding; I specifically requested dealing with Mr Savage himself."

Max started to turn and make his way back outside, when Seth quickly spoke.

"Mr Seminov please, Mr Savage has every intention of being here, but he is temporarily delayed, perhaps I can offer you a drink, or would you like me to show you around?"

"Too early in the day for a drink, as long as Mr Savage is on his way, I suppose it won't hurt for you to show me around."

Seth had warned Max in advance that Savage would possibly do this, but also Max was pleased he had thrown Seth with his disguise, he was sure Savage was watching close by.

About an hour later after Seth had shown him through the entirety of the boat, explaining things along the way as if he was a genuine customer, Max turned impatiently towards Seth as he realised they were back in the plush lounge where they had started.

"Obviously Mr Savage has no intention of showing up and I take this as a personal insult; today has been nothing but a waste of my time!"

"I'm sorry…"

"Mr Seminov?"

Max noted the look on Seth's face and knew Savage had finally decided to make an appearance, despite Seth's description of him, he was surprised at the size of the man. Max was guessing him to be at least six three, he himself stood at six two and the man seemed to tower above him and his large frame, which by no means was overweight, he had to almost turn sideways to fit through the door. His face, which was virtually devoid of a wrinkle or character line and judging by his unnaturally black hair, he was guessing that he was much older than his smooth face would have one believe.

As Savage walked towards him, his gaze was drawn to the man's dark menacing eyes. Max could well understand how his overall appearance could instil fear, especially in a small man like Seth.

Not surprisingly Savage was also scrutinising Victor Seminov, but Max was confident the man would not see past his disguise and moments later Savage held out his hand.

"Mr Seminov, I'm Michael Savage, I hope Seth passed on my apologies for not being present upon your arrival?"

"Yes he did and he was kind enough to give me a thorough tour of the boat."

"Good. Well there is no point explaining the excellent

craftsmanship and thought that has gone into building this yacht, I am sure you have seen that for yourself."

"Yes, I can make no fault there, but then that is not the real reason I'm here today, as you well know."

"You're obviously a man who doesn't like to waste time on small talk, although I've noticed you have come alone," replied Savage.

"I feel it draws less attention that way."

"True, but what about carrying such a large sum of cash, Seth did explain that the initial down payment was to be in cash of non-sequential serial numbers?"

"Yes he did, as I said, an old man carrying a briefcase draws far less attention than one being escorted with a bodyguard."

Max walked over towards the low table in front of the lounge chair and placed the briefcase on top, after quickly punching in his security code to unlock it; he opened the lid so Savage could see the contents.

"One million dollars, as per the agreement."

Savage walked forward and pickup up each bundle to ensure they were all one hundred dollar notes and not padded with blank paper. Satisfied, he turned towards Seth and gave a quick nod, which in turn he immediately unlocked one of the cupboards near the bar and pulled out a briefcase, similar to the one Max had brought on board. Seth quickly placed the case on the table, before stepping back, ensuring he was out of camera view and then pushed the button to turn on the camera. Normally in these proceedings he opened the briefcase for the client, but he needed proof of Savage's involvement, there was a good chance this video would be used as evidence in court, something he had no intention of being a part of.

Seth tried to keep his face devoid of expression as Savage looked at him questioningly and Max instantly picked up on what Seth was trying to do.

"Well Mr Savage, do you plan on allowing me to sample the product or do you expect me to trust you in good faith?"

"Of course Seth…"

"Who no longer needs to be present, this is after all a business transaction between you and I, is it not?"

"Of course."

Not waiting to be dismissed, Seth quickly left the room, leaving Savage to unlock the briefcase and carry on with the proceedings. Max pulled his small testing kit from inside his jacket pocket and poured liquid from one of the vials into another, Savage handed him a clean paperknife and Max took a small sample of the white powder, placing it in the vial with the liquid and after sealing the lid he gave it a quick shake. Within seconds the substance turned dark like the colour of coffee and Max smiled and turned towards Savage.

"Definitely five stars, it will be a pleasure doing business with you." Max said as he held out his hand.

"How about we seal the deal with a drink?"

Max didn't want to carry on this charade any longer than necessary and looked at his watch, giving the impression he was pushed for time, when suddenly he noticed the date, it was the eighteenth of January, Michelle's birthday.

"Something wrong?" Asked Savage.

Max realised for an instant he had allowed Savage to see behind his mask, as the man was looking at him suspiciously. His mind raced trying to think of a plausible excuse that would remove any suspicion from Savage's mind.

"Have you ever forgotten a woman's birthday?"

A smile suddenly came to the man's face and he nodded his head knowingly.

"You know it is an unspoken rule never to ask a woman her age, but if you happen to forget her birthday, there will be hell on earth to pay!" Exclaimed Max.

"I find flowers and a booking at her favourite restaurant plus some bauble from one of the finest jewellers, does the trick."

"You've done this before."

"Trust me, it works every time."

Max rose to his feet, feeling he had managed to put Savage at ease.

"Well it's been a pleasure doing business with you, but if I'm not going to be drawn, quartered and hung out to dry, I better get a move on," said Max as he closed the briefcase before taking possession of it.

"I'll see to it that Seth makes all the arrangements for delivery of your purchase; welcome to the world of luxury boating Mr Seminov."

Max stood and both men shook hands, before Max made a hasty exit, knowing it would not draw any further concerns from Savage.

Later that evening, all four viewed the video of the transaction between Victor Seminov and Michael Savage.

"Well there is no court on earth that will allow Savage to wriggle out of that one!" Exclaimed Jasmine.

"With the data I've gathered from his computer and Seth's recant of how the operation was run, including the demise of Malcolm Microbe, he's going to live out his retirement behind bars," said Max.

"I think this, calls for a celebration!" Replied Seth.

"Not just yet, I've lived up to my part of the bargain, now it's your turn. Where is my daughter?"

"She's about half an hour from Brisbane Airport," replied Seth.

"Impossible!"

"I agree with Max, I was in the air for at least forty-five minutes in the private jet, I made a point of looking at my watch after take-off and then before the blindfold was replaced before landing and I swear it was about a thirty minute trip in the helicopter!" Exclaimed Blade.

"Yes that's correct, but what you didn't realise, the ride in the private jet was to throw you off; you actually landed back at Brisbane Airport," replied Seth.

"So the jet was virtually a joy ride," commented Max.

"Yes, every aspect of what she is doing is illegal, she

cannot afford for anyone to have even the slightest clue where she lives or the event takes place!"

"That's why no one has been able to find her until now," commented Jasmine

"Correct, also Blade managed to survive the fight, but many haven't, what do they do with those that don't, as far as I know there have never been any reports of a body or bodies found with multiple knife wounds?"

"Are you suggesting that she buries the bodies on her property?" Asked Jasmine.

"It's a big property."

"Seth is right, it also explains why I couldn't find a possible landing area for the jet working on the times Blade gave me, even if I varied those times; it wasn't possible," stated Max.

"So where exactly is this place?" Asked Blade.

"Have you ever heard of Cooee Mountain?"

"Are you kidding me?" Asked Blade incredulously.

"Nope."

"Holy Shit!"

"Well?" Asked Max looking at both Seth and Blade.

"It's only one of the most exclusive properties in the area, possibly all of Queensland," stated Blade.

"Well, that sounds like exactly the kind of place Salina, better known as the 'Mistress' would hide out," commented Jasmine.

"Ok Seth, what can you tell me about the security of this place?" Asked Max.

"I'd say it's probably better than the Perth Mint."

"Dogs?"

"Yep and they're mean bastards too, wouldn't surprise me if they feed the victims to them."

"Oh my god!" Exclaimed Jasmine.

"So it will have to be an approach from the air," commented Max.

"No way, the sound of an approaching helicopter would immediately put the guards on alert," replied Seth.

"Who said anything about a helicopter."

"How else?" Asked Blade.

"Small plane, about twelve thousand feet."

"Hang on, I'm not jumping out of no plane, especially at that altitude," replied Blade.

"Oh, look who's chicken shit now they're the one having to jump out of an aircraft," taunted Seth.

"Twelve thousand feet is a hell of a lot different to a few feet above a rooftop and you were attached to a winch," replied Blade angrily.

"Ok enough, I never said anything about you jumping out of a plane; if you'll shut up and listen I'll explain how we're going to do this."

Max looked sternly at both men, who immediately looked contrite.

"Blade, you've been to Michelle's room…"

"Michelle?" Asked Blade.

"Rusalka is only a stage name, now do you think you would be able to find it once inside the building?" Asked Max.

"Yes."

"Ok, let's take a look at this place on a satellite image," said Max as he sat in front of the computer.

All looked at the available images that the programme was able to produce.

"It's certainly a large property, I'm assuming one of these buildings is the stadium, plenty of room to land a dozen helicopters, I'm surmising this is how the guests also arrive," commented Max.

"You guessed it and blindfolded as well."

"Ok, well here is a good image of the property entrance and the road leading up to it, plenty of trees and foliage for you to hide your vehicle out of sight, while you wait for me to disable the alarms and open the front gates," said Max.

"Yeah, but the sound of an unauthorised vehicle approaching is still going to draw attention from the guards, as well as the dogs," explained Seth.

"Not if their busy elsewhere, I've got a few little tricks up my sleeve to create a diversion."

"Sounds good, so what do you want me to do?" Asked Jasmine.

"You're going to contact your friend in blue and show her that video of Rusalka on YouTube and tell her she is forced to do this and is currently being held by the elusive Mistress…"

"You want them to know that your daughter is responsible for killing god knows how many men?"

"No! You must never mention to anyone that Rusalka is my daughter and that goes for all of you, because if you do, I will personally rip out your tongue!" Exclaimed Max.

All three looked at Max in shock, but all knew, if they even so much as hinted at the fact, he would carry out his threat.

"Now, I know Salina is on the top of the list for questioning over the illegal smuggling of young girls for the purpose of prostitution, among other things. I'm sure if that video of Rusalka doesn't gain their attention, the whereabouts of the Mistress will, but I don't want you to give them her location until Blade has managed to get my daughter off the property."

"It's not going to be easy withholding that information," stated Jasmine.

"I'm sure you'll be able to come up with a plausible reason."

"Jeez, well obviously this is something I will be doing days before, what about on the actual night, what do you want me to do?"

"Trust me; you're going to have your work cut out keeping the location quiet until I give you the signal. Don't worry, you'll get your story, after all you're the only reporter privy to what's going to go down, you'll have plenty of time to have your crew in place for a Frontline News exclusive."

"But…"

"No butts Jasmine, the last thing I need to be worrying about, is you getting yourself into trouble because you've got into your pretty little head, that you're some kind of Lara

Croft!"

Jasmine bit back an angry retort and just glared at him, *you'll keep Max Steel, just wait till I have you in the interview chair!*

CHAPTER TWENTY-SEVEN

Max looked at the altimeter that was strapped to his wrist, the plane had almost reached twelve thousand five hundred feet, when he moved himself into position at the open door and waited for the all-clear signal from the pilot.

Moments later he received the thumbs up and Max exited the plane headfirst, a method he preferred, shortening his free fall of ten thousand feet to less than a minute, reaching speeds just under two hundred kilometres an hour.

He looked at the luminous dial on his altimeter and the moment he had reached two thousand five hundred feet, he deployed his parachute and flipped down the night vision goggles attached to his helmet. With the use of his GPS and night vision he could now see below him, he steered his parachute towards the intended target, the northern side rooftop of the main building.

As he had done many times before, the moment his feet touched the ground he twisted his upper body in the direction of the wind, a much safer method as it slowed down his ground speed. Once his landing roll was complete he quickly detached his chute so he wouldn't be dragged off the roof.

He secured the chute out of sight, so it wouldn't blow in the wind alerting the guards to his presence, then pulled a rope from his backpack, first anchoring it to a secure point before rappelling down the side of the building, where Seth had told him he could gain access through a side door. Max knew once he opened this door it would trigger the alarm countdown, he had a thirty-second window before the alarm would sound and send a signal out to the response centre; this countdown was designed to allow the homeowner time to enter in their code once entering their premises.

Seth had told Max where the control panel was located and it took him less than twenty seconds to remove the alarm panel and cut the wires. After triggering the electric front gates, he then proceeded to plant some small explosives to divert any security guards away from the main entrance.

"Seth, you copy?"

"Loud and clear."

"Proceed to the entry gates; they should be opening as we speak."

"Gotcha."

Seth moved the vehicle forward, out of the shadows a short distance from the estate's entry, by the time he had turned the vehicle into the drive the gates had completely opened. Blade kept an eye out for any sign of guards, or menacing security dogs, while Seth kept his eyes on the road ahead.

Jasmine had also been parked in the shadows, but what neither of the men realised, was she had followed them at a safe distance. She couldn't just stand back on the sidelines, not after coming this far and hoped it wouldn't be too long before she could reveal her exact location to Tracey, she knew her boss would not allow her and her team to wait on the sidelines for too long. Suddenly her phone vibrated and she knew without even looking at it, that it would be Tracey, this would be call two, *how many more would there be before she could answer?*

Michelle paced the room, she was more than ready for the fight tonight, after her birthday had come and gone without so much as a Happy Birthday, she had gone from a bout of deep depression to pent-up rage. She'd barely touched the food that had been sent to her room, she felt more in the need of a stiff drink, but drinking wasn't allowed for at least forty-eight hours before a fight.

She looked at the clock on her desk, the guard would be here any minute to escort her to the stadium, suddenly there was a loud explosion and she heard the sound of running feet outside. She raced over putting her ear up against the door, hoping to learn what was happening, she could hear raised voices and then there was another explosion. Desperate to know what was causing the explosions, but not being able to open the door, nor wanting to suffer the consequences if she could, she raced over to a window, pushing her face up against the glass in the hope she could see something. Suddenly there was a rattle at the door as if someone was trying to open it and moments later the door burst open with such force, it nearly snapped off its hinges. The last person Michelle expected to see was Blade and they both stared at each other momentarily, Blade noting she was in costume and realised she had been getting ready for a fight, but his lack of speech caused Michelle's anger to bubble forth.

"It's about bloody time!"

"Jeez, is that all the thanks I get for risking life and limb to get you out of this place?"

Michelle looked at him and realised her comment had been unfair, in actual fact her anger was more directed at her father, a man who was supposed to have been in the Special Forces, rescuing people from places like war-torn Afghanistan, *but when it came to finding his daughter, in his own country, a girl just about turned grey waiting!*

"Sorry, I just wasn't expecting to see you again."

"I told you I would."

"Yeah well a lot of guys have told me things, but never follow through."

"Well I'm not a lot of guys, now are we going to stand here all night and discuss your issues with past boyfriends, or are we going to get the hell out of here?"

"Of course I want to get out of here, but you're forgetting these babies." Michelle said as she clicked her bracelets together.

"Surely you don't think I wouldn't come prepared."

Blade removed his backpack and pulled out a disk shaped object that was attached to a 9v battery.

"How's that going to help?" Asked Michelle.

"It's an electromagnet; it has enough power to fry the electronics in your bracelets, rendering them useless."

Blade held the magnet to each bracelet and turned on the

switch, once all four bracelets had been done he put the magnet and battery back in his pack then pulled out a knife and handed it to Michelle.

"Let's go."

"Hang on a minute; surely you don't expect me to believe a simple magnet can reduced these things to nothing but pieces of metal?"

"Yeah, why not?"

"Trust me, I've tried to walk through that door before with these things on and I'm not about to do that, unless you have the device the guard uses so I don't get fried!"

"Michelle, trust me."

Michelle looked at him in shock, *how did he know her name, she had never told him?*

"Yes, I know who you are, who do you think is responsible for the diversion outside? He told me this device would work and after spending some time with him, I believe him."

Michelle stood and looked at the door and then cautiously moved forward, bracing herself for the moment when she stepped out into the hall.

"Do you think we could speed it up a little, I'm sure your father has just about exhausted his arsenal by now!"

Michelle opened her eyes and realised she was standing in the hall; suddenly she heard the sound of the Mistress's voice, sparking her into action. She immediately turned and started walking quickly in the opposite direction Blade was heading.

"Where the hell, are you going?"

"Something I've been wanting to do for a real long time!"

"Michelle, Rusalka!"

Blade tried using both her names to get her attention, but she ignored him and broke out into a run down the hall.

Suddenly Blade heard a crackle through his earpiece.

"Blade, what the hell's taking you so long, I'm waiting out here like a sitting duck?" Asked Seth.

"Apparently someone has a score to settle before she's ready to come out."

"Holy shit!"

"Seth, Blade, why aren't you moving out? I want my daughter off the scene before the cops arrive!"

"Yeah well your daughter's got other ideas!" Exclaimed Seth angrily.

"Tell Blade to man up and do whatever it takes to get her out of there, now!"

"Blade…"

"Yeah, I heard, he obviously doesn't know his daughter very well!"

Blade caught up with Michelle just in time to see her land a bone crunching punch in the middle of the Mistress's face, dropping her to the floor, out cold.

"That's for making me miss my birthday you bitch!"

The two bodyguards immediately stepped forward and Michelle brought up her knife.

"You really want to mess with me guys, even after seeing what I can do with this baby?"

Both men stepped back and put their hands in the air.

"That's more like it, now pick up that sorry piece of shit that calls herself a woman and head for the front door!"

One of the guards did as she asked and Michelle followed close behind both men, letting them know she wouldn't hesitate to use her knife.

"What are you doing?" Whispered Blade.

"Making sure this bitch gets locked in a cell where she belongs, by the way, how come I haven't heard any cops, surely all the explosions should have brought them here with their guns blazing?"

"Your father wanted you off the property before they stormed the place, but I think you destroyed that idea," said Blade as he heard the faint sound of sirens in the distance.

"Yeah well I'm sure you're in radio contact with him; tell him I'm not leaving till I personally throw this bag of shit in the back of a paddy wagon!"

"Max, we're on our way out the front door, but your

daughter says she's not leaving till the boys in blue arrive."

"You…"

Blade immediately pulled off his earpiece; he had no intention of having the wax blasted out of his ears. Unfortunately both Seth and Jasmine hadn't had the foresight to do the same, both suffering a ringing sound in their ears for a period afterwards.

Despite Jasmine disobeying Max's orders and following Seth and Blade onto the property, she had remained in the safety of her car after nearly having her leg bitten off by one of the vicious Rottweiler security dogs. She did her best to film what she could through the windscreen of her car, all the while relaying what she could see to her handheld recorder. Suddenly Jasmine's phone vibrated for the umpteenth time and she knew it would once again be Tracey; she could ignore her no longer.

"Hello."

"Bloody hell Jasmine, what in god's name is wrong with you? You beg me to back you up in some James Bond style operation and then you ignore all my calls!"

"Sorry, I was just following orders!"

"Orders, Christ almighty, I've been sitting here twiddling my thumbs for the last hour, I've had my boss screaming in one ear and been copping crap from my team in the other, who are also sick of waiting around!"

"Sorry, I can tell you the location now."

"I'm pretty sure I already know, after receiving multiple reports of hearing world war three taking place in the Cooee Mountain area, which I am sure is where you are…"

"Yeah, look I'm really sorry Trace, but he wanted to get Rusalka out before you guys arrived!"

"So he's protecting her, he doesn't want her charged with murder. What is she to him anyway?"

"I'm sorry I can't tell you that."

"God, you've definitely got it bad for this guy, but mark my words, if this woman disappears for a second time, your head will be the first on the chopping block!"

"She won't."

"How can you be so sure?"

"Because Rusalka is waiting to personally assist her into the back of the paddy wagon."

"But you said..."

"Yeah well apparently Rusalka has a mind of her own."

"Good for her. So where are you now?"

"Doing my best to get a story from inside the safety of my car."

"I know I'm going to regret asking, but why?"

"Because there are two vicious dogs waiting outside my car, eyeing me off for dinner."

"Jeez girl, what you'll do for a story!"

Moments later a convoy of police vehicles arrived with lights flashing and sirens blaring, aside from the diversions Max had created to keep the guards away from the front door, he had noticed a paddock that had numerous helicopters, which meant the stadium was full of people, *Rusalka was supposed to fight tonight!*

He disabled the helicopters; he wanted to ensure no one left the property without first being questioned by the police. Even though these people had no actual part in the fights, they were complicit in their actions by paying to watch, which had forced Michelle to kill god knows how many men, just to survive.

He could still remember the face of the first man he killed, something he would never wish upon anyone, least of all his own daughter. He knew she was strong in every sense of the word, *but was she strong enough to put the faces of those men who died at the end of her blade behind her and move forward?*

He was annoyed that Blade hadn't used brute force to get Michelle off the property before the police arrived, but then on the other hand he could understand why she insisted on staying. On reflection, he would have had great satisfaction in being able to throw Microbe in the back of a paddy wagon, assured he would be locked up, suffering the indignities of prison life till his dying days, but Savage robbed him of that pleasure. Yes the man was now dead, but Max still felt as if that chapter was unfinished.

Tracey was in the passenger seat of the lead vehicle, but this was her show, she was in charge. However it all started going pear shape when Jasmine not only refused to reveal the location but also wouldn't answer her calls and it was looking more like she was going to be left with egg on her face.

The scene in front of her was surreal; it looked more like part of a James Bond movie than her usual arrest of a suspect. She found it hard to believe, that the video of Rusalka on YouTube was real and it was only Jasmine's insistence that she knew the exact location of the Mistress, which had compelled her to be here.

As the vehicle neared the elaborate entrance of the house, Tracey couldn't help but gasp in shock, for standing in full costume with a lethal looking knife in one hand, was Rusalka, she had one foot on the lifeless body of a woman and two muscle men were kneeling on the ground nearby with their hands behind their backs.

"Well I'll be dammed; if I didn't see it with my own eyes I wouldn't believe it!"

Tracey looked across at the constable who was driving the car and noticed his mouth had dropped open in disbelief, but also admiration at the sight of Rusalka.

"Don't even think about it Barnsey, not only will it cost you one hundred grand, but you have to dance the fight of knives first!"

"It'd be worth it!"

Tracey laughed, she had to admit the girl was beautiful and in full costume it was certainly a striking pose. Tracey alighted the vehicle and made her way up the few short steps, suddenly taking note of the big muscle guy standing to the right of Rusalka, wondering why she hadn't noticed him before.

"Hello, I'm Sergeant Roberts, I believe you are Rusalka?"

"Correct and this piece of trash laying on the ground is the

STEEL JUSTICE

Mistress, I don't know her real name, but trust me, she is scum and I'm sure when you run her fingerprints through your system, it will set the alarm bells ringing!"

"You don't have to convince me, in fact we have been after her for some time, now if you would like to give Constable Barnes your statement…"

"I'm not moving until I throw this bag of shit in the back of the paddy wagon!"

"I understand you're angry, but by law because she is unconscious and bleeding, she has to be attended to by a paramedic."

"Yeah and they'll take her to the hospital and next we know she has disappeared!"

"She'll be under Police guard."

"Yeah, I've heard that one before!"

Jasmine had finally been able to get out of her car, after two officers restrained the dogs and put them in the back of a vehicle, she had walked up to the front entrance just in time to hear the conversation between Tracey and Michelle.

"Can I make a suggestion?"

Everyone turned to look at Jasmine.

"I know you, you're that chick who busted into the Mistress's building and rescued the girls," said Michelle.

"That's right, did you watch the show?"

"Show?"

"Frontline News, I was the reporter, Jasmine Bronson."

"Nah didn't see that, but I saw you that night, you just didn't see me."

"I'm sorry, but I did get a glimpse of you when I watched the video the following day."

"Video, I didn't see any cameras."

"I had one disguised as a pendant around my neck, one of the girls that was rescued told me who you were, which led us to Blade and eventually here."

"So I've got you to thank for getting me out of here?"

"I just played a small part, now what I was going to

suggest, seeing as you have been incarcerated for a long time, how about you ride in the ambulance that takes this woman to the hospital and they can check you over to ensure you are fit and healthy and have no underlying problems following your long confinement."

"I don't want…"

"Rusalka she's right and besides that way you can be sure the Mistress doesn't escape," reasoned Blade.

Michelle looked from Blade to Sergeant Roberts and then Jasmine, feeling as though she had been hemmed into a corner. Looking past them, taking in for the first time how many police cars and officers were on the property, noting some people were being questioned, while others were handcuffed and put into the back of a police vehicle. Suddenly her gaze came upon a man who was wearing dark clothes and his face had been darkened with camouflage paint, she knew instantly it was her father, causing a lump to rise to her throat and tears pricked in the back of her eyes.

Overcome with an emotion she couldn't explain, for the first time in her life she looked at him as her father, not some regimental nutcase that went out of his way to make her life difficult. Despite his blackened face and the distance between them, she could see the look in his eyes, knowing he was overcome with the same emotion, she finally understood his reasoning behind keeping his daughter a secret; he had been trying to protect her from something like this.

Jasmine noticed what passed between father and daughter, she knew it was taking all of Max's strength not to run forward and hug her. Like Michelle, she understood why he stayed rooted to the spot. Michelle looked at Tracey and stepped back from Salina, who was now moaning as she regained consciousness.

"Ok."

Tracey immediately signalled the paramedics to come forward, who in turn copped a barrage of abuse for taking too long to give her something for the pain.

"She might look and dress like a lady, but trust me, she's far from it!" Exclaimed Michelle.

"I think everyone already agrees with you on that one," commented Jasmine.

A couple of hours later when everyone had either given their statement or been taken down to the Police Station for questioning, Tracey came up to Jasmine.

"Just got off the phone to my Senior Sergeant, apparently while my team and I were waiting for your call, they received a large parcel at the station. Once the bomb squad had ascertained that it wasn't a bomb, it turned out to be a briefcase containing, about one hundred grams of cocaine and a video of an actual drug deal going down. It also contained a USB memory stick containing some very interesting information."

"Really, do you know who sent it?" Asked Jasmine.

"I was hoping you could tell me," replied Tracey.

"What makes you think I would know anything about it?"

"Well after they arrested a Michael Savage, who even the drug squad was unaware of, it was discovered he has links to Salina."

"Really?"

"Why do I get the impression you already knew this?"

"I have no idea what you're talking about."

"You know, you're not a very good liar."

CHAPTER TWENTY-EIGHT

Michelle was given the all clear from the hospital and once Salina had recovered from surgery to her broken nose, she was transferred to the prison infirmary. With Deanne's blessing Jasmine handed over to the police all the information she had that Dr Robert Shoal had left for his daughter. It was enough evidence to exhume the bodies of Robert Shoal, Reymont Skinner and Edwina Mary Dolton; whose daughter Leanne was more than happy that her mother's death was going to be re-examined.

As much as Jasmine wanted to run with her story on Frontline news, she knew the importance of waiting for all the facts. Other News stations had already posted snippets of information, much to the annoyance of her boss, but Jasmine wasn't concerned. By the time the other News stations got word that something big was happening at Cooee Mountain, the police had sealed off the property, so she had been the only reporter who had managed to be on the scene, but also a part of the lead up to the event.

Fortunately, for forensics, Dr Cook had been able to obtain a sample of the experimental arthritis drug, which was believed to be what Salina used to kill her victims. After Max and Jasmine had questioned him about the death of Robert Shoal, his friend, he realised that he had entrusted him with the leather satchel for more than one reason, he wanted him to find this drug, because he knew it would be the only way to prove Salina's guilt.

After finding large traces of the drug in their bodies, their deaths were now listed as murder and police had the monumental task of trying to locate other possible victims, during the time Salina had posed as a nurse. The families of Salina's victims, whom she profited from, received Justice in the courts for all monies unlawfully obtained, plus accrued interest from the time of their death.

STEEL JUSTICE

When Michael Savage's fingerprints were run through IAFIS (Integrated Automated Fingerprint identification) it brought up a match to a Graham Black. Not only had the man been on the most wanted list, but it was believed he had died in a fire. After examining the file of those involved in the autopsy of the burnt corpse, it was soon discovered one person involved in the handling of the DNA, was killed in a car accident not long after the report was presented. Immediately bank records of this person were recalled and it was discovered a large deposit had been made to his account around the time of the autopsy.

As both Max and Jasmine suspected, Dr Shoal was killed because he was the surgeon who performed the procedure, which changed the appearance of Graham Black.

From the computers seized from Salina's home, police were also able to bust a paedophile ring that was not only linked to the one Jasmine had exposed on Frontline News, but also the two men Seth had murdered.

With all the information that had come to light, Jasmine was now able to run with her story and to her boss's delight, there was enough to stretch it into a series. After the first show went to air, Frontlines News became number one in the ratings and Jasmine Bronson had now become a household name.

As promised, Max organised a new identity for Seth and he was now the proud owner of one of Savage's luxury yachts. Seth couldn't wipe the smile off his face as he popped the cork on a bottle of champagne and poured a glass for the small party, which consisted of Max, Jasmine, Michelle and Blade.

"Here's to the start of a new life," said Seth.

"I'll drink to that!" Exclaimed Michelle.

"Here's to Justice," replied Max.

"Yes, Steel Justice," stated Jasmine.

Everyone clinked their glasses in agreement.

"Max how'd you do it, how did you manage to not only get Seth a new identity, but also, this yacht, it must have cost a fortune?" Asked Blade.

"You know after working with you these past months, seeing the stuff you do, I can understand the new identity, but to be able to wrangle me the yacht, hell, I really didn't expect that!" Exclaimed Seth.

Max smiled and everyone looked at him questioningly.

"Dad, I hope you're not going to say you spent my inheritance so Seth could have his boat?" Asked Michelle.

"Of course not, the price tag on this girl is far more than my bank account could ever handle."

"Come on Max; tell us how you managed it," responded Jasmine.

"Firstly Seth, is there anything about this particular yacht that is familiar?"

"Of course, it's the one I took you through the day we set up Savage."

"Well as Victor Seminov had already made a down payment of one million dollars, whom by the way the police are trying to track down and as the boat had been impounded, due to the fact it had been sold for the purpose of transporting drugs, it was virtually unsaleable. The Company wanted it moved from their berth; so I made an offer to get it off their hands."

"Hang on, you were Victor Seminov, which brings me to where did you get the million in cash from?" Asked Seth.

"Savage himself."

"What, how?" He asked incredulously.

"Yeah Max, how did you manage it?" Asked Blade.

"It was quite easy, after Seth had gained me access to Savage's computer; it was child's play siphoning amounts of money, that wouldn't draw any attention, from his many accounts."

"Very clever!" Said Seth and everyone nodded in agreement.

"So how much did it cost you to take it off their hands?" Asked Blade.

"One hundred thousand."

"Damn, there goes my inheritance!" Exclaimed Michelle.

"Jeez man, I didn't expect for you to dig in your own pocket on my behalf!" Exclaimed Seth.

"I didn't, I took it from Savage."

"Good work dad, I hope you took enough to leave a nice little nest egg for me?"

"No Michelle, Even though Savage is a low life, I wouldn't transfer money from him for my own gain, that would be sinking myself to his level. At the time I took the money, I knew not only that I had to obtain a boat for Seth, I also knew its value would be greatly reduced by the arrest of Savage. I made a guess that as there had already been a down-payment of one million dollars, the company would be willing to take virtually anything to be rid of it."

"But Savage was the company," stated Seth.

"Yes, but he also had a lot of shareholders who have a vested interest in his legitimate enterprises and I dare say the directors of these companies have been working overtime to cut any links between them and Savage, trying to maintain the reputation of their businesses. Just because he has been arrested and his personal property seized, it doesn't bring a halt to the running of those companies that had no knowledge or involvement in his drug dealing."

"You never cease to amaze me Max Steel, who would have thought the day I held a gun to your girlfriends head, it would turn out to be the smartest thing I ever did!" Exclaimed Seth.

"Girlfriend, you and Jasmine?" Exclaimed Michelle.

Jasmine looked across at Max, also waiting for an answer.

"It's nothing like that, circumstances just happened that caused Jasmine and I to team up to find you. I got my daughter back and Jasmine got her story."

Michelle looked across at Jasmine who took a gulp of her champagne and nodded her head.

Suddenly Max's hearing was attuned to a sound he hadn't heard in a long time; instinctively he looked to the skies, trying to pinpoint its location. Suddenly focussing on a small dark speck, that was quickly becoming larger as it headed directly towards them.

"Dad, what sort of chopper is that?" Asked Michelle.

"It's an EC-665, made by Eurocopter."

"I've never seen anything like it," she Replied.

"That's because it's an attack helicopter, better known as the Tiger, you won't normally see one of these guys unless you're in a war zone."

"What the hell is an attack helicopter doing here?" Asked Blade.

"I was wondering the same thing, but we're soon to find out."

"Surely he's not going to land here at the marina?" Asked Jasmine.

"Looks like he's going to use the helipad at the end of the dock," replied Max.

"God I hope he's not here because he found out I got this boat?" Asked Seth.

"I doubt it; I'm guessing he is here to see me," replied Max.

"Why?" Asked Michelle, now having to yell because the noise was so loud.

Max didn't bother to answer, he wasn't about to yell that he had been using his army contacts to not only rescue her, but also instigate the demise of Savage and Salina. From their vantage point, he had a clear view of the chopper and watched, as the pilot put the machine through it's cool down process and then exited the chopper, making his way towards where Seth's boat was docked.

"Captain," said the pilot as he saluted.

"At ease Lieutenant, I'm a civilian now."

"Permission to come aboard sir, I've been instructed to deliver this to you, it comes directly from the Major General."

"Permission granted."

As the lieutenant stepped on board, Max noted the look on Seth's face; he was gritting his teeth at the sight of his black boots on his highly polished timber deck. To Max's annoyance he once again saluted before handing him the letter. Max walked a short distance away and read the contents. Michelle could tell by the look on his face it wasn't good news.

"Dad, what's wrong?"

Max folded the letter and walked towards her.

"Apparently my past has come back to haunt me."

"Sir, I was also given instructions not to leave without you," said the Lieutenant.

"Well I'm afraid you'll have to," replied Max.

"Sir, I'll rephrase that, I was ordered not to leave without you."

"Dad go; I know you really want to."

"Michelle, I made a promise to you years ago…"

"Don't stay on my account, I'm a big girl now, besides I was planning on hanging here with Blade, we've been talking about me going pro."

"You can't be serious, what about your dream to one day become a skipper?"

"Yes I am serious and dreams can change; one thing I learnt while being held prisoner by Salina, Sayoc Kali is in my blood, of all the hair brain schemes I came up with looking for that big thrill, nothing ever gave me the adrenaline rush I got every time I stepped out into that ring. Dad I know you miss the life you had before I came onto the scene and living life on the edge, I know this because I'm your daughter and I inherited this from you."

Max looked from his daughter to the lieutenant and the helicopter in the background. His daughter was right, his hands were itching to get hold of those controls and if he was realistic, after the past events of not only trying to find Michelle, but bring down Microbe, Savage and Salina, he hadn't felt so alive in a very long time, he then looked towards Jasmine.

"You know what this means don't you?"

"Yes, you won't be able to keep your promise of an exclusive interview, its ok, I understand."

"What about your boss?"

"I'll think of something."

"Do you think she would settle for an exclusive interview with Rusalka?" Asked Michelle.

"Are you serious?" Asked Jasmine.

"Hell yeah!"

"Michelle, think about this…," said Max.

"Dad, firstly, Blade and I have been talking and we've decided for various reasons that I should officially change my name to Rusalka…"

"Over my dead body!"

"Dad, think about it, all those years I had to keep secret the fact you were my father, now you are planning to go back to your old life, wouldn't you rest more easy if the world believed Michelle Brown perished at sea, the day Josh crashed Microbe's helicopter. I can't speak for the Lieutenant, but I trust everyone else here and I know they would never reveal the true identity of Rusalka."

"Max she's right, I've never mentioned to my boss, Michelle and Rusalka are one and the same. I can tell Jodi, sadly, the rumour of Michelle being alive was not true. I'm sure Michelle, or should I say Rusalka can come up with a plausible story, from all the information I got from Maliha and you gathered from Savage's and Salina's computer about the whole setup. Jodi will jump through fiery hoops to ensure Frontline News has the exclusive on Rusalka, in fact if she had to choose between the two of you, Rusalka would win hands down."

Max looked at his daughter and could see for the first time in her life, she had actually met her match with Blade and as much as he hated to admit it, he couldn't be leaving her in safer hands and then he looked towards the lieutenant.

"Well?"

"Sir, I'm truly sorry for your loss, honestly I had no idea you had a daughter, but without sounding rude, as you have nothing holding you here; will you accompany me back to headquarters?"

"On one condition."

"Sir?"

"You let me fly this baby back home!"

"It would be an honour and a privilege Sir," said the lieutenant as he saluted.

Max hugged his daughter and shook Blade's hand while he leaned into his ear and whispered.

"You do anything to upset or harm my daughter in any way; I will personally hunt you down."

Blade nodded his head in acknowledgement and Max then shook Seth's hand.

"Enjoy your new life, and try to stay on the straight and narrow."

"Yes on both counts and it was a pleasure working with you," said Seth as he saluted with a smile.

Max then looked towards Jasmine.

"Good luck with the story."

"Thank you."

A sense of disappointment came over her as he turned and walked down the few steps to the wharf, admiring his physique and remembering that night, taking another gulp of champagne as he made his way towards the helicopter. He stopped suddenly and turned, surprising the lieutenant and those watching as he ran back towards the boat and bounded up the stairs. Before Jasmine realised what was happening he took her in his arms and kissed her passionately, before whispering in her ear.

"Thank you."

Before Jasmine could respond, he turned and bound back down the stairs and toward the worried lieutenant. Jasmine could feel the eyes of everyone on her, but she stayed focused on Max as he climbed into the helicopter and secretly smiled into her glass. Once again, they braced themselves as the whirling blades created a loud deafening noise, watching until the helicopter became but a mere speck in the sky and disappeared from sight.

"So what was that all about?" Asked Michelle.

"Sorry, I'm not one to kiss and tell."

Jasmine turned from her questioning eyes and put her fingers to her lips, which still tingled from Max's passionate kiss and smiled to herself.

~~~~

Thank you for purchasing *Steel Justice*, could you please take the time to post a review on the site you bought this book, I would love to hear your thoughts.

Jenni Boyd.

Other intriguing titles by this author are available through;
http://www.jenniboydbooks.com/

Contact the author or comment at:
https://www.facebook.com/JenniBoydBooks

Made in the USA
Charleston, SC
14 August 2014